MEET ME HALFWAY

MEET ME HALFWAY

LILIAN T. JAMES

Crystal Pages Publishing
is an imprint of Aleron Books LLC

First printing edition 2022

Cover Design : Murphy Rae
Editor : Allusion Publishing
Floorplan Designs : Elizabeth Garber
Chapter Header Designs : Etheric Tales & Edits

ISBN-13: 978-1-7378899-3-9

To the people whose wings were clipped, but who figured out how to make new ones, one feather at a time.

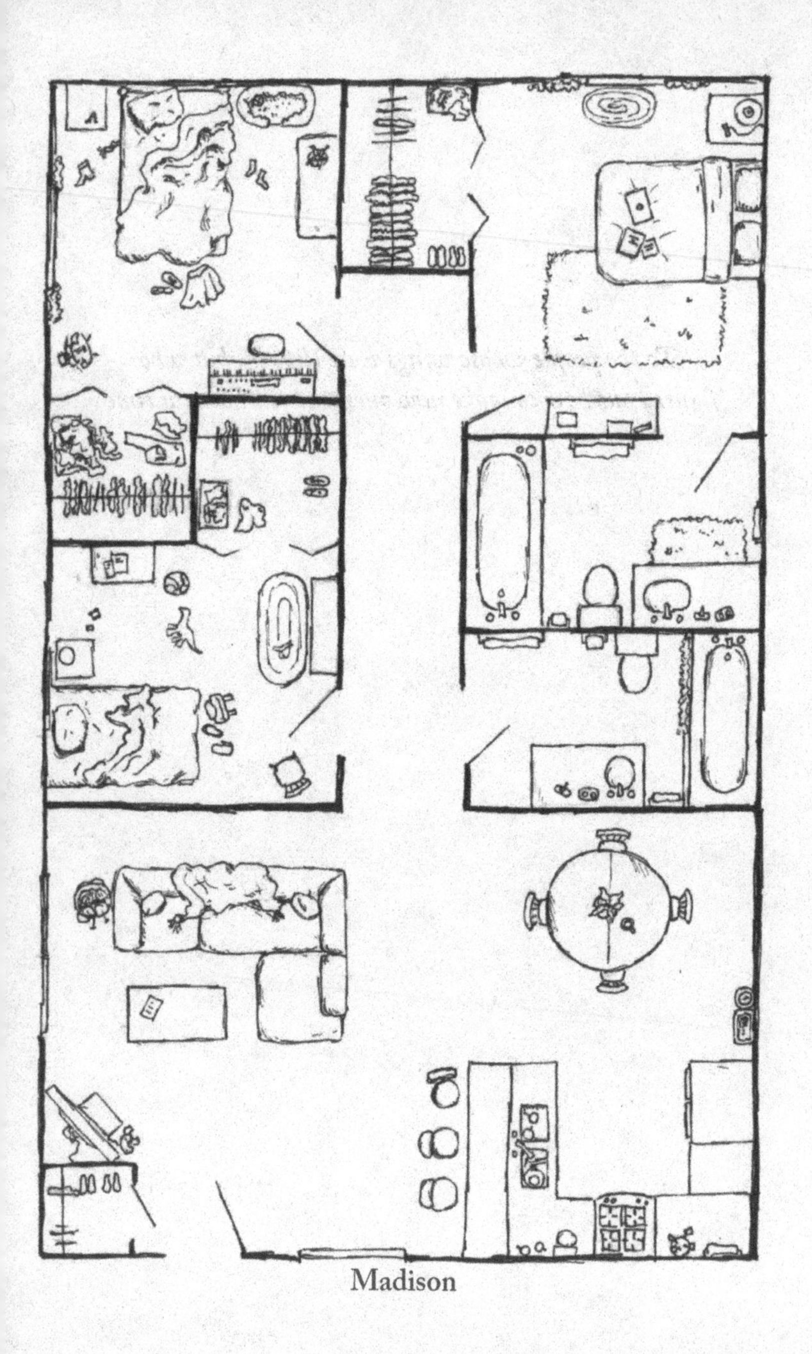

Madison

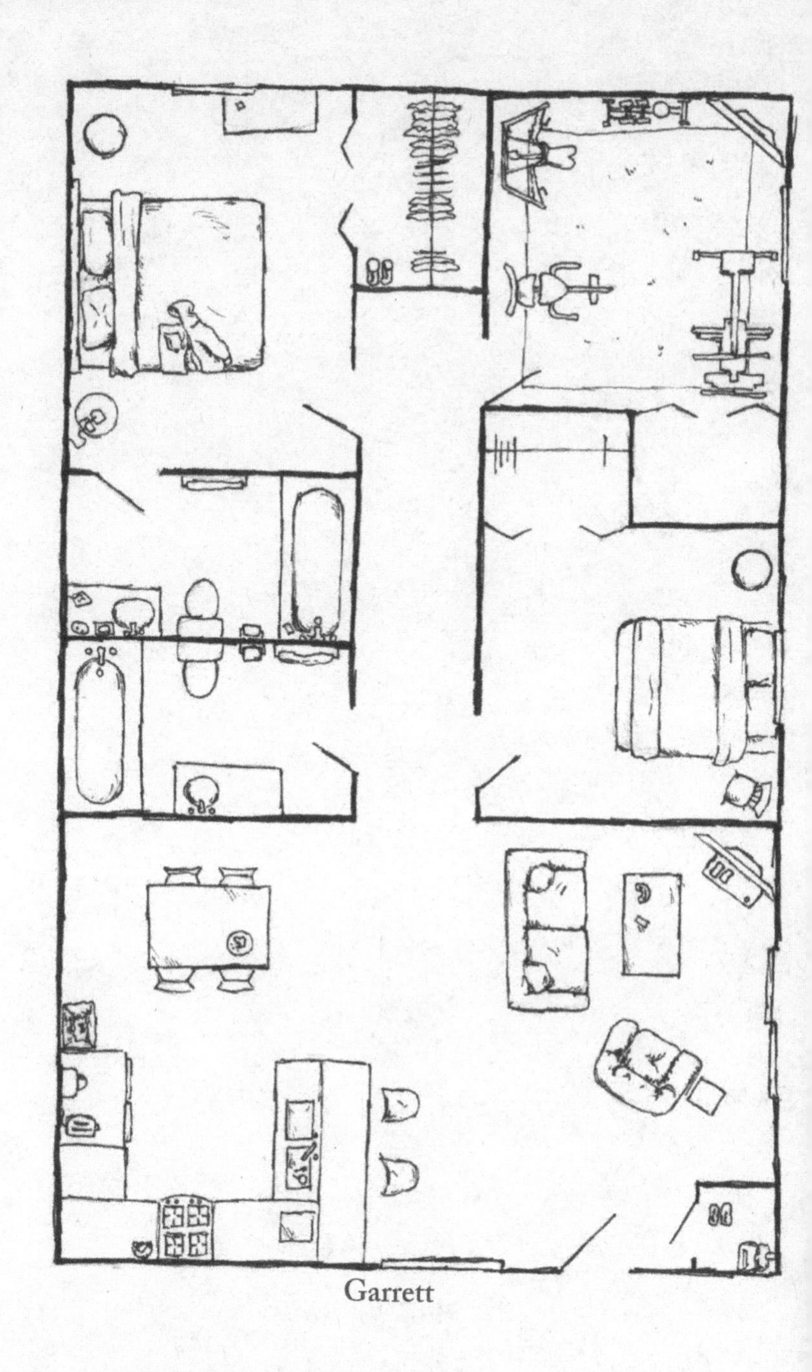

Garrett

Author's Note

Includes sexually explicit content, topics such as mental and emotional recovery from previous spousal abuse, stalking, alcoholism, sexual harassment, and assault.

Preface

It's difficult to put into words what this story means to me. To be honest, it was difficult to put this story into words, period.

Madison's exact story is fictional, but the aspects of it are very much real to many women who are single parents, had children young, and/or are rediscovering themselves after an abusive relationship.

I've been an avid romance reader my entire life. Even as a child, I was invested and in love with the "happily ever after" of fictional characters in movies and shows.

However, after I had my son, I began to notice a lack of parenting in romance novels. It isn't surprising that many authors avoid the subject since a large portion of readers prefer romance to only have children in the epilogue or not at all.

But I've been a mother since I discovered I was pregnant at the age of 16, and I wanted to see it reflected in the books I read. I wanted young mothers. I wanted single mothers. I wanted to *relate* to the main character.

To be fair, those books do exist, they're just harder to find and often portray motherhood as a characteristic of the woman, rather than the life-altering struggle it can be. The main characters own homes but only have one job, and never seem to worry about bills. They also often have college degrees, but there's never any explanation as to *how* the character accomplished that as a single parent. Not to say all that isn't possible; it is. It just wasn't true for me.

In *Meet Me Halfway*, Madison works seven days a week, balancing three jobs, because that's what *I* had to do to make ends meet. Madison takes night classes and is sleep deprived in order to obtain a degree because that's what I had to do. Working over 60 hours a week, I didn't have time to do college any other way. It was one of the hardest things I've ever done.

This is the brutal reality for young, single mothers—specifically the ones who have an absent partner. For most, their lives are not polished, not pretty, and far from perfect.

Fictional stories are just that, fiction. They don't have to be realistic, and often aren't. I love magical men with wings as much as the next fantasy reader, but representation is also important. I wanted to feel *seen* and *connect* to a main character, and one day I realized I was more than capable of writing it, myself.

Whether you're married or not, whether you have children or not, anyone can read and enjoy Madison's story. But for those of you who relate to her:

I wrote this book for you.

I wrote this book for me.

And I wrote it for every young mother who comes after us.

Chapter 1

I PUT MY hand across his face, waving it up and down to block his eyesight in a last-second attempt to cause him to crash.

"You can't! I won't let you!" I screeched, but he ducked under my arm, determined to stay on the road. I snatched my hand back and clenched the object in my lap with both hands.

"No!" he yelled, "Stop!"

I ignored him, tightening my hold and focusing, swaying my body back and forth as if my movements might assist in his demise.

"You won't always beat me, it's time you learned what it's like to suffer. I'm going to dance over your corpse!" I was so close. So damn close. Just once. All I needed was to come out on top *once*.

I was feeling good, high off the adrenaline of kicking ass when he hit me directly in the back, sending me spinning out of control and smashing into the wall.

And just like that, I was the loser all over again. Same outcome, different day.

"God dang, Jamie!" I yelled, dropping my controller, and throwing my hands up in defeat. "A red shell? Really? How long were you holding on to that?"

He crossed the finish line, laughing maniacally, the deep, foreboding sound of an evil mastermind. Or as close to it as his scrawny, prepubescent voice could get.

"I get my skills from my uncle. You'll never beat me." He set his controller down, smiling at me and pretending to crack his knuckles. I could practically smell the smugness emanating from his skin.

"Whatever, dude. I'll get you next time."

"You say that every time."

"Yeah, but this time I mean it."

We both giggled, wrapping the cords around our controllers, and setting them on top of the gaming system that sat on the floor next to our puny excuse for a television.

It was our ritual. Every night, on the nights I was home, we'd play three rounds of racing and whoever lost had to clean up the living room. "Whoever" always meaning me. I might as well legally change my name from Madison Hartland to Loser Neverwin. The kid was flipping ruthless.

"All right, bud, you know the drill, go brush and wash your face while I clean up."

He immediately stood and shuffled in the direction of the hallway right behind our couch. His lack of complaint or eye roll instantly had my mom senses tingling.

"That means you have to actually go into the bathroom," I hollered over my shoulder, not even bothering to turn around.

"Ugh, how do you always know?"

"Eyes in the back of my head." I chuckled, hearing him grumble to himself before the sink turned on and drowned him out. I wasn't buying it and was one-hundred percent going to smell his breath before he climbed in bed.

At eight years old, he'd never looked a thing like me. His dirty blond, straight hair and ocean blue eyes were polar opposites of my dark brown, spiral curls and chocolate eyes. Honestly, it was no wonder people assumed I was his babysitter.

His personality; however, might as well have been a carbon copy of mine. He was sneaky as a fox and stubborn as a bull. It made me want to rip my hair out most days, and I had only myself to blame. Lord knows my mother found it hilarious and exactly what I deserved.

But for as stubborn as he was, he was a sweet kid. He enjoyed hiking and exploring, but he wasn't a rough and tumble kind of kid. He was just as happy vegging with me at home as he was hanging out with friends at school. I considered myself beyond lucky.

Crawling on my hands and knees, I made my way across our small living room, picking up the pillows we'd strewn across the floor. Prior to our match, we'd partook in a pre-game, epic fight to the death for the last package of gummies. He may have escaped with his life, but I won that battle.

Was he in elementary school? Yes. Did he only come up to my shoulder in height? Yep. Did I go easy on him because of that? Not a chance. Sweets were rare in our house. He knew the stakes.

I had just finished brushing crumbs off our faux-wood coffee table and readjusting the rug when he opened the door and walked out.

"That was fast. Did you wash your face?"

Insert dramatic eye roll. I didn't even need to see him to know he was doing it. "Yes," he said, drawing out the end like a snake.

I glanced up, narrowing my eyes. His skin didn't look damp, and there wasn't even the tiniest hint of pink to his cheeks. "You sure?"

He stared at me for a second longer before he turned without a word and stomped back into the bathroom.

Kids.

I sat back on my heels, pushing up off my knees to stand. "Come on, time to go potty," I told the covered mound next to me. Nothing. Shaking my head, I lifted the blanket off the black-haired, sausage roll of a dog hidden underneath. "Don't you ignore me."

Said sausage roll glared up at me, and I swore if she could talk, she'd be telling me to fuck off. You'd have thought she was seventy rather than six by the way she acted. If food wasn't involved, she wasn't interested.

She was a short-haired, miniature dachshund and had been

a puppy no bigger than my hands back when we bought her. I remembered back then that we'd had her for a few days, and for the life of me I still hadn't been able to pick a name. So, like the genius woman I was, I decided to let my two-year-old name her.

"What's your favorite thing?"
"The rug!"
"Okay, what's your second favorite thing?"
"Pants!"

And thus, Rugpants was named. Genius woman, indeed. I nudged her limp form. "Come on Rugsy, outside, let's go."

She rolled off the couch like a potato on a kid's project ramp and trotted her short, stubby legs toward the patio door. It was literally two feet away, but she still found time to stretch and yawn on the way over.

Yanking on the handle, I forced the door to slide open as far as I could while it fought against me. I sighed, mentally adding 'call the landlord to fix patio door' to my never ending to-do list.

Rugpants looked up at me, pure sass in her buggy eyes. "Don't give me that look, it won't open any farther. You can fit." I nudged her out, leaving the door ajar so she could make her way in when she was done.

Walking backward, I plopped onto the couch, closing my eyes and listening to the cicadas serenade me through the opening and praying no mosquitoes took advantage of my laziness.

Jamie would come back any minute with a book, and I was dreading it. Not because I didn't enjoy reading with him, I loved his interest in books, but because reading time meant nighttime, and nighttime meant schoolwork. No matter how much I tried to enjoy them, the evenings were never long enough.

I allowed myself one more minute of self-pity and then sat up, breathing deeply and clapping my hands together. "It's bedtime, let's go!"

I heard the faint clatter of something in the bathroom—I didn't even want to know what an eight-year-old boy was doing in there—before the creak of the door echoed out, and he darted into his room.

"Are we reading out here or in there?"

"In here!" he yelled.

Of course, we were. Lazy bum. Slapping my hands on the couch, I heaved my butt up and trudged toward the first bedroom in the hall, directly across from the bathroom.

We'd moved in last week, and Jamie had been so excited to have his own bedroom and bathroom. It'd been a struggle not to burst into tears at his excitement over something he'd always deserved to have.

I crawled into bed next to him, shoving my toes under his legs to warm them and biting back a laugh when he hissed and slapped at me. We didn't fit on his twin mattress, but I'd keep squeezing in as long as he'd let me.

"I have several chapters I have to read for class later, so do you mind doing most of the reading tonight?"

He shrugged. "Sure."

I settled in, leaning my head on his shoulder and listening to him read a novel about dragons. We were currently on book three of an ongoing series, and he was loving them.

I'd made it a point to read to him every night growing up, no matter what. When he finally got old enough to read on his own, we began taking turns and it was, by far, my favorite part of each day.

I could see his eyes start to droop when I took my turn, and I smiled. He was getting so big, but sometimes I still caught glimpses of my baby boy hiding underneath. "Let's end here. You have school tomorrow, and I need to get started on my own reading."

"Do you have a test?"

"Not tonight, thankfully, just some reading." I laid his book on his nightstand and stood, throwing his blanket over his head.

"About what?" he asked, not even bothering to move it.

"Well, one of them is an overview of the research results regarding car wash employees stealing change from vehicles. I have to write up a report naming any issues with validity and reliability."

I watched his fingers slowly creep out and drag the blanket down his face. His nose was scrunched up tight. "That sounds awful."

"It will absolutely, without a doubt, be awful." I laughed, flicking his light off. "'Night, bud."

"'Night, Mom."

I closed his door, turning and staring at my own bedroom. I could practically hear the sheets calling my name. They were probably ice cold and fantastic. Fuck, I was tired. Tipping my head back, I sighed, turning and making my way to the kitchen tucked into the corner of our living room.

Twenty-five and there I was, spending the night prepping a cup of dollar store coffee in tie-dye sweats, mismatched socks, and curls plopped on top of my head like a pineapple. I was the antonym of sexy.

Dressing up my coffee with more sugar than my daily allowance recommended, I made sure Rugpants had wandered back inside, and then heaved the door shut, ambling into my room.

The duplex was the largest place I'd ever been able to barely afford. 'Barely' being a key detail. With three beds and two bathrooms, it was more space than we'd ever had in our previous one-bed, one-bath apartment.

The master bedroom was the same size as the other bedrooms, but I didn't have to share so it was a winner in my book. I set my "World's Best Hooker" mug my friend had gifted me on my nightstand and wiggled my butt down onto my cheap, three-inch mattress, next to the four-legged child that'd already crawled in.

"Here we go," I muttered, cracking my neck. I set my laptop on my crossed legs and logged into the university website. Once it was loaded and my planner spread out next to me, I promptly pulled up my nightly companion: streaming music.

I couldn't afford the commercial-free version, but you wouldn't hear me complain. It was the only thing keeping me awake most nights. Even eyecare commercials were more entertaining than silence.

I pulled up the report I'd been assigned, a research project conducted by one of my professors. He'd assigned it to the class, camouflaging it as a practice assignment when in reality, he was using us to find errors in his work for him.

I was pretty sure it would be considered highly unethical, but whatever. Setting the music station to Top Hits, I rolled my shoulders and got to work.

I'd suffered through the entire report and was summarizing my findings when a knock came on the front door. I startled, straightening up and spilling the majority of my coffee down the front of my top. Cursing, I leapt off the bed and attempted to quiet Rugpants's barking while she tried to uncover herself from the comforter.

Who the hell could that be? I set my mug down, wiping pointlessly at my wet chest, my heart already in my stomach. I didn't know anyone in this town besides my parents, and they wouldn't be knocking on my door this late at night.

I slid out of my room, closing the door behind me to lock sausage butt in so she hopefully wouldn't wake Jamie. Part of me didn't want to answer the door at all, but what if it was an emergency? I knew more than most that emergencies could happen at any time of night.

I made my way down the hall and across the living room. It didn't take long to cross a one-thousand-square-foot home, and I found myself wishing I'd walked a little slower.

I stood on my tiptoes and peered through the small window on the door, nerves shooting through my limbs and making my fingers shake. There was no one there. I paused, refusing to blink, waiting for someone to step into my view. But nothing happened.

"Don't open it," I told myself. "It's probably someone waiting off to the side, ready to kidnap you and chain you to a basement wall." I stared at the doorknob. "Oh Lordy, I'm an idiot," I muttered, unlocking the door and cracking it open an inch.

"Hello?" No one answered. No shuffling, no crickets. Nothing.

I pulled the door open a little wider, dredging up the small amount of bravery I was surprised I actually possessed. But I was promptly put right back in my place of cowardice when I spotted movement in my peripheral.

I flinched violently, smacking the side of my head into the door frame, and shrieking in an undignified manner. Heaving, I clutched at my chest, positive I was about to have an aneurysm.

It was a ripped piece of notebook paper. The little square of gray tape at the top indicating it'd probably been attached to my door before I so elegantly arrived.

Bending slowly, just in case anything jumped at me, I snatched it off my porch, holding it up to the light to read the chicken scratch.

Some of us are adults with jobs and need sleep. Be more considerate and turn down your music.

My face heated, and I glanced around anxiously. I didn't see anyone, but that didn't mean someone wasn't still out there. It'd only been a minute or two since I'd heard the knock. The someone obviously being the neighbor I shared a wall with.

Having only moved into the duplex a week ago, I still hadn't met the person sharing the duplex with me, aka my wall neighbor. I'd caught a quick glimpse of a man sitting in the forest green Chevy Nova parked out front once, but that'd been it. I didn't even know if anyone other than him lived there, or if he was actually the person living opposite me.

A sudden crunch to the left of the porch caught my attention, and I snapped my head to the side, squinting into the dark.

"Hello?" I called, clenching the note tighter in my hand and waiting, but I didn't see or hear anything else.

Keeping my spine straight, I backed up, letting my rear push my propped door open so I could slip back inside without turning my back to the shadows.

I was embarrassed. I knew the set up for the other side of the duplex was likely the same, meaning my room would share a wall with the other master room, but I never really thought much about it. I certainly didn't think my music was that loud. I had Jamie sleeping down the hall for God's sake, I wasn't blaring it.

I tried to brush it off. Neighbor man, or whoever lived there, was the one keeping himself awake by writing a damn letter and stalking over to my door in the middle of the night. Joke was on him.

Lost in thought, I fanned the paper back and forth, the motion chilling the large damp spot on my chest and making me shudder. I wiped at it subconsciously only to freeze when I grazed my nipple.

I looked down in horror, my eyes locking onto the hardened peak beneath my fingers. It was glaringly obvious through the wet fabric of my white sleep tank. Standing under my porch light, I might as well have had a neon arrow pointing right to it. *Come one, come all, to the nipple show.*

I groaned, my embarrassment hiking up to humiliation status. It was fine, no one had been out there. The sound I heard was either a cat or my irrational anxiety playing tricks on me. Probably the latter.

All I knew for sure was I was too tired for this shit. Frustrated, I slapped the paper onto the bar, the sound echoing out louder than I'd anticipated and setting off Rugsy's insufferable yapping again.

"Shush! Lay down!" I whisper screamed, running down the short hallway. I'd barely opened my door and toed her body back when another door clicked open behind me.

"Mom?"

I sighed. At this rate I was never going to finish my assignment. "Sorry, bud, I know we're making a racket. I'll keep her quiet, I promise. Go back to bed."

"What's all over your shirt? Is someone here?" he asked, rubbing the heels of his palms into his eyes.

I crossed my arms over my chest. "Besides the creature under your bed? Nope."

He dropped his hands, glaring at me. "He's not there anymore, I checked." His voice was raspy with sleep.

The effort of keeping a smile off my face was a battle. "Oh? Where do you think he went? Maybe to find a kid with a little more meat on his bones?"

"No," he said, stepping through his doorway. "I'm pretty sure I saw the clown in your shower drain eat him."

Speechless, I stared at his closed door a moment longer. That was a visual that would stick with me for a while. Thank God I hadn't planned on sleeping for a few more hours.

I'd made the mistake of telling him about the first horror film I'd ever watched and how I'd been at a sleepover and had to lay in a pitch-black room while the TV screen was off but the surround sound was on. I'd been forced to fall asleep listening to the sounds of kids screaming and dying. Fifteen years later, I still had nightmares about it.

Shuddering, I made my way back to my room, grabbing a t-shirt from my closet and replacing my nasty top. The remainder of my coffee was ice cold at this point, not to mention I'd have to study in silence now. Great.

I propped my pillows against the wall and snuggled back in, shaking my head when Rugsy instantly re-burrowed under the comforter at my feet. How she breathed way down there, I'd never know.

This was our routine every night, or at least every night Monday through Thursday. I'd enrolled in a local community college when I was around twenty, thinking I'd stay two years and come out with something to help me get a job. I'd received enough federal assistance to pay for it, so it could only help, right?

Three years and four associate degrees later, I was still waiting for it to help me land a full-time job rather than the part-time ones I currently had. My dream was to work directly with delinquent teens in a youth correctional facility, but instead I was stuck earning minimum wage making copies and serving food.

I'd graduated with a 4.0 GPA and had been so proud until the moment I'd realized no one else cared. If it wasn't at least a bachelor's, my GPA didn't matter to employers. Period.

So, I'd applied for a few scholarships and transferred to the university in the next city over. I was currently in my last year of full-time, online courses for Criminal Justice, and I was starting to run on empty.

Research results and court rulings were boring to read during the day, but at night it was giant, face-altering-yawn-level boring. But I was pushing through anyway, determined to finish and determined to maintain my GPA.

The thing was, getting pregnant at sixteen meant the world had stopped expecting anything of me. I probably sat at home with my seven baby daddies, milking the system while I refused to get a real job. I mean, that's what all single moms did, right?

My neighbor had only further proved that narrow viewpoint by his comment insinuating I wasn't an "adult with a job."

I'd been a single mom for years; I was used to it. I was going to graduate *summa cum laude* if it killed me. Not because I had anything to prove to the world—society's views on teenage moms were never going to change—but because I was determined to prove it to myself.

Three hours and a few more assignments later, I was dead.

I was head bobbing harder than an emo at a concert and had nearly face planted into the screen. I closed the computer and glanced at my alarm clock, internally crying.

Five hours. If I fell asleep right now and skipped a morning shower, I could get five hours of sleep. I lifted my arm, sniffing. The waft of vanilla and strawberries hit my nose. I could definitely pull off one skipped shower. Sweet.

Making sure my alarm was set, I scrunched down into my bed, chuckling when Rugsy shuffled up to curl behind my knees. It'd make turning difficult, but I didn't move her. Jamie had stopped cuddling with me years ago, so knee-pit, dog snuggles were all I got these days.

Thank God I only had one six-hour shift tomorrow. It was one of my easy days, and I was beyond grateful. Most people hated Mondays, counting down the days until the next weekend, but for me, weekdays were my break.

Just this year. I just needed to finish up this last year of school and then I'd be free to get a better job. *One* job.

I laid there, crossing my fingers and toes as I fell asleep. If you wished hard enough and worked hard enough, it was bound to come true eventually. I had to believe that.

Chapter 2

TIPPING MY HEAD back, I squinted at the popcorn ceiling and tried to make out shapes like I was an astrologer. Ceilingologer. Ceilologer?

"Madison, are you listening to me?"

I groaned, closing my eyes. "Yes, Dad, I'm listening."

"You've been here several weeks now, there's no reason for the dishwasher to still be broken. When was the last time you called him?"

I rolled my head forward, letting it drop, and imagined submerging myself in the sink full of soapy water. "I called last week. It's not a big deal, I don't mind hand washing. We don't exactly have many dishes anyway."

"It is a big deal, it's his property. It's his job to keep it in working order. You pay more than enough rent for it," he argued, leaning against the counter next to me. Realizing he wasn't going to drop it, I set the rag down and glanced up.

John Hartland was a large man, coming in at six-foot, two and well over two-hundred pounds. He could look menacing as hell when he wanted to as long as you didn't know him. To me, he was just one big ass, balding teddy bear.

I twisted my body, wrapping my arms around his waist and giving him a hug, nonchalantly drying my hands on the back of his shirt. His narrow gaze told me I wasn't as sneaky as I'd thought.

"It's fine, Dad, I promise. I'll call again tomorrow if you sit your butt down and relax."

"I just care about you."

"I know." I smiled, stepping back and turning to finish the few dishes we'd used for dinner. We had dinner with my parents a couple times a month, taking turns hosting. On our own, Jamie and I were happy eating meatless spaghetti or sloppy joes, but I used our hosting nights as an excuse to try new meals. I actually enjoyed cooking when I had the opportunity.

A loud cheer burst from my son's room, making both of us chuckle. My mother was currently in there playing cards, and she was similar to me in the sense that she wasn't going to go easy on him. She was vicious. I don't think I ever played a game where she didn't throw down a stack of wilds and force me to draw more cards than I could hold.

My parents raised me in the Midwest up until I graduated high school, including helping me with Jamie my final years. But then my dad accepted a higher management position within his company, and they moved out here to North Carolina.

I should have moved when they did. It's hard to imagine how my life might have ended up if I'd moved with them instead of moving in with *him*. But we all make dumb choices I supposed. Nothing I could do about it now.

Jamie and I had been here for a few years now, and although we'd moved a couple times, we'd always stuck to the same town my parents lived in.

I didn't grow up around much family, and Jamie already only had my side of the family that he knew, so I wanted to make sure he stayed as close to his grandparents as possible.

"Those are some deep thoughts you got swirling around."

I blinked, realizing I'd been standing at the sink, holding the same dish for several minutes. "Sorry, just sort of spaced out."

"You look tired, punkin'." He'd moved to the kitchen table and polished off the cider he'd brought with him. The fact that he could see my dark circles from there made my already suffering self-esteem deflate like a balloon, but faster. More like a whoopie cushion.

To complete the self-deprecating image I'd mentally crafted of my self-esteem's death, I blew a long, drawn-out raspberry. I threw myself in the chair across from him, waving my hand dismissively. "That's just what every woman wants to hear."

He didn't even bat an eye. He knew me too well to know when I was trying to brush off a subject. "You know what I meant. You're working too much, Madison."

"I'm fi—"

"Don't bother saying you're fine. We all know you're doing

too much when you don't need to." Hand it to my mother to enter a conversation with a flourish.

I looked up to see Beth Hartland standing in the hallway, giving me a mock glare. But even the severe expression couldn't dull her beauty. With a heart-shaped face and high cheekbones, accented by her light brown straight bob, she had the type of face that instantly made you love her.

She'd been trying to convince me to take money from them for a while now. I knew they just wanted to help and didn't care about the money, but I did. The entire idea stung.

I was paying my bills and keeping us fed. There was no reason, other than lowering the number of hours I worked, for me to accept money from them. I wasn't so stubborn that I wouldn't take money if I suddenly lost my jobs and couldn't make ends meet, but thankfully, I wasn't at that point.

"How's Brenden?" I asked, aware my obvious turn of conversation wasn't fooling anyone.

"Pull back a little, Madison. Let yourself focus on finishing school. It's not healthy for you to keep doing what you're doing. You've been through enough—"

I held up my hand, cutting her off when I locked eyes with the boy standing behind her. His brows were drawn down in a frown and his lips were pursed.

"Hey, bud, grandma and grandpa are going to be heading out soon, why don't you go ahead and hop in the shower before I whoop your butt at racing tonight."

He shuffled his feet, glancing between us. "Yeah, all right."

Watching him walk away, I made eye contact with my

mom. I knew she wouldn't say anything else on the matter with him around. She was firm and opinionated when it was just us, but she'd never undermine or lecture me in front of Jamie.

"I know you love us, Mama. I love you too. But we're doing okay. We're actually pretty happy here. It's roomier and the neighbors are quiet." Although they might not say the same about me, I thought.

She gave me a sad smile, coming up to kiss me on the head.

"So really, how's Brenden doing?" I asked, standing and walking them toward the door.

"He's good. He snagged a few more gigs and is feeling pretty good. He did the sound for an event on some sports station, you'll have to ask him about it."

"Dang, that's cool," I said, honestly believing that but knowing I wouldn't call him. I loved my brother, and I applauded how hard he'd worked for his dream job, but we just weren't super close.

Brenden was three years older than me and living in Los Angeles. He'd gone to school for film, and as soon as he'd graduated, he'd promptly moved to the west coast to work his way up. He hadn't made it big yet, but he'd made several connections, and I was proud of him.

We chatted for a few more minutes before they left, my dad promising to make my favorite meal next time if I promised to call the landlord. I didn't need any more motivation than that. Fried potatoes were the key to my heart.

As I watched them pull out of my drive, I caught sight of something on the ground near the property's mailboxes. Like someone had thrown a pile of trash out of their car window while they'd driven past. Irritated, I walked down the steps, carefully tiptoeing around nature's confetti. The last thing I needed was a stick stabbing me through my bright orange socks.

It was the neighbor's mail. The flap to his mailbox had been left down, and his mail scattered across the ground beneath it. Either the man rarely emptied his mailbox, or he was a big receiver of credit card offers and grocery sale fliers, because it was one heck of a pile.

I cocked my head, staring at it. To anyone watching me, I probably looked like an idiot who'd never seen a letter before, but I found it odd. I was sure it wasn't uncommon for a postal worker to not shut the box all the way, but for it to *all* fall out?

I glanced back at his side of the house. I had no idea if he was home. His vehicle was parked out front, but I didn't know if he had another one or a roommate whom he could be out with. I didn't see any sign of a light on, but then again, I never did. He was either a vampire or had some seriously good blackout curtains.

Should I knock on his door and let him know? I chewed my lip, the idea of knocking on his door after his note was cringe-inducing. I chuckled, maybe I'd leave a note, myself, about it. It would serve him right.

Sighing, I shoved the thought out of my head. I wasn't that type of person, no matter how much he deserved it. I walked up to his box, grumbling to myself when I had to step off my driveway and onto the grass.

I squatted, snatching each piece, and making a point not to

examine any of them too closely as I piled them on my thighs. Messing with mail was frowned upon by most, and I didn't want anyone accusing me of snooping through someone's shit.

It didn't take me long, but I could feel the cold damp of the grass soaking through to my feet. Lovely. "Farewell, beautiful fuzzy socks. I guess it wasn't meant to be tonight."

"Are you talking to yourself?"

"Shit!" I jumped from my delicate squat, sending the perfectly piled mail right back to the ground. Heart practically in my throat, I turned and looked at the woman standing directly across the street. "Oh my God, you scared me."

She didn't bother apologizing or replying at all. She had a sharp face with a pointed chin and a nose on the longer side. Her hair was pulled back into a tight bun, and she had a swipe of vibrant plum eyeshadow visible above each eye that matched the pant suit she was rocking.

She lived in the single-family home across the street, so I'd seen her before, but this was the first time she'd ever spoken to me. From what I'd gathered, she lived there with her significant other and two children. Her lips tightened, and when she raised an eyebrow, I realized she'd asked me a question.

"Oh, yeah, I guess I was." I forced a laugh, brushing my palms down my thighs. "I'm Madison, we moved in a few weeks ago. It's nice to meet you."

She didn't move to approach me, and I certainly wasn't going to walk across the street in my wet socks to shake her hand.

"Kathy Newman. I'd been planning on coming to welcome you to the neighborhood, but I didn't know what hours your husband worked and didn't want to impose."

My entire body stiffened, and I had to take a deep breath. I couldn't tell if she was being genuine or not, but I had a feeling she was fishing, trying to figure out why she'd yet to see a man here.

"No husband here, it's just us. I work a lot, but we're home most weekday evenings. You're always welcome to pop by," I offered, trying to keep my bitch face controlled.

"That's a shame. Does he travel often for work?"

My mask slipped at the look on her face, the tightening of her lips and the crinkle of her nose, but I forced a smile. You'd think I'd be used to the assumptions by now. *Is that your little brother? Are you the babysitter?*

"I meant I'm not married at all."

"Oh. It's just you?"

"And my son, yes, ma'am."

"Oh," she repeated, tightening her hold on her purse and taking a step back like she thought my unmarried status might rub off on her. "He must look older than he is." Bitch.

"No, he's as old as he looks. His name is Jamie, and he's eight."

"And he's yours?"

Like a motherfucking shapeshifter, my forced smile disappeared, transforming me into ten shades of pissed off. Of course. How silly of me to assume she'd think the child *living with me* was actually my own child. Lord knows it was more believable that I'd married an older guy with a kid than the idea I'd had him myself.

I widened my stance, crossing my arms and not even trying to sound polite. "I shoved his big ass head out of my vagina, so yeah, I'm pretty sure that makes him mine."

Did I need to provide a stranger with that visual? Nope. But the look of horror I glimpsed on her face before she spun back toward her house was worth it in every way.

I'd been shamed more times in the last eight years than I could ever count, and ninety-nine percent of the time it was by women. Sister code only held up if you abided by their rules and views. Step out of line and women could be fucking vultures.

I huffed out of my nose like a bull, mentally calling her a bitch in every way I knew. She had a boy close to Jamie's age. It was frustrating and disappointing to know she'd probably never allow her son to talk to mine.

I tried to brush the encounter off, squatting back down to pick up the mail for the second time. I'd made a nice pile, largest on bottom, smallest on top, and had begun carefully angling and twisting it Tetris-style to get it into the mailbox when I realized the owner of it was now standing on his porch. Staring at me.

Well, fuck. This looked bad.

Should I continue what I was doing and explain? Or give it a good shove and run? I stared at him, bug-eyed and frozen.

He must have realized I'd developed a gargoyle complex because he stepped off his porch and took several large strides toward me. "Something I can help you with?" His voice rang out across the distance, deep and raspy.

Trying to ignore the instantaneous clench in my gut, I clutched the pile to my chest, making sure to shut his box before walking over, eyes at my feet. "I'm sorry, I was outside, and I noticed your mailbox was open. I was trying to put it all back in so it wouldn't blow away."

I stopped a few paces away before I braved glancing up and making eye contact, and boy was it a mistake. The man appeared to be in his mid-thirties, and he was fan-your-face gorgeous. Easily the most attractive man I'd ever seen.

His espresso brown hair was shaved short on the sides but shaggy and unruly on top, and it stuck up in a few places like he'd just run one of his giant hands through it. It took one hell of a man to pull off messy bed hair. I was blatantly staring at that point, and his brows lowered over a pair of bright hazel eyes framed by long lashes.

Holy balls.

It wasn't difficult to be taller than my five-and-a-half-feet height, but this man towered over me. He had to have been at least six foot three, six foot four. And if that wasn't enough, the breadth of his shoulders was practically double mine, and they sloped down to a trim waist.

He was wearing a pair of rugged jeans that showed off tree trunk thighs and a fitted, long-sleeve black Henley that left very little of his biceps to the imagination.

It took me a minute before I realized the set of full lips resting above his square jaw were moving. "I'm sorry, what?" I blinked a few times, pulling myself out of creeper status.

"I said my box being open doesn't explain why you have my mail." He raised one thick eyebrow like I was a porch pirate, and he was waiting for me to stutter my way through an extravagant lie.

"It was all over the ground? I was just trying to put it back for you. Here." I held the stack out toward him. Maybe he'd take it as a peace offering and forgive me for both hugging his mail and the whole music incident.

"How would all of it have fallen out?"

I'd seriously never met anyone with such a low, masculine voice. I swore I could feel it wrapping around me as he spoke.

"Uh…I don't know." I bounced my arm up and down. "Can you take it?"

He stared at me for a moment before unfurling his muscular arms and grabbing the stack from me. He tucked it under one arm, tipping his head to the side and appraising me. His eyes roamed from my fuzzy feet, up along my pajama pants and too-large t-shirt. He narrowed his eyes, apparently disappointed in his findings.

I reined in a sigh. Sexy he was, friendly he was not. "Look, I wasn't snooping through your mail. I happened to be outside and noticed it on the ground. I live next door to you, my name's Madison."

He nodded, whether because he believed me or was simply acknowledging he'd heard me, I had no idea. When he didn't introduce himself in return, I stuck my hands in my pockets and rocked back on my heels. "All right, well…"

"Garrett," he grunted, albeit reluctantly.

I offered a smile. "It's nice to meet you, Garrett."

His name had barely left my lips before he twisted back toward his porch. Well, alrighty then. I watched him go, not at all noticing his perfectly toned ass as he walked up his stairs and through his front door.

I honestly wasn't sure what to do with myself. People like Kathy I was used to, but that? He'd just dismissed me like I'd handed him a pamphlet about my Lord and Savior rather than his own damn mail.

Shunned by two neighbors in one day. That might be a new record.

I made my way back into my house, ripping my ruined socks off the second I stepped through the doorway. I couldn't hear the shower going, so Jamie was set to walk out any minute.

I grabbed a new pair from my dresser and opened up my planner, plotting my assignments for the night. Tonight wouldn't be so bad, I might actually hit six hours of sleep for once.

I was heading back down the hall when the sound of my ringtone echoed from the kitchen. Assuming it was my mother calling to finish our conversation, I took my time walking over and picking it up.

Caller ID: *Don't Answer.*

My fingers gripped the phone so tight my knuckles turned white and every muscle in my body locked. I stared at the two words I'd replaced his name with, no longer hearing the ringing. Why was he calling? What did he want?

I wasn't sure how long I stood there staring at the phone screen, long after it'd gone to voicemail before Jamie's voice yanked me out of my funk. "Mom?"

Shaking my head, I glanced up to see steam pouring out

around him like a graveyard scene in an old horror film. "Sorry, bud, I zoned out. You ready to play?"

"You mean, am I ready to destroy you? Yep."

"Bring it, short stack."

Chapter 3

"ALL RIGHT, THERE'S Genesis, Exodus, Leviticus, Numbers, Deut—Deuter—"

"Deuteronomy?"

"Right, Deuteronomy, Joshua, Judges, Ruth, first and second Samuel…"

I clicked on my blinker, listening to Jamie rattle off the rest of the books, trying not to chuckle at his pronunciation of Ecclesiastes. He'd been stressed out all morning about a math test he had, so to distract him, I'd challenged him to see if he could remember all of books of the Old Testament in chronological order.

His school had made him learn them back when he was in kindergarten, and I was honestly impressed that he still knew them. Although, truth be told, I didn't know them so if he messed up, I wouldn't know.

"See, told you I knew 'em."

I darted a look over my shoulder. "Yeah, yeah. You know, the amount of random information you have stored in your brain is honestly alarming." I barely remembered the details on a court case an hour after reading it, and here he was remembering useless names he'd memorized years ago.

Jamie was a student at a private Christian academy a few minutes across town, but not because we attended the church. We weren't *not* religious; we just weren't devout either. I'd been raised Catholic my entire childhood, but I hadn't set foot in a church since graduating high school. The only reason he was enrolled there was because it was the best school in the area, bar none.

I remembered being ecstatic when Jamie had turned five and was finally old enough to start public school. I was beyond ready to save the hundreds I'd been spending on daycare each month, but the school district we'd lived in was in a shady part of town. And I don't mean a little shady, I mean, at one point I'd received a phone call informing me a man with a gun had led police on a wild chase through the play yard.

No, thank you.

So, I'd registered him at the academy, paid the non-refundable enrollment fee, considered selling my left boob to afford it, and plopped his butt in private school. It was actually the main reason I worked the hours I did. The monthly tuition alone cost more than half my rent. But I couldn't regret my choice.

I pulled into the lot, circling around to the front, mentally cheering when there wasn't a long line in the car rider lane. "Good luck on your test, bud. I know you can do it, and no matter what, you're awesome!"

"Thanks, Mom. Bye." He snatched his bag and jumped out of our old, white Jeep, slamming the door behind him.

I immediately rolled down my passenger side window. "*I love you!*"

His shoulders scrunched around his ears, and he spun slowly to look at me, eyes wide, like I didn't do this to him regularly. Muttering a quick, "Love you too," he took off in a power walk that rivaled grandmas doing rounds at the mall.

I chuckled, not feeling at all guilty for the things I made my kid put up with. He wasn't scared to throw it back at me. I switched off the orchestra music he'd been listening to and clicked aimlessly through stations before turning it off. I wasn't a fan of morning shows, and it was nearly impossible to find a station playing only music this early in the day.

Luckily, it didn't take me long to get to my weekday job. Living in a town of around 21,000 people had its perks. I didn't desire the congestion and traffic of a larger city at all.

I parked next to my boss, taking a deep breath and holding it in for as long as I could before exhaling. I actually enjoyed this job a lot, and I loved Evaline, my boss, but desk jobs were difficult when you didn't sleep much.

I grabbed my heels from behind the middle console, swapping out the flats I'd been wearing. Hopping out of the Jeep, I adjusted my black pencil skirt, pulling it down and making sure everything was covered and in place.

My white button-up blouse was a little wrinkled, but I could look worse. It was nearly impossible to keep my clothes from wrinkling when I had to travel to do laundry and didn't own an iron. Evaline was used to it.

I worked for the security side of a sister company business. One side handled security, private investigations, and running background checks, while the other side handled home and business alarms. Our side happened to be in the middle of renovations, so I'd been having to use the alarm side's door. And I hated it.

"Good morning, Madison dear, how are you today?"

Swallowing down the anxiety I always felt walking through their side, I smiled down at the seventy-year-old, white-haired woman who loved red lipstick and handled the front desk. "Good morning, Ruth."

Ruth had worked for the company for the past thirty years but had recently dropped to part time. She hadn't officially announced it yet, but she'd hinted she was ready to retire. I'd almost cried, knowing their side would make me take over her job rather than hire someone new.

I enjoyed working for Evaline, but she was a close family friend of the man heading the alarm side. So she had no qualms with sharing me and still expecting me to keep up with my current responsibilities. Her trust in my abilities was forty percent comforting, sixty percent frustrating.

"How's the little one?"

I smiled, loving how Ruth still referred to my son as little.

It was nice to know someone else didn't like him growing up. "He's good, thank you."

I passed through the lobby, inwardly cringing at the prospect of walking by a certain desk that faced the hall. The one and only hall leading to my side of the building.

I turned the corner and didn't even try to hide my heavy sigh when the desk sat unoccupied. My relief was staggering. But I made sure to speed up anyway, taking advantage of his absence. He never took a day off, so he was hiding around here somewhere. I had no intention of running into him if I could help it.

Tossing my purse under my desk, I signed into my computer, spinning my chair in circles aimlessly while I waited for it to log me in.

"Madison, is that you?" a soft voice laced with a hint of a southern accent called out.

"Yes, ma'am."

"Can you come help me with something real quick?"

"Give me a second to log my time and then I'll be right in!" I stuck my leg out to stop my chair's motion and sat up straight, pulling up my timecard form. Double clicking on my email icon next, I cringed at the number of unread notifications.

"How was your evening?" I asked, making my way toward her office. "Want me to start coffee first?"

"Yes, please! Will you grab my prints while you're in there?"

"Sure." It was just Evaline and me down here, but there were three offices, so we'd spent a day transforming the office in-between us into our official break room. I'd brought in a mini fridge I'd owned since high school, and she brought in a fancy coffee machine.

She couldn't offer me more than thirty hours a week or pay more than minimum wage, but I still considered myself lucky. Sometimes when we were slow, she even looked the other way and let me study.

Inhaling the aroma of the brewing coffee, I grabbed an orange off the table, snatched the papers off the printer, and marched into her office.

"Oh, honey, that skirt looks good on you."

"Thanks! I found it at the thrift shop downtown last week. I snagged my hose when I climbed into my vehicle this morning, but I didn't feel like going back in to change into pants."

"If anyone ever figures out how to make a cheap pantyhose that doesn't get runs every time I sneeze, I'll die a happy woman."

I laughed, sinking into a chair and handing her the printed documents. Evaline was crazy, but I adored her. As blond as could be and coming in at barely five foot tall, she was a petite woman all the way around. If I looked up "delicate" in the dictionary, I was pretty sure Evaline Grayson would be a synonym.

"What can I help you with this morning?"

"I need help figuring out how to set up an account on a website, but we'll get to that in a second. I actually wanted to tell you, Jim and I were talking this morning, and he has a few new jobs he'd like you to do."

I'd been in the process of peeling my orange but paused at the name. Jim was Evaline's husband, and he happened to head the security side of the company. "What does he need me to do?"

"Do you remember the big case we took last week?"

"The one about all the credit card fraud claims at the fast-food place?"

"That's the one. Jim and Tony finally finished all the interviews yesterday, and he'd like you to transcribe them." She pushed her glasses higher up her nose, worry lines appearing on her forehead like she truly thought I might say no.

"I don't know how great I'll be at it, but I can do it. Was that all?" I tossed the peel in the garbage and pulled off a few chunks of fruit, shoving them into my face.

"He wants you to apply for an Unarmed Guard license this week so you can take over a few shifts at the community college."

I choked, burning citrus juice shooting straight up my nose. I gasped, patting my chest and blinking away tears. "What?"

"We're picking up companies faster than people are applying. We're understaffed, and he's hoping you can pick up an occasional weekend shift."

"Me though? Like...seriously, me? He wants *me* to take a guard shift at the college?" I was not an intimidating woman. I ran from spiders and peed myself when I saw snakes. I was not, in any way, cut out to be a guard.

"You have the educational background to qualify for it, and it'd only be when we have no other choice." She smiled at me, but it was a forced expression, and it was clear she didn't exactly agree with her husband on the matter.

"Okay, I guess. But I'm only available for a day shift on Saturday."

"That's perfectly fine. I'll let him know your answer and send over the information for the license later this afternoon."

I knew I was still sporting a grimace as we discussed the rest of the day's schedule, going over client deadlines and the transcription assignment. My primary responsibility was running background checks, but we were getting in so many new clients I wondered how I'd fit in anything else when I only worked there thirty hours a week.

I'd been starting, stopping, rewinding, and replaying an interview for about an hour, and was diligently concentrating when fingers curled around my shoulder and warm breath tickled the back of my neck. Goosebumps erupted across my skin, and not the good kind. More like the kind you get before an evil spirit appears.

I'd been sitting hunched over my keyboard with my legs crossed in my chair, so when I slammed into the back of my chair, I smashed my knees into the underside of the desk and nearly tipped over. Ironically enough, it was the bear-sized grip still attached to my shoulder that kept me steady.

The feel of his breath stuck to my neck, and I slowly lowered my headphones and looked up at the man standing behind me. A few inches over six feet, Rob Spencer stood above my seated form like a fucking skyscraper on steroids. The guards and security technicians who sometimes came through the office had even nicknamed him after a famous, bald-headed wrestler.

A solid decade out of the military, Rob still maintained a high and tight haircut and always kept his sharp jaw shaved clean. He was thirty-eight and could have been an attractive man, if he wasn't such a goddamn creep. Just being alone in my office with him was sending all sorts of bad vibes up my spine.

"Something I can help you with, Mr. Spencer?"

"As much as I enjoy hearing you say my name that way, darlin', I've told you a hundred times to call me Rob." He smiled at me, and he had the nerve to caress his thumb along the top of my arm. I looked down at his hand and back up at him.

"Rob. Something I can help you with?"

"Many things." He smirked, and I vomited slightly in my mouth. "But today I'm actually here to help you."

I leaned away from him far enough to send a signal for him to drop his hand. "What?"

"Your unarmed guard license."

"Oh." I turned away, pulling random background requests from the stacks on my desk and looking them over even though I'd already finished them. This couldn't be happening. I didn't want him here. Did Evaline know he was here? She knew how I felt about him.

He circled me, folding his large body into the cheap, wooden chair in front of my desk and crossing an ankle over a knee. He looked ready to settle in for a while, and my stomach roiled.

I'd never forget my first day of work, how he'd walked up behind me similar to how he'd just done, and I'd smiled up at him, humming with the excitement of starting my first job within the criminal justice field.

I remember my smile twitching as he stepped into my personal space, remember trying to bury my personal issues and stay polite. I'd introduced myself, but instead of shaking my hand, he'd kissed it. And not some brush of the lips. He'd actually left a wet film on my knuckles. And when he'd moved to leave, he purred in my ear. Fucking *purred*.

Each and every meeting since had only furthered his level of ick. Looking across my desk at him now, I had the sudden desire to throw my stapler at his face. "Are those for me?" I asked, finally noticing the papers he'd been holding in his non-harassing appendage.

He handed them over, and I made sure to keep our fingers as distanced as possible as I took them. It was an application packet for the license. "I offered to train you, but Jim said you can only work Saturdays." His lip curled on one side.

Rob worked part time at a hardware store on the weekends, thank God. "I appreciate the offer. So, is this all?" I asked, wiggling the application.

"Yeah, darlin', that's all you got to do. Send over an email when you're done, and I'll figure out who I can schedule you with to shadow." He pushed up off his knees and stood, leaning over my desk.

I flinched back, but he continued reaching over and gently pulled on one of my curls. "Have a good day."

The door to the hall had barely shut before I was barging into Evaline's office.

"I'm sorry, Jim asked you to do what now?"

I sighed, knowing full well how this conversation would go. My dad knew Jim Grayson personally. He'd been the one to put me in contact with Jim in the first place.

My dad's company had been a client and hired out guards from them a few years back. I'd be surprised if Jim didn't wake up in the morning to a strongly worded email from my father.

"He wants to keep me on the back burner so I can take shifts when they have no one else. Just daytime rounds at the community college on the weekend when no one is there."

"That makes no damn sense, Madison. What in the hell are you supposed to do if you find a man breaking into one of the buildings? You're not equipped to handle those kinds of situations."

"Gee, thanks, Dad. That didn't sound sexist at all."

"Don't get smart with me. You know what I meant. You shouldn't be putting yourself in that kind of situation." His stern voice echoed out through the speakers of my Jeep while I headed toward Jamie's school.

"I won't be the only female guard under their employ."

"They're not my daughter. I don't care about them. With your history—"

"Please don't go there," I interrupted, ten seconds from hanging up. I'd called as soon as I left work to talk to my mother and get her opinion on taking an extra weekend shift, but my dad had been the one to answer.

"I need to go, Dad, I'm almost to Jamie's school. Just tell Mama I called and have her call me later if she has the time."

"Yeah, yeah, I'll tell her, but you and I are going to talk

about this more the next time you come over for dinner."

"Love you! Goodbye!"

"Love you too."

I turned my music up, trying to drown out the thoughts going through my head and failing. It's not like I wanted to work yet another shift. Saturday was the only day of the entire week that I didn't work during the day. I was tired enough as it was.

But the worst part was I'd be sacrificing even more of my time with Jamie. I knew he understood, but I hated it more than I could put into words. And who would be with him while I was gone? I couldn't keep sending him to my parents. They had lives and full-time jobs too. They deserved a break on the weekends.

I tightened my grip on the steering wheel, breathing out slowly, but the more I thought about it, the more that thick, suffocating feeling slid through my limbs, weighing me down. No matter how hard I swam, I couldn't ever seem to pull myself out of it enough to not let it suck me back in.

I felt the telltale burn of tears, and I blinked rapidly to contain them. The last thing I needed was for Jamie to see I'd been crying. "Keep it together, Madison."

But the moment the first tear leaked, I lost complete control over all of them. They poured down my face silently, not caring even the slightest about the mascara they were sure to ruin.

I knew who I needed to call. Who would tell me the truth and could help me get my shit together. The only person who could. Not letting myself second-guess it, I clicked on my Bluetooth and voice dialed.

"Well, hey, baby mama."

"Hey, I'll be pulling up to Jamie's school soon so I can't talk long, but do you have a second?"

"Who do I need to beat up? I can head out first thing tomorrow."

I laughed, wiping at my face. Leave it to my best friend to instantly know how to pull me out of my funk. "Put down the shank, Jethro. No murdering today."

"Why does it sound like you've been crying?"

Of course, she'd pick up on it right away. I'd known Layla since we were ten. We'd seen each other through our worst phases, our awkward phases, and our too-drunk-to-function phases.

She'd been the one to hold my hand for fourteen hours while I gave birth. She knew what I sounded like when I screamed, when I laughed, when I cried, and when I took a shit. She knew everything. So I wrapped myself in the comfort of our friendship and let myself fall apart a little.

"Am I a bad mom for being gone so much?" I heaved in a shaky breath, ignoring the car stopped next to me at the light. Lord only knows how deranged I looked.

"What? No. Who told you you're a bad mom for working?"

"No one." I sniffled, wiping at my nose. "Evaline asked me to take another position which would make me work a few random Saturdays, and I said yes. Not that I had much choice in the matter."

"You gave up your only day with Jamie?"

"Yes," I whispered, hating to admit it out loud.

"Who's going to hang out with him?"

"I'm not sure yet, I'll probably have to ask my parents." As much as I didn't want to ask, I knew they'd do it. They may not have been happy when I wound up pregnant at sixteen, but they loved him with every piece of their hearts.

"Bitch, I've told you I'd move there and help you. You know I will."

"I know." The line went silent for a minute, apart from her shuffling the phone around.

"Well, I'm pulling into Jamie's school, so I have to go. I just needed to verbally process my emotions."

"You still have a spare room?"

"Yeah."

"Perfect. Call me later and we'll talk details, but I'm coming. Don't even try to argue with me. I have nothing important holding me here right now. It'll cut both our rent payments in half, and I can help watch our son."

I huffed through my nose, "Layla Davis, I don't—"

"What's that you say? You see Jamie walking to the vehicle and can't argue? No worries, I'll call you later, bye!" She yelled it all out in the span of a single breath, and then the bitch hung up on me.

I'd squatted down to grab a new soap dispenser from under the sink when I heard the clink of a dish being set on the counter. I twisted to look over my shoulder. "And just what do you think you're doing?"

His face puckered like he'd stuck an entire lemon in his mouth, and he threw his head back, groaning. "I don't want to wash the dishes tonight. Not having a dishwasher *sucks*."

"Do you know what you sound like right now?" I asked, narrowing my eyes.

"Ungrateful."

"Ungrateful." I agreed. "You have dishes. You have food. You have running water."

He looked at his feet, shuffling them back and forth. I knew he hadn't meant it that way, he was just a kid who didn't want to do a chore, but I also didn't want him growing up not appreciating everything we had.

"You have two choices, bud, you can wash the dishes, or you can clean your room. I stepped on no less than four building blocks the last time I walked in there."

"I'll clean my room," he said over me, already halfway out of the kitchen. Looking at the pile in the sink, I decided he had the right idea.

I let out a heavy breath, I didn't want to wash the damn dishes either. Promising myself I'd do them before bed, I decided to take advantage of Jamie being busy and poured myself a glass of wine from the half-empty box in the fridge. Closing the door as quietly as I could, I stepped out onto the porch.

"Leave me the hell alone."

The words were spat out so harshly, I reared back, plastering my back against my front door. I stood there frozen, hand clenching my cup, eyes darting around the dark to find the source.

"I don't really fucking care, Courtney."

It was then I noticed the small red glow of a cigarette out in the neighbor's driveway and made out the outline of his body, pacing back and forth near his Nova.

"I. Don't. Care. Have a nice life, or don't. Preferably the latter." He ripped the phone away from his ear and took a deep drag of his cigarette.

I wasn't even the woman he'd been yelling at, but I felt just as small and exposed as if I were. What was it about men that made them believe their size gave them permission to talk to women that way?

As soon as I thought it, I squinted an eye, chastising myself. I didn't know him or that Courtney woman. For all I knew, she was a nutjob sister or an ax murderer.

He suddenly whipped toward me, and I panicked, eyes widening, scared I'd accidentally spoken my thoughts out loud. He stared at me, smoke billowing out of his nose in a steady cloud.

Taking several large strides toward me, he stepped into the halo of light cast by my porch lantern, and I was able to see he was wearing a dark shirt with a logo on the breast I couldn't quite make out. I'd thought his arms had looked muscled the other day, but in a t-shirt, the unblemished, defined curves of his biceps and forearms were on full display.

His lips were flattened into a straight line and his brows drawn low over his eyes. He looked pissed. With my free hand, I blindly reached behind me, feeling for the door handle. He'd just opened his mouth to speak when I found it. Not waiting for him to yell at me for eavesdropping, I shoved my door open and ran inside.

I locked the door and spun around, feeling like I was fifteen again, getting caught sneaking out of my house in the middle of the night. Looking up, I spotted Jamie's head peeking out of his room. "Did you spill your drink all over yourself again?"

Yes. Yes, I did.

Chapter 4

A WEEK AFTER my phone call with Layla, I somehow found myself on a small airplane at five o'clock on a Saturday morning, heading to my home state. It really was crazy how life could change in the span of one day.

Layla had called me the day after my mini-breakdown and demanded she come live with us, refusing to take no for an answer. We'd struck a deal; she'd move to North Carolina as long as I flew to her and made the cross-country drive with her.

The one-way ticket had been surprisingly affordable, so if I was being honest, I didn't argue hard against the idea. She was my best friend, and I missed the shit out of her every day.

So there I was, smashed in the middle seat between two armrest hogs, on my connecting flight to Kansas. Thankfully, the time zone went back so I'd gain a few extra hours during the trip and arrive by eleven o'clock. I couldn't afford to take more than two days off from any of my jobs, and my parents couldn't watch Jamie on the weekdays anyway.

Layla would be picking me up from the airport, and we'd be heading straight over to get the moving truck. At that point, we'd load up her boxes as quickly as possible and immediately start the twenty-hour drive to North Carolina.

We were planning to drive straight through in order for me to make it to work on time Monday, but we'd pulled so many all-nighters in our lives, I had faith we'd do all right. As long as we took turns, it couldn't be *that* hard.

I shifted in my seat, fiddling with the "I love mommy" bracelet Jamie had made me a few years ago. I wasn't sure what had made me decide to wear it, but as I was packing, I'd suddenly felt the need to bring a piece of him with me.

It'd been only the two of us for so long, I suppose I just needed some reassurance. It felt weird to know I'd be in a different state than my child. I'd never done it before, and it felt wrong somehow, like I'd abandoned him.

In the rational part of my brain, I knew those toxic thoughts weren't accurate. But when you spend years being ridiculed and critiqued for every parenting choice you ever made, it's hard not to join in and judge yourself right along with the haters.

Jamie knew I was traveling to Kansas to visit Layla, but he thought I was taking a "girl's vacation." He didn't know she'd be coming back with me, and I couldn't wait to see his face. He'd been in love with her since he could speak.

Back when he was about five years old, Layla had brought

her boyfriend at the time over, and Jamie had burst into tears because he'd wanted to marry her. I had a feeling she was eagerly waiting to tease him about it.

Declining a drink from the flight attendant, I pulled out a highlighter and one of the three college textbooks I'd managed to squeeze into my carry-on bag. Laying it out across my lowered tray, I prayed I could study without the motion of the aircraft making me nauseated.

"You studied *both flights?*"

"What else was I going to do? Crochet?"

"Sleep, Mads, you were supposed to sleep."

I shrugged. It was so rare for me to get daylight hours to study, and I was already going to miss out on time during our return trip. I felt like it was only logical to take advantage of the flights. I doubt I could've slept in the middle seat anyway. That was just asking to wake up cuddling a stranger's shoulder.

When I'd landed, Layla had been waiting at the airport coffee shop. Dressed in a baggy sweater and leggings, she hadn't noticed me when I first arrived. She'd been hunched over a book with large, square glasses resting on her freckle-dusted nose. Her hair was loose, landing about mid-waist and was an eye-popping, vibrant blue. I might have hugged the ever-loving shit out of her.

Since I hadn't needed to check a suitcase, it didn't take us long to reach the parking garage and cram ourselves into her tiny

Miata. I'd landed early afternoon, so as long as there weren't any hiccups with the truck rental or packing up her stuff, we were looking good to put some miles behind us before it got dark.

"So..." she started, merging onto the highway, and I already knew where this conversation was going to head. "Meet any hot guys lately? Maybe a new guard at work, or a nice, scruffy gas station attendant?"

I rolled my eyes. Layla had been on me for years now about *getting back out there*. She knew me well enough to know I was lonely, but she also knew me well enough to know I had neither the time, nor the desire, to date.

In my experience, there were only four things the human male species was accomplished at: donating sperm, exaggerating the number of recipients they'd donated to, bragging about where the sperm was deposited, and disappearing the moment said deposit did its intended purpose.

I told her as much.

"You're too young to be so damn cynical, Mads."

I bristled at her disapproving tone. "It's the truth and you know it. And that's with me not even mentioning male number two who came after that."

"You're seriously the most pessimistic person I've ever met."

I puckered my lips, pretending to consider it, then shrugged and nodded my head. She was right, I was pessimistic as hell. Life had made sure of it.

"Speaking of male number two...when was the last time you called him?"

My entire body tensed, her words triggering my fight or

flight response. And since there was no safe way to fly, I went with the first choice.

"Why would I call him?" I demanded. "I haven't called him since the day the divorce was finalized."

She darted her gaze at me, her eyes narrowing and lips curving down. "And when was the last time he called you?"

"Does it matter?"

"That recently, huh? What a fucking asshat. Seriously, I hope someone takes a shit in his exhaust pipe."

I sighed, reaching up to rub my temples. It was too early in the trip to already be touching on sore subjects. "He's called me a few times, but it's always random and spaced out." I paused, clasping my hands in my lap. "He called last week, late evening. Don't give me that look, I didn't answer."

"Good. I'd fucking castrate you if you did. He was probably drunk."

I nodded in agreement, but internally flinched. Her statement wasn't meant to sting, but it did all the same. When we were together, Aaron had only cared about me when he was sober. Once we separated, he only cared when he was drunk.

A half-hour later, we were driving onto the gravel parking lot of a…company? Where in the hell were we? "Layla, are you sure this is the right place? It's kinda shady looking."

"Yeah, this is the address the guy gave me, and look, there's the moving truck and car trailer parked over there." She turned off her Miata, but neither of us moved as we glanced around, the same look of apprehension on our faces.

"O—kay. Let's get this over with then. Keep your key

between your fingers."

She pinned me with a side glare, shoving her door open and hopping out. But as we rounded the vehicle, I could see the key sticking out between her fisted fingers.

Two grimy men, some suspiciously wrinkled paperwork, and one hour later, we were gunning it out of the parking lot. "Okay, you were right, that place was shady as fuck," she said.

I responded with an exaggerated, wide-eyed nod. It had been the right place, they'd had paperwork ready for us and everything, but it had been the most awkward experience I'd had in a while.

The two men hadn't even assisted us with getting Layla's car onto the trailer. In fact, they'd acted like they'd never done it before in their lives, so we'd had to figure it out ourselves. It'd taken longer than we'd wanted, and we were now behind schedule.

"At least it was cheap."

We arrived at the apartment she'd been sharing with a friend from college. We were both starving, but neither of us had felt confident attempting to grab a quick bite with the truck and trailer.

We'd be lucky if we made it the entire trip without getting stuck somewhere as it was. Our driving skills weren't something to brag about even on the best of days.

But two hours, two sets of sore, shaking arms, and two pairs of sweaty pits and tits later, we were done packing.

"Why do you have so much stuff? Where are we going to put all of this?" I asked, sagging against the driver door. The thought of raising my noodle arms to hold the steering wheel for the next few hours sounded horrendous.

"It's not as much as it looks. It's mostly clothes. And shoes," she said, walking toward the apartment door one last time.

I huffed a laugh. My fashion sense tended to be 'thrift store snazzy,' whereas Layla's was 'come get me sexy.' She'd always had the most amazing closet.

"I really don't think all your bedroom pieces and your music stuff will fit in the room, Layla. The rooms are small."

"Eh, I'll shove it all in the garage since you don't use it. The acoustics will be bomb in there anyway." She disappeared into the apartment to give one final look over and to grab her fur baby.

I walked around and gripped the rope to pull the rolling door shut, eyeing Layla's keyboard and sound system. She'd been singing and performing since she was old enough to hold a guitar, and there was literally no one who could hold a candle to her. Banjo, violin, electric, twelve string, she could play them all.

During middle school, she'd even added piano to the mix. I was just patiently waiting for her to become famous and support me for the rest of my life like the dependable baby daddy she was.

Confirming the back was latched and wouldn't fly open, I'd just started turning when something slammed into the backs of my knees, sending me forward and smacking my forehead into the truck.

"What the hell, Sadie?" I yelled, shooting a glare at the wet nose and lolling tongue staring up at me. That adorable face silently watched me rub my forehead while her butt moved a mile a minute. "Yeah, yeah, hello to you too, mutt."

Sadie was a pit-bull, golden retriever mix, and at only a few years old, she was as sweet as she was rambunctious. We'd already shoved her giant bed in-between the captain chairs of the truck cab, and I opened the door, letting her leap in.

"We all set?" I turned to see Layla locking the front door with a licorice stick hanging out of her mouth.

"Yup. Let's get on the road, bitch!"

***

Wine shot out of my nose, sending flames through my sinus passages and tears to the corner of my eyes. I flailed my hands in front of my face, coughing and wheezing. "Tell me you didn't."

"I did."

"In the same weekend?" I somehow croaked out in the midst of my coughing fit. I closed my eyes and squeezed the bridge of my nose. Wine would be sloshing around my brain for at least a week after this.

She continued, unfazed by my near-death experience next to her. "I mean, I would've voted for us to all join together, but sadly they weren't down for crossing swords. Shame, but we can't have it all, I guess."

I dropped my hand, squinting my eyes open to look at her.

"You're joking."

She burst out laughing, reaching over to pat my thigh. "Yes, you poor sap, I'm completely full of shit. I don't like to share, you know this."

Shaking my head, I took a—carefully controlled this time—sip of my rosé. It was Thursday evening, five days after Layla and I had packed up her life.

We'd arrived half-dead, but safe, to the duplex late Sunday night, and it'd already been one of the best weeks I'd had in years. I hadn't realized just how lonely I'd been, how deprived I was of non-work-related, adult interaction.

Jamie's reaction had been icing on the cake. We'd picked him up from my parents Monday morning, and he'd been jabbering so much, it'd taken him a solid two minutes to realize she was sitting up front with me. He might have actually stopped breathing for a moment.

His eyes had resembled a shining pair of anime eyes, and his voice had screeched out a shocked, "What?!" when she informed him she'd moved in with us.

Every day since had been amazing. After work Monday, I'd actually been able to shower *before* bedtime without feeling guilty about sacrificing Jamie's and my evening game session. Layla had talked so much smack about beating him that he'd challenged her to take my place.

She'd turned and winked at me when he rushed to start up the system, tipping her head toward my bedroom door. I'd almost kissed her.

Tuesday, I'd picked up Jamie and came home to find dinner

cooked and ready; a slow cooker meal that made the entire house smell like fall. Not having to prepare a meal had given me an entire extra hour to study, which in turn, meant I got an entire extra hour of sleep that night.

Yesterday, I'd walked in the front door to find her folding our freshly laundered clothes while our pups wrestled on the floor at her feet. I didn't know where she'd gone to wash them, but she could have washed them in a river, and I wouldn't have cared. It was one more chore marked off my never-ending list.

Granted, I knew things would change when she started working, but I was going to soak up the help while I could.

Now we were outside, slouched in white, plastic chairs she'd purchased yesterday from the dollar store, and drinking. Not wanting to make numerous trips inside and risk waking Jamie up, we'd brought the entire box of wine out with us. Throw in a full bowl of popcorn and our comfiest sweaters and leggings, and we were over here living our best lives.

Layla pulled out her phone to play music, but I made an excuse about wanting to enjoy the peace and quiet. If I told her about the note my neighbor left, she'd only demand to blare the music even louder. She didn't take anyone's shit.

I was known to bite when provoked, usually because of people like the bitch of a neighbor, Kathy, but I didn't enjoy it. Confrontation made me itchy.

"Seriously, though, Mads, what do you do for fun? If you suddenly had an entire weekend of paid vacation and your parents watched Jamie, what would you do?" She took a giant handful of popcorn, cramming it all into her mouth and looking at me like a deranged chipmunk.

"Sleep."

"Fuck off, I'm serious."

I reached between us for the wine and poured another glass. Did I need it? No. But I was about to have a weekend full of double shifts, so I was determined to enjoy my last evening at home this week.

"I'm serious, too. I wouldn't even know what else to do. The few times I'm relaxed with Jamie and not studying, I'm building a train set with him or watching animated movies."

I shrugged, pausing long enough to toss a few pieces of buttered goodness into my mouth. "Even the thought of going out to a bar or spending the weekend on a beach with a sexy, hazel-eyed, dark-haired, muscled stranger has me riddled with anxiety. I've officially forgotten how to socialize."

Her drink, which she'd been lifting to her face, froze an inch away from her mouth. A disturbing smirk graced her lips, and her eyebrows were closer to her hairline than her eyes. "That is quite a specific description of a stranger, my dear Madison."

I waved my hand flippantly, dismissing her observant—and irritatingly correct—assumption. There was no way I was going to tell her about Garrett, my rude but hunky as hell wall neighbor. "It was just an example."

"A very precise one. What an imagination you must have." She wiggled her brows. "I suppose when the only thing getting you off is your hand and imagination, you have no choice but to get good at—" She ducked, cackling and dodging my attempt to smack her.

I shook my head, laughing despite myself. It was true, it'd been years since anyone other than myself had touched me. I didn't usually mind, but there were definitely days when I craved the feel of a man's hands sliding across my skin, the brush of lips along my neck, and the eruption of butterflies during a breathtaking kiss.

But I didn't let those days trick me into thinking I *needed* a man. I didn't. Jamie and I were scraping by just fine, and as much as Layla liked to joke, my hand and imagination worked a hell of a lot better than any man ever had.

"Teasing aside, Mads, do you really have no interest in dating again?"

"I don't know. Relationships take time, and I don't have that to give to someone right now. Not to mention, unless I meet a guy at the grocery checkout who isn't sneering at my EBT card, or some nice single dad enrolls his child in Jamie's class, I don't go anywhere *to* meet someone."

She tipped her head back, pondering that. "What about online dating? That's how I met Sam," she said, referring to her ex-boyfriend.

She suddenly sat up, growing more excited as she worked through her thoughts aloud. "Actually, it's perfect for you. You can post the truth about your situation so only those who don't care will contact you, and then you can weed them out from there."

"I don't think men our age use those sites. They just pick up women downtown near the college."

"Which is why you need to look for an older man."

My mind instantly flickered to Garrett, like a string had yanked on my thoughts and plopped me at his feet. I shook the image of his chiseled features and muscled biceps away, busying myself with brushing kernel pieces off my lap.

"Can I put 'looking for sugar daddy' in my bio?"

She spread her hands out in the air, mimicking a banner. "Must have a big dick and deep pockets."

I drained the last of my wine. "If I can't fit inside his pockets, I don't want him." We tried to keep straight faces, but failed, erupting into laughter.

"And they said romance was dead."

I froze at the sound of that voice. A familiar rasp that rumbled through the air and danced across my skin. Leaning forward to see past the side railing of the porch, my eyes latched onto the arresting, damn near haunting, view of its owner.

Cast mostly in shadow, with the porch light illuminating his face like a beacon, Garrett stood a foot away from the railing, staring right at me. His hands were tucked into his pockets, the sleeves rolled up to expose his forearms, and a cigarette was perched between his lips.

He looked untouchable. Unattainable. The kind of man your mama warned you about, but the kind you'd willingly crawl on your hands and knees for anyway. He was dressed in only a plain white shirt and black sweats; his feet bare on the cement. It was obvious he hadn't planned on coming over. He'd likely just stepped outside for a quick smoke when he overheard our immature conversation.

I was struck speechless, but Layla didn't miss a beat.

"There's nothing wrong with telling someone what you're after up front. Honesty is always the best way to begin a relationship, wouldn't you say…?" She stretched out the last word, holding her hand out and tilting her head in an obvious indication she was waiting for his name.

He didn't give it to her.

He just continued staring at me with that same flat expression, and I swore beneath it was a hint of disappointment. My skin itched, and I felt like sinking down into my chair and hiding behind my legs.

Garrett pulled the cigarette from his mouth, plumes pouring from his nose. "Is it *honest* to sit there objectifying men for their bank accounts and dick sizes knowing tomorrow you'll be the first to ridicule men online for objectifying women for the size of their tits or homemaker status?"

My eyes felt like they were going to fall out of my head, and I suddenly regretted my extra glass of wine. I couldn't come up with a single, decent response. "We were just joking," I said, hoping to prevent his face from growing any angrier. It did the opposite.

"If a man said that, you'd call it an excuse and tell him to *do better.*"

I moved to argue, but stopped, letting my mouth hang down like a fish for a second before snapping it closed. He was being a dick about it, but I could see his point. If I'd stepped out of my home to have a moment of peace and overheard two men talking about women's worth being based on their bodies and employment status, I'd have taken offense.

So instead of yelling at him, I was about to apologize and tell him he was right. That is, until his next comment sucked the words right back down my throat.

"It's no wonder you aren't dating anyone. Women like you give women everywhere a bad name. Nothing but a leech wrapped in a pretty package, looking for a sugar daddy to take care of you while you sit at home, drink wine, and go shopping." Each word lashed out harder than the one before, his anger finally clawing through.

He stepped right up to my porch and put his cigarette out on my railing, sneering up at me as he did. I stared right back at him, refusing to look away first. I knew my entire face was flushed, and my ears burned like Hades himself was mouth breathing against them. I didn't know what to do with my body, let alone my face.

I wasn't unfamiliar with people judging me. I'd been given the scarlet letter at sixteen and called a slut more times than I could count, along with every possible synonym for it.

But this was worse. It reminded me of the time a college-aged coworker had approached me while I was pregnant, offering to pay me for sex. My rounded belly had apparently screamed "I'm Madison, and I'm easy. You don't even have to wrap it up because I'm already pregnant. Enjoy the risk-free ride."

I was still living at home and going to school but had daycare to pay and couldn't afford to quit, so I'd had to continue seeing the asshole every shift.

This felt much like that. He'd basically called me a sleazy

gold digger, and it didn't matter that I knew it to be untrue. Just like the guy back then, I was stuck in his vicinity, unable to walk away and never see him again.

My eyes burned, and I shifted in my seat, submitting defeat and glancing away. I sensed, more than saw, Layla straighten to her full five-foot-ten height, locking her spine for battle. She knew me better than I knew myself and could probably sense my quickly rising anxiety.

"Well, you can fuck right off. If you want to run your mouth, go do it in your own home. You couldn't have made it more obvious you don't know her at all."

He gave a dry mockery of a laugh. "And I don't care to."

Ouch.

He twisted, the movement catching my eye and convincing me to look up, only to be ensnared in his accusatory gaze. He looked me up and down, and then gave me his back, his long strides taking him back toward his side.

Layla launched out of her chair, snatching her glass and the near-empty box of wine. I could practically hear her grinding her teeth, and for a second, I thought I saw actual flames in her eyes.

Wrapping my fingers around my own glass, I took my time following her inside, trying to give myself every possible second to withstand the storm she was about to unleash upon me.

The lock hadn't even fully slid into its home for the night when her nails dug into my shoulder, whipping me around. "I *knew* it, you dirty little slut!"

That was not at all what I was expecting. "Wait, you knew what?" I asked, legitimately confused.

She leaned down into my face, raising both hands and making air quotations. "A hazel-eyed, dark-haired, muscled stranger? How convenient the man who just approached your house like he's already intimate with it, just happens to look like that. Spill."

"I'm not sure how to answer that."

She grabbed my shoulders again, shaking me like a rag doll. "Spill!"

I stepped back, slapping at her arms. "He's not intimate with my side unless he knew the residents before me. I've only spotted him a few times and only talked to him once before this. It didn't go much better."

"He's fucking hot."

"Yeah," I agreed. There was no reason trying to deny it. He was calendar model hot. I threw myself face down on the couch. There was no way I was accomplishing any studying tonight.

Layla sat on top of me, slouching down and getting comfortable. "However, he's also a fucking, judgmental asshole."

"Seems so."

She sucked on her teeth. "I bet he's quick on the mark. Shame. Those arms are delicious."

"Careful," I said, my voice muffled by the cushion smashed against my face. "You're objectifying him."

She laughed, smacking me on the ass. "He's really our immediate neighbor?"

"Yep," I said into the couch.

She twisted her lips to the side. "I don't know how I feel about that."

"Me neither."

Chapter 5

WE WERE GOING to be late. Between the wine and the drama—frankly just about everything last night—I'd forgotten to set my alarm for the first time in years.

Thankfully, my body was so used to getting minimal sleep, sleeping in equated to only an extra half hour. However, when you only give yourself one hour to wake up, get ready, drop your kid off, and get to work, it's a problem.

I'd been mid-roll when I suddenly had that intuition that hits you when you just know something's wrong. My eyes shot open, quickly followed by my mouth as I shouted an expletive, I prayed Jamie didn't hear.

He had. That blessed boy had gotten himself up and was eating a bowl of cereal when I ran out. His blond hair was sticking up in every possible direction, but at least he was up and wearing pants.

Plucking the spray bottle off the bathroom counter, I doused his hair in mist, causing him to squirm and spill milk down his chin, before pushing a hat on his head. It'd have to do.

Five minutes later, I jogged back out, tucking my blouse into my slacks as I went. My hair-tie was clasped in my hand and my shoes tucked in my armpit. "Are you ready, bud?"

"What do you think?"

I glanced up from my pants to see Jamie standing at the door, shoes on and backpack slung over his shoulder. He was sticking his tongue out with crossed eyes.

"Okay, I deserved that one." I chuckled, grabbing my frizzy, third-day curls and throwing them into a bun on the top of my head. I didn't have a lick of makeup on, and my head was already letting me know it didn't appreciate the lack of morning coffee. "I'm ready, let's go."

"Rugsy looks like she needs to pee. Also, you don't have your purse."

I wasn't going to curse. *I wasn't going to curse.* "Go ahead and buckle into your seat, I'll be out in a second," I said, handing him the keys and running to snatch my purse from my room.

Layla cracked her door as I passed, her half-lidded, mascara-smeared eyes watching me. "I'll deal with Rug, you go ahead and go." Her voice was rough with sleep, and I instantly felt guilty for waking her up.

"Are you sure?"

"I was planning on taking Sadie to a dog park I found. I'll bring Rug along with us. It's fine."

"She'd like that." I moved again, then paused, looking back at her. "Are you still good with hanging out with Jamie tonight, or should I drop him at my parents?"

"Nope, we're good. Now go before you get fired and have to take up hooking to pay the bills."

I ran toward the door, flipping her off behind my head as I went.

"It's been a long time since I've seen you with your hair pulled up. I almost forgot how cute your ears are."

I closed my eyes, taking a deep breath and praying to every deity of every religion to give me the patience to deal with this fool today. I hated it when anyone talked about my ears, but especially when he did.

My ears weren't big by any means, but they stuck out from my head rather than lay flat. I didn't use to care until my ex made a habit of referring to them as handlebars. I had a feeling Rob would be the kind of man to do the same.

I was currently standing at the copy machine on his side of the building because we didn't have a machine capable of copying multiple sheets at the same time on our side yet. I'd been begging Evaline to get one so I wouldn't have to come over here, but she didn't want to until all the construction was done.

Keeping my back to Rob, I continued working, hoping if I ignored him he'd get the hint and walk away. The only consolation I had was that we were standing in the middle of the hallway so at least he wouldn't try to touch me. Should I have known better at this point? Probably.

His thick fingers slid against the shell of my right ear and instant panic set in, making me flinch away and twist toward him. His eyes flared; his hand still outstretched.

Fuck, I hated reacting like that in front of people, it made me feel weak and stupid. And if there was anything I did not want to appear like in front of someone like Rob, it was weak and stupid.

The feeling of not having control over your body or emotions was one of the most humiliating and debilitating experiences. And one of the hardest to overcome.

"Please don't touch my ears, Mr. Spencer." Stepping back up to the copier, I grabbed my pages and shuffled them into a neat stack. I hadn't finished, but I'd just do the rest one at a time on our small printer.

"I was only playing around, darlin'. I didn't mean to startle you." He smiled at me like my reaction to his touch was adorable.

"I would prefer it if you didn't touch me."

His smile fell, and he pulled back a little, flattening his lips and giving me a stiff nod. "All right. Well, I have your guard uniform in my office. Jim forgot to ask your size, but I'm pretty sure I ordered the right one."

Because that wasn't creepy as hell or anything. "I need to finish what I'm working on, can you set them in my box, and I'll grab them later?"

His jaw flexed, and the skin around his eyes creased. He wanted to argue, I could see it in every inch of his posture, but someone, somewhere, smiled down on me. "Sure. Swing by and talk to Jim on your way down, he's wanting you to shadow Saturday."

My grip tightened on the pages, digging the edges into my palms. "This Saturday?"

"Why, do you have plans?"

I turned, ignoring his question. "I'll talk to Jim about it, thanks." He muttered a reply, but I was already halfway down the hall.

After confirming with Jim that he did, indeed, want me to take a six-hour training shift on Saturday, I ventured back to the alarm side of the building ninja style and found the uniform tucked into my box. Taking it into the bathroom, I tried it on so I could let him know if it wouldn't work. I couldn't decide if it was convenient or disturbing that it fit perfectly.

My day had drastically improved after lunch. I'd finished everything on my calendar, completed and aced a quiz during my lunch break, and since Evaline was out of the office for the afternoon, not a single soul bothered me. Solitude was the key to my heart some days.

Right at three o'clock, I was pulling out of my work parking lot, singing out of tune with the radio, and trying to hype myself up about my waitressing shift that night.

My schedule was insane but consistent. Monday through Friday, I worked for Evaline from eight in the morning until three in the afternoon. Friday night through Sunday night, I worked at a restaurant in town known for its chicken wings and beer. My shifts there started around four in the evening and ended whenever we closed, usually around midnight or one in the morning.

The hour in-between shifts gave me just enough time to grab Jamie from school, drop him off at my parents' house, and change clothes before heading right back out.

On Sunday mornings, I worked another six-hour shift at a shipping company for a man named Ken, inputting driver timesheets and processing the week's payroll. All of it added up to over sixty hours. That wasn't taking into account any guard shifts I might occasionally pick up as well.

I was still a few minutes away from the school when my phone rang with an incoming call. I glanced down at the screen to see the caller ID showing Jamie's school. Shit.

I pulled into the lot, edging my Jeep into a tight parking space. The call had been the secretary, asking me to come into the office to get Jamie rather than the car rider line. Thinking he'd been hurt, my stomach had dropped, sending a nauseating sensation up my chest and into my throat.

She'd assured me he was fine, and that Mrs. Brueger just needed to speak with me. Considering Mrs. Brueger was the principal, I couldn't say it made me feel a whole lot better. I yanked the tie out of my hair, re-working it into a tighter, more presentable bun, and peeked at myself in the mirror. Go figure it'd be the day I didn't wear any makeup.

I glanced at the clock, frustrated. If I didn't hurry, I would be late for work for the second time in the same day. Slipping my heels back on, I made my way into the school, the click of my shoes on the linoleum echoing out like the inevitable countdown of a bomb.

My meetings with the principal never ended how they started. We'd begin by swapping tight smiles and each sit, clenching a metaphorical item in our hands—me, a matchstick, and her, a lighter. Then she'd lean forward, slowly, politely, and set it aflame, smiling at me all the while. I'd begin to sweat, watching the minuscule flame eat closer and closer to my skin. And just when I'd think I'd lucked out and it began to die off, she'd throw fucking gasoline on it.

Mrs. Brueger may have allowed Jamie to attend the school, but only because she had no actual reason to deny him. My money was as good as anybody else's, and she despised both it and me. She hadn't always. She'd frowned on Jamie's first day when I'd explained I was his mother, but that was it.

Then one day, I made the mistake of forgetting to deposit my month's worth of tips into my bank account, and I'd had to pay Jamie's tuition in mostly ones and fives. If I'd brought in a dead body, she wouldn't have shown as much horror and disgust as she did when she saw that cash.

She'd assumed the worst and hated me ever since.

The secretary ushered me into Mrs. Brueger's office, telling me she was going to retrieve Jamie from his classroom and have him wait for me.

"Good afternoon, Ms. Hartland." I looked at the dark-haired woman sitting at the desk, not missing the way she stressed the *Ms.*

I took a seat across from her, giving her the usual practiced smile and sat back, crossing my legs. The office was small and always made me feel trapped. "Good afternoon."

"I'll make this quick. Something with Jamie has been brought to my attention, and I feel it is prudent we discuss it."

"Okay." I intertwined my hands in my lap, already wanting to throttle her by her tone alone.

"His teacher, Mrs. Rener, said Jamie hasn't been completing assignments and has been lying about—"

"My son doesn't lie."

"—it, saying he turned them in."

"If Jamie says he turned something in, he did. He sits at our table several nights a week and works on assignments."

Ignoring me completely, she kept on going, rolling a pen back and forth between her thumb and pointer. "Mrs. Rener also said he regularly ignores her lectures and reads books under his desk."

"Then he's bored."

She opened her mouth, but I continued. "Look, I'm not saying it's okay for him to ignore the lesson, it's not, and I'll talk to him about it. But he has an A in every subject, so he understands what's being taught, he's just not handling it in a great way."

She set her pen down, leaning forward onto her elbows and resting her chin against her steepled fingers. "Is there anything going on in his life that might account for his sudden disinterest in school? Any changes?"

I deserved an award for containing my eye roll. She was blatantly disregarding everything I was saying. "We moved out of our apartment and into a new home a few weeks ago."

"Ah," she said, as if that explained everything. "That's probably it. Suddenly having a new bed and new people around is a lot for a child his age."

My hands clenched each other so hard, a few knuckles popped. "We didn't move in with anyone. It's still only us, and he sleeps on the same bed he always has."

"Are there male figures coming in and out of his life?"

"Excuse me?" My face grew hot, my ears raging infernos on either side of my head. Was she fucking serious?

"I'm just trying to find out if there's anything going on that might be causing him anxiety and to feel like he has to escape into a fictional world, Ms. Hartland."

"I do not have *men* coming in and out of my home, Mrs. Brueger, and I do not appreciate the insinuation that I do."

"My apologies. I suppose it was presumptuous of me to accuse you of allowing your dates to meet him." She didn't sound apologetic at all. She sounded like she was so full of shit that it was packed all the way up to her tonsils.

"I don't date."

"Is his father—"

I stood abruptly, the chair scraping across the floor like nails on a chalkboard. "If that's all, Mrs. Brueger, I need to go. I'd rather not be any later to work than I need to be. I will email Mrs. Rener to apologize and to discuss providing Jamie with higher level work. I will also speak with him tonight about his behavior in class."

Her mouth hung open, like she was genuinely shocked I'd cut her off and would leave. "Yes. Please do."

I was fuming, practically foaming at the mouth when I re-entered the main office. Jamie jumped off his seat, eyes wide and white knuckling his bag. I didn't acknowledge the secretary as I stormed out. I couldn't. I was ten seconds away from exploding.

Jogging to keep up with my pace, Jamie didn't say a word as he buckled into his seat, but I could feel his eyes on me. I ripped off my heels, throwing them on the passenger seat and watching them bounce off onto the floorboard. I curled my hands around the steering wheel in an iron grip, blinking rapidly and trying to clear my vision enough to get us home.

"Mom? Are you mad at me?"

Awesome. Superb parenting, Madison. Meet with your child's principal and then leave pissed and not say a word to him. That won't give him the wrong idea at all.

My head dropped forward to rest my forehead against the wheel. The burn in my eyes finally easing as the tears won the battle and slid down my cheeks.

"No, bud. I'm not mad at you." I applauded myself on how smooth the words came out even while my soul was splintering on the inside.

"Am I in trouble?"

Leaning back, I futilely swiped at my eyes and forced myself to put the Jeep into reverse and leave Satan's playground. "Your teacher is frustrated with your lack of interest in class. She said you're ignoring lessons and reading books. I agree with her that the behavior is disrespectful. You know better. But no, you're not in trouble as long as you promise to stop."

"Then why are you sad?"

His question made me feel even worse, guilt surpassing anger. Parenting was fucking hard. Hell, adulting, in general, was hard. My mama had warned me, but she hadn't warned me enough.

"I'm not sad, I'm angry." And humiliated. Vulnerable. Exposed. "But it has nothing to do with you. I'm sorry for worrying you."

I took a deep breath, mentally bitch slapping myself to get my shit together. All it was doing was clogging my nose and upsetting my child. And Lord knows I wouldn't make any tips tonight if I showed up with a puffy face.

I called the restaurant as soon as we pulled up to the house, letting them know I'd had to go into the school and would be late. Then I climbed out, circling the vehicle to open my passenger door and find the heels I'd thrown.

I'd just leaned down when my skin tingled, the hairs on the back of my neck standing at attention. I twisted my neck and glanced over my shoulder to see Garrett standing in the middle of his yard with a push mower.

His eyes, which had been on my ass, snapped up to my face. I frowned at him, straightening and tucking the heels under my arm before shutting the door.

His gaze zeroed in on my face and lingered. He worked his jaw back and forth, narrowing his eyes slightly before they finally dropped to the child stepping up next to me. Jamie stared back at him, a defiant look on his face, and I watched Garrett's eyebrow arch before he turned away, effectively dismissing us. Fine by me.

I ushered Jamie into the house, hearing the rumbling of the mower start up as I closed the door.

"What the hell happened?" Layla barreled toward me like a bull that'd spotted a red flag.

I cleared my throat pointedly, flicking my eyes to Jamie and back. "Nothing. We'll talk later, but I need to go." Dropping my purse on the bar, I ran toward my room, throwing off my clothes and yanking on my uniform. Five minutes later, I had on the barest of makeup and was running back out, shoes and apron in hand.

"Thanks again for hanging out with him. Try not to destroy the house, you two."

Layla hadn't moved a muscle. She was looking all over my face with squinted eyes while I shoved my feet into my shoes. Crossing her arms over her chest, she said, "I make no promises."

I gave Jamie a loud, smacking kiss on the cheek which he instantly rubbed off. "Behave, love you."

"Love you too."

Locking my spine, I walked out, prepared for another stare-off with Garrett, but both he and the mower were nowhere in sight.

Chapter 6

AN HOUR INTO my shift, and I'd already added a new stain to the shins of my pants. I groaned, tempted to stamp my feet. Solid black and snug in all the right places, they were my most comfortable pair of work pants. Go figure.

I wiped my hands on my t-shirt, uncaring if I got it dirty, and started grabbing plates of wings, smelling them and stacking them in order along my arm. I'd been working at the restaurant long enough, I could tell the flavor of each wing sauce by smell alone. It made my job a whole lot easier since the cooks had a habit of not labeling them anyway.

Turning, I bumped the swinging door open with my hip, dashing out to each meal's designated recipient, smiling and refilling drinks before heading back into the kitchen to do it all again.

Overall, I didn't mind waitressing. It wasn't always easy, but the tasks themselves were fairly straightforward and it kept me busy. The only slow time I ever had was at the beginning of my shift during the grace period before the dinner rush.

Which was why my boss hadn't batted an eye at my late arrival. He was younger than I was and high as a kite most days, so he was pretty laidback. It bugged me more about being late than it had him.

I'd stressed about it the entire way here, deciding I would start taking my uniform to the office to change so I could drop Jamie off and head right back out. Layla was about to start her new job soon, and I'd have to start dropping him off at my parents again anyway. It made sense to cut out as much wasted time as possible.

About halfway through my shift, I finally got a lull in my tables. It was times like this I envied the smokers who had an excuse to step out back for a break. If I had the money to spare, I'd buy a pack and light one up and hold it, just so I could join them.

Checking on the few customers I had, I made sure they'd be set for a bit and then made my way to the bar. Nate always worked the same nights I did, and he was my favorite person here. "Hey, Nate."

"Hey, Curly, where has your cute ass been all night?"

"Working. We can't all laze about, twiddling our thumbs behind a bar." I grinned at him.

Nate was a damn good bartender, and he had the giant jar of tips to prove it. Around the same height as me, he had black hair slicked back, tattoos covering every inch of his arms, and big green eyes that worked like a charm when he needed something. He had a mysterious and dangerous vibe to him but was a gooey pushover on the inside.

He also happened to be a horndog with a firm belief in open relationships and group activities. I'd lost track of the number of times he'd tried to convince me to give the lifestyle a shot. Not with him, but in general.

My answer had always been the same. No, thanks. Reverse harems were sexy in books, but the female anatomy could only take so much. I swore my vagina clamped shut just thinking about more than one dude climbing on top of me in a twenty-four-hour period.

"Guess I'll be too busy twiddling my thumbs after close to make you a drink then."

Recoiling, I clutched my chest and dropped my mouth open. "You wouldn't dare." He just pointed at me, making me chuckle.

I tapped my hands on the bar, getting ready to head back to check on tables when a familiar face snagged my attention. I froze, blinking several times, unsure if it was actually him or not.

Dressed in jeans that pulled taut around his thighs and a dark green Henley, Garrett sat perched on a stool at the far end of the bar. He was leaning to the side, one elbow resting on the bar while his other hand curled around a bottle of beer in his lap.

He wasn't alone. Sitting next to him, blessed with his undivided attention, was a woman. She could've been a stranger I supposed, but his posture was relaxed, and his face lacked the tension I'd begun to think was a permanent feature. It seemed like he knew her, *liked* her.

I wondered what it was about her that enticed him, what he preferred in his women. Looks could often be deceiving, but she appeared to be in her early forties with thick, luscious curves, and long, coppery waves that fell about her shoulders. She was gorgeous.

I liked to think I had a decent ass, but there was nothing luscious about my thighs, and no one would be writing ballads about my B-cup breasts. Biting my lip, I forced myself to snap out of it. Who cared what he saw in her? It's not like I wanted his attention.

Before I could force my body to move, his eyes traveled over the woman's head and landed right on me, widening almost imperceptibly. I could have looked down and seen a sniper's dot on my chest, and it wouldn't have caused my heart to stop as much as his stare did.

I should've walked away right then. I didn't owe him anything. I knew that, but some neighborly part of me wanted to repair the rift between us and at least say hello.

With each step I took in his direction, his face seemed to close down more and more, until it finally settled into that flat look I was accustomed to. His companion, sensing his attention was no longer hers, looked over her shoulder at me. Her brows rose, and her eyes darted back and forth between us.

In perfect Madison fashion, I gave her an awkward wave, and then looked back into Garrett's unfriendly, yet still stupidly attractive, face. "Hey, Garrett. How are you?"

"Fine."

He took a swig of his beer, his tone sharp enough to slice a chunk out of me if I stepped too close, and I couldn't help but feel irritated. He was never going to see me as anything more than a gold digger. It was time for me to get over it and stop wasting my time. I *wasn't* like that, so his opinion didn't matter.

No matter what, I refused to let him think his attitude affected me. Pasting on my biggest waitress smile, I said, "That's great to hear. I've got tables I need to check on so I'm—"

"I thought you did something else for work."

"Um..." I froze, wondering where he was going with that. Both his tone and the curl of his lip told me he thought I was being sketchy. Was he trying to imply I didn't actually work here? For his intellect's sake, I sincerely hoped not. I was wearing an apron, for fuck's sake.

"I do."

He wanted to ask another question. I could see it in the way he tapped his fingers along his half-empty bottle, the way creases appeared across his forehead and his tongue pushed against the inside of his cheek. In the end, his desire to ask won out against his desire to ignore my existence.

"Then why are you working here?"

The motherfucker really thought I was lying about something. Was he that dense, or just convinced of his own superiority that he couldn't fathom the idea he'd been wrong about me? Either way, I blamed my pent-up anger from the day's worth of shit interactions that fed the fire on what I did next.

Gracing him with the most insincere expression I could

muster, I stepped into his personal space, just shy of straddling his knee. The side of my pinkie brushed the top of his hand as my fingers wrapped around his beer.

I pulled it from his grasp, knocking my head back and downing the half-full bottle in one go. Bringing my face a few inches from his, I ran my tongue across my bottom lip, his eyes tracking the movement.

"Because I've yet to find a sugar daddy with a large enough…" I dropped the empty bottle directly in his lap, letting my eyes linger on it, "pocket."

The look on Garrett's face was worth every crushing wave of anxiety I was inevitably going to suffer from later, likely when I tried to sleep. I stepped back, keeping my eyes on his surprised ones, and letting my face drop into my best bitch face. "Have a good night, Garrett."

I made my way back to the kitchen, ignoring Nate's attempts at grabbing my attention. What the hell had I been thinking? I had no idea if anyone other than Nate and Garrett's companion had seen that, but I could only hope the answer was no.

I'd like to say I held my head high and worked around my asshole neighbor, but I didn't. I avoided the bar like the plague for the next hour or so, going so far as to bribe another coworker to deliver my tables' alcoholic drinks.

It wasn't until Nate finally found me and told me Garrett had left that I stopped hiding like a little bitch. I may have no issue showing fangs when threatened, but you bet your ass I'm going to tuck tail and run as soon as it's safe.

By the time the last straggler left for the night, and we'd

locked up to start closing duties, it was sometime after midnight. Sadly for me, nothing assisted my brain in dredging up things I'd rather forget than monotonous, boring chores.

Refilling condiment containers? I was thinking about how good Garrett looked in his favored Henleys. Mopping the floor? I was remembering the way our hands brushed and how I'd wrapped my lips around the same bottle he had a few minutes before. Wiping down the bathroom? I was physically cringing at what'd I'd said and done.

I might as well have dug a hole, climbed in willingly, and started scooping in dirt. If he thought I was a whore looking for a sugar daddy before, he definitely believed it now. I didn't know why it bothered me so much. Maybe because we shared a wall, and as long as I lived there, I'd regularly see him. It just would've been nice to get along, I guess.

"You ready yet, Curly?"

I looked up from the table I was sitting at to see Nate with his jacket on, his foot tapping away. I'd been counting up my cash and zoned out. I hadn't even realized we were the only ones left. "Yeah, I just need to go cash out real quick."

"You want your usual?"

"Please."

He gave me a mischievous grin, and I knew he was waiting to push me about my encounter with Garrett as soon as we stepped outside.

Sure enough, as soon as my butt landed in a seat and I'd curled my feet underneath me, he'd handed me my cranberry juice and rum and gone straight for blood.

"You got any hot plans tonight?"

The way he exaggerated the word 'hot' had me narrowing my eyes. "Nope."

"Curly, with the amount of tension pulsating off you and your mystery man, I thought for sure you were gonna get you some after work. I thought maybe he was a new boyfriend, and ya'll were doing some role-playing shit."

If I'd have been taking a drink, it'd have gone straight to my lungs. "Jesus Christ, Nate. No."

"I don't know, I felt like I was watching the foreplay scene for a porno. It was hot."

I set my cup down, hiding my face in my hands and shaking my head. "Oh my God, you need help."

"And you need to get yourself laid."

I examined the contents of my drink, taking a swig and giving Nate a side-eye. "There is not nearly enough alcohol in here for this conversation."

It was almost two o'clock in the morning when I pulled into my drive. I was worn out, but at least I didn't have to study. As a whole, I enjoyed weekdays more. I'd always rather hang out with Jamie and study than work a double shift, but tonight, my brain was thankful it didn't have to function academically.

Removing the keys from the ignition, I looked over at Garrett's side. There was an unknown car parked behind his Nova, and I could only assume it was the woman I'd seen with him. My stomach tightened, and an oily feeling curled up inside me. Jealousy.

Not that she was with him, but because of the simple fact that two adults had the opportunity and desire to enjoy each other's company and bodies. And I'd be over here, continuously going home alone like I had been for years.

Maybe I'd sleep on the couch tonight. The idea of hearing Garrett shaking the sheets as his reward for strutting through life as a dick was more than I could bare. Especially when I'd likely be snuggled up against a pillow just to feel like someone was sleeping next to me. Maybe I'd shove Layla over and crash in her room.

"Hey, mama bear."

I startled, dropping the keys I'd yanked from the lock. Layla was lying across the couch on her stomach, knees bent and feet criss-crossing back and forth. She was looking up at me over her reading glasses, a notebook and pen in front of her. Neither dog was present, probably curled up together in one of our beds.

"I didn't realize you'd still be awake, it's two o'clock in the morning. Did anything happen with Jamie?"

"Yes, his room caught on fire, and while we were running outside to escape, a copperhead bit him on the ankle. Also, he has mono. I just thought it best not to call and tell you any of that."

I rolled my eyes skyward, praying to the ceiling constellations for patience. This woman was lucky I owed her, or I would've sat right on her face. "So why are you still up? Music muse?"

"Something like that." She toyed with the pen, pressing the

end button in a rhythmic tune. "I slept for a little bit but woke up hungry. I came out here for some Oreos and an idea for a song hit me. So here we are."

"If you give a Layla a cookie."

"Ugh, you're such a mom."

I plopped down on the floor, letting my head fall back to rest against her thigh and exhaled heavily, I was so ready to pass out. "Really, though, did he behave?"

"Yeah, of course. We had a great time. He missed you though. He beat some time record on Rainbow Road and turned to tell you before remembering you weren't home."

My heart fell, straight through my feet, the floor, the ground, the goddamn planet itself. Layla could've shot me, and it wouldn't have torn a gaping hole in my chest as savagely as those words did.

It wasn't the first time, nor would it be the last, of me disappointing him. He learned to hide it more now that he was older, but I knew he wished I was home on the weekends.

No matter what I did, what choices I made, I always lost. If I only worked one job, we'd be homeless. If I worked two jobs, we'd be back sharing a one-bedroom apartment. If I worked three jobs, I could finally provide my child with a home, but at the cost of our time together.

Sometimes I wondered if the person who first said money can't buy happiness ever knew what it was like to be poor. To struggle. Did he or she ever have to take a calculator to the store just to find a way to afford a month of groceries?

Inspirational quotes weren't made for those of us living near the bottom. They were made for people at the top to feel better about their privileges. To tease us bottom dwellers that if we tried harder, reached farther, or if we just learned to appreciate what we currently have and not what we *could* have, we could be just as happy and content as them.

It was bullshit wrapped in fancy words and a flowery background to overpower the stench. The world wasn't made for us losers to win. The best we could do was simply finish the game unscathed.

Chapter 7

I'D LOST MY mind. I stood in front of my mirror, staring down at my body. A gray button down tucked into black slacks, and a giant, gaudy security badge stared back at me. I'd even been given a flashlight and pepper spray to attach to my belt. Freaking *pepper spray*.

The only thing that made me feel the slightest bit better was even though I may have been stupid enough to accept this job, Jim Grayson was even more stupid for asking me. Nothing against female guards, women could rock any damn thing they set their mind to. I just wasn't one of those women.

Throwing a sweater over my uniform, I snatched the scuffed, black shoes I'd worn the night before and stumbled out of my room. Saturday morning was the only day during the week I got to sleep in, but due to this training shift, I'd only been able to steal four measly hours. Taking this shift had me questioning all my life choices.

Thankfully, there'd been zero moaning sounds through my bedroom wall, so I'd at least been able to crash in my own room. They'd either already finished their business by the time I fell face first onto my mattress, or they were especially good at keeping quiet. Even still, I was feeling grumpy.

I made a pit stop at Jamie's door, cracking it open and peering inside. "Psst, Jamie." I rapped my knuckles lightly on the wood. "Morning, rise and shine." Sheets rustled, and I could make out the lump of his body twisting on the bed. He mumbled an incoherent sentence.

"Sorry, bud, I have work today. Up and at 'em if you want breakfast." A muffled groan was the only reply. Good enough. I shut his door as quietly as I could, trying not to rile Sadie in the next room.

Layla was still crashed and would be for several more hours. She was meeting some guy today to play music with. She'd run into him at a coffee shop in town, and they'd hit it off after discovering their shared love for Martin guitars.

Part of me was apprehensive about her meeting up with someone we didn't know, but the other part of me was happy for her. I'd been worrying lately that she was going to regret coming to live here, but if she started dating, she'd hopefully put down a few roots and make a home here as well.

A scratching noise caught my attention, and I glanced to the right to see Rugsy dancing in front of the patio door, whining. "I know, I'm coming."

Dropping my shoes, I put my body weight on the door, shoving it open as far as I could, hissing when the frigid morning air battered against me. "Make it quick, sausage roll, it's freezing out here."

I left her to do her business, sliding my socked feet across the kitchen floor and aiming for the coffee pot. There were a lot of things I'd given up over the years to save money, but coffee would never be one of them. I'd shank a bitch if someone tried to take away my caffeine.

I hummed a random children's song to myself and scooped in the butterscotch-flavored grounds. I was filling up the water reserve when I heard the patio door shifting and creaking and stepped back, looking over the bar to see Jamie. "You got it shut all the way?"

"Yeah." He rubbed his eyes, readjusting his crooked pajama pants and stomping his big feet into the kitchen. I wasn't any happier about being awake on a typical day off than he was, so I decided to give him a free ride on the sassy train.

Tossing some bagels in the toaster, I began mixing up a big glass of chocolate milk to help pump up his mood. "Layla won't be home, so you'll be staying the night at grandma and grandpa's tonight."

He dropped into a chair, crossing his arms over the table and laying his head on them. "I know, she told me."

I offered up a small smile, hoping he wasn't too mad about me and her both being gone on our hangout day. "This won't happen often, I promise. I just have to go in for training today."

The bagels sprang up, and I plucked them out, tossing them

on the counter and sticking my semi-burnt fingers in my mouth. "You'll have fun, and I'll try to swing by and see you before I head out tonight."

He nodded over his arms but said nothing, and the guilt that had eaten me up last night hit me again like a speeding bulldozer. I swallowed it down, putting a smile on my face and telling myself I was doing the right thing.

I handed him the chocolate milk and an apple, the guilt I felt thicker than the topping for his bagel. "Regular cream cheese or strawberry?"

***

A half hour later, I herded him out the door, amazed we'd managed to walk out on time. We'd both lazed about, daydreaming about our pillows rather than actively getting ready.

We each zipped up our jackets and walked out front. Technically we had a one-car garage, but the door sounded like a herd of stampeding dinosaurs, and I was scared of it breaking and trapping my vehicle inside, so we didn't use it.

"—so nice. I wish you'd come out more often, you don't have to stay home all the time."

My head swiveled to the side at the sound of a woman's voice. Jamie and I paused mid-walk, looking at the three individuals also walking out of the house next door.

Garrett wore gray sweatpants that hung off his hips in a way that felt indecent, and a black tank that showed off every ripple of muscle all the way to his shoulders. It was unfair how attractive he was without even trying.

His hair was tousled like he'd just rolled out of every straight woman's wet dream, and when my wandering gaze finally made it to his face, those hazel eyes were fixed on me.

I'd been right, the vehicle belonged to the woman from last night. She stood next to him in the same clothes she'd worn the night before. Normally, that would've indicated they'd had a one-night stand, but the third individual threw me off.

He was older than Garrett, maybe around his early fifties. He had what society would label a "dad bod" with a salt-and-peppered beard and matching hair that was pulled back in a ponytail. He stood with a similar air to Garrett and had his arm wrapped around the woman's shoulders.

Had they all spent the night together? My eyes widened of their own accord. I hadn't heard a damn thing, and the wheels of my mind were working overtime. How did one have a threesome *quietly*?

Ignoring Garrett's continued stare, and the now two extra sets of eyes on us, I opened the passenger door, setting my purse and Jamie's overnight bag on the seat.

"Are you heading to work?"

The deep, gravelly voice slid up my spine, stopping at the base of my neck. I turned to find him a few steps closer, arms crossed over his chest, glowering at my slacks and work shoes with such intensity that I subconsciously stepped back.

It was only one step, one small, singular movement, but I might as well have quaked like a leaf and waved a white flag to my observant, overprotective son. By the time I'd finished the lone step, Jamie had shoved in front of me, crossing his arms and mimicking Garrett's stance back at him. "Who are *you?*"

Oh my God. Darting forward, I wrapped my hands around his shoulders, pulling him back against me. "That's Garrett, he lives in the other half of the duplex." Jamie's face didn't relax. If anything, his frown deepened.

Addressing the glowering man, I answered, "And yes, I work today."

I sneaked a glance back at the Jeep, about to pull Jamie toward his door when the woman reached out and smacked Garrett in the back of his head. "Fix your face."

A chuckle tried to burst out, and I hastily sucked it back in, a choked, wheezing sound escaping me. He didn't flinch at her parental-like assault, his eyes just traveled up my body before he turned his glower on her instead.

I exhaled, feeling like I could breathe again. The woman, unfazed by his irritation, *tsk*ed at him and shook her head. Walking toward me, she waved her hand in his direction and said, "Don't mind him."

She extended the same hand to me as she continued, "We met yesterday. Kind of." She laughed, like the memory from last night was a treasure she was savoring. "So, you're the neighbor. I'm Sarah, Garrett's sister-in-law."

Attempting to mask my surprise, I reached past Jamie, who remained statue-still in front of me, and took her hand. "Yes, that's me. I'm Madison Hartland, it's nice to meet you."

Sarah smiled, and it lit up her entire face. Sporting wrinkled clothes and smeared makeup, yet she was somehow still gorgeous. She hooked a manicured thumb over her shoulder at the man who'd had his arm around her. "That's my husband, Harold."

Harold let out an irritated grunt that had her erupting in giggles, and I wondered if she was maybe still a little tipsy. Unfortunate brother-in-law aside, I decided I liked her, and I knew Layla certainly would.

"He'd prefer it if you called him Harry." Her eyes twinkled, and I couldn't help but smile back.

Dropping her gaze to Jamie, she asked, "And who's this strapping young man in front of you?"

I'd been prepared for the question and immediately slapped bricks down, building up my defensive wall with superhuman speed so my disappointment at her response wouldn't show on my face. I wasn't ashamed of Jamie, not even a little, but that didn't mean it was always easy to stomach responses with a smile on my face.

"This is my son, Jamie." I gave his shoulder a small pat and waited for it—the slight nose curl most people did without even realizing it. But it never came. In fact, she didn't react at all besides reaching a hand toward him to shake.

It was Garrett who caught my eye. His double-take was subtle enough that I would've thought I'd imagined it if it weren't for his face. It was like I'd told him the earth was square.

His eyes widened, deep creases appearing across his forehead as his brows rose. His arms fell slack to his sides, and he darted his gaze back and forth between Jamie and me.

I could've guessed word for word what was going through

his brain. He was calculating, adding and subtracting our apparent ages, trying to figure out if I looked younger than I was or if Jamie looked older.

"Garrett, why didn't you tell me you had such a handsome neighbor?" Sarah asked, winking at Jamie, and my heart warmed at the open smile he gave her. She'd made his entire day with that comment alone, and I was tempted to hug her.

Garrett sighed in the way all people did when their siblings were being annoying as hell. He looked to Harry for help, but Harry only chuckled, clearly not tempted to help him out at all.

Accepting defeat, Garrett walked forward until he was even with her and looked down at Jamie. "It's nice to meet you, Jamie."

Then he smiled—a small one, no more than a tilt of the lips—but it morphed his entire face, relaxing the harsh edges and exposing the barest hint of dimples.

I gripped Jamie's shoulders to keep myself from stepping forward in a daze. Garrett's smile was like the fucking sun, sucking me into its gravitational pull against my will. I was pretty sure my panties disintegrated on the spot. The man had fucking *dimples*.

In hindsight, I should've known better and paid more attention to my reaction. Jamie, more aware than I ever wanted him to have to be, took my snug grip as a sign that I was uncomfortable. The grin he'd given Sarah disappeared, and he openly glared at Garrett, muttering the most unfriendly hello ever to be released into the world.

But instead of looking insulted, Garrett appraised him. He roved his eyes over his face with a contemplative look, and I fidgeted, wondering what he saw. Could he see the stress radiating from Jamie's small body, the fight response vibrating just under his skin?

Garrett's eyes finally twitched the tiniest bit, and then they snapped up to me. For the first time since meeting him, he seemed to see me, and the fluttering sensation occurring in my middle in response was a clear indication it was time to go.

I looked to Sarah, who was watching us with a devilish smirk on her face, and tipped my head toward my vehicle. "It really was nice meeting you, but we need to head out."

Her hand went to her chest, worry lines gracing her face. "I'm a talker, I'm so sorry, I hope I didn't make you late."

I gave Jamie a gentle push, whispering for him to buckle in. "No, no. I don't have a set time this morning, I just have to get in a required number of hours, and I can't afford to be late tonight."

Garrett's mouth opened and then snapped shut, the muscles in his jaw flexing as he re-crossed his arms.

"All right, well, bye." I gave a wave, circling back around the Jeep and climbing in. Knowing Jamie was watching me, I reined in the natural urge to grip the steering wheel and backed out of the drive.

I waited patiently for the mini explosion that was coming, and I didn't have to wait long. We'd barely made it to the end of our road when he detonated.

"Why did he talk to you?"

"You don't think people would want to talk to me? I'm cool." Yep, I was deflecting like it was dodgeball.

"No. He was being nosy. He shouldn't be asking about your work."

I flicked my eyes up to the rearview mirror. He was staring out the window, hands clenched in his lap, and his face was strained. "He lives next door, bud, he was trying to be friendly."

"He didn't look friendly."

"Honestly, I think that's just his face. You know how Layla tells me I always look angry when I zone out? I think Mr. Garrett suffers from the same thing."

I glanced up again, but he didn't crack a smile. "You shouldn't have told him anything. You should've told him to worry about himself, like you tell me all the time."

Nausea coiled in my stomach. I'd slowly been sewing up all the holes Aaron had carved into Jamie's heart, soothing his stress and avoiding things that set him off, but my irresponsibility with my reaction to Garrett had ripped it all open again.

I didn't blame Garrett; it wasn't his fault his size and general vibe were intimidating. The only person who deserved the blame was Aaron.

"Yeah, maybe you're right, but he wasn't being malicious. He and Sarah were just talking and being neighborly. It's always good to get to know your neighbors in case of an emergency."

He finally turned, making eye contact with me for a moment through the mirror. "We have each other for that, and Layla."

I sighed, wishing I wasn't driving and could sit next to him and force him to give me a hug. "We can't be scared of every man who talks to us, bud. That's not how I want to live, and that's not how I want you to live. We deserve more than that, don't you think?"

He huffed a heavy breath, and his voice came out sharp and angry. "I wasn't scared of him. I just didn't like him looking at you like that."

Deciding not to feed the flames, I raised my invisible flag. "The coolest thing about choices, bud, is they're *yours*. You don't have to like anyone if you don't want to. You should never be rude without cause, but there is nothing that says you have to like Mr. Garrett."

"I just don't think *you* should like him."

I pushed down a laugh. I honestly had no idea how I felt about our burly, hot-to-cold neighbor.

~~~

After Jamie had sprinted into my parents' house with a shouted "Goodbye!" I'd stood outside for a few minutes, chatting with my mom. She'd scheduled several things for them to do over the weekend, and I was thrilled. A solid distraction was exactly what he needed.

I'd be swinging by to see him before working tonight, and I planned on waking up early so I could see him tomorrow morning before I did my payroll shift, but other than that, he'd be with my parents the entire weekend.

I had no idea how we ever would've made it without them, how any single mother, teenage or not, could ever make it without some sort of help. Single parents were expected to work
~~~

full time yet stay home with our kids, be educated yet not abuse federal assistance, and somehow afford rent, bills, food, clothes, and gas by ourselves.

And heaven forbid we ever need to hold up a register line to pull out a WIC check.

I knew, without a shadow of a doubt, I never would've brought Jamie and me to the comfortable point we were at if my parents hadn't been available to watch him while I worked, and if I hadn't been willing to accept that help. Not everyone in my situation was that lucky.

I nodded, excited for the things Jamie would get to do with them. He'd have a blast, and my mom was always good about taking lots of pictures when they did stuff without me.

"All right, I'm going to head out, but I'm only required to shadow a guard for six hours, so I'll have time to swing by this evening. And tomorrow morning I'll be here bright and early to make breakfast for everyone."

"I can't promise we'll be up."

I rolled my eyes. She and my dad were the definition of morning people. They'd absolutely be up. Jamie, on the other hand, I'd have to hit with a pillow.

Walking onto the community college campus was a crazy feeling. I hadn't stepped foot on it since I graduated, and now here I was being trusted to guard it. I wasn't necessarily scared of something actually happening, it was more of a fear of disappointing people.

When people put their faith in me, I wanted to show them they were right to. I was motivated and determined, and when I set a goal, I accomplished it. But I didn't feel any of that confidence with this job, and that's what stressed me the most.

Reaching for the handle to the building, I yanked. No go. I pushed. No go. Confused, I stood there frowning hard enough to create new wrinkles before I stomped around the building looking for another entrance. Nothing.

I didn't have the guard office's number, just Jim's cell. Rob had given me his, too, but I'd flipped off the email and refused to save it like the petty bitch I was.

Stepping back up to the door, I gave three hard raps on the glass pane and looked around, fidgeting. After what seemed like ten minutes and several more knocks, the door finally flew open.

The man standing on the other side was dressed identical to me, but he definitely pulled it off better. He gave off a Hollywood bootcamp sergeant vibe, except for the ten-watt smile he was currently giving me.

"You must be Madison. I hope you haven't been standing here long. I've been sitting in the office waiting for you to give me a call that you'd arrived." He stepped to the side to let me pass.

"No, sir, just a few minutes. I don't actually have the office number, so I knocked a bunch." I offered a small laugh, "I'll happily take that number now though."

It didn't take long for me to begin to feel more comfortable with the job. My trainer seemed to understand my apprehension and knew what to say or do to show me how I could accomplish a task.

My primary job would be to drive the perimeter of the campus in the company suburban and then park and begin the on-foot patrol. He walked me through each building, showing me where lights were and explaining what all I'd need to check. Once that was all done, I was free to sit in the office until the next round of surveillance was due.

Overall, it had significantly helped ease my fears and made me feel way more prepared and capable. I was still nervous about how I'd handle anyone who got pushy about being on campus, but I supposed I'd cross that bridge if I ever came to it.

By the time I got home, I was dragging. I'd already started wearing down by the end of the six hours, and that was before I'd gone to my parents' place. Waitressing involved a decent amount of walking, some nights an insane amount. But patrolling around, into, and through every building on a college campus, numerous times, involved a lot of walking and a lot of stairs.

Then when I'd swung by to see Jamie, he'd asked me to throw his new boomerang around with him. By the time we'd moseyed back inside to annihilate some chocolate chip cookies, my feet and legs were aching.

So now here I was, sitting in the driveway, wanting nothing more than to curl up and sleep, fully aware I'd feel even worse when I woke up tomorrow. But I needed to move, I only had maybe five minutes to change and reverse back out.

Dragging my sorry ass out of the vehicle, I was audibly

groaning and mumbling when the feeling of being watched hit me. The hairs on my neck raised, and the air around me seemed to almost condense, pressing down on me. I already knew who it was. The only person who had a stare intense enough to feel from a distance.

Garrett had the hood of his Nova propped up and was leaned over it, a rag thrown across his shoulder. He was sporting his usual jeans with a white long-sleeve. The sleeves were rolled up, and his muscles flexed as he extended his arms on either side of him and rested his weight.

He was staring right at me, scrutinizing me. It should have ruffled my feathers to have a man blatantly staring at me with no care, but I was doing the same to him. I'd never been a car girl, I couldn't tell one car from another, but seeing him leaning over the front made me want to invest in a photo calendar…or a wrench and pliers.

His eyes left my face, drifting about my body like he expected me to show up with a broken leg or something. Once he was satisfied with his findings, his gaze snapped back to mine, and for a second I thought he looked relieved. But it was there and gone in a flash, replaced by his usual pressed lips.

I gave him a silent nod of greeting and dashed away, now down to only three minutes to change.

Sadly, for my sanity, but luckily for my eyes, he hadn't moved an inch in the few minutes I'd been inside my house. I'd had to let the dogs out to pee, and it'd taken me a few extra minutes, so I ran out, digging through my purse for my keys.

And like I was living in a goddamn comedy, when my

fingers finally closed around them and yanked them out, I moved too fast and tossed them to the ground. The grumbled curses that exited my mouth were not graceful or attractive in the least.

I snatched them from the cement, twisting to make it to my Jeep, but came to an abrupt stop when I noticed Garrett had moved closer, his hands tucked in his pockets, watching me fumble.

I uttered an awkward hello and then forced myself to ignore his domineering presence and climbed into the vehicle. He was still standing in the same position, watching me with that eerie intensity, a pinch in his brows, as I reversed out of the drive.

I had no idea what his deal was, but I really hoped he'd figure his shit out and stop staring at me soon, because apparently, I had no idea how to act like a rational human being when he did.

Chapter 8

I'D BEEN RIGHT. I felt even worse after sleeping. I couldn't fathom how anyone could run several miles every day. All I'd done was walk more than I normally did—plus stairs, so many stairs—and everything hurt. My bones, my brain, my eyes. I swore even the fat cushioning my body was twitching.

My shift last night had been insanely busy due to the game that was playing, and I'd brought home more tips than I had in a long time.

There were times when drunk patrons forgot to tip, but more often than not, they tipped way more than they needed to. Usually because they were too gone to count or because they wanted in my pants.

Either way it was good for my pocket, but it also meant I worked past one o'clock.

When I'd texted Layla to tell her I had a feeling it'd be a late night, she'd offered to pick Jamie up this morning so I could get an extra hour of sleep. God bless that woman, I'd needed it. I owed her an actual, real bottle of wine…and maybe a male stripper. She was the kind of partner every parent needed.

Flopping myself over the comatose dachshund under my comforter, I rolled out of bed, whining every bit of the way. If this wasn't my sign of how severely out of shape I was, I wasn't sure what would be.

I made my way to my bathroom like a glob of silly putty, turning on my shower and lying across the counter while I waited for it to heat up.

Shucking off my pajamas, I climbed under the hot spray, hoping the sauna-like temperature would bring some life back into both my soul and my face. The circles under my eyes were officially setting up permanent residence to the point I'd considered naming them.

After spending a solid five minutes unmoving under the shower head, I went about my routine. For a curly girl, the routine went something like this, condition, condition again, condition some more, scrunch.

It was time consuming, but I'd learned years ago, spending a few extra minutes babying my curls was the difference between "Yes, girl, work it," and having animals bow down to me as their new king.

Wrapping my wet mane into a t-shirt on the top of my head, I headed to the closet to change and wiggled my butt into a fitted, knee-length black dress.

Practically dislocating my shoulder, I reached back and zipped it up before buckling a skinny white belt around my waist and grabbing a yellow cardigan for a pop of color. Digging around the floor, I found my favorite black flats. There was no way my sore ass was putting on heels today.

My mother taught me, if you ever feel like shit, make sure to at least dress cute as shit because it's a whole lot easier to feel awful if you also look it. So, I made sure to spend the necessary time to properly dry my hair and apply makeup to convince myself otherwise.

I stared at myself and practiced my 'I can do this' smile, but it quickly fell. Even I didn't believe it, and I was glad Jamie wasn't home to see the exhaustion my makeup couldn't hide.

I tried to prevent him from ever seeing how truly tired I was, but it was really damn hard some days. Not to mention the effort of pretending I felt otherwise often made me feel even more run down.

It's challenging to keep a mask in place around the people you love. One of the more difficult lessons I'd learned was if someone you cared about easily masked their emotions around you, they weren't as invested in the relationship as they tried to make you believe.

Everyone hid pain at one point or another, but the key was how often and how *effortlessly* and *consistently* someone could hide things from you.

Locking the door behind me, I descended the stairs, pulling my cardigan closer and wishing it had buttons as the wind batted against me. I'd have to dish out some funds soon to buy a coat since my previous one had finally met its maker, but I'd deal with that issue another day.

I hadn't walked far enough out yet to see onto Garrett's porch when I realized he was outside. I'd been preoccupied with my thoughts and hadn't immediately noticed it, but he had what sounded like soft rock playing. When I finally approached my vehicle and had a straight-on view of his front door, there he was.

Sitting on his front steps, he was leaned over, elbows resting on his bent knees, head hanging heavy between them, with one hand cradling the back of his neck while an unlit cigarette dangled lazily from the other. He looked as exhausted as I felt.

His music wasn't blaring but had apparently drowned out my steps, and he didn't seem aware I was outside. For once, I was the one doing the scrutinizing.

The smart idea would be to jump into my Jeep and get to work on time without a run-in with Garrett's foul mood, but I hesitated. How many times had I sat outside during those bad months, wishing for a friend to talk to? Wishing for somebody—anybody—to see I needed help and offer it?

Setting my purse on the hood, I walked toward him, stopping a few feet away from his legs. "Garrett?"

His head whipped up with such speed I instinctively stepped back, stumbling, and almost fell on my ass. Righting myself, heat filled my cheeks, and I waited for the frown or even a curt word telling me to get lost, but he didn't do either.

His eyes, which had first gone to my face, lowered, caressing down every curve of my body and then lingering on my legs. He pulled his bottom lip into his mouth, taking his time as those hazel eyes slowly retraced their path back up.

Warmth coiled in my middle, at odds with the cold wind hitting my cheeks, and I shuddered. Goosebumps decorated every inch of my body, but they weren't from the cold.

Taking a shaky breath, I tried again. "Hey, I'm sorry to bother you. I know we're not friends or anything, but I was heading to work and saw you sitting here. I just wanted to make sure everything was okay."

Surprise flashed across his face, there and gone in a second, but he said nothing. He just rolled his cigarette back and forth between his fingers, watching me. I could practically see the thoughts swirling behind those full lips, but I had no idea what they were.

I shifted on my feet, feeling stupid and irritated. It was one thing to not seek me out or be a chatterbox but ignoring me to my face when I was trying to be a decent person pissed me off.

I'd put up with a man treating me that way for far too long, I sure as hell wouldn't continue to do so.

"Look, if you have a problem with me, tell me to my face. Ignoring me is childish, and at the age you appear to be, I'd like to think you're more mature than that. I'm not a sleazy ass woman, I was only trying to be nice. I'm not interested in you, and that includes both your dick and your pockets."

His lips parted, and his tongue pushed against the inside of his cheek. I wasn't sure if he was actually listening or if I was pissing him off, but I wasn't done.

"I walked over here without an invitation, so that's on me.

Trust me, it won't happen again. But this whole judgmental bullshit you have going on isn't working for me. I get enough of it from everyone else, I don't need it at my own damn house."

I crossed my arms. "We can either be cordial all the time or not talk at all, but you have to quit this hot and cold thing you got going on. Be civil or fuck off completely…which is it going to be?"

My entire face down to my neck was flushed, and my chest heaved in and out. But whatever reaction, or lack thereof, I thought I'd get from him, I didn't expect him to drop his cigarette and practically launch off the porch.

One second, I was looking down at him, hands on my hips, and the next he was only a foot away, towering over me. Adrenaline shot through my veins, and I reared back, battling the urge to retreat several steps.

Instead, I held my ground, tipping my head to keep eye contact, but he wasn't looking at my face. His eyes focused on my neck, his jaw clenching before they snapped up, freezing me in place.

"You're right."

I dropped my gaze to his mouth, confirming that it had, indeed, opened to speak to me. "What?"

"You're right. I've been an ass."

I was transfixed by those fucking lips, watching the corner curl to create the beginning of a smirk and wasn't at all paying attention to my own mouth. "Can I get that in writing? Maybe a nice note on my door?"

He chuckled, a dark rumbling sound that seemed to

originate straight from his chest. The sound hadn't even finished making love to my ears before I already wanted to hear it again.

"I'm sorry for accusing you—"

"Of being a jobless, privileged, high-maintenance bitch?" I smiled, batting my eyelashes and hoping he couldn't hear the erratic pounding of my heart.

He rolled his lips in, dipping his head. I swore his eyes lit up, and if I didn't know any better, I'd say he was trying his damnedest not to smile.

I extended my hand. "Here, I'll meet you halfway. I promise not to fuck you for money, and you promise to stop glaring at me like you hope I catch on fire."

The second I uttered the words, I instantly wanted to rewind time and draw them back in. Holding my smile in place, I prayed my eyes didn't give away my internal face palm.

He raised a single brow, grasping my outstretched hand and engulfing it with his own. His grip was firm, and the light scrape of callouses against my palm sent tingles straight to my core.

"You don't enjoy a little heat, Madison?"

Fucking hell.

I was fairly certain I might have experienced a mini orgasm at the way his deep voice caressed along the syllables of my name, and it was shocking, to say the least. I couldn't remember the last time a man had drawn a physical reaction from me to the point I'd begun to think there was something wrong with me.

I'd had sex when my ex wanted to, and I'd enjoyed it, but I'd never felt the rush of excitement or pleasure people described. I'd always had to sneak away afterward and finish the job myself.

But I couldn't deny the heat coiling up inside me at his words and the way he was looking at me.

I pursed my lips, pretending to contemplate his question. "Oh, I enjoy it, but I've found the best heat comes from my own fire, not from a man's."

His nostrils flared, his hand tightening around my own, and for a split second he seemed to shift forward. I tugged my hand out of his grasp, ice instantly replacing the warmth.

Teasing comments were all fun and games, but it would be wrong to lead him to believe it was anything more than that, especially when I'd just convinced him I wasn't a gold-digging hoe.

The truth was, I wasn't interested in a relationship with anyone, and I didn't do casual. Tucking my hands safely under my armpits, I shuffled back. "Well, it was nice to officially meet you, Garrett…?"

"Rowe."

"Garrett Rowe. But I really do need to get to work. Friends?"

He tracked my retreat, dropping his clenched fist at his side and inclining his head in a half-nod of acknowledgment.

"Friends."

Chapter 9

GROCERY SHOPPING WAS the devil's favorite activity. It was like my own personal hell cloaked in elevator music and cereal boxes. If somebody told me they enjoyed it, I would instantly assume, with no hesitation, they were secretly a serial killer.

I hated it with a passion, and that hatred only escalated when I moved out on my own and had to apply for assistance. Because it didn't matter how well I dressed or how sweet I was, the second I pulled out my EBT card, people's mannerisms changed.

It was degrading and frustrating. Purchase a frozen meal because it costs less than five dollars? I'm a lazy parent. Apply for assistance to afford ingredients for a homemade meal? I'm abusing the system. I'm damned if I do and damned if I don't.

So, suffice to say, by the time Jamie and I loaded up the Jeep and left the store, I was close to losing my shit. Turning up hi music—which was an orchestra playing some video game them song—I focused on the lingering echo of ignorant looks anc comments. I allowed myself a full sixty seconds to stress, over-analyze, and second-guess myself, then I shoved it the fuck ou of my head.

Pulling up to the house, I glanced in the rearview mirror planning to ask Jamie what sides he wanted with dinner tonight, only to be met with a lolling head and gaping mouth. The kid was out cold. I parked, pushing open the door as silently as I could.

Jamie had stopped napping years ago, so for him to crash just while driving across town, he had to be thoroughly wiped. Hopefully he'd be able to nap a few more minutes while I unloaded the Jeep.

Layla was due to be home soon, and she'd have no problem poking at him and re-energizing his mood. She'd been gone a lot lately, playing music with the guy she "wasn't dating" so Jamie would be thrilled we were both home.

I was excited for the evening because I'd gotten ahead in my classes over the past week and didn't have to do more than read over a few articles tonight. I'd be able to relax and just enjoy hanging out.

I clicked my back hatch open, lifting it stealthily, and pouted at the number of bags staring back at me. I didn't have the time to shop weekly, so I always bought several weeks' worth of food as soon as the money came in. It was convenient to only go once or twice, but it sure was annoying putting it all away.

Making the only logical choice there was, I grabbed as many bags as I could, stacking them down my arms like a conga line of sloths. I took a deep breath, heaving my arms up and speed walking to the door muttering a string of "fuck, fuckity fuck" when it felt like the bags were slicing through my bones.

I dropped them at the door as carefully as I could before making my way back for round two, cradling my tomato-red forearms. Only a half dozen more trips to go. No biggie.

"Would you like some help?"

I twisted, whacking my head on the side of the hatch frame. My eyes watered, and I rubbed my head as I looked up into an amused pair of eyes. I hadn't seen or spoken to Garrett in almost a week since our cease-fire, and the sight of him sent a thrill through me. He stood a few feet away, hands tucked into the front pockets of his jeans, looking unfairly good in a black pull-over hoodie.

"Oh. No, I got it. Thanks, though."

"You sure? It looks like your helper is down for the count."

I smiled, looking over the outline of Jamie's unconscious form. I'd always been jealous of how deep of a sleeper he was.

Garrett's gaze followed my own. "How old is he?"

I tensed. I couldn't help it, the reaction second nature. "He's eight."

"He seems like a good kid," he said, grabbing several bags in each hand.

"He is—hey, you really don't need to do that." I held my hands up, waving him off like a stray cat. "I promise, it's fine."

"I know it's fine, that's why I'm doing it." Rounding me, he headed to my front door, hollering over his shoulder, "I'm being neighborly, Madison, you should really quit this hot and cold thing you got going on."

I scrunched my nose, pushing my lips up to meet it. I think I preferred it when he didn't talk. Determined not to let him do it all, I grabbed as many bags as I could and power-walked my ass to the porch with as much sass as I possessed.

He shook his head but was smart enough not to say a word. After the last trip, I again tried to wave him off, but the stubborn man refused to budge. "Let me help you carry them inside."

He looked so earnest standing there, holding a shit ton of my groceries, but I'd been deceived by a pretty face and kind gestures before. I was very much aware that if I invited him inside, there wasn't a soul who would hear me yell unless Jamie woke up and wandered in.

My thoughts must've been playing across my face because his expression softened. "I'm just trying to be civil, no ulterior motives. I'm not a gold digger either."

A stray laugh escaped me, and despite my hesitancy and general common sense, I drooped in defeat. "All right, but don't look to me for help if Rugpants chews your leg off."

"Rug what?"

Unlocking my door, I shoved it open, stepping inside to flip the closest light switch before snatching my bags back up and leading Garrett Rowe into my house.

Sadie sprinted around the corner from Layla's bedroom first, and I danced to the side, barely avoiding her collision. She moved on to Garrett, sniffing around his legs and wagging her butt at him while he tried to set the bags on the bar without tripping over her.

Freeing his hands, he reached down to scratch her head. "Is this Rug…man?"

The second his voice graced the air, a muffled yapping sounded from my bedroom, and I giggled. "Rugpants, and no, that's Sadie."

Yapping turned to growling when my dog entered the hall, her stubby legs working hard to bring her to the intruder. "*That's* Rugpants."

He leaned down to give her the same scratches, but she snarled, hair rising along her back. I stepped forward to apologize and grab her even though I'd told him I wouldn't, but he surprised me by chuckling. "My grandmother had a long-haired dachshund. They're feisty things."

I picked her up, snuggling her angry body into my chest. "Yeah, she's all bark but no bite. Come on, Sadie." Setting Rug down at my feet, I fought against the side door and forced them both outside. She was still barking, but at least it was a little less ear-splitting.

When I turned back, his eyes were analyzing my patio door before they slowly moved around the living room. "It's nice."

I gestured him back to the door for the rest of the bags. "It's the same as yours, just opposite, I assume."

"It is, but it feels homier here."

I tried not to show it, but his comment warmed my heart. For years, I'd wanted nothing more than to give Jamie a home. Hearing that someone else thought I'd succeeded made me feel like the sun itself was rising inside of me. "Thank you."

He tipped his head at the basket of yarn and half-finished blanket by the couch. "You knit?"

"Crochet, but yes. Not as much now as I used to though."

He grunted in acknowledgment, and I swore the corner of his lips twitched. "Why don't you go ahead and wake him up, I'll start unloading."

"Oh, no, that's okay—"

"I know, Madison. I know you can do it on your own, but I'm here and have nothing else to do. Let me finish helping, and then I'm out of your hair."

I rubbed the back of my neck. I needed to chill. He was being a friend, probably trying to make up for his asshole behavior before. I needed to stop being so pessimistic and assuming the worst out of everyone. He knew I had a roommate, and my son was right outside. He wasn't going to do anything.

"All right, thank you."

He looked at me over a box of pasta. "Was that so hard?"

I gave him a flat look. He had no idea. I hated admitting when I needed or wanted help. "I'll be right back."

Jamie slid out of the Jeep like a slug, dragging his feet next to me while we walked. He wasn't a morning person, and that general description held true post-nap as well. "What has you feeling so drained, bud? Tough day?"

"Not really. Just didn't sleep well last night."

I frowned. He hadn't mentioned anything this morning. He used to suffer from nightmares right after everything happened with Aaron, but I didn't think he'd had one in a long time. I glanced at him wanting to ask, but knowing he'd deny and deflect. He was a lot like me that way.

So instead, I opted to perk him up. "Layla will be home any minute. We'll throw together some dinner and then have the ultimate game night. Sound good?"

We stepped onto the porch, and I could feel his eyes on me. "How long will you be able to play?"

I winked, holding the door open. "As long as you want, bud. I don't have to study tonight."

He dropped his backpack to the floor, swinging in front of me, eyes bright. "Really?"

"Pinkie promise." I looked over his head to Garrett, who had just about finished emptying all the bags. He'd been watching us from the second we walked in and met my eyes.

"Hey, bud, you remember our neighbor, Garrett?"

Jamie whipped around, frantically looking where I'd indicated and, spotting the large bulk of a man in our kitchen, plastered his small back to my front.

"Why are you in our house?" It was phrased as a question, but the way he demanded it, it sounded more like a hidden order for Garrett to leave.

"He saw me struggling with the groceries and offered to help." I stepped around him so I could see his face. He looked furious, but underneath it was alarm.

"That's what *I'm* for."

"You're right, I'm sorry. Next time, I'll wake you up." I pressed a loud, smacking kiss to his forehead. "But just know I'll make you carry all the bags."

I walked into the kitchen, Jamie hot on my heels, and tilted my head to look up at Garrett. I wouldn't embarrass Jamie by apologizing for his rude question, but I hoped Garrett would understand he meant no harm.

His eyes searched my own, looking for an answer I didn't know how to give. When he finally opened his mouth to speak, it wasn't to me. "I noticed your gaming system over there. You any good?"

Jamie scoffed, arrogance coating the sound. "Yeah."

Not fazed in the least by my child's obvious dislike of him, Garrett nodded. "I have a few systems over on my side, but not that one. I haven't seen one of those since I was young."

I had to hand it to the man, he knew the right thing to say. Jamie's eyes lit up, excitement and interest warring with his determination to stay angry. Jamie loved all things video game-related.

My dad owned a few systems, and they always played or watched walk-through videos when he visited. He wanted to ask about Garrett's, the words were practically slamming against his lips, trying to get out.

Somehow Garrett managed not to laugh at the constipated-like expression on the kid's face and took pity on him. He leaned against the bar, telling Jamie all about his gaming stash and what all he'd played.

I began putting the groceries away, listening to them chat and smiling as Jamie reluctantly thawed and probed our neighbor for details. Once finished, I headed over to see if the dogs were ready to come back inside when the front door flew open.

"Wench! I'm hungry, where's my—oh. Well, hello there." Layla's eyes widened, and she rolled her lips into her mouth, kicking the door shut behind her. "Mads, there's a man in the house."

I exhaled, blowing out my cheeks. "Yes, this is Garrett. You've met him before."

She raised a hand, stopping me. Dropping her bag by the door, she shucked off her shoes and pointed a finger at him.

"Hold up, isn't he the one who called you a leech hidden in a pretty wrapper or some shit?" She cringed, her eyes cutting to Jamie. "I mean stuff."

I gave her an exasperated look, and in my peripheral, I could see Garrett shifting as Jamie looked at him with narrowed eyes again.

Ignoring her question, I crossed my arms, letting my head fall back and addressing the ceiling. "Garrett, this is Layla."

"Her wife. Sugar *mama*, if you will."

Garrett widened his stance, accepting her challenge. "Do you often refer to your wife as a wench, Layla?"

She smirked, lowering her lashes over her eyes and fluttering them. "I have many pet names for her, but not all can be voiced in current company."

"Pet names mean nothing if you don't put a ring on her hand." He looked over at me pointedly, and I struggled not to snort.

"Rings are materialistic and lack uniqueness. Pet names and affection are specific and personal," she countered. "I've cleaned up her vomit, wiped away her tears, slept in the same bed, and held her hand while she pushed out that kid's watermelon of a noggin."

Garrett raised his hands in defeat, and a hint of a smile graced his lips. "Fair enough."

"I don't have a watermelon head." Jamie stood to the side, glowering like he'd received the worst insult in the world. Considering he was in love with Layla, it probably was. I couldn't help but laugh, ruffling his hair as I passed him on my way into the kitchen.

"If ya'll are done with your pissing contest, I need to get started on dinner. Would you like to stay and eat, Garrett?" I looked at him over the bar, offering the friendliest smile I could.

He'd already been looking at me before I spoke, and if anything, his gaze seemed to spark with my question. Nate was my only experience with having a male friend, and I suddenly wondered if I'd crossed a line. Did he think I was hitting on him?

My face heated under his attention. "It's nothing fancy, I'm making spaghetti and steaming up some veggies. But I tend to always make too much, so you're more than welcome to stay."

He shifted his weight, leaning his elbows onto the bar. "I don't think I've ever known someone who didn't make too much spaghetti."

I chuckled. "True."

He watched me wander the small kitchen, setting out pots and ingredients. "Is there something I can help you with?"

"No, I got it, why don't you go relax. We don't have cable or any streaming services, but there's a container of movies in the coat closet."

He paused, pushing his tongue against the inside of his bottom lip. "You mind if I fire up a game with Jamie?"

"That's fine—" I started, but I trailed off at the two inches of flat stomach that greeted me when Garrett raised his hoodie over his head. He folded it across the back of a barstool, and I quickly averted my gaze while he adjusted his shirt, hoping he hadn't noticed me ogling him.

Luckily for me, my little eavesdropper overheard Garrett's question and was bobbing his head up and down next to the neighbor he'd sworn he didn't like. I rolled my eyes and pointed at him. "Make sure you kick his butt."

The kid nodded seriously. "I will."

Chuckling and sending the boys away, I raised my brows and looked over at Layla, who'd been watching the entire thing with a 'bitch, you got some shit to tell me' look on her face.

"Get in here and help."

She sucked on her teeth, putting her hands on her hips. "You just told him you had it under control."

"Yeah, and I do, because you're going to come chop up the veggies for me."

Like a lion on the hunt, Layla marched into the kitchen, cornering me while I was elbow deep in dish water and couldn't escape. I could tell by the glint in her eye, I wasn't going to like whatever it was she had to say.

While we'd cooked, she'd told me more about Rick, the musician she'd finally admitted to hooking up with, and I was happy she'd found someone besides me she enjoyed spending time with.

The problem was she'd used her new relationship as an excuse to poke at me about my own dating life, again trying to convince me to try online dating. I'd brushed it off with an "I'll think about it."

For the most part, I'd been able to turn the conversation back to her throughout the evening and got a small reprieve while we'd all eaten. We'd all sat at the table, trading small talk and teasing Jamie about finally getting whooped on his game.

I smiled, remembering how appalled Garrett had looked when I'd scooped up my spaghetti and dumped it on a slice of buttered bread. I'd made sure to make direct eye contact when I shoved it in my mouth. I was serious about my food, and spaghetti sandwiches were a staple in my house.

Overall, it'd been a wonderful evening, but as soon as Jamie hopped in the shower, Layla had twisted, beelining for me. Garrett was still over, but he was in the living room, wrapping up the controllers and putting the system away. I'd told him not to worry about it, but he'd only looked at me like I was an idiot and done it anyway.

"So."

Continuing to scrub the pan in my hands, I asked, "So, what?"

She groaned, smacking her hand on the counter. "Online dating! You said earlier that you'd think about it."

"And you believed me?" I laughed, leaning to the side,

trying to keep the rinsed pan over the sink while reaching for the towel I'd inadvertently left near the stove.

A large hand appeared in my peripheral, grabbing it and handing it to me from over the bar. I offered him a look that was half smile, half grimace, thankful while simultaneously wishing he'd go back into the living room so he wouldn't hear our conversation.

Determined to make a point, Layla transferred her attention to him. "How old are you, Garrett?"

"Thirty-six."

"Okay, so a little older. And have you ever met someone online?"

"Once."

"And?"

He grunted. "And what?"

"Did you at least get laid?"

"Jesus, Layla, don't ask him that." I did not need the mental image of Garrett's body sexing some other chick. Wait, other? No, *any*. Any chick.

She shrugged. She and I had never viewed sex the same way. She saw it as a simple activity for mutual pleasure that anyone could, and should, participate in whenever they wanted. I saw it as something personal. I'd never had a one-night stand. In fact, I'd only ever slept with two men, and both had been serious relationships.

"I'm just saying, it's a win-win for you. Maybe you meet the man of your dreams, maybe not. But you could at least get a good night out of it. Lord knows your strung-out ass needs it."

I glared at her, slapping the towel back onto the counter and reaching for the last pot. "Hard pass."

She groaned. "Your soulmate could be waiting for you right now, and you don't even know it."

That had me bursting out laughing. "No man is waiting for this hot mess express. My baggage has baggage. I got suitcases and carry-ons, backpacks and purses. The entire fucking plane is full. If a man attempted to board, we'd plummet from the sky."

She flung her hands forward, fingers spread wide, enunciating each of her words. "That's why online dating is perfect for you. Put it up front that you have a kid and work a lot. Only the guys who are accepting of all that will message you."

"Plus, the ones who want to take me out with the intention of slipping me a roofie." I forced a laugh that didn't quite match my eyes, but Layla didn't accept the white flag I was clearly waving. She knew I was trying to brush off the conversation, and she'd decided she wasn't playing anymore.

"You can't be scared of men forever."

Aware of Garrett's vision burning a hole in the side of my head, I turned to face her fully. "I'm not scared of men, Layla. I'm just not interested in dating. I'm stretched thin as it is."

"It's been years, Mads. We're social creatures, we're not meant to be alone."

"I'm not alone," I said, but it came out snappy and defensive. Smoothing my voice back out, I said, "I'm happy with how things are."

She shook her head, backing out of the kitchen. "No, Mads,

you're not. You've just decided it's easier to let him win." She raised her hand in farewell to Garrett, turning toward the hallway. "I'm going to steal your shower since Jamie's in this one. Goodnight, Garrett."

I watched her disappear into her bedroom, Sadie at her heels. The house was suddenly too quiet, the only sound being Jamie's shower. My eyes stung, and I didn't know what to do with my face.

Layla was brutal and honest, and she could be a real bitch, but she was rarely ever wrong about me. I loved the hell out of her, but sometimes I hated how see-through I was to her.

"I'm going to step out for a smoke before I head home. Come out, you look like you could use some air."

I cut my eyes to Garrett, taking in the lines of his face and letting him do the same to me. I wasn't sure how he knew, but that was exactly what I needed. "Sure. Give me a second to go let Jamie know where I'll be."

He could have gone ahead and stepped out, but he didn't. He waited for me, pack in one hand, hoodie in the other. Opening the door, he stepped to the side, letting me pass.

Foregoing the chairs—because I wasn't sure the thin plastic could handle Garrett's bulk—I dropped down onto the stairs, cradling my knees to my chest and breathing in the crisp eastern air.

He lowered himself with significantly more grace than I had and sat next to me. He didn't push, and I was thankful. We sat in companionable silence, each swimming in our own pool of thoughts.

I wasn't sure how long we'd been out there, but I was jarred to the present when something covered my face. I panicked, spine snapping straight before I could suddenly see again.

A raspy chuckle sounded next to me, and I looked down to realize Garrett had pulled his hoodie over me.

"You're shivering so hard you're shaking the cement."

"Asshole, I was not." But I laughed, pulling it the rest of the way down and tucking my legs inside of it like a small cocoon. It was warm from being rolled up in his lap, and it smelled like him. When he finally stood and bid me goodnight, I watched him go, feeling oddly relaxed.

It wasn't until later, after I'd read to Jamie and crawled into bed, two things became clear. One, I was enjoying the feel of sleeping in a man's clothing way more than I should, and two, the entire time we'd sat outside, he'd never actually lit a cigarette.

Chapter 10

I LAUNCHED UP from the bed, scaring the daylights out of Rugsy and whipping my head around to look at my alarm clock.

"Shit. Shit, shit, shit!"

The textbook splayed open near me told me everything I needed to know. I'd unintentionally crashed before setting my alarm. Again. *Shit!*

Dressed in only my borrowed, over-sized hoodie and underwear, I half-fell to the floor in my haste, flinging my bedroom door open and racing toward Jamie's room. I cracked the door open enough to peek in and, remembering Layla passed out in the next room, whisper-yelled, "Get up, bud, we are so very late!"

Seeing him flinch awake, I raced back to my room, looking at myself in the mirror. God help everyone who had to look upon me today, for their eyes would truly be punished. My hair was a lost cause, more frizz than curl, so up it went into a tight, librarian-style bun.

I opted to skip makeup completely, instead shucking my clothes off and throwing on the first work dress I saw. The knee-length, pencil skirt bottom at least gave me some shape, and the leopard print, ruffled top added some much-needed flair. I'd even wear heels. It'd have to do.

Following Rugsy's waddle, I made my way to the living room, knocking on Jamie's door again. "Jamie, get dressed, we gotta go!"

His door flung open. "I'm ready. What happened?"

"I'm sorry, I fell asleep reading and forgot to set my alarm. I think we still have a few of the emergency fruit pastries. Go run a brush through your hair and your toothbrush over your teeth, and I'll grab a package for you."

I checked the time on my phone. He would be at least a solid fifteen minutes late to school, which meant I'd be even later than that to work. I cursed, dialing Evaline to let her know.

She clicked her tongue. "No problem at all, honey, I'm just sitting here online shopping for new office chairs anyway."

Of course, she was. "Thanks, Evaline, I'll see you soon."

Hanging up, I grabbed my purse and slipped into my heels. I felt like I was beginning to lose the tight grip I'd been holding onto my life and everything in it. I'd never been late before, and now it felt like it was becoming a regular occurrence. Next thing you knew, I'd be missing assignments. The thought alone had me queasy.

We ran out to the Jeep like the chaotic creatures we were, and I'd never been so thankful to not run into Garrett. It'd been several days since I'd invited him into my house, and I'd be lying if I said I hadn't worn his hoodie to bed each night since. Not because I was a lonely social creature in need of a man to date, but because Garrett smelled amazing.

One quick drive—only a smidge over the speed limit—and several nasty glares from school employees later, I pulled into my work parking lot. A half hour late.

I sighed, resting my head on my steering wheel and wasting one more minute to breathe. I could do this. A bad start to a day didn't mean it would be a bad day overall. It would be fine.

Shuffling the papers, I rearranged them in order to make another set of copies. I really needed to use the larger machine, but I'd already ditched my heels and didn't feel like putting them back on to walk to the other side. I could only imagine Jim's face if he caught me strutting through the building with only hosiery covering my feet.

Adding the newest set to the pile on the table next to me, I frowned when I heard the door to the hall open and close. Evaline was at her weekly lunch with her daughters at the golf club and would be gone for a few hours. Maybe Jim was checking on something?

I was about to call out when the heavy, familiar thud of boots made its way toward me. Why? Why me? Why today? I cringed, listening to the steps grow louder and pause near the doorway to my office. A second later they started up again, close to the middle room I was in.

I imagined this was how the characters in a horror film might feel if they could hear the suspenseful music that played for viewers right before they inevitably had their heads chopped off. There was something even more unsettling about a situation when you *knew* it was coming but couldn't escape it.

The steps paused again, but I didn't stop what I was doing, continuing to feed papers into the printer one at a time. I refused to turn or acknowledge him, hoping he'd get the message and walk back out. This was not his side of the company. If he had a question, he could easily call either myself or Evaline's direct extension.

There was zero need for him to be on this side of the building.

Of course, he didn't get my neon sign. I could feel his sticky presence behind me, watching but not speaking, as if enjoying the opportunity. Creepy ass fucker.

The smart choice would've been to inform him I was aware of his presence, a simple "Hello, Rob" would do. The next smart choice would be to get the hell out of dodge and avoid being in this wing of the building completely alone with him. But I didn't.

Something about this man made me revert into the worst version of myself, the version that rolled over and shut up. I knew it, saw it. Yet I couldn't seem to stop it.

Rob's version of intimidation was different than Garrett's.

Garrett was intimidating in the strong, silent way, like a bodyguard. Rob was intimidating in the way he would push me just to feel good about himself. He liked to see me squirm. I might as well have been cornered in a room with Aaron, and that's what terrified me.

His clothing rustled as he shifted his weight and took another step. He still hadn't spoken, and I had to swallow down the uneasy feeling crawling up my throat like a thick sludge. The irony that this was a security company, yet we had no security cameras on this side of the building, wasn't lost on me.

Taking a small breath—when I really wanted to heave—so he wouldn't see my rising panic, I finally turned my torso to face him, going with smart option number one. "Hello, Rob."

"Good morning, darlin'." It was afternoon. "You look amazing today."

My nose curled. It wasn't low self-esteem that had me disagreeing with him. I genuinely looked a mess today, which meant he was solely referring to the shape of my body in my dress. I'd never understand the nerve of people like him. Did he truly have no shame, or were social cues just that difficult for him?

Choosing to ignore his comment, I asked, "Is there something I can help you with? Evaline should be back from lunch soon. I'm sorry if you called one of us, I've been stuck making copies for several minutes."

"I knew Evaline was out." His eyes trailed down my body, and I took an instinctual step away, bumping into the printer and shifting it back an inch with an ear-cringing screech.

"Okay, well, I'm trying to head out to lunch myself soon, so I need to finish these up. Leave a note on my desk for whatever you need, and I'll get back to you."

"Let me take you to lunch."

"Oh." Not a chance in hell. "No, thank you. I was planning on heading home during my lunch break today." I wasn't. It'd take my entire break to go home and get back.

"Dinner then." He closed another foot of distance, and my panic was now clawing at me, closing off my throat.

"I can't. I have class in the evenings during the week and work nights on the weekends." My internal dialogue screamed at me to just tell him no, I wasn't interested and never would be. "I'm sorry."

His brow creased. "Where else do you work?"

Fumbling for the stack of papers next to me, I picked them up, holding them to my chest like a shield. "I work several places." I forced a laugh. "I'm just really busy so again, I'm sorry. If you'll excuse me."

I moved to edge around him, but he reached an arm out, blocking my path. "I want to see you outside of work, Madison. Tell me what day, and I'll make it happen."

My body was tensed so tight, I'd shatter if I fell. "I can't, Rob. Will you please let me pass?"

His eyes narrowed on me like I was misleading him in some way. "Do you have a boyfriend? Is that it? I've never heard you mention one."

"I don't. I told you, I work a lot."

He leaned in, his cologne stabbing into my nostrils,

tempting me to hold my breath. "I'll take you somewhere nice. You can get all dolled up with your hair down and a pretty dress."

Is that really what he thought would change my mind? All that sounded like to me was a lot of damn work. And for what? A free meal and a gag-worthy one-night stand? Hard pass.

"No, thank you. Please let me by, I need to finish these up before I leave."

I nudged my stack of papers against his arm, internally begging him to move. He regularly pushed past my comfort zone, but he always pulled back before it went this far. It gave me a bad feeling, and I'd bet my paycheck Jim wasn't in the building either.

He dropped his arm, but instead of allowing me by, he replaced it with his chest, smashing my personal bubble into a million pieces. My eyes widened of their own accord, and the sound I made was something I'd remember long after this nightmare ended.

"I know women like to play hard to get, but I have to say, Madison, I'm not impressed."

I hugged my arms closer, digging my nails in until I broke skin. "I'm not trying to impress you; I'm trying to leave. You're making me uncomfortable."

"I know you want me."

"Excuse me?"

His arm darted forward, wrapping around my ass and squeezing, pulling me against him. "You wouldn't wear these short, sexy dresses if you weren't trying to get my attention."

My dresses weren't even short. I didn't own a single one that went more than an inch above my kneecaps. Not that it would matter anyway. I could wear a leather mini skirt, and it still wouldn't mean I was asking to be touched. I dressed to make myself feel pretty, not to please cocky, egocentric men.

His lips coasted over my ear, his breath leaving a damp film in its wake. "You teased me on purpose. You can't offer dessert on a silver platter and then refuse to share a bite."

The feel of his tongue gliding up my earlobe was going to haunt me, and my shoulders shot up to block him. My mind splintered, the past and present mixing together into a toxic combination and sending black spots into my vision. I could taste bile. "Let go."

"Stop lying to yourself, darlin'."

He smashed his mouth onto mine, ramming his tongue against the seam of my lips trying to force them open. I twisted my head, blindly kicking at his ankles. I wanted to fight, to flail and slap and scratch, but my arms were pinned against me, the papers slicing into the tender skin on the inside of my arms.

He didn't let up. He *groaned*, like my fight was everything he'd ever imagined, like I was playing right into his fantasy. He ground against me, the lump in his slacks digging into my inner thigh.

I couldn't move, couldn't fight back. I couldn't even open my mouth to scream without his tongue shoving through. So instead, I did the opposite.

I shut down.

I went to the dark corner of my mind, the one I hadn't had to escape to in years, and I stopped. I stopped twisting. I stopped fighting. I stopped thinking. I. Just. Stopped.

If there was one harsh truth I'd had forcibly ingrained in my head in my twenty-five years, it was that some men liked their women willing, and some liked them unwilling. But very few liked to grope a boneless shell.

In the safety of my corner, I was curled up in a fetal position, raging and tearing my hair out. But on the outside, I was motionless, my eyes wide open, staring over his shoulder at a spot on the wall. I let him paw at me, refusing to give him the satisfaction of witnessing another second of my emotions.

He increased his attempts at first, each action growing wilder and more desperate than the one before. He squeezed my ass hard enough to bruise, and when that didn't pull anything from me, he bit my lip.

Only then, when I'd still failed to react, did he pull back. I didn't avert my eyes from the spot on the wall, and it took everything in me not to wipe at the smears of saliva across my lips and chin.

Keeping my voice as flat and calm as I could manage, I asked, "Is there anything work-related I can help you with?"

His head pulled back another inch, brow creased, and his lips thinned. He released me, dropping his arms at his sides. He stared, his expression tight, and for a moment he looked nervous. But he wiped it away with an arrogant smirk. He raised a hand, wiping his thumb across his mouth.

"Not work-related, no."

"Then I need to go," I said, rearranging my armload of bent pages. "Excuse me."

He stepped to the side, and for one glorious moment I thought he'd actually let me pass without another word, but he snatched my elbow in a firm grip. "Don't make this into something it wasn't. No one needs to know what we do in private."

Was he trying to convince me or himself? If he thought I was running to Jim's office to report him, he was wrong. Why would I waste my time? I'd verbally complained about Rob to both Evaline and Jim several times, and nothing had ever been done. Rob was just being *friendly*.

So no, I wouldn't run to Jim. I was going to walk my butt right back into my own office, sit at my desk, and finish preparing the list I'd promised Evaline.

Only then would I address the issue in a written email, sent directly through the company network. Hopefully, he'd finally take me seriously this time.

I calmly unhooked his fingers from my elbow, knowing I only succeeded because he let me, and walked out of the room. He followed me, stopping at the doorway to my office, watching me.

It didn't bother me; I was still safely tucked away in my corner. So, I ignored him, pulling my chair up to my desk and going about my job. He said something before he left, but I was no longer listening.

A hurricane was screaming around me, debris crashing at my feet, hair whipping across my eyes, but I sat through it, signing my name on document after document. It was fine.

It'd all be fine.

❧❧❧

"Quit."

"I can't quit. It's my main source of income."

Layla's string of expletives echoed out of the speakers of my Jeep, "If they don't fire him before you show back up tomorrow, fucking quit, Mads."

"He will be."

"He better."

I was confident he would. The speed with which Jim arrived at the door of my office before his lunch was even over, beat even what I'd anticipated. My email to him had been short but clear.

Mr. Grayson:

Attached you will find a spreadsheet documenting every interaction that has occurred between myself and Rob Spencer since the first date of my employment. It includes each date, the occurrence in detail, and whether or not I approached yourself or Mrs. Grayson.

The list is up to date, including today's occurrence. I would like to schedule a meeting at your earliest convenience.

Sincerely,
Madison Hartland

Something else I'd learned in life, between college and

abuse, was that written, dated notes were *everything*.

Our meeting had been brief. Everything that needed to be said was documented in my email. He'd apologized profusely and been adamant that Rob would no longer be welcome at the company. Although I was relieved that he wasn't trying to blame me, I refused to thank him for taking action only after being forced into it.

Jim wasn't an awful person, nor was he necessarily a bad employer, overall. He just hadn't taken my complaints seriously until now. He fell under the long list of people who brushed "harmless" harassment accusations under the proverbial rug. "That's just how he is" or "He was just flirting." I wasn't even angry, only disappointed.

Jim sent me home immediately after, promising to pay me for the rest of the day, and I'd called Layla the moment I started my vehicle.

"Do you want me to come home?"

I turned into my driveway, wanting nothing more than for this day to be over. But hey, glass half full, at least I'd gained a few hours to laze about the house before I needed to pick up Jamie.

"No, enjoy your time with lover boy after work. I'll probably take a shower and rest."

"Bish, no you won't. You'd make it one minute before picking up a damn textbook."

I laughed, the sound feeling foreign in my husk of a chest. She knew me way too well. "I'm hanging up."

"Love you, wench."

I turned off the ignition and stepped out onto the drive, heels dangling from my hand. Something looked different. I tilted my head, examining the house, trying to pinpoint what it was. My brows met my hairline. My yard was mowed, and my fence was…white.

From the day we'd moved in, it'd been almost solid green from the massive amount of pollen that saturated the air each year. The landlord never came out to do anything—hello, broken dishwasher—and I didn't have the means to do it. I didn't even own a garden hose.

I allowed my heart to get a little excited. Sure, he was supposed to call before showing up, but if he'd done this, then maybe he'd actually fixed the dishwasher as well. I crossed my fingers, hoping this was a sign that life was going to give me a break.

"Madison?"

My heart plummeted, excitement dying quicker than it'd come, and pure, unfiltered panic filled my chest cavity where it used to reside. It couldn't be. Not today. Not after everything I just went through. I must have imagined it. Layla joked that my karma was cursed, but even this was pushing it.

"Madison."

Fuck. I'd know that voice anywhere. I knew how it sounded when it whispered sweet words, how it dropped to a husky tone when he slid his hands across my skin, just as well as I knew how it sounded when it screamed and spit at me.

With my entire soul, I didn't want to turn around, knowing how much it would hurt to lay eyes on him. I was so emotionally drained from the encounter at work, I couldn't take another one. I'd splinter the rest of the way open and be stuck on my hands and knees, desperately scooping up the pieces.

But continuing to give him my back, where I couldn't anticipate his movements, would be worse. I turned, meeting a pair of moss green eyes flecked with gold that had appeared in some of my happiest and worst memories.

I hadn't set eyes on him in three years, and he looked the same, yet different. His hair was still a beautiful auburn hue, but he'd grown it out from the military cut he'd been required to have back then. It fell in soft waves above his ears, accentuating his eyes.

He'd thinned out, a pale, angular face staring back at me instead of the full, boyish cheeks he used to have. He'd never been what society would consider gorgeous, but there'd been something about him that had pulled me in all those years ago. That'd kept pulling me in, even when it should have pushed me away.

There was no pull left. Nothing but the chill of a tile floor and the throb of invisible bruises. "What are you doing here, Aaron?"

His smile twitched, becoming less relaxed. "You're ignoring my calls."

I inhaled and exhaled slowly, clenching the straps of my heels until my nails dug crescent moons into my palms. We were outside, in public. He wouldn't touch me. "How do you know where I live?"

"Layla gave me your address, although the lack of numbers

on the house did make it a little harder to confirm. I had to go through the mail to figure out which one you were in."

Horror sliced through me. He said it with so much fucking pride, like it showed how devoted he was rather than psychotic. He was the one who'd gone through Garrett's mail that day; he'd known where I was this entire time.

"You're lying."

"Maybe a little bit." His grin kicked up again, and he moved forward. "She did give it to me, but I may or may not have misled her. She was more than happy to share when she thought I was your thoughtful brother trying to send a surprise gift to his nephew."

The fucking bastard. Contacting Layla for my address was exactly something my brother would do to avoid a lengthy conversation with our mother. Aaron had always been sneaky; it was his specialty. A sly fox in a fluffy, sheep package.

"What are you doing here?" I repeated.

I wasn't falling for his flirty looks and words. I had no desire to play whatever game this was, and he must've seen it on my face because his smile dropped away entirely. "We need to talk."

"No, we don't. I don't want you here."

"Why do you always have to be dramatic? I just want to talk. If you would have answered my phone calls, I wouldn't have had to come find you."

"There's nothing you can say that I want to hear. Please leave."

"I have a right to talk to you." He closed more distance between us, stopping only a few feet away. Standing at five foot seven, he didn't stand over me, but that made it almost worse. I'd never been given the freedom of having someone yell at me from a foot above me. No, he'd done it nose to nose.

He raised his arm—to hug me, grab me, who knew—and I flinched violently, my own arm coming up to cover my face. A sneer ruined his mouth as he dropped his proffered limb. "Don't fucking do that, Mads, I hate when you do that."

"I'm pretty sure she asked you to leave."

Both our heads twisted in sync, looking toward the individual standing on the other side of the driveway.

Aaron's head whipped back to me, fury darkening his features into something foul and all too familiar. "You want to explain who the fuck that is?"

I didn't get the chance to reply. It'd taken Garrett less time to reach us than it had for Aaron to finish the accusation he'd threaded in his question.

"It's time you head out. She's made herself very clear."

Aaron's eyes were boring into me so hard; I'd be lucky if I didn't wind up with dents in my face. Dropping my eyes to his feet, I wrapped my arms around my body, not even knowing when I'd dropped my shoes. "Please, Aaron. Just leave."

"No, you're being ridiculous."

Warm fingers brushed my arm, resting right above my bent elbow, and my head snapped up. The look Garrett gave me wasn't far off from the way Aaron was looking at me, and it should have terrified me. But it didn't.

His touch was gentle, and his anger soothed the creature crouching in the corner of my mind. Because he wasn't angry at *me*. He was angry *for* me.

"Go inside. Make some coffee and put on a pair of those crazy socks you like."

I nodded dumbly; my focus tied to the thumb gently moving across my skin before he dropped his hand. I turned away, refusing to look back at my ex. I didn't want to see his expression. I already knew it'd be full of a hatred fueled by his own bitter misery.

I made it as far as opening my front door, still shoe-less, before Aaron finally comprehended I really wasn't going to talk to him. He broke, lashing out one last time. "Fuck you, Madison!"

Stepping over the threshold, I turned and caught a glimpse of Garrett standing over Aaron, staring down with his fists clenched at his sides. He was speaking, but I couldn't make out what he was saying before I slammed the door shut.

I moved mechanically, starting a pot of coffee and walking into my bedroom. And it was when I reached back to lower the zipper of my dress that I finally snapped. I tore it off, scratching myself in the process, but I didn't care.

Tears pooled in my eyes as I wadded the garment up and threw it across the room with an anguished yell. I'd never be able to wear it again after today. I'd paint it in flames if I could.

I threw on a pair of soft shorts and paused, naked from the waist up. Fuck it. I needed the comfort. I grabbed the over-sized hoodie and threw it over my head, the hem reaching past my shorts. I already felt better.

There was something about large, baggy clothing that made

me feel safe. Similar to how you felt as a kid when you'd throw a blanket over your head to hide from the imaginary monster in your room. It was like nothing could touch you when you were enveloped in warmth.

Standing in the center of my room, I stared at the small filing cabinet I kept in the corner. I edged toward it, nausea coiling inside my stomach as I opened it and pulled out the well-worn stack of records tucked into the back. The messages, photos, screenshots, and medical reports.

Always. I'd always had to pull them out when I thought of Aaron. Always had to remind myself of what lived deep in his heart, what crawled and prowled under his skin waiting to eat me alive. As I moved to sit on the edge of my bed, I stared at the front page, not moving to flip through them.

For the first time since leaving him, I didn't feel the need to. And it was the single most freeing moment of my life. I hugged Garrett's hoodie closer, breathing in the faint scent of him still clinging to it, and chucked the papers in my nightstand.

Moving to my dresser, I opened the top drawer and stared at the bright neon colors. Garrett hadn't just come to my defense; he'd also somehow known the two things in the entire world that helped me relax: coffee and fuzzy socks. I pulled a pair out, squeezing them in my hand, and a weird sensation bubbled in my chest.

A few minutes later, I was standing in the kitchen, adding creamer to my coffee when a harsh knock sounded against my front door. I froze, my throat drying out. I should've known he'd come back. Aaron never gave up when pushed. If anything, it only encouraged him to push back harder.

Gripping my mug how I was, I nearly dropped it in my relief when Garrett's voice permeated through the wood. "Madison."

I set the mug on the bar, shuffling over and unlatching the door. Pulling it open, I hid behind it, embarrassed. I knew I'd have to thank him eventually; I just hadn't realized it'd be right now.

He removed his shoes, never taking his eyes off the side of my face peeking around the edge. "Is it okay that I'm here?"

I nodded, stepping around the door to shut it. "Yes. I made coffee; would you like some?" I watched him set his shoes—and mine—on the floor and wrang my hands, aware I looked even worse than I had that morning. The thought was depressing.

When he didn't reply, I looked up, worried he was already regretting getting involved in my mess. His eyes were on my exposed legs, and his lips pressed into a flat line as he trailed his gaze up to my face. He cleared his throat. "Is it spiked?"

That drew a laugh from my throat. The man never failed to catch me off guard. "I wish. Liquor is usually above my budget, but after everything that happened today, I might make an exception." I offered him a tentative smile, walking back to the kitchen.

He cleared his throat a second time, eyes darting away. "Coffee would be great."

Thankful for something to do, I grabbed a second mug and poured him a large cup. He looked uncomfortable, and I had a feeling it had to do with my choice in clothing and the fact it was his. And why wouldn't it? I'd practically answered the door looking butt naked underneath his hoodie.

Good job, Madison. Now the neighbor thinks you strut around naked in his clothes. Perfect.

"So, you going to tell me what that was?"

I handed him his coffee, pushing the creamer toward him. "It was nothing. I'm sorry you had to deal with it. I promise I don't normally have drama." At least, not anymore.

"I'm going to need you to do better than that. He told me he was your husband."

He might as well have struck me. "No! I mean, he used to be. But we've been divorced for about three years, so I don't know why he'd tell you that."

I felt Garrett's gaze like it was nestling inside my chest, making itself at home and searching for answers. "You said everything that happened today. What else happened?"

"Just something with an asshole guy at work."

"What do you mean? What'd he do?"

"Decided he was entitled to something he wasn't." I flicked my wrist. Rob was definitely not something I wanted to get into right now. "It's fine; it was taken care of."

His jaw tightened. He wanted to ask more. So, I did what I did best. I wiped the pained expression from my face, morphed it into something calm, and changed the subject.

"Did you see the landlord when he came out today?"

His brow creased. "No, but I was at work for most of the morning. Why did he come out?"

I took a sip of my coffee, leaning over the counter and sliding my socked feet back and forth across the tile like an ice skater. "I'm honestly not sure. I've been sending in fix-it tickets for my dishwasher and patio door, and he's never shown up." I shrugged, looking up in time to catch his eyes darting back to my face from wherever they'd been.

"Then how do you know he was here?"

"He cleaned up my fence and yard."

"Huh." His expression shuttered, becoming suspiciously neutral.

"I'd thought maybe he'd done it while he was here fixing the dishwasher, but it doesn't appear so."

"What's wrong with your dishwasher?"

I waved my hand. "No idea. I've watched a few how-to videos to try to fix it myself, but I always end up staring at it like a deer in headlights." I laughed.

He set his mostly full mug on the bar. "I'll take a look at it."

"No, it's fine. I wasn't trying to guilt trip you into looking at it. Ignore me, I tend to ramble sometimes."

"I don't mind, I like fixing things." He shrugged, a hint of a smirk gracing his lips almost faster than I could see, and I suddenly realized what his earlier look had meant.

My mouth felt uncomfortably dry as I asked, "The landlord didn't stop by, did he?"

He didn't answer, stepping around the bar and into the kitchen, stopping right in front of me. "Madison."

I craned my neck back. "Garrett."

"Let me take a look."

Chapter 11

"PULL IT FARTHER over on your side."

"I can't, it'll hang to the floor and block the doorway."

"Well, it's not going to stay up back here, the chair is too tall. The blanket will slip, the entire thing will crash on top of us, and one of us will choke on popcorn and die. What's more important, a doorway or living?"

Standing on the arm of the couch, I stared at Layla incredulously. "We are not going to choke and die from a blanket falling on top of us."

"Says you. This is thick, Grade A quilting. If it whacks you in the face during a scary scene, and you suck a kernel straight down your throat, I'm not performing the Heimlich on you."

I could make out Jamie's muffled giggles from underneath our makeshift tent. "Fine, you wretched woman." I yanked on the blanket, evening it out across the couch and dining chair as best I could before hopping down. Adjusting the hoodie I'd come to wear every evening down over my leggings, I placed my hands on my hips and admired our creation.

Honestly, I was pretty damn proud of us. We didn't own many blankets and our couch was as puny as it got—Garrett's knees had practically touched his chest the night he'd played games with Jamie—but the fort was large enough for the three of us to crowd into. Whether it'd stay up after we let the dogs out of Layla's room was another story.

"You better not be eating all the popcorn, dude face." I leaned down, poking my head under the edge of the quilt, and searched for his face in the dark.

"I make no promises."

Laughing, I raised up, walking over to our DVD player to start the movie. Most people would've thought our lack of a TV stand was trashy but having a television directly on the floor was incredibly convenient for movie parties.

Layla was spending the night at her boyfriend's place, but when Jamie had asked her to build a tent and watch a movie with us, she hadn't batted an eye. She'd called Rick and let him know she'd be late. I smiled at her, feeling lucky as hell to have her as a role model for my kid.

Cracking open the sodas I'd treated us to, we snuggled up on the floor, pillows strewn about everywhere. We shoved popcorn in our faces, likely all smearing butter across our chins, and watched a Halloween movie about a house trying to eat children. It was exactly what I needed to recover from the absolute hell this week.

It'd been three days since the debacles with Rob and Aaron, and I'd barely slept since. Work had gone fine, the supervisors on both sides of the company sitting down to make sure I was doing all right, yet I couldn't lose the tension in my shoulders.

I kept waiting for Rob to appear somewhere to punish me. The idea was ridiculous, the reality being I'd probably never see him again, but my imagination wouldn't listen.

And I hadn't heard a peep from Aaron. No text, no call, no random car on the street. Nothing. I should be high off my relief, yet my stress level was the only thing that was high.

Although I'd never admit it out loud, I was struggling. I couldn't get myself to focus on anything the way I needed to, but I also couldn't relax. I was stuck in a vicious circle of losing, and honestly, I was a catastrophe waiting to happen.

But lying on the living room floor, piled up with my two besties, for a moment I could breathe and forget everything outside of our tent of happiness.

When the movie ended, and we'd all climbed out, I stared at the mess. I was usually a nut case about cleaning and always made Jamie help, but right then, I couldn't have cared less.

"Hey, Mom?"

"Yeah?"

"Do you think I could sign up for soccer?"

I turned to give him my full attention, seeing Layla do the same. Jamie rarely asked for anything that wasn't video game or book-related. Sports weren't typically his thing. "What made you want to try soccer?"

He looked down, toeing the carpet nervously. "I've always liked soccer. I play it with my friends every day at recess, and my P.E. teacher thinks I should sign up."

My brows dropped into a frown. "Always? Don't get me wrong, I think that's awesome, bud, but I've never once heard you talk about it. We don't even have a soccer ball."

He pushed his toes around some more, not meeting my eyes. Low, almost at a whisper, he said, "I didn't want you to have to get another job if I asked to play."

My arms went limp at my sides. My heart clenched tight, stopping the flow of blood from circulating through my body and sending a chill through me. "What?"

He glanced at Layla before looking at me. "The school league is expensive. I didn't want you to have to work more to pay for it." He put his hands up, as if worried I'd agree and shut the conversation down. "But my P.E. teacher told me there's a form you can fill out so you wouldn't have to pay for me to join. You'd only have to pay for the uniform."

I swallowed. And then swallowed again. He wanted to play a sport. He'd always wanted to play a sport, and he'd hid it from me because—fuck, I was going to lose it. The cracks in the dam were spurting and crumbling, and I could do nothing but hold on for dear life and hope to make it to safety before it crashed completely.

"Yeah, bud," my voice cracked, and I had to force down the lump in my throat, "you can join. When are sign ups?"

His eyes lit up like it was Christmas morning. "Next week."

"All right. Go brush up and get ready for bed. We'll talk

more about it tomorrow and figure out what I need to do."

He spun, running around the mass of blankets, but stopped at the hallway entrance. Turning to look at me over his shoulder he said, "I love you, Mom."

I watched him disappear into the bathroom when the first tear pooled in the corner of my eye. My time was up.

"Go on." Layla tapped me on the arm and pointed to the front door. "Go break down, it's okay, mama bear. I'll read with him tonight. You want me to stay home?"

I choked, the tear escaping down my face as more pooled and burned. "No, I'll be fine."

She gave me a small smile that didn't match her eyes. "Yeah, you always are. Now go."

I practically ran, my only goal being to get outside before Jamie came back out and saw me fall apart. My ass had only grazed the cement when the tears fell in earnest, leaving hot trails down my cheeks to drip off my jaw onto my clothing.

I curled in on myself, tucking my head into my knees and raising my arms to wrap around the back of my neck. My chest heaved as I pulled in large gulps of air, the silent tears forming a drenched trek down my thighs.

I tried everything, counting, counting backwards, reciting court case information I needed to test on, pinching myself, and holding my breath. But the tears kept coming, and now I desperately needed to blow my nose. Fuck. Why did it feel like every time I climbed an inch up, something kicked me in the face until I slid back a foot?

My heart hurt; a physical pain that wouldn't lessen no

matter how hard I tried. Nothing could make me feel worse than realizing I hadn't known my child wanted something as simple as playing a freaking sport because he'd been too nervous to tell me. Nothing.

"Hey, everything okay?"

But that might come close.

My head snapped up, my swollen eyes and damp nose on full display for a man who could not have looked better. I pulled my sleeves down over my wrists, wiping at my eyes and wishing with all my might that I had an invisibility cloak I could slip over myself.

Garrett stood a few feet from my porch, appearing like a shadow in his black sweats and t-shirt. He had to be freezing, and the sudden knowledge I had his hoodie on inflamed my face. So now I was wet, swollen, and bright ass red while using his clothing as my own personal tissue. Perfect.

I thought about lying and saying I was fine, but it would've just made me look stupid. I was very clearly not fine. Denying the obvious would be pointless. "No. Not really."

"Yeah, that was a dumb question."

I winced, wiping my nose discreetly on my knee and tucking my legs in tighter to my chest. "What are you doing over here?"

He shifted his weight, tucking his hands in his pockets. "I was walking to my car and thought I heard something."

I glanced at his feet, my eyes narrowing, which wasn't much since they were practically swollen shut. I hadn't thought I'd made any noise.

"You were going somewhere with no shoes on?" I

hiccupped, making my words come out squeaky and pathetic.

His tongue darted out before he pulled his bottom lip into his mouth. I subconsciously clenched my thighs closer together, eyes pinned to his mouth for reasons I didn't want to explore.

"I was…looking for something."

"Oh."

He pulled a hand out of his pocket, gesturing to my stoop. "Mind if I have a seat?"

A little, yes. I'd come outside to avoid an audience to my meltdown, not advertise it to the hottest man I'd ever seen. But I was taken back to that day when I found him in a similar position—minus the tear stains.

"Sure. I mean, sure, like it's fine," I hiccupped again and ducked my head, breaking our stare. Why was I the way I was? If awkward had a name, it'd be mine.

Garrett climbed up, slowly bending those long, thick legs to sit next to me. We couldn't have even been a foot apart, and his warmth and smell surrounded me even more than the hoodie did, the two somehow both calming me and waking me at the same time.

It wasn't until I smelled the real thing that I realized his hoodie had long ago stopped smelling like him. I'd worn it to bed too many times, covering it in my own, less sexy scent. At least that would make it easier to convince myself to return it. Which I would do…as soon as he left.

"You want to talk about it?"

"It's nothing. I just needed a minute."

"It doesn't look like nothing, and I'm a good listener."

Fresh tears spilled down my cheeks. Now that I'd started, I couldn't seem to shut it off. "It's fine."

He leaned forward, resting his arms on his thighs and side-eyeing me. "Is it about your ex-husband?"

I inhaled sharply, choking on my own saliva and proceeding to have a mild hacking fit. "No," I croaked out.

"You sure? I could always go break the fucker's nose if it'll bring a smile to your face."

I laughed then, loud and full. It was shaky and not at all attractive with my congested nose, but it felt freeing. A few bricks that'd been sitting on my heart fell away.

His head whipped in my direction, and he stared at me in a way I didn't quite understand, but it made me feel like he was searching for something. I wiped my hands over my face again, worried I had snot smeared, or something else horrifying. "I'll take a raincheck on that."

He didn't push, seeming to understand that I needed the silence to center my thoughts. I sat up straight, stretching my legs down the stairs and fighting the irrational urge to rest my head on his shoulder.

"Jamie wants to join a soccer team. Apparently, he's wanted to for a while."

Garrett tipped his head back, his brow furrowing at the explanation for my tears. "And that's bad?"

"I didn't know. He said he plays every day with friends, and I didn't even know he liked it. He didn't want to ask me because of the money. He was afraid I'd have to get another job. As if he thought he wouldn't be worth it."

I took a shuddering breath, fisting my hands in my lap and mentally swearing I wouldn't start crying again. I was an adult, dammit.

He bent one leg, turning to rest it on the porch so he could twist toward me. "How many jobs *do* you have?"

"Three."

"You just, do what? Interchange them to match full time?"

I gave a hollow laugh. "No. I work the same schedule every week, usually between sixty and sixty-five hours."

He reared back, barely avoiding smacking his head on the railing. His eyes were the widest I'd ever seen them. "The fuck you do."

"I do."

"Every week?"

"Every week."

He stared at me like I'd not only grown a third head, but a magical unicorn one. "You don't get any kind of assistance from your ex?" He worked his jaw, looking out toward the road. "Sorry, that's none of my business."

I ignored the implication that Aaron was Jamie's father. Most people assumed that, and I was too emotionally depleted to hash out my entire moldy history.

"It's all right. No, I don't get child support or anything. I've tried for years, but he takes jobs that pay under the table, so it's never happened."

I didn't like thinking about how much easier our lives could've been if the sperm donor had just been willing to assist with the child he'd helped procreate.

Garrett's tongue pushed into the inside of his cheek, and I could tell by the way he was looking at me that he wanted to ask something else, but he didn't. "So, your son sacrificed something he enjoys, trying to make your life easier?"

My face crumpled, tears pooling all over again. Putting it that way fucking *hurt*. My chest was filling up with blood from the knife wound Garrett had just graciously given me. "Yeah," I sobbed, "I guess so."

"You must be one hell of a mom for that boy to love you that much."

"No, he's just an amazing kid all on his own." I sniffed, pulling my legs back to my chest like an infant.

He leaned toward me and I froze, but he only flicked a mosquito off my wrist. "My parents divorced when I was a little older than Jamie. My dad…he wasn't a good person. It took longer than it should have for my mom to gain enough confidence to leave him."

He trailed off, removing a pack from his pocket and pulling out a cigarette. I couldn't speak; I couldn't fucking breathe. I knew how those stories played out, how it'd played out not only for me, but for Jamie. And my heart ached for the child Garrett was and what he might have witnessed.

"Anyway, my point is that I can guarantee without a shadow of a doubt, I wouldn't have turned out half as good as I did if I'd had to live with my dad. A kid can be born happy, but it's the love they receive that teaches their heart to be gentle."

He glanced at me, and a faint blush painted his cheeks when he saw me blatantly staring at him. There was a whole lot more to this man than I'd have ever guessed after our first few interactions. I'd gotten a glimpse of the cinnamon roll hiding underneath his sexy, stoic coating, and I liked it.

I smiled and gave in to my urge, tipping my head to rest against his shoulder. "Thank you."

"I didn't do anything," he said, voice gruff, but he didn't pull away.

Finally experiencing a touch of contentment, I watched his fingers roll the cigarette back and forth. "You know, not to be a mom or anything, but you really shouldn't smoke."

He huffed, curling his fist around it. "I haven't lit one in almost two weeks."

That would explain the unlit one the other night, I supposed. "Does holding one help with the craving?"

He shifted, and my head rose and fell with the slight movement of his shoulder. "Gives me an excuse to sit outside."

I nodded against him but wasn't sure what he meant. Why would someone need an excuse to be outside? Unless what that someone actually wanted, was an excuse to see if his neighbor was outside. I brushed the errant thought away. The idea was ridiculous.

We sat there like that, neither feeling the need to speak, until the sound of my front door opening had me shooting up. It was just Layla. She stepped out, coming up short when she saw us on the stairs, and her eyebrows met her hairline.

Seeing Garrett had stood and stretched out his hand, I took it, letting him pull me to my feet.

"I better go inside. Here—" I grabbed the hem of his

hoodie, pulling it over my head before folding it in half and holding it out to him. Left in the brisk air with only a thin top, I shivered. "Thanks for lending it to me. Sorry I smeared my tears all over it."

He stared at it for a moment before reaching out and taking it. His eyes dipped to where I nonchalantly tried to hide my peaked nipples, and his fists tightened around the fabric.

"No problem." The words came out sharp like a curse, and I frowned. Why did he look angry?

"Well, goodnight then."

"Goodnight, Madison."

I watched him walk off, aware of Layla's demanding ass behind me. Shaking off Garrett's sudden change in behavior, I turned to see her texting. "What's up?"

She shot me a glare. "I told Rick I can't come after all. I'm heading to pick up some wine. Get inside and sit your ass on the couch. You have tea to spill."

Chapter 12

IF THERE'S ANYTHING you shouldn't do while tired, it's play Battleship. Literally nothing knocks you out faster. I stared at the red and white markers, seeing double of everything as my eyesight went unfocused.

"I think you sank my last ship, but honestly I can't make out the rows anymore so I'm not sure."

"That's just another way of saying you suck at this game."

I arched an eyebrow, peering at Jamie over the top of the game. "Respect your mother, I suck at nothing."

He giggled.

"Trust me, bud, if there's anything your mom *isn't*, it's a sucker."

I blinked, turning my head with horror-film slowness to my best friend, currently curled up with the dogs on the couch, strumming her guitar.

Picking up a carrot stick from our snack bowl, I threw it at her face—missing completely. "You do enough of that for the both of us."

"And it is glorious!" She threw her arms in the air, terrifying both dogs awake.

Jamie looked up from his board. "Why would sucking at something be glorious? I hate being bad at stuff."

I burst out laughing, absorbing the moment of joy so I could bask in it later. "Never grow up, bud. You're perfect just like this."

"O-kay."

"Perfect!" I slammed my game board shut, or as shut as it could be with pieces still in place. "Now let's play Twister or something."

He folded his arms across his chest, frowning. "You squished me to death last time."

"But did you die?" Stretching my limbs and groaning, I rolled onto my back to sit up, but ended up lying there like a chalk silhouette of a dead body.

"Mom. Come on. One more game."

"I'm exhausted. Plus, I went through the effort to sign you up for soccer today, so I've done my parental duties for the day. I'm calling in sick now." I flopped to my side, slowly pushing up into a sitting position like a half-dead mermaid.

He rolled his eyes, turning to the love of his life. "Layla, do *you* want to play a game of Battleship?"

"Depends, do you want to cry?" She gave him a grin I could

only describe as predatory as she got up and moved to take my place.

It was Thursday, my last free evening before a weekend of hell, and I didn't feel the least bit ashamed about grabbing a blanket and sneaking outside. Not only did I have my usual doubles this weekend, but I had my first guard shift Saturday, and I was officially overwhelmed.

I was considering calling out of the restaurant since I knew a few girls who'd been wanting extra shifts. With Layla paying a portion of the rent and utilities, I was getting ahead with bills and could afford to cut back for at least one weekend.

Climbing onto one of the porch chairs, I ignored the fact that it needed to be wiped off and laid my head back, staring out into the night. I loved how quiet it was here. Not as quiet as my childhood home where we lived miles down a dirt road, but it was so much quieter than any of the places Jamie and I had lived before. Especially the military base.

There was barely any breeze, the warmest night it'd been in a while. Fall could never be considered warm here, but at least it wasn't freezing.

Deciding to take that as a positive sign, I yanked up my blanket and dragged it out onto the small section of yard next to the driveway.

Spreading it out like a giant rectangular cloud floating on the grass, I kicked off my damp socks and dropped down. It was a little chillier off the porch without the blanket wrapped around me, but I'd come this far so I was determined to follow through.

I stretched my limbs starfish style, and gazed up at the clear, night sky to search for constellations. When I was younger, I used to sneak out at night sometimes, just to look at the stars and see if I could find the Big Dipper.

The sky was one of the things I missed the most about living in the Midwest. The landscape where I'd lived was flatter than a pancake, so the stars reached as far as you could see. Anyone who called the Midwest ugly had never seen a Kansas sunrise.

A familiar smell pulled me out of the fog I'd been lazing in, drifting in my nose, and shooting tingles all the way to my toes. I turned toward it, curling up and wishing I could climb inside and rub it all over me. I loved that man's damn smell.

Wait.

My eyes snapped open, blinking a few times to clear the spots, only to discover a limb next to me. A limb I'd just been snuggling my face into. I jolted up, upsetting a fleece throw blanket that'd been tucked over me.

"Hey."

I rubbed at my eyes, trying to figure out what I was seeing. Garrett. Garrett was next to me, lying on his back, with one arm—my cuddle buddy—straight at his side, and the other tucked underneath his head. His legs imitated his arms, with one stretched out while the other was bent at the knee. He looked comfy as hell.

"Hey," I greeted back.

He laughed, a deep sound straight from his chest that left a weird, warm sensation in my gut. "You should see your face right now."

I ran my hands across my eyes and down my cheeks, sitting

up fully. "I'm a little confused."

"So was I when I stepped outside and noticed your unconscious form sprawled out in the yard. I about had a heart attack before I noticed the premeditated, perfectly laid-out blanket underneath you."

I flushed. "Oh God, I'm sorry. How long have I been here?" I pinched the fleece blanket, rolling it back and forth between my fingers.

"Not sure how long you were here before I noticed you, but I've been here for about twenty minutes. I didn't want to wake you, but I also didn't want to leave you alone." He tilted his head, looking at me under lowered brows. "It's not safe to be sleeping in the middle of your yard."

"Thanks, Dad."

His eyes lowered farther. "I'm not *that* much older than you."

I scrunched my lips, fighting a smile, and looked at the night sky. "You're what, twenty years older?"

"Eleven," he growled.

I chuckled. "Seriously, thank you for bringing a blanket and making sure I was safe. I hadn't planned on falling asleep, I just wanted to look at the stars and breathe for a minute."

"Yeah, you don't look so hot."

"Thanks."

He curled his stomach into a crunch, smoothly sitting up and gestured at my face. "I meant you look tired."

Normally, my sensitive ass would've felt like crap that a hot guy had pointed it out, but I didn't. I *was* tired. "Are you always this smooth of a talker?"

Fiddling with the sleeve of his shirt, he shifted uncomfortably, as if he might actually be embarrassed.

"I'm joking. I look like complete shit, it's okay, you can say it."

He huffed a laugh under his breath, slanting his eyes in my direction. "I don't always sleep well either. I spent a lot of years in the Marine Corps, several of them deployed, and it messed with my ability to sleep for eight straight hours. So, I get it."

His admission piqued my interest, waking me the rest of the way. I felt like I should've known, but as much as media tried to portray all military members as stereotypical "jarheads," that was rarely the case. You couldn't always tell.

"How long have you been out?"

"Only a couple years, although it feels like longer."

I nodded, I didn't have experience with what being enlisted was like, but I'd lived on an Army base. I'd heard people talk about how difficult it was returning to civilian life. "Were you stationed around here, or did you move here after?"

"Most of my enlistment was spent here, but I'm from California."

I popped my lips, watching my toes wiggle in front of me. "That's a big change, California to here." I wanted to ask why he'd chosen to stay here, rather than go back after he'd gotten out, but he looked uncomfortable enough as it was.

He coughed, rubbing at the back of his neck and cringing slightly. "So, what about you. What keeps you up at night, Madison?"

I pressed my legs together, biting my bottom lip to keep my face from displaying the irrational thoughts his voice sent through my head. I swore the way he said my name was like ear porn. I glanced at him in time to catch a small flare of his nostrils.

"School," I blurted. Slouching over the blanket, I lowered my voice. "I'm taking online courses at the university."

His eyebrows shot up, the hazel of his eyes appearing more brown in the darkening evening light. "Like administrative courses for your job or something?"

"No, I'm enrolled full time. I have a few associate degrees I transferred with, but I'm focusing on my bachelor's right now. It's honestly not awful, I just do it at night because of my work schedule."

"And you're a mom." He shook his head, releasing a heavy sigh. "Jesus fucking Christ, Madison."

Before thinking better of it, I reached over and patted his knee. "It's really not as bad as it sounds."

His eyes darted down, focusing on where I touched him. Feeling like I'd crossed an invisible line, I pulled it back, but his eyes stayed pinned on his knee.

"I get it now, why you told Layla you don't—"

My phone's shrill ringtone filled the silence, cutting him off and making me jump. I bundled the blanket up and tossed it in his lap, lifting my legs and searching for the phone hidden somewhere beneath me.

It was probably Layla calling while she watched us from the living room window like a voyeur. I'd answer, and she'd likely greet me with a dirty comment about Garrett. I was already chuckling over the imaginary conversation when I located the device.

Caller ID: *Don't Answer*.

My fingers clenched around the screen involuntarily, and my body tensed. How many years would it take for me to stop reacting this way? How many years away from him before the thought of his voice no longer sent me into a downward spiral of self-hatred?

I closed my eyes, willing it away, but when I opened them, the contact name was still across my screen, laughing at me. I'd known his silence wouldn't last forever. Why couldn't he just leave me alone? Forget me? It wasn't hard, Jamie's sperm donor had proved that much.

Angry at myself for my inability to keep from obsessing over past mistakes, I smashed the power button harder than necessary to silence it, and looked up at Garrett. "Sorry about that. What were you saying?"

But he wasn't looking at me. In fact, I wouldn't call what he was doing 'looking' at all. He was glaring down at the phone in my hand with such vehemence that I legitimately wondered if he might light the device on fire with nothing but the flames of his eyes. He looked furious, and it instantly had me backtracking.

"I'm sorry, I shouldn't have tried to answer my phone while you were talking, that was rude of me."

I chewed the inside of my cheek, trying to come up with something to say or do that would ease the sudden tension between us. I wasn't sure when my mind had decided to consider this man my friend, but it had.

He raised his eyes to mine slowly, reluctantly, like he feared my phone might leap up and stab me in the chest if he removed his gaze from it. He exhaled through his nose, squeezing the fleece blanket between his hands like he wished it was someone's neck.

I frowned down at the helpless fabric. Was he angry that I'd cut him off to pick up my phone, or because of who'd been calling? It couldn't have been the latter. Even if he saw the contact, it wasn't a name. And why would he care anyway?

Feeling confused, I mumbled, "All right, well, I should go back inside. I'm surprised they haven't come looking for me yet." I gave him a small smile, the pressure in my chest lessening when his face relaxed minutely.

"Would you…" I hesitated, unsure if it was okay to invite him inside. Besides Nate, whom I'd never seen outside of work, I hadn't had a male friend since high school. I didn't have experience with where the lines were in a male-female friendship.

"I feel like it's all I ever offer you, but I was planning on making my fiftieth cup of coffee for the day. Would you like some?"

He grunted, and I chose to take that as a silent agreement. Slapping my thighs, I said, "Come on, it's cold out here."

Getting up, I nudged him with my foot. Whereas I'd had to shove off my knees and heave myself up, he rose in one smooth movement. His gloriously thick thighs doing all the work.

Good Lord, what was wrong with me? Thoughts like that were *definitely* crossing the line of friendship. I grabbed the blanket and shook it out to distract myself before heading toward the house.

Both dogs instantly went for him, one in excitement, the other in furious outrage. I rolled my eyes, walking toward my little family who'd moved to the table and were now playing a game of Guess Who.

"Child of mine, shouldn't you be getting ready for bed by now?"

"I was going to go outside and ask you if we could play one more game, but Layla told me not to bother you. She said you were having a mental crisis and would come back in when you were done asking the sky for the answers to life."

I slid my eyes to the woman behind that statement. I was going to kick her in the ovaries when she least expected it. I opened my mouth but didn't get the chance to reprimand either of them when Garrett's rumbling laughter echoed out right behind me, sending shivers up my spine.

I glanced back, but he was standing so close, I only got an eyeful of chest. Tipping my face up, I squinted my eyes, but that only made him laugh harder.

"That sounds about right, J-man."

I flung my hands up in defeat. "I hope you all get restless leg syndrome the second you try to fall asleep. Which, speaking of sleep, you seriously need to finish up and get ready, bud. It's past your bedtime, and you have school tomorrow."

He grumbled, flicking the remaining plastic figures down and loading the game back into its box. I watched him shuffle to his room, Sadie at his heels. She'd taken to sleeping with him lately, and although he wouldn't admit it, he was eating it up.

"Coffee still okay with you, Garrett? I could also do tea or a glass of water?" He looked down at me, close enough I could feel the heat from his chest, and I fought the urge to press my chilled body against him for warmth.

"Coffee's fine."

I gave him a thumbs up, setting to work and chatting with him and Layla about their plans for the weekend. Layla seemed to be the only one with anything exciting happening.

"You sure you don't need me to stay home to watch Jamie for you Saturday?"

I waved a hand near my head. "Nope, my parents are excited to have some extra time with him. You and Rick go off and have fun. Hike, get some vicious leg cramps, sweat profusely, attract mosquitoes, all that fun outdoorsy stuff."

She gave me an unimpressed look. She and Rick were not, in any way, the outdoorsy type. They'd probably stay in and write new, amazing music all day.

Garrett had moved to the bar to watch me work. He looked so out of place with his huge mass of a body trying to get comfortable on our cheap barstool. "Which jobs do you do on the weekend?"

Grabbing the finished pot, I poured it into the two mismatched mugs I'd pulled out. "Payroll on Sunday and waitressing each night. Although, I honestly think I might call out from the restaurant. Someone recently told me I look awful so I think maybe I should pull back a bit."

I winked at him over my shoulder and swore his eyes flared in response. But by the time I turned to slide him his mug and creamer, he was back to his normal, stoic expression.

"I actually start a new position Saturday as well."

He wrapped his long fingers around the cup, and my gaze was drawn to his full lips as he pursed them to blow across the top. "Another one?"

"Kind of. I'm just a fill-in, nothing permanent." I leaned back, gesturing to my body with an exaggerated wave. "You're looking at a newly licensed, unarmed guard. Saturday's my first solo shift."

His mug hit the counter with an abrupt *thunk,* causing my head to jolt back. I could practically see the anger seeping from his pores. The man's moods were going to give me serious whiplash one of these days.

"You're fucking with me."

I grimaced, unsure what to do with the unapologetic audacity he was flaunting at me. "No."

"You have no business being a guard."

"Excuse me?" He was one-hundred percent correct, because I was a complete scaredy cat. But I sure as hell wasn't going to agree with him to his face. Not after he'd just laid my pride on a log and slammed a freaking sledgehammer into it.

"You want to explain that one to me?" I tightened my hold on my mug, trying to keep my voice low so Jamie wouldn't come running out of his room.

Garrett didn't back down. "You're what, five foot three? A buck thirty, soaking wet?"

"Five foot five, actually." As if that tiny detail mattered in the least.

"Where." The word was wrapped in aggression, and it made the air around us thicken to an almost unbearable level. My shoulders drew up, and in my peripheral, Layla straightened to attention.

Fighting back my body's conditioned response to livid men, I took a shaky sip of coffee. It was still too hot and burned my tongue, but I ignored the pain, refusing to let him see how much his tone had unsettled me. "The community college."

"And what exactly will you be doing?"

"Patrolling the campus."

"Alone."

It wasn't a question, but I answered like it was anyway. "Yes."

"Unarmed." Another statement.

"I'll have Mace," I snapped. He was hitting on every insecurity I already had about the job, and it pissed me off. I didn't need to be reminded that I was doing something I didn't feel qualified to be doing.

"Mace," he scoffed, shoving off the stool and prowling around the counter toward me. I retreated a step, heart rate increasing, but he kept stalking closer until we were chest to stomach, my back pressed against the fridge.

"Go ahead, Madison." His face loomed inches above my own. "Reach for an imaginary Mace canister at your side. Let's see if you can do it before I incapacitate you."

My chest started heaving, my blood pressure building to an unhealthy point, and angry tears stung the corners of my eyes. I raised one arm to the side, holding up a hand to stop Layla, who looked ready to castrate the man in front of me.

Never looking away from him, I moved, but I didn't go for anything imaginary. I shot my hands straight up, wrapping them around the sides of his head, and pressing my thumbs over his eyelids—not enough to hurt, just to make a point that I could.

His hands clutched my waist, making it impossible to pull away. I rammed my knee up into his thigh, just to the side of his groin, and he grunted.

Slipping my hands farther up, I grabbed two fistfuls of his hair and yanked his head down. Several silent tears had escaped, trailing down my flushed cheeks, but I still looked him straight in the face. His grip on my waist immediately slackened to a gentle hold.

"I feel like we've been here before," I whispered, doing the opposite of him, and tightening my grip, "with you assuming something about me and looking like an asshole."

I tilted my head, sucking on my teeth. "You're right, I'm no match against a man of your size who truly wants to do me harm, but I'm not without claws. I may not win, but you better believe I fight back now."

More tears fell, the angle of my head causing them to drip over my lips, and his eyes flared, fixated on my mouth. "Madison—"

We were suddenly jarred to the side when a body slammed into his, catching us unaware and knocking him to the side. He'd barely centered his footing, holding me upright along with him, when the same small body shoved between us, pushing against Garrett's chest with all his might.

"You *get away from her!*"

I darted forward, snatching Jamie's flailing limbs and wrapping my arms around him from behind. "Stop! Stop, Jamie! He's not hurting me."

His arms fell, and I hugged him harder, trying not to sob at the shaking I could feel coursing through his frame. "I'm fine. I promise, I'm fine."

Unlocking my arms, I twisted him, planting my hands on his cheeks, and making him meet my eyes. "Garrett wasn't trying to hurt me. I'm safe, okay? You're safe."

He nodded, but I could tell he didn't quite believe me as he wrapped his arms around me in a strangling hug.

Movement over his head caught my eye, and I looked up to see Layla ushering Garrett to the door. His face had shut down, his signature flat expression in place. I locked eyes with him and silently mouthed, "It's all right."

I stood there long after they left, hugging my child and staring at the abandoned coffee mugs on the bar, wishing I could remove every bad memory from his head. Every heartache, every fear, every pain. All of it. I wanted to write a book with a perfect, magical world and transport him there where nothing could ever hurt him.

There was nothing crueler than wanting to give someone everything and knowing you couldn't. Knowing you were already predetermined to fail at it from the very beginning but trying your damnedest to succeed anyway.

Chapter 13

I'D BEEN WORRIED for no reason. Patrolling the campus was, by far, one of the easiest jobs I'd ever had. It felt like I was being paid to be on vacation. No one was talking to me, touching me, or asking me questions. I wasn't studying, and bonus, I was getting exercise.

It was amazing.

Obviously, there was the chance something could go wrong. The campus was closed besides a couple of straggling professors, so yes, unwelcome people could show up and cause an issue, but I'd decided to see the glass as half full for once. I was determined to enjoy the small sunlight the sky had finally bestowed upon me.

It was a surprisingly calm day, the eastern breeze napping for the time being. Wearing a beanie and a thin black jacket over my uniform, I was warm and comfortable as I made my way to the next building.

The only terrifying thing to happen to me so far occurred during my walk-through of my second building. I happened to be standing next to a maintenance room when the heater kicked on, and I almost jumped out of my shoes, I ran so fast. And once you've had a kid, being scared is no joke. I nearly peed myself.

Thinking about Jamie put a damper on my mood. The other night had been a hard one, but an important one in a way. When we'd finally left the kitchen, we'd curled up on my bed and talked about what he'd seen and how it'd made him feel.

I'd explained that Garrett had just been worried about my safety and hadn't gone about it in the right way, but that didn't mean he wanted to, or would ever, hurt me.

It shouldn't have been as easy to admit as it was, because by all accounts I didn't actually know my neighbor all that well. I didn't know his past, other than his military history and the little he'd said about his parents.

But the thing that stuck with me was he didn't put his hands on me other than to hold me steady. He didn't shake me and demand I not go even though he might've wanted to. He'd simply pushed me metaphorically to see the truth for myself.

It'd been a dick move, and in the end, it hadn't been necessary since I'd already been second-guessing the shift, but I understood the intention behind his method, as stupid of a method as it was. Hopefully it wouldn't be an issue here soon anyway.

I had no desire to take many guard shifts. I could use the

extra income, but I didn't *need* it to survive. I just needed to get through each day until graduation, when I could hopefully get a full-time job and quit all these others.

God, I couldn't wait to graduate. A higher-paying job wasn't a given, I knew that. I also knew how hard it was for females to get a job in my field. But I was determined, and I had a thing for proving people wrong.

Finishing my on-foot patrol, I meandered through the abandoned courtyard, heading toward the building with the security office so I could ransack some vending machines. But as I approached the parking lot of the building, I frowned.

As a whole, there weren't many vehicles on campus. Apart from the college-owned vehicles, I'd only seen one or two other cars. So, when I spotted a truck parked in the middle of the empty lot, it caught my attention. When I realized there was a man leaning against it, I halted mid-step.

My first instinct was to continue on my path to the building. It was the first rule in the "Woman Alone in a Parking Lot 101" handbook we had drilled into us since birth. My second instinct was to curse and remind myself that it was literally my job to go investigate.

Jesus, I was not cut out for this. Cutting across the yard of the building, I prayed to God the man was only using the campus's convenient location to meet up with someone. Preferably not drug-related.

The stranger was wearing a ballcap-style hat, with a hoodie and jeans, and he was leaned back against the side of the truck, watching me. I felt insanely exposed walking toward him out in the middle of an empty lot.

When I was a few yards out, he pushed off the truck, pulling his hands from his pockets to remove his hat and run his fingers through his dark hair. The action had lightning spearing through me.

I knew that mannerism, and I knew that face. The head tilt, the cut of the jaw, and even the unruly hair that always seemed to look sexy no matter what. It was ingrained in my mind. As I closed more distance, I recognized the black hoodie I'd worn to bed for an inappropriate number of days.

Garrett.

Without taking his eyes off me, he tossed his hat through the open window of the truck. "I wondered if you were ever going to come back around this way."

I blinked. "I'm working."

"I can see that." His eyes dipped to my uniform. There wasn't much to see, the uniform did me zero favors.

I didn't respond, but my thoughts must have been clear on my face because his expression flickered, concern flashing through for the briefest second. "Look…"

I held up a hand. "If you're about to apologize, it's not necessary. I'm not mad. I've come to realize you tend to err on the side of caveman more often than not."

His full lips twitched. "I may not be the best at communication," he offered.

I slapped a hand to my chest, inhaling sharply. "Gasp. You?"

He closed his eyes, shaking his head, and my smile slipped free. "In all seriousness, I appreciate having a friend who cares enough about my safety to speak his thoughts and tell me."

His eyes snapped to mine, and something sparked in their depths. "Does that mean I can keep the lunch I brought you?"

Perking up, I glanced around him for a bag of goodies. "Were you trying to earn my forgiveness through my stomach?"

"Depends, would it have worked?"

My stomach chose that moment to elicit a deep, unending growl, and I squinted one eye shut, grimacing. "I feel like any comment I make now would be rather pointless."

A dark chuckle escaped his lips, drifting across the fall air and lifting my spirits. He twisted back, reaching his arm through the open window, and pulled out a white bag baring a red and yellow logo.

Swallowing the pool of saliva that'd appeared in my mouth, I tipped my head to the side, eyeing the bag like a fucking raptor. "What if I said I didn't like their food?"

"You'd be lying. Now tell me, can you eat, or do you need to get back to work?"

I pulled my phone out of my pocket, checking the time. "I have time to eat. I was already heading to the office for my lunch break anyway. Although, this beats a vending machine buffet, ten to one."

"Perfect." He walked around to the front of his truck, giving the hood a rough smack. "You need help up or can your short, little legs make the jump?"

I narrowed my eyes, choosing to ignore his comment in the name of new friendship and delicious chicken sandwiches. "I didn't even know you had a truck. I've only ever seen your Nova."

He shrugged, hopping up on the hood with ease. "It's my work truck. I don't usually drive it around outside of work, but the Nova's in the shop."

"Oh. I feel kind of bad for not even knowing what you do for a living."

"I'll tell you once you stop being a pussy and get up here to eat."

I went from raptor to dragon in two-point-five seconds, flaring my nostrils and setting my palms flat on the hood. Pushing off with as much grace as I could, I shoved up and twisted, with the full intention of landing on my ass and staring smugly into his stupid, perfectly proportioned face.

Halfway through my twist, the gaudy security buckle on my belt caught on the grill, disrupting my momentum, and making my fingers slip on the smooth surface. I fell forward, face planting right into his lap.

I flailed and reared back, my mind fully determined to make a run for the building and never speak to him again. But his hands were already grasping my waist, hauling me up and setting me beside him.

Adjusting myself into a more comfortable position, I clasped my hands in my lap, looking anywhere but at the man whose crotch I'd just face snuggled.

"You know, your ears turn red when you're embarrassed."

I fidgeted, still not looking at him. "They turn red when I feel anything other than apathy. I know. I've lived with them for twenty-five years."

"It's pretty fucking cute."

My eyes whipped over to him, my face, neck, and ears now flushing for an entirely different reason. He held out a wrapped sandwich, giving it a playful shake. I accepted his peace offering; I was embarrassed, not insane.

"Okay, I'm up here. Now tell me what you do for a living." Unwrapping my gift with a flourish, I took a bite, moaning over the gloriousness that was grease on a bun.

I looked over at Garrett, preparing to lather him in my heartfelt thanks as soon as I swallowed, but paused mid-chew at the dark look he was sending my way. Mouth stuffed, I muttered an unattractive, "What?"

He glared down at his lap, brushing off imaginary crumbs. "I do contract work with turbine engines." His face softened at my blank expression, and he chuckled, "For helicopters and small aircraft. It's, more or less, the same thing I did in the Marines, just on civilian aircrafts now."

"That's pretty cool. Did you ever want to do something else, or do you like it?"

"I like it. Growing up, I wanted to be a pilot, mostly because I wanted the ability to fly my mother somewhere nice." He pushed his jaw out, as if he'd said something he hadn't meant to. "Anyway, it's steady work, and I'm good at it."

With those hands, I bet he was good at a lot of things. "Well, I'm glad you enjoy what you do, that's always a good thing."

He nodded, still looking at me. I pulled my legs up, sitting criss-cross applesauce as I dove back into my food and tried to ignore the feeling of him watching me eat.

"Sarah and Harry are coming to visit tonight."

It took my brain a second to catch up to the mildly familiar names and random turn of conversation. He was talking about his siblings?

"They'll be staying over if you'd like to pop by and say hello. I'm pretty sure Sarah fell in love with you the moment she saw you at the restaurant." He trailed off, taking an overly large bite of his sandwich.

Raising my brows at his weird behavior, I huffed out a laugh. "I'd love to meet them more officially. Actually, I prepared an ungodly amount of chili in the slow cooker this morning if you'd all like to come over for dinner."

He looked uncomfortable at my offer, but I had a feeling it was over the idea of me feeding everyone rather than the invitation itself.

"We're usually stuck eating it for a solid week straight, so it's no big deal. It's up to you, there will be plenty if you change your mind."

He considered me for a moment before tipping his head, and we fell into companionable silence as we ate.

Once we'd both finished and polished off the potato wedges, I steeled my spine and looked up at him. I was pretty sure I knew the answer to my question, but I wanted to hear him say it anyway.

"True or false. You came out here with an apology meal as a ploy to check and make sure I was still alive."

His eyes were pinned to my hand as I brought it to my mouth and licked the salt off the pads of my fingers. He twisted away from me, exhaling and shoving his hands into the front pocket of his hoodie.

"True."

⁂

I could get used to this. It was still early evening, and I'd had time to shower, dry my hair, find something decent to wear, put a dash of makeup on, and prepare appetizers to go along with the simmering chili.

I'd felt sheepish when I'd called out at the restaurant, but I couldn't claim not to be loving every second of my free Saturday night. I felt like a real human being for once, and it felt *good.*

"Will you grab my pop out of the fridge and toss it to me?"

I looked up from the stove. "No, but I can grab your soda if you'd like." I smirked as Layla raised her arm and flipped me off behind her head. Pop, soda, purse, pocketbook. I'd been on the east coast long enough that I was used to the differences in terms here versus the Midwest, but it drove Layla nuts. I made it a habit to annoy the hell out of her with them any chance I could.

She and her boyfriend, Rick, were currently cuddled up on the couch, watching some sci-fi movie he brought while I finished up dinner. I switched off the stovetop burner and pulled open the fridge to grab her drink. A pair of giant ass eyes stared back at me from the center shelf, and I cursed.

"Seriously, Layla? The fridge?" Witch-like laughter met my ears, and I glared over the bar, launching the toy at her.

A few years ago, she and I had each started a collection of

these creepy, bug-eyed stuffed animals. We'd randomly found one at a gas station once and had both continued buying them. I couldn't remember who'd started it, but not long after she moved in, we'd made it a game to hide them around the house, scaring the shit out of each other with them. Lately, she'd been one-upping me.

I shook my head, glancing toward my front door for the hundredth time. I don't know why I was so nervous about meeting Garrett's family again, but I was. And honestly, I was more than a little excited to have people over. I couldn't remember the last time I'd hung out with a group of people who weren't family members—or over the age of eight.

Dressed in a pair of distressed jeans that fit me like a second skin, and a loose, off-the-shoulder sweater, I didn't feel like an overworked mom. I felt like *me*. And I'd really missed me.

Two hard thumps against the door snagged my attention in a way that should have embarrassed me. I shot out of the kitchen, tossing the can on Layla's lap, and smoothing down my wayward curls in a futile attempt to make them behave. "Do I look okay?"

Layla squinted her eyes at me over Rick's shoulder. "And just who are you impressing tonight, and why don't I know about it?"

"Garrett's sister-in-law, Sarah. She's married, but my hope is to woo her and replace your nagging ass."

She pursed her lips, dipping her head in a silent, 'fair enough,' manner, before curling back up into Rick. A nasty emotion swelled up inside my chest at the sight of them practically cuddle fucking on my couch, but I swallowed it down, forcing it to the pit of my stomach like a bad taste. Jealousy didn't look good on anyone.

Taking a deep breath, I opened the door, only to be accosted by what I could only describe as a puppy in human form. She strode right in with no preamble, kicking off her shoes and folding me into a giant hug.

"It's so nice to see you again, Madison. I almost peed myself when Garrett told us you'd invited us all over for dinner."

She was about my same height and was wearing a maroon romper with a floor-length, cream cardigan. Her hair was styled in that perfect messy bun straight-haired people were capable of creating, and it tickled my face as she squeezed me.

Releasing me, her head whipped around the house, landing on the two figures on the couch and heading straight for them, her mouth already moving in greeting. I watched her in shocked silence, still frozen from where she'd accosted me.

"Please excuse my wife, she might be a little tipsy."

Garrett scoffed, "Drunk, you mean. She might be a little drunk."

Seeing the two men standing next to one another in decent lighting, I could see the distinct similarities in them I hadn't been able to see the first time. Garrett was an inch or two taller, and his brother carried a few extra pounds around the middle, but their stances, the way they both stood straight with their arms crossed over their chests was nearly identical.

I held to my original estimation that Harry was around his early fifties, maybe late forties. Although his face wasn't quite as cut from stone as his brother's, he was also incredibly attractive.

I looked back and forth between Garrett's smooth face and Harry's trimmed beard, trying to decide which look I preferred more.

As if sensing my attention, Garrett's eyes cut to mine, searing me in place before dipping to my shoulder. His jaw clenched, the movement sexier than it had any right to be, and I immediately had my answer.

Layla hollered from the couch, pulling me from my thoughts, "So what you're actually saying is Sarah here is winning, and the rest of us are behind?"

"Oh, I like her. Not to worry though, we came bearing gifts. Harry, where's our gift?"

Sarah made her way back to her husband, taking a bag from him I hadn't noticed and rising on her toes to give him a deep kiss. Plunging her hand in the bag, she pulled out a large bottle of amber liquid. "Who wants to play a game?"

Layla and Rick both whooped, the latter giving the first a firm butt smack as they hopped off the couch. I shifted on my feet awkwardly, suddenly second-guessing where this evening was headed.

"Maybe we should eat the food that was prepared for us first?" Garrett addressed Sarah, but his eyes were still on me.

"That's probably best," Layla sang, passing me to slip into the kitchen and grinning evilly. "Mads here, is a complete lightweight on a full stomach. You don't want to imagine her on an empty one."

I frowned. "I'm not that much of a lightweight." I just rarely drank liquor. I was fine sipping wine or beer, but liquor made me uncomfortable. I hated the feeling of not being in total control of myself. Some people liked that out-of-body feeling, but I hated it. It never led to anything good.

Dishes clanged off the counter as Layla set bowls out for everyone, laughing as she did. "I beg to differ. Remember that time you showed up to school drunk, and ended up puking on a teacher before breaking your nose on a toilet when you passed out over it?"

Every head turned my way. Sarah burst out cackling while Harry and Rick both fought back smiles. Garrett simply raised an eyebrow, waiting for me to confirm or deny it.

The daggers I shot Layla would have terrified a lesser woman. "I'd taken shots of Everclear, and I was fifteen."

Rick set his full bowl at the table, patting my back in commiseration as he walked by. Given his lifestyle, he probably had firsthand experience of the mayhem Everclear could create.

He could be a little obnoxious, but overall, I didn't mind the guy. I gave him a grateful smile, but it fell when tingles shot across the back of my neck. I peered over my shoulder to see two slits of hazel eyes looking at me.

I frowned, wondering what I'd said wrong. Maybe he just didn't find my story as funny as the rest of his family? I tilted my head in silent question, but he looked away, accompanying his brother into the kitchen.

***

"Okay, so the game is simple, we each take turns saying

something we don't think anyone has ever done. If you *have* done it, you take a shot. If no one has done it, the person who asked takes a shot. But don't ask boring questions…I'm looking at you, Garrett."

I chewed the inside of my lip, listening to Sarah animatedly list off instructions. I'd played the game many times before, back when I hadn't been old enough to do so, but not since having Jamie. In fact, I hadn't played a drinking game at all in years.

I raised my hand, waving it above my head. "I'm going to sit this one out since I happen to be the only one who works in the morning."

We'd all piled our dishes in the—thanks to Garrett—working dishwasher and were now squeezed in around my table. The men had grabbed a few extra chairs from Garrett's house while Sarah set up the bottle of whiskey, a liter of soda, and a stack of red plastic cups.

The sight itself sent me back in time. I felt like I was a teenager again, standing in the middle of a wheat field, scooping spiked punch from a cooler while someone blared music from a pickup truck.

Layla nudged my shoulder. "Don't be such a mom, Mads. You can have fun. It's allowed."

"You literally just called me a lightweight earlier, and now you want me drinking Jack and Coke less than twenty-four hours before I have to work." I smashed my lips together, resting my chin on my palm.

She dipped her head. "Touché. All right, you can have wine then." She jumped up, and thirty seconds later, I had a glass of white wine set in front of me.

"There. Now let's play. I'll go first." She was practically jumping in her seat as she glanced at me, and I knew no matter what I had in my glass, she'd made it her mission to get my "high-strung ass" drunk.

She tapped her fingertips against her cup rhythmically, each click of her calluses making me more apprehensive of what she'd say.

"Never have I ever shoved a full-fledged human out of my body."

"Are you fucking kidding me?" I snapped, shoving her hard in the shoulder.

She only cackled like a deranged hyena and pointed to my glass. I grabbed it, taking an irritated sip. I was an annoying drunk, and I puked easily, so I had no idea why she thought it'd be good for me.

It wasn't until I caught her discreet glance at Garrett that I realized what her true game plan was.

This bitch didn't want me getting drunk just for the hell of it. No, she wanted to get me drunk so I'd want to get *laid*. Well, she was going to be thoroughly disappointed because that wasn't happening.

Sitting to her right, Rick was next, and his question was exactly what I'd expected from him. "Never have I ever done shrooms." No one moved apart from an exaggerated eye roll from Layla, forcing him to take a drink.

Garrett was next, sitting directly across from me. "Never have I ever been pulled over." Unsurprisingly, everyone at the table picked up their cups. I caught his eye, but he quickly looked away.

The game continued on, each question ridiculous, yet harmless. Stealing, skinny dipping, and evading arrest. Then it got back to Layla. That beautiful, frustrating—had my best interests at heart but needed to calm the fuck down—woman stared hard at Garrett before cutting her eyes to me and blurting, "Never have I ever, gone the last five years without fucking someone."

Sarah and Harry set their cups on the table, cracking up like it was the most ridiculous question to be asked all night. But it was the heated pair of eyes I could feel on the side of my face that had my heart picking up speed and a flush creeping up my neck.

With as straight of a face as I could maintain, I downed an overly large amount of wine.

Rick coughed, his eyes widening comically. "Wait, I thought you only got divorced like three years ago?"

"I did."

"What, you just didn't sleep with your husband for two years?" he asked.

"We were separated for a while before I was finally able to file for divorce."

Sarah stared at me like I'd grown another head, and she wasn't the only one. "You seriously haven't had sex in five *years?*" She pointed to her husband. "I'd fucking explode if we went that long, and not in the good way, obviously."

Garrett grimaced at the visual of his sister-in-law he clearly didn't appreciate, but he was looking straight at me. "You said finally able to file. Why couldn't you file before then?"

My grip on my cup tightened, and I cursed myself when his eyes caught the movement. Giving him a practiced smile, I said, "That's not how the game works, and it's not your turn."

Layla leaned forward. "Oh, stop. He's just curious because you're hot as sin and none of it makes sense."

I opened my mouth to defend myself, but she plowed on. "She stayed married and faithful to Aaron's stupid ass for two years because he was deployed. Bullshit, if you ask me. If anyone deserved to be dropped in the dirt, it was that motherfucker."

I reached down, pinching the tender flesh of her thigh. She yelped, flinching away from me. I could literally feel the weight of Garrett assessing me, and I met his gaze, putting a challenge in my own. His mouth parted, but Rick spoke first.

"Never have I ever done butt stuff."

I'd never been so thankful for a change in conversation, and I nearly burst out laughing when Harry looked pointedly at his untouched drink and sighed before then looking at his wife.

Deciding it couldn't be more embarrassing than what I'd already admitted, I reached forward, fully intending on chugging the rest of my wine and saying to hell with the consequences. I knew Garrett was watching me, he'd never stopped, and the heat was setting me aflame.

I dared a glance, feeling my heart pick up when his eyes tracked my movement. Setting the cup against my lips, I was not at all prepared for him to reach forward and grab his own cup. Holy fucking hell. Did that mean he'd done it to someone else or…

The people around us disappeared, I didn't even know if anyone else moved to take a drink. I was entrapped by the man across from me, nearly convulsing in my seat as molten lava poured in my core. The cobwebs that'd been covering my libido were long gone, burned up as if they'd never existed.

Not once did he break eye contact with me as we each tipped our heads back. The roll of his throat as he swallowed was possibly one of the most erotic things I'd ever witnessed, and I was suddenly too hot in my own skin. If he'd been able to touch me, just one touch, I might have shattered right there at the table.

And by the way his nostrils flared, he knew it.

Fuck.

Chapter 14

I WAS DEATH.

That was, if death looked like a pile of dog shit that'd been run over by a golf cart full of polo-wearing, sweaty men before being scooped up and tossed in a lava pit.

I hadn't woken up hung over. I actually only had a minor headache, which was the surprise of the century for me, but I'd barely slept a wink. I'd passed out within minutes of crashing but had woken soon after with a brain that refused to shut down.

A few hours later, and I was fucking dragging. I'd had to take a scalding shower and drink two large cups of coffee just to find the energy to get dressed for work. I was now slouched on my couch, listening to a lecture about the inefficiency of school drug programs while I worked on a crocheted baby blanket to keep myself from falling asleep a half hour before I needed to leave.

It was going well so far. I'd only had to restart the lecture three times when I'd failed to comprehend a word and re-do the same row of stitches five times when I kept losing count.

I'd finally given up on the lecture and was staring at the half-finished blanket resting in my lap when a knock sounded at my door. My head shot up, wondering who would be here this early. Rick and Layla were passed out in her room, and my parents wouldn't have brought Jamie back yet.

Creaking the door open, my tongue got lodged in my throat at the sight of Garrett in his hoodie and a pair of sweats, holding a plate of cinnamon rolls. If delicious was a view, this would have been it. He had a slight shadow dusting his jaw, and his hair was tussled in an incredibly endearing way.

"Hey."

"Good morning."

His half-lidded eyes took in my work clothes before glancing down at himself. "Were you about to head out?"

I shook my head, opening the door wide enough for him to step through. "No, I still have a few minutes before I need to leave. What's up? By the way, I'm desperately hoping those heavenly smelling morsels are for me."

He smirked, handing me the plate. "Sarah made them this morning. She practically kicked me out of my own home to bring them to you before you left, as a thank you for dinner. She said to tell you nothing goes with chili better than cinnamon rolls."

I half-laughed, half-squealed. "No one else on this coast does that! God, Harry better be ready for a fight because I might steal his wife."

"You a fan of polygamy?" he poked, resting his fine rear on a barstool while I slapped a roll on a clean plate and put it in the microwave.

"Not particularly. I was just going to replace Layla with her. After last night, I'm sure you can understand why." I busied myself with grabbing a paper towel, slapping myself internally for bringing up the previous night.

"She's a feisty one."

"That she is."

Pulling my prize from the microwave, I didn't even care that I had an audience as I stuffed my mouth with gooey, breakfast perfection.

His eyes sparked, a laugh hiding in their depths, but he turned, gesturing to my mess of items littering the living room. "So that's what you do when you should be sleeping?"

"Jealous?" I asked, sticking my thumb in my mouth and sucking the icing off like the glutton I was.

His lids lowered. "Yes." Clearing his throat, he stood, walking toward the couch and balancing his butt on the edge. "Your free time looks positively exhilarating."

I joined him, closing my laptop and moving it out of the way so he could sit. "Don't knock it till you try it."

He raised his eyes to the ceiling, lips moving like he was either praying for patience or talking to the popcorn.

"I see I'm not the only ceilologer."

His head snapped back down, brows heavily creased. "A what?"

"Uh..." Why did I never think before I spoke with this man? I swore my social cues seized up completely when he was around. "Nothing." I picked up my crochet hook, fiddling with the tip.

He stared at me for another moment, probably coming to terms with the fact that I was really fucking weird. No shade. I was. "What are you working on?"

I looked down at the soft bundle of pink and white yarn, feeling self-conscious. "A baby blanket."

"Are you an aunt?"

"No. I do have a brother, but he doesn't have any kids. I make blankets to donate."

He continued watching me in that silent way of his, asking questions without actually asking them. I sighed, knowing there was no reason for the subject to embarrass me.

"There's an amazing local organization that assists teenage mothers. I donate baby blankets to them."

His jaw worked, and his eyes dropped to the blanket, watching my hands as I folded it up and carefully placed it in a canvas bag.

"It's actually the kind of organization I'd like to work for, or even head, someday. Many teenage mothers turn to drugs or alcohol to cope with stress. A program dedicated to keeping them clean could do so much good." I bit my lip, realizing I'd just told him something I hadn't even told Layla or my family yet.

"Anyway, I'm behind on how many I usually make..." I trailed off, not sure why I was rambling about something he had no interest in. What grown man wanted to discuss crochet?

"I have never been so wrong about a person as I was about you," he said.

I looked up, smiling. "I don't know. If a rich, old guy offered to buy me a house in exchange for a few titty shots a month, I might say yes."

I'd meant it as a joke, but his eyes darkened, dropping to the high collar of my blouse before coming back up. "Is that all it would take?"

My breathing quickened. He needed to stop looking at me that way. I didn't know how to use my mouth or my fucking limbs when he looked at me like that.

I licked my lips, looking at the clock we had sitting by the television. "I mean, I'd also ask for my bills to be paid. As you know, I'd much rather go shopping and drink wine than have to work."

His raspy chuckle caressed my skin, lighting me up from the inside out. He followed my gaze to the time and stood. "Shame. All I have to offer are cinnamon rolls."

I watched him walk away, admiring the way his sweats shifted over his ass. "You didn't even make them."

He winked over his shoulder, pulling the door open. "And you didn't get all the icing off your chin."

***

Jamie hadn't stopped talking since I picked him up after work, but I was soaking up every bit of it. As nice as it'd been to have a parental break for a night, I'd missed him.

"Did you know that rat poison is so effective because rodents are incapable of vomiting?"

"Huh. That makes sense I suppose."

"Yeah, it's kind of mean though. Did you know sloths sometimes mistake their arms as part of the tree and end up falling to their deaths?"

I darted a glance away from the road long enough to look back at him, but all I could see was his forehead hovering over the upheld animal book. "Is there a reason all these facts are about death?"

"Well, the next fact after the rats was about female koalas having more than one vagina, but I thought you'd appreciate the sloth one more."

I blinked at the road. "Feel free to wash that out of my ears with a different fact, bud."

"No, I think I'll leave you with that one." He giggled as we turned into our drive, but his laughter died when he jumped out of the Jeep and spotted Garrett to the right of us, leaning against his work truck with his phone to his ear.

The second Garrett saw Jamie, he uttered a quick, "I'll call you back," and hung up. "Hey, J-man, you have a good time at your grandparents' house?"

I came around the vehicle in time to see Jamie kick at some loose gravel, his head down and arms wrapped tightly around his book. He couldn't look more sheepish if he tried. "Yeah."

It didn't faze Garrett, and the way he smiled at my child made something stir in my middle, feeling a lot like indigestion.

Jamie opened his mouth. Closed it. Then repeated the

action a second time. A determined expression crossed his face and he nodded, almost to himself. He handed his book to me and marched right up to our neighbor, extending his hand toward him.

"I'm sorry I yelled at you. My mom told me you're her friend and were just trying to help her."

Garrett's face softened as he shook my child's hand and leaned down. "Never, and I mean *never*, apologize for defending your mom. You were right to yell at me."

I forced myself to stay silent and let them hash it out when I really wanted to butt in and give my opinion. Jamie looked so much older than his eight years as he stood there, looking a grown ass man in the eye.

"We good, J-man?"

He gave a serious nod. "I would be okay with being friends."

"Yeah?" Garrett's smile lit my heart, giving that indigestion feeling a hard squeeze.

"Yeah." Jamie released his hand, stepping toward me to grab his book. "But only if you promise not to make her cry again."

Garrett's smile fell, his face turning to stone as he locked eyes with me. "I promise."

His words drifted to my heart and prodded at it, seeking entrance. I hadn't trusted a man in a long time. Trusting someone meant opening yourself up for hurt, and I'd done that enough to last me a lifetime. But I believed him, and the knowledge of that had me sweating under my skin.

"Cool. So, you wanna come to my soccer game next Sunday?"

I choked on a laugh, pressing my fingers against my eyelids.

For as protective as the kid could be, he was also completely guileless.

Garrett's tongue poked the inside of his cheek, and an amused grin formed on his lips. "If you play soccer even half as well as you play games, I'll be there."

"Yeah, I'm basically the best."

I laughed, snagging his shoulder and twisting him toward the door. "All right, hot shot, time to go inside."

He grumbled an irritated, "Fine," before also adding, "My mom will text you the time and place if you want to go." He darted away, avoiding the playful smack I aimed at the back of his head.

I returned my attention to Garrett, feeling my pulse race when he shortened the distance between us to lean against the side of my Jeep. "Don't let him guilt trip you, you don't have to go Sunday."

His face seemed contemplative, as he stuck his hands in his pockets and looked over my head toward the house. "You work, don't you?"

I lowered my eyes, adjusting the strap of my purse over my shoulder. "Yeah, it's at eleven in the morning, which is in the middle of my shift."

"I'll go."

"You don't have to—"

He cut me off again, straightening to his full height and stepping into my personal space until I had to tip my head back in order to maintain eye contact.

"Text me the address. I'll go. I'll even bring him home

afterward. It's not like it's out of my way." He smiled slowly, and it was sinful.

My lungs forgot how to work, and I had to swallow before I could answer. "I don't have your number."

"Give me your phone."

What I should've done was scrunch my nose and told him I don't take orders from men towering over me. What I should not have done was inhale his clean, male scent and hand my phone over without so much as a word.

A few seconds later, a *ding* came from the back pocket of his jeans, and he smiled. I reached to take my phone back, but he ignored me, leaning forward and pushing it into my purse. The way his face hovered over mine while his fingers eased the device through the open crevice of my purse straps should not have had me squeezing my thighs together, but my body officially had a mind of its own.

Feeling way in over my head and suddenly needing a cold shower, I side-stepped, putting some much-needed space between us. "I better go check on Jamie, he's probably stuffing his face with snacks and ruining his dinner."

His eyes dipped to my neck, then traveled up to my ears before resting back on my eyes. I retreated a few more steps, suddenly nervous my thoughts were written across my face.

"Have a good night, Madison."

"Yeah, you too." I took off, walking faster than was necessary until I'd shut the door, effectively cutting off his relentless stare. I dropped to the ground, my pulse erratic.

A buzzing sound caught my attention, and my stupid,

idiotic heart picked up. Gripping my phone somehow felt intimate and dirty after the thoughts I'd had over his handling of it.

I unlocked my screen, and promptly burst out laughing, startling the dogs who'd come to greet me. Jamie poked his head out of his room, but I continued smiling down at my phone, wider than I had in a long time. I knew, without a shadow of a doubt, I was in so much trouble.

He'd put himself in my phone as Sugar Daddy.

Chapter 15

CRADLING TWO FOIL-WRAPPED hot dogs and two steaming Styrofoam cups, I made my way up the bleacher steps, focusing every bit of concentration on not tripping in my skirt and heels. If I'd known I would be here today, I would have dressed in a damn pantsuit. Or packed jeans and an extra sweater. Hindsight was a bitch.

I'd missed the entire beginning half of Jamie's first game but had at least arrived in time for the second half. My boss made a deal with me. He allowed me to slip out as soon as I'd finished payroll and paid me for a full day on the promise that I would babysit his granddaughter for free in a couple weeks.

Was it ethical? Probably not, but I'd agreed in a heartbeat. I was excited as hell to surprise Jamie.

I'd scanned the area for my parents, knowing they'd be here

somewhere, and found them sitting in foldout camping chairs closer to the field. But like a damn planet drawing me to his gravity, my eyes were pulled to the bleachers.

Sitting several rows up, right above a group of school moms I recognized, was a familiar black hoodie hugging a body I couldn't miss if I tried. By the way the women before him were glancing back, they hadn't missed it either.

He had what looked to be a gray beanie pulled down over his head, and he was leaned forward, elbows resting on his thighs, rubbing his hands together for warmth. I hadn't realized how much I'd missed seeing him. I'd only caught quick glimpses of him the past week, and he hadn't responded to my text when I'd given him the field location.

Seeing him felt like a sun was settling inside me. The man had no idea I would be here, yet he'd shown up. For Jamie. I pressed my handful of items against my chest, trying to dampen the uncomfortable pressure there, and began the climb.

Making it to his row, I shuffled my way past a few long legs and knobby knees, trying not to stab my heels into toes or knock over beverages. A gust of wind shoved into me, yanking and pulling loose curls across my face. Hands full, I made do with shaking my head and blowing a few pieces off my nose while cursing.

Garrett's head whipped in my direction, and he half-stood, eyes lighting up as a slow, panty-melting smile formed on his lips, his dimples on full display.

The moms who'd been watching him like he was the game rather than their actual children, gaped openly. I was torn between half of me completely understanding while the other, irrational half wanted to shove them down the bleachers.

Garrett straightened to his lumberjack, six-foot whatever height as I made my way toward him. His eyes trailed from my heels, up my pencil skirt, and lingered on my lilac sweater.

Either he was a secret fashion connoisseur with an eye for thrift shop finds, or he appreciated the half-inch of visible cleavage my scoop-neck sweater showed.

By the darkening of his eyes, I was pretty sure it was the latter. I pushed down the thrill the thought sent me. It wasn't necessarily me he was ogling, I told myself. Garrett Rowe was simply a boob man. The idea he might enjoy someone else's rankled, but I pushed that down too. All my idiotic thoughts could have a damn party down in the pit of my stomach.

"I come bearing gifts."

His eyes dipped down once again, and the corner of his lips quirked up. For a moment, I swore he was about to make a dirty joke about what my gifts were, but he refrained. Instead, he sat back down, taking the cups from me and setting them on his other side out of the way.

"Hot chocolate and hot dogs?" He quirked an eyebrow, and I chuckled, ungracefully plopping my butt next to him.

"They were out of coffee, and you looked cold." I unwrapped my foiled meal and looked out onto the field to try to pinpoint Jamie.

There was a beat of silence before he bumped my shoulder with his and said, "Thank you."

I replied by reaching over to toast his wrapped hot dog with the tip of my own. Taking a giant bite of the rubbery, luke-warm food, I desperately wished I had some mustard and relish to drown it in.

I chewed, watching miniature humans chase after a ball. I had no idea what the rules were or who was winning. To be honest, I wasn't into sports at all. Growing up, I'd only participated in the school dance team and my brother had been into cross country, so soccer was outside my bubble of knowledge.

"He's done really well."

"Hm?"

"Jamie. He's played almost the entire game so far, and he's done well. He's a good team player, which I doubt is common at this age."

I smiled around my food, pleased, but the feeling didn't last long.

"Glad you were able to make Jamie's first game, Madison. You almost missed it."

The comment came from Tristan, the woman sitting in the center of the mom trio in front of us. I'd run into them a few times before, and they were no fans of mine.

They were the kind of people who enjoyed using their religion for attention and glamor but were the first to turn a blind eye and ignore everything they claimed to believe in when it was convenient for themselves.

Brushing off her passive-aggressive tone and letting it flow past me like I was a damn river stone, I glanced away from the field to answer her. "Thanks, Tristan, I'm glad I was able to make it too."

I didn't know Tristan's exact age, but I knew she was about mid-thirties. She was pretty in a small-town-pageant-winner type of way. Wavy, volumized blond hair, blue eyes, and bright, extravagant makeup. She had a lean face with straight square teeth and was always dolled up in name-brand items, from her coat down to her shoes.

Batting her eyelashes at Garrett, she smiled up at him. "It's nice to finally meet you. There for a while, we all thought you were imaginary." She giggled, and I had a nasty urge to pour my drink on her head.

He lowered his eyes, giving her that flat, uninterested look I'd been the personal victim of before. "Should I know who you are?"

I coughed, choking on my half-chewed bite, and he immediately leaned over, handing me one of the hot chocolates while continuing to look down at Tristan. If stone-cold granite was a person, it'd be freaking Garrett Rowe.

She pulled back, blinking furiously in offense. "I run the PTO at your son's school. I even designed the boys' soccer uniforms this year." She pursed her lips, like second-grade uniforms were the epitome of a life well-lived.

"Huh," was all he said before dismissing her and looking back out at the field. No explanation, no denial, no "he's not my kid." Nothing. I stared up at him, baffled. I didn't know of a single man who wouldn't have corrected a beautiful woman about his parental status.

She frowned, or at least I think she did. It was hard to tell with her perfect, Botox face. "How long are you staying in town for?"

He took his time dragging his eyes from the field, making it very clear she was interrupting. "I live here."

Her lips formed a perfect "oh" and her eyes darted to me, calculating. I sighed, setting my cup down and hardening my spine. I could fill an entire notebook with all the reasons I disliked this woman.

"Tristan, this is my neighbor, Garrett. Jamie invited him to the game." Which is why we're trying to watch it, you gossip whore, I silently added.

Her bell-chimed laugh hit my ears, banging all the way to my eardrums, and making me wince. The other two women—Carolyn and Lara, if I remembered correctly—laughed along with her like they all somehow knew the same joke. It instantly had alarm bells taking off, joining the still-ringing sound of her laugh.

"My apologies, Garrett. That makes so much more sense."

I sucked my lips into my mouth, trying to let the comment pass. Same shit, different day. We'd only spoken a handful of times, but she always found a way to insult my single-parent status each time. Inhale, exhale. Her comments didn't matter. *She* didn't matter. I was a motherfucking river stone, and I was here for Jamie.

"And why is that?" The question rumbled out of the broad chest next to me, and my head turned his way, but he wasn't looking at me. If Tristan had wanted his undivided attention, she now had it.

She batted her lashes again, and I imagined if they were any longer, she'd fly away. Turning around more fully, she had the audacity to rest a hand on his knee. Her very much married hand.

"I meant it as a compliment. You don't seem like the kind of man who would have had a child *with* a child." She laughed again. "But that's what I get for assuming."

The underhanded insult shot through me, and I set down my Styrofoam cup to keep from squeezing it in half and throwing it at her smiling face.

I waited to hear his reply, hear him knock her down a peg or give her his unimpressed expression. But he didn't. He just stared at her hand on his knee, the muscles along his jaw flexing.

The cold, plummeting feeling in my stomach definitely wasn't disappointment or embarrassment. Nope. I was probably just coming down with a sudden case of the flu.

Pushing down the feeling—that I was leaving unnamed—I pasted my very best customer service smile on my face, lining it with a hint of disdain.

"Thank you, Tristan."

She glanced over, eyebrows raised, and her hand still resting on Garrett's knee. "For what?"

"For always reminding me how young I was when I gave birth. You'd think I could remember since I was the one who laid there for fourteen hours and shoved his body out of my vag, but it's so difficult sometimes. Probably because my brain hadn't fully developed yet. So, thank you."

I kicked my smile up a notch, sweetness oozing from the

corners. I hoped she fucking drowned in it.

She sneered, finally pulling her hand off my neighbor to point a long, manicured nail at me. "I'd say I'm surprised by your crass, juvenile comment, but lying is a sin."

"Ah, yes, we wouldn't want Jesus thinking you were anything but a stand-up Christian woman."

Her jaw jutted out, and she huffed loudly. "Not all of us are as comfortable spitting on our values and beliefs as you are, *Madison*."

I clenched my fists to keep them from visibly shaking. It was physically painful to keep my face neutral when my heart was racing, and my neck and ears were reddening.

"Turn around and watch your son, Tristan. I'd like to watch mine play since, as you so graciously pointed out, I already missed the first half."

Disdain filled her eyes, her lips curling and twisting to form the poison I could sense was about to spew. "Your son wouldn't even be here if it wasn't for the tuition payments parents like us pay." She gestured to herself and the moms on either side of her.

I could ignore a lot, but implying my son didn't have a right to his education was a hard ass line. Forcing my jaw to unclench enough to speak, I said, "I pay the same tuition you do."

Her bell-chimed laugh burst out, but it was tainted, no longer carefree. "Please. You receive financial aid, and everyone here knows it. How do you think your son was able to join the team? Did you think it was *free?*"

My face fell, and she scoffed. "People like you love working the system, and rather than be grateful, you turn your greedy rear around and butt into our social circle like you belong here."

Her voice had picked up in volume, and the people sitting around us were now watching, salivating over my humiliation like vultures circling a rotting carcass. I could hear my pulse in my ears and my eyes were beginning to burn.

I sniffed, blinking rapidly, refusing to let a single drop fall. I was used to this. I could handle this. It was fine. Everything was fine.

"You're right, Tristan. I didn't pay for Jamie to be on the team, but not because I was unwilling to pay. However, I pay the same tuition as every family here, and I do it on my own. I get up and go to work every day to earn my son a spot here. And as an unemployed mother whose husband works to pay for her child's spot, you have no right to comment on it."

"You, of all people, are going to judge me for being a stay-at-home mother? How unsurprisingly hypocritical of you."

I slid my sweaty hands down my thighs and gripped my knees. I could feel the heat of everyone's eyes, and nausea coiled inside me.

"You're putting words in my mouth so you can manipulate your way into being a victim. I won't play that game with you. My son is here because he deserves it and because I work for it. End of story."

Carolyn and Lara were both tapping at her shoulders, telling her to drop it, but she was a wildfire, blazing with no care of who or what she torched. "You can sit there in your second-hand secretary costume all you want, but we both know the only job you're qualified for doesn't require clothes."

I flinched, my shield crumbling under the combination of her venom and the continued stares. A single tear leaked out, and I dashed it away only for a second to quickly follow. I stood, intent on running away to bawl in the privacy of my vehicle, but a firm grip around my wrist stopped me.

I looked down, blinking to see through the blur in my eyes. Garrett had a hand around me, but he wasn't looking at me. He was staring at Tristan, and he was radiating with fury.

"You may not care about actually watching your children do something they enjoy, but we're here to watch the game. Remove yourselves so we can do so."

She pulled back, verbally exhaling, like she couldn't believe he'd actually told her to leave. But Garrett didn't give a shit. If anything, his gaze grew even harder as he leaned forward. "Now."

The idiot still looked ready to fight, but Carolyn suddenly shoved into her shoulder, muttering who knows what in her ear. Tristan made sure to shoot me one final condemning look, but she listened, getting up and sashaying away with her nose in the air.

It didn't matter to me whether she'd left or not. I didn't want to be there anymore, but the hand around my wrist refused to loosen, tugging me back down to the bleacher.

"I'm sorry, Maddie."

I twisted toward him so fast, I was surprised I didn't get whiplash. No one called me Maddie. I'd demanded my family switch to Mads back in middle school because I'd thought Maddie sounded like a kid's name. So why did it sound like fucking sex on a stick coming from Garrett's mouth?

"What," I swallowed, wiping more rogue tears away. "What do you possibly have to apologize for? I'm the one who embarrassed you."

He slid his hand from my wrist to my palm and clasped his fingers around mine. His eyes were still pulsing with anger as he looked down at my tear-streaked face.

"I should have stopped it before it got that ugly." He cursed, holding my hand tighter. "I was afraid of saying something to that woman that I couldn't take back, and even more afraid I'd do something that would fall poorly on you or Jamie with the school."

I was barely breathing at that point, staring up into his eyes and losing myself in the knowledge he'd felt that way on my behalf. The idea of having someone—especially him—in my corner, was intoxicating.

"What were you afraid you'd do to her?" I whispered.

He leaned down until we were almost sharing breath. "Honestly? I wanted to slap her in the face with my wiener."

I blinked, speechless, until he slowly raised his free hand. I glanced down to see the still-foiled hot dog, flattened like he'd squeezed the ever-loving hell out of it, and I lost it. I laughed so hard a high-pitched, piglet snort escaped me, and my stomach muscles screamed in protest. And then Garrett's baritone laughter was joining me.

We sat there, with who knows how many people watching us, dying over the fact that he'd suffocated his wiener trying not to pummel a woman with it.

More tears dripped down my face, and they felt good. With each laughter-induced tear that fell, my lungs expanded farther, and my heart settled. Looking up at this man, each of us fighting to control ourselves, I couldn't remember the last time I'd laughed hard enough to cry.

We sat shoulder to shoulder, still holding hands while we watched the last quarter of the game. It didn't feel weird or romantic, just comfortable, and a nagging whisper in the back of my head told me I could get used to it.

"Does she bother you often?"

"No. With my work schedule I can never attend school events, so I rarely see her or any of the other parents. But to answer the follow-up question I'm sure you want to ask, yes, she is always like that when I do. Although, usually she sticks to passive-aggressive comments. I may have poked the embers a bit today."

"All because she disapproves of your age? Isn't it a religious school?"

"Yes and no. The age I got pregnant bothers all the parents I've met, but it's that combined with me being, not only single, but single and divorced. It's a three strikes and you're out club, so I never even made it through orientation." I shrugged.

After eight years, I still sometimes struggled to bear people's judgmental comments, but I also knew I wasn't missing out by being excluded from their circles. I had no desire to befriend people like that anyway.

"Can I ask you a personal question?"

"You just told me you wanted to wiener whip a lady. I think

we're past the point of needing permission to ask questions."

He laughed, deep and full, and butterflies took off in every fucking direction, making me lightheaded. "Point taken." Sobering, he asked, "What made you and Jamie's father divorce?"

I tensed, my immediate knee-jerk reaction being to jump ship and not answer. But we'd basically just traded imaginary friendship bracelets, so he deserved the truth. I pulled my hand away, trying not to read too much into the way his fingers clenched the empty air.

"My ex-husband, Aaron, the one you met? He's not Jamie's dad."

His eyebrows shot up, not necessarily in shock but rather mild surprise, which I'd expected. He'd already hinted once before that he assumed them to be one and the same.

"When I was sixteen, I dated a guy who was four years older than me. We were together less than a year before we broke up, and then I found out I was nine weeks pregnant. I was seventeen by the time I gave birth. He was twenty-one. In the state of Kansas, I was of legal age to consent, but it obviously didn't go over well with my family."

I laughed humorlessly, watching my son chase the ball and successfully steal it from an opponent.

"He'd always been controlling, telling me what to wear, how to act, making me straighten my hair and wear certain makeup. But he got nasty during my pregnancy and started following me around and obsessively calling my phone." I looked down, distracting myself with pushing back my cuticles.

"In the end, my parents threatened to put a restraining order on him, and I was induced at the hospital under an anonymous name. We even tried to get his parental rights removed. It was denied, but the court ruled he had to attend parenting classes and anger management before he could have non-supervised visitation with Jamie."

"And did he?" he asked, his tone indicating he already knew the answer.

"No. He disappeared soon after when he realized he had no control over me or Jamie. I haven't heard from him since. I don't regret any of it because it gave me Jamie, but the guy was just a nameless sperm donor. Nothing else. And I'm finally at a point in my life where I'm okay with that."

"That's a lot to go through at such a young age."

I nodded absently, chewing the inside of my lip and feeling uncomfortable. "Anyway, I'd already known my ex-husband through mutual friends during all of that, and we eventually eloped when I turned 18. The rest you know."

"Shit."

"Yeah," I agreed. "Like I said, my plane is packed the fuck full." I stood, gathering up my purse and trash. "Let's go, it looks like the game's over."

I felt bad for how little I'd actually paid attention. If it wasn't for the scoreboard, I wouldn't even know they'd won. But when it was all said and done, it didn't matter. The look on Jamie's face when he saw Garrett and me standing near the field was the most beautiful sight I'd ever seen. He hugged me so hard, I almost popped an ovary, but I hugged him back, congratulating him on the team's win.

When I turned, Garrett had approached my parents and was shaking my dad's hand, introducing himself. My conveniently timed indigestion reared its head at the sight.

There was a pull on my arm. "Grandpa said we could go get frozen yogurt after the game."

"Did he now?"

I should say no. None of us had consumed anything remotely resembling healthy food today, but I figured go big or go home, right? Jamie had won his game after all. I may not have paid attention, but a win was a win, and we could celebrate it.

Turning to see both my dad and Garrett looking over at us, I offered a goofy smile. "Apparently, we're going out for frozen yogurt, would you like to join us, Garrett?"

He smiled, stuffing his hands in his pockets. "Does anyone ever say no to frozen yogurt?"

"Nope," I said, enunciating the word. "It was a rhetorical question. Get your butt in gear, and let's go."

Chapter 16

I STOOD ON my porch, watching Jamie chase Garrett across our yard, hollering. The day after his first game, we'd come home to find a brand-new soccer ball waiting for him on the porch. Jamie had instantly dropped his bag to the cement and snatched it up, running his hands over it like he'd found the heart of the ocean.

I'd felt Garrett before I saw him, that familiar tingle running along the back of my neck. But it was the feeling that had run through my chest that worried me.

He'd been leaning against his Nova, which was finally out of the shop, watching us with an expression I couldn't name. With a hat pulled low on his head and a leather jacket sitting over his hoodie, he'd looked off limits in the most enticing way.

The swift putter of my heart as his eyes had locked with mine had me questioning how smart it was to continue our friendship. He didn't walk over, nor did he say a word. He'd just winked at me, sending that quivering beat lower than my stomach, and pushed off, making his way into his house.

Now here we were a few days later. Garrett had been outside when Jamie and I got home, and the kid hadn't batted an eye about asking him to kick the new ball around. Garrett scoffed, making some playful comment about wiping him across the ground, and they'd started up a competitive game of one-on-one.

Incessant whining behind me demanded my attention, and I stepped back inside. Both dogs were at the door, beside themselves wanting to go play. Layla was out for the evening, and neither of them appreciated being left alone.

Pulling out the bag of treats we kept in the kitchen, I tossed one to each, shooing them out before digging into the fridge for dinner.

I heard Jamie's laughter before I heard the click of the door opening, and it was one of best sounds in the world. As much as I worried about my growing feelings for Garrett, I could never regret having an extra person give my child the time and affection he deserved.

I poked my head around the bar, scrunching my nose at their flushed faces. "Ya'll better not be sweaty and filthy."

A smirk formed on Garrett's face, and I knew better than to let him reply. "Never mind, don't answer that. Go wash up, bud, dinner's ready as soon as the potatoes are."

"'Kay!" He took off, contentment oozing from him in such waves, I couldn't help but smile.

"Garrett, would you like a baked potato or a sweet potato? I'm cooking two of each, and I can eat either."

He was kneeling, in the process of giving Sadie a belly rub, but at my question he lifted his head. I realized I hadn't even asked if he wanted to stay for dinner, just assuming he would.

"You don't have to—"

"Sweet potato." He stood, not taking his eyes off me while he slowly slid his jacket down his shoulders. He had two other layers on underneath, but the motion was unintentionally seductive, and I had to turn toward the stove to hide the heat creeping up my neck.

An hour later, I was curled up on the couch. The still-unfinished baby blanket was sitting in my lap, and I had a crochet hook clenched in my fist, but I wasn't focused on a bit of it. My eyes were too busy watching back muscles flex and shift underneath a white shirt while Garrett moved about my kitchen, cleaning up dinner.

After we'd all annihilated our meals, he'd pushed back from the table, grabbing each of our plates and all but told me to get lost. I'd argued, demanding he was my guest, and I could clean my own dishes, but he'd turned that intense, unblinking gaze on me until I relented.

"Go relax, Maddie. I mean it. No homework. No cleaning. Go put on your PJs and curl up. I got you."

So here I was, curled up on the couch, "relaxing," while a man took care of the cleaning. It reminded me of my parents. For as long as I could remember, my dad had always said if my mom cooked, he'd clean. Watching Garrett do the same felt domestic. But more than that, it felt normal and *right*. And that scared the hell out of me.

I wasn't sure how long I stared at his working form, but he eventually turned to look at me, a towel slung over his shoulder. "How long do you think you'll be working on that?"

I frowned at the untouched project in my lap. "I'm not sure. Probably up until Jamie goes to bed since you didn't give me much of a choice." I raised an eyebrow pointedly. "Then I'll have to study. I have a test this week."

He nodded, folding the towel into a rectangle any perfectionist would appreciate, and rested it over the stove handle. I scooted over to make more room on the couch, but he didn't come toward me. He went to the door and shoved his feet into his untied boots.

"Wait…you're leaving?" Why was there a hitch in my voice? The man had no reason to stay, I was lucky he'd stayed as long as he did and helped clean up.

"I'm just going to grab something. I'll be right back." And with that, he dashed out the door, his departure pushing a gust of cold air through the living room and making me shudder.

Jamie's door instantly opened. "Did Garrett leave?" He tried to ask it nonchalantly, but I could hear the mild disappointment in his tone.

"No, he said he had to go get something. You finish cleaning up your room?"

He stared at me, sighed, and walked back in his room without a word. I was still chuckling when Garrett barged back through the front door carrying a grocery bag and setting my furry security alarm off.

Giving Rugpants a small scoot with his foot, he ambled toward me, and if I didn't know better, I'd say he was nervous.

"Please tell me that's dessert."

He froze, looking down at the bag in his hand. "I can go get dessert if you'd like."

"No, thanks, I'm much more interested in what you have." I smiled at him, and a blush dusted his cheeks, which only made me smile wider. "Come on, show me."

I patted the cushion next to me, and he fell onto it hard enough to make me bounce. He scratched his chin, his nails scraping against the stubble. "It's not perfect."

"All right."

"My second one is turning out better."

I shoved his shoulder, which rocked me back rather than moved him. "Oh my God, Garrett, just show me."

Darting one more glance my way, he untied the plastic handles and reached in, pulling out a blue bundle and handing it to me.

"Is this…a baby blanket?" I laid it out flat in my lap over my own. Although it wasn't a perfect shape from several stitch miscounts in the middle rows, it was definitely a blanket.

He rubbed the back of his neck. "I told you it was bad."

I gripped the blanket to my chest, eyes wide. "You *made* this?"

He nodded, pulling out a second, partially finished one in the same color. "This one is turning out better. It's way harder than you made it look."

I squeezed the first one tighter, pushing it against the chaotic beating in my ribcage, trying to settle the rogue organ. "What made you decide to learn to crochet?"

He nudged my knee with his own, a half grin peeking out. "The organization is important to you, and you seemed upset to be donating less than your usual amount. I thought I'd help."

"How are you single?" The question burst out of me with such force, I was surprised I didn't scream it. But even so, I couldn't have stopped the impulse to ask if I'd tried. It didn't make any sense for this man to be single. None.

He didn't answer at first, scooting back to lean against the cushions and pulling the attached skein and hook out of the bag. He wrapped the yarn tail around his fingers and pulled up a loop, beginning a slow, slightly unsteady, row of single crochet.

Watching the way his fingers worked the hook in and out of the stitches was pornographic, and I had to do a self-check to make sure I wasn't drooling.

"I was engaged."

The desire to stare at him and see the subtle changes in his face was almost debilitating, but I knew how difficult it was to discuss the past while someone studied you.

Forcing myself to pick up my own project, I said, "You don't have to tell me if you don't want to."

"I want to." His voice was gruff and firm, but he continued working on that squishy blanket with intense focus. "We'd only been together half a year when I proposed. I'd fallen quick and hard and was about to deploy. My desire to have someone miss me deluded me into thinking she could fill that role."

I knew the story, or at least ones very similar. Living on a military base, I'd seen several guys marry girls they barely knew just because they were deploying. Seldom had those scenarios worked out long term.

"What happened?"

He breathed deep, tightening the yarn tail until I was sure his stitches would be two times too small. "A few weeks into my eighteen-month deployment, during one of our phone calls, she told me she was three months pregnant."

I swallowed, a wave of nauseating anxiety hitting me with where this story was headed. Given Garrett was alone and had never mentioned a kid, it couldn't be anything good. But I listened quietly as he continued.

"I was upset. Not because she was pregnant, but because neither of us had noticed before I left, and I was going to miss out on all of it. I've always wanted to be a dad, wanted to see a woman I loved swollen with my child."

He cleared his throat. "I checked in as often as I could, asking her about appointments and updates, making sure she got plenty of money to buy anything she needed.

"Being deployed is something you have to experience in order to understand. It's miserable. But I couldn't imagine how hard it was for her to live alone, carrying the baby of a man who wasn't around and could rarely call. I felt guilty the entire time. Every month, every week, every fucking day."

He dropped the blanket onto his lap, clenching his fists over the top of it, and my heart paused its beating. I wanted to take his hands or lean over and rest my head on his shoulder.

Something. Anything.

"I got back home expecting to find my fiancé with an almost one-year-old son. Devin." He stopped, glaring down at his hands.

"Had she never been pregnant?" I asked.

He laughed, and it was a dry, ugly sound. "Oh no, she'd been pregnant. Turned out, he just hadn't been mine."

That nauseating feeling increased, pressing up into my throat. I set my project to the side, turning my body to face him. I couldn't not look at him anymore, not with that torn expression distorting his face. "I'm so sorry, Garrett."

"She'd already been pregnant with someone else's child when I proposed." He scoffed. "Which made more sense since I'd never fucked her raw, but I'd been too blind to see it before. Worst part was she admitted it freely. She wasn't even ashamed."

My nails dug into my pajama pants, and with all my wicked heart, I wished it was this unknown tramp's face I was clawing at. "Why the hell would she say yes, if she was with someone else?"

"Money."

That one word clanged through the room, hitting every wall, splattering across the ceiling and floor, coating every inch in a nasty film.

"What was her name?" I demanded.

He twisted to look down into my eyes, and I knew he could see every bit of the fury I didn't bother hiding. "Why?"

"Because I want to bitch slap her right across her worthless face."

His nostrils flared, his eyes darting down to my mouth before looking away, a muscle twitching in his cheek. "Her name was Courtney, but don't you lose any sleep over it, it happened years ago. I took a paternity test to make sure the boy wasn't mine, and then essentially told her she was dead to me."

I recognized the name. I'd overheard him on the phone with her once, forever ago it seemed. Satisfaction shot through me when I remembered how vividly he'd told her to fuck off. "Does she contact you often?"

He shook his head. "No, she's only called me once since I left, and it was to ask me to dig through some old insurance documents for something. I refused, and she hasn't called again."

I rested my hand on top of his, curling my fingers around his fist. "I'm sorry."

"Don't be. She's not worth your time or anger, Maddie."

"Although I disagree strongly with that statement, that's not what I'm sorry about."

He turned his hand, opening it to allow my fingers to lace with his. "Then what are you apologizing for?"

"For the conversation you overheard when we first met. I'm sorry for ever making a joke about using men for money. I hope you know, I never meant it."

He squeezed my hand. "I know you didn't."

I smiled, pulling my hand back and shifting to my original spot to give him his personal space. Something crossed his face, but it was there and gone in a moment, and I wasn't sure I'd even seen it.

Picking my blanket back up, I asked, "So is that when you

moved into the duplex?"

He mimicked me, grabbing his project and settling back into the cushions. "Yeah, I needed a new start and had my brother here to get me a connection with a job. Pretty cut and dry."

"What made Harry move out here?"

He grunted. "Sarah."

That didn't surprise me. Anyone with eyes could see that man was head over heels in love with her. I had a feeling he'd move to Antarctica if she asked him.

"How often do you and Harry see your mom? If you don't mind me asking."

He didn't immediately answer, setting his hook between his lips while he pulled a few stitches out to redo. "We usually fly to Cali to see her for a week or two during the summer."

I was about to ask him more, but clamped my mouth shut when Jamie's door creaked open behind us. We both turned, eyeing the messy head that poked out.

"Can I come out yet?"

"Did you finish your room?"

"Is your room done?"

Jamie's eyes widened, darting back and forth between the two of us as we both spoke at the same time. I peered at Garrett to see a grin pulling at his lips.

I relented, giving in to the kid's miserable puppy dog face. "All right, come hang out for a little, but I expect you to finish before bed."

"Deal." He ran out, almost tripping over Sadie's sleeping

form on the floor. Standing next to the TV, he clapped his hands together, smiling mischievously.

"So, who wants to play first?"

"What did you just say?"

"I said your fighting skills are worse than your soccer skills!"

I squealed, leaping out of the way when Garrett dropped his controller and leapt at Jamie, smooshing him to the ground and giving him a noogie. "Take it back."

"No!"

Good Lord. I stood, folding the almost-completed blanket back in its bag and dropping it in the corner. Watching them roll around laughing was as fun as it was painful. It was exactly what Jamie had been deprived of.

I tried to be everything for him, the qualities often seen in a mother as well as a father, but there were some things I'd never be able to do. I knew for a fact, with our history, he'd never let loose and tackle me to the ground. And part of me wondered if Garrett knew that somehow.

They wrestled around, hollering for a few more minutes before they finally tired, lying across the floor like floppy noodles.

"All right, you crazies, it's time for bed."

It was surreal walking around the living room with Garrett, cleaning up while Jamie changed and brushed his teeth. It was even more surreal when Jamie brought his book out, and he and

I read on the couch while Garrett stretched out on the floor, eyes closed and hands behind his head, listening.

One chapter and a heart full of emotional flutters later, Jamie was tucked away in his room with Sadie for the night.

Garrett had stepped into the bathroom, so I went to my room to set up my textbooks and laptop for the night. I was reading through my planner when a light tap sounded on my door.

"Hey, I'm going to head out."

I busied myself tracing the words on my planner, pretending to be jotting something down so I wouldn't have to turn around. Hearing his voice in the privacy of my room felt intimate, and I wasn't sure I could hide my thoughts if I looked at him. With how flushed I felt, it was sure to be written all over my face.

"All right."

I could sense him standing at the door, waiting for me to say something else, and I hated how ridiculous I was acting. I was being a wuss, and I didn't want him to leave without telling him what I'd wanted to say earlier. What he needed to hear.

I twisted around, right as he began edging back out of the room. "Garrett, wait."

He paused; his fingers curled around the door frame.

"I just want you to know, your ex was an idiot. *Is* an idiot. I'd like to think most women aren't like that. Don't let it keep you from being happy. You're an amazing man, and one day you're going to make some lucky woman the happiest person alive."

He pushed the door open to accommodate his wide

shoulders, and I dropped my gaze, watching his feet cross the floor until they stopped directly in front of me. One more step and he'd be touching me.

I was frozen, staring at his socked feet and considering my options when he pressed a quick, chaste kiss to the side of my head.

"Thanks, Maddie. And not just for that."

Goosebumps erupted all down my arms, and I had no idea what to say. You're welcome? My brain had logged out the second he entered my room, and at the touch of his mouth, it'd officially erected an Out of Commission sign. By the time I looked up, he was already pulling the door closed behind him.

Later that night, long after I'd heard the front door shut, I sat in bed staring at the same textbook I'd been holding for an hour. Still feeling the imprint of his lips against my head, I finally acknowledged what I'd been afraid to admit, even to myself.

I cared for Garrett Rowe much more than just a friend. Much, much more.

Chapter 17

WHEN I WAS pregnant with Jamie, I puked numerous times a day during the first five months. I lost weight and struggled to go to school because of how often I got sick. It wasn't pretty. There wasn't a single thing about me that had the pregnancy glow.

This felt kind of like that.

I'd woken around three in the morning and had to sprint to the bathroom when flames shot up my chest and through my mouth, not stopping to collect go.

I was on the floor, curled around a cleaning bucket I'd pulled from under the sink, when Layla's alarm went off. It was now six. I'd been on the floor for hours, and it didn't seem to be fading anytime soon.

I didn't know what to do. I'd taken the entire past weekend

off from my night shift. Even with Layla's help, I couldn't afford to take more than a few days off.

Lurching up, my stomach clenched, and I dry-heaved over the bucket. Fuck my life, there was no way I could go in. Standing with the bucket hugged to my chest, I made my way out of my room, knocking on Layla's door.

She opened it wearing only shorts and a bra, a curling iron dangling from her hand. Her eyes widened when she took in my disheveled sight.

"What the hell, Mads?"

"I think I might have food poisoning."

"No shit. I told you that taco salad looked fucking iffy. You look like you're on death's door. Like, you legit look awful."

I looked up from my new plastic best friend to my old best friend, glaring with all the muster I could gather. "Thanks."

She set her curling iron on her side table and grabbed a top to pull over herself. "You're calling in to work…right?"

"Obviously," I groaned, squeezing my eyes together and trying not to gag in her face. "Can you take Jamie to school on your way to work?"

"Yeah, I'll handle it, babe, go back to bed."

She didn't need to tell me twice. I formed my body into a fetal position on my bed and called Evaline to let her know I wouldn't make it in.

It'd taken almost two hours before my stomach settled enough to finally venture out. It was either risk inducing another puke fest or die by severe thirst. I chose the first option. It felt like my entire mouth had been invaded by a colony of cotton balls.

Water in hand, I shuffled to the couch to prop myself up, staring at the blank screen of the TV and wishing with all my heart we had cable.

Rap, rap, rap.

I shot forward, knocking my—thankfully empty—bucket to the ground and almost dumping my water glass across my lap. The sudden movement had spots dancing across my vision, and a wave of dizziness washed over me. I had to plant my head between my knees to ward off the overwhelming sensation of passing out.

Rap, rap, rap.

"Madison?" A voice asked, muffled behind the wood.

Neck still bent between my legs, I allowed myself a moment to wail. Why me? It'd been days since he was last here. Why would he choose today of all days? I could ignore him and pretend I wasn't here, but my Jeep was parked out front. Fuck.

Pulling myself off the couch with painful slowness, I dragged my feet to the door. My head was swirling, but I took a steadying breath and unlocked it. All I needed to do was keep my shit together until he left. I could do that. I'd given birth, I could control the urge to vomit in this man's vicinity.

"Madison?"

"Garrett."

"I was getting ready to head out when I noticed your Jeep still here. Everything okay?"

He tilted his head, trying to see me through the two-inch crack I'd allowed. He was dressed for work and had a lunch pail sitting on the porch next to him. My stomach rolled harder.

"Yep." One-word answers. I could handle one-word answers.

"What's wrong?"

"Nothing."

He glared at me, and even through the gap, it seared into my skin. "I just don't feel well. Something I ate. It's nothing." I settled a hand over my middle, breathing in and out.

His eyes narrowed, dipping down before coming back to rest on my face. He pushed the door, and I reactively pushed back, trying to prevent him from coming inside. It was the wrong thing to do.

I looked up at him, eyes wide and mouth parted in horror before I whipped around, sprinting for the bathroom.

The sound of heavy footsteps was my only warning life was not going to take it easy on me. Of course, Garrett had invited himself inside. Of course, he didn't stay in the living room when I had my head buried in a toilet and hair plastered to my face.

I heard a few sliding sounds I couldn't quite place and then more footsteps.

"Put these on and step in the shower."

"What?" I croaked, cracking an eye open and trying to focus up at his face.

"You heard me." Something soft dropped onto my thighs, and I glanced down to see a pair of clothes. *My* clothes. A black tank top and cotton briefs to be exact.

"You went through my dresser?"

"It was either that or I saw you naked. Figured you'd prefer it this way."

"Excuse me—"

"If you sass me right now, Maddie, I swear to God, I'll strip you down and toss you in there when it's still ice cold."

Was it possible to feel nauseated and incredulous at the same time? "I'll puke all down your back," I threatened, not sounding nearly as strong as I wanted.

"No, you won't. From the sounds of it, you got nothing left in the tank. You'd just gag, and I gotta tell you, baby, gagging doesn't bother me."

I stared at him, his words settling between us with a heaviness I shouldn't have felt given the current circumstances.

He walked farther into the bathroom, pulling back the curtain and turning on the shower. Turning to look down at me with his hands on his hips, he asked, "So what's it going to be? You gonna meet me halfway here, or am I tossing you in?"

I narrowed my eyes, unsticking my head from the toilet seat and gripping the clothes in my lap. "Are you going to at least leave?"

"With you looking two seconds away from passing out? Not a chance. I'll face the hall while you change, but don't you dare try to climb over the tub edge without help."

I grumbled out a curse at his back that had his shoulders tensing, but I did what he said. It took me longer than I wanted to admit, but he never complained or peeked.

"Okay." Part of me understood I was standing in my bathroom in only underwear and a thin tank, but I couldn't muster up the energy to care. I didn't even bother to glare when he placed a wrist over my forehead.

"Fuck, you're burning up."

"I think...taco salad."

"What? You know what, never mind. Let's get you in." He gripped my waist like he thought the small step over the tub edge might send me sprawling face first into the shower wall, and pulled the curtain partly shut behind me.

I stood under the spray with my eyes closed, letting the lukewarm water run down my body and drench my clothing. I lifted my arms to push some rogue curls out of my face but froze when my fingers brushed against something firm. My eyes shot open, a cracked squeak leaping from my mouth.

Garrett stood mere inches away, wearing only his shirt and boxers, his bare feet almost touching my own. I hadn't heard him undress, let alone step in. "What are you doing?"

"Helping you."

"I'm f—"

"The word 'fine' better not leave your mouth."

I smashed my lips together, unwilling to agree but also knowing I couldn't argue an obvious fact. I sighed, accepting defeat and closing my eyes again. If I didn't look at him, maybe I could trick my mind into thinking he wasn't there. But less than a minute later, his hands wrapped around my shoulders.

"Turn around so I can wash your hair."

I resisted his attempt to twist me. "It's—" I cut myself off. Great, I was never going to be able to use that damn word again. "My hair doesn't need to be washed."

"The vomit clinging to the strands by your face beg to

differ." His eyes drifted down, but I refused to follow his gaze. If I saw even a hint of vomit on my person, I'd lose it all over again.

"I can wash my own hair, Garrett. My curls are picky, and I have an entire routine, and... Why are you smiling at me?"

He twisted me again, catching me off guard and turning me until the back of my shoulders grazed his chest. "Shut up and let me take care of you. I know what I'm doing."

I watched his arm snake down in front of me to grab my bottle of no-poo shampoo from the corner shelf.

"You...do?"

"My mother's hair is blond and not quite as curly as yours, but it's similar. My grandpa used to call her his Shirley Temple because of it."

A tired chuckle escaped me. "My dad called me the same thing."

I couldn't see him, but somehow, I knew he was smiling, and I wondered if I'd see a hint of his dimples if I looked back. I heard the click of the bottle opening, felt the brush of his arm as he returned it, and then his fingers were sliding though my hair.

He cleared his throat. "When I was younger, I made the mistake of telling my mother about the abundance of hair tutorials online."

If I'd have had the energy, I would've laughed, knowing what he was about to say next. But then his fingers started drawing circles along my scalp, and a deep, uncontrolled moan exited my mouth instead.

His hands paused their ministrations, his nails digging in for a fleeting moment before continuing their path.

"She made me sit and play video after video for her, writing down all the tips and tricks."

I tilted my head up to see him, leaning the back of it against his chest, and caught the tail end of a nostalgic smile.

"Anyway, my point is I know all about pineapples and plopping." He looked down, meeting my gaze while working his hands down the sides of my head.

The brush of his fingers against the tops of my ears sent a shiver racing down my spine, and I closed my eyes, allowing myself to enjoy a moment of weakness.

"Thank you, Garrett."

"Don't thank me, baby. I got you."

⁂

Consciousness eased in slowly, gently, coaxing away the lull of my heavy eyelids and warm limbs. I was comfortable and felt surprisingly well-rested. I cracked an eye open, blinking away sleep and focusing on the wall across from me.

It took me a second to understand I was in my bedroom. In bed. In the middle of the day. I pushed up onto an elbow and rubbed my face. The damp edge of a bunched-up t-shirt around my head brought the morning's activities slamming to the front of my mind.

Vomiting. Garrett. More vomiting. *The shower*. Holy shit. My sticky skin told me two things. One, my fever had at least broken while I slept, and two, I'd have to take an actual shower all over again.

I flushed, remembering all the sounds I'd made when Garrett had tipped my head back into the spray and massaged all the product out. No one had ever done that for me before. It was, by far, one of the hottest things to happen to me, and if I hadn't had puke breath and a raging fever, I might've climbed him like a tree.

He'd been a gentleman the entire time, never once even ogling the nipples I knew were visible through my soaked tank. He'd helped me out and bundled me in a towel before disappearing to let me change back into pajamas, and returning with a t-shirt to squeeze the excess water from my hair.

He'd wrapped my wet locks up off my neck, tucked me into bed, spoon-fed me children's acetaminophen, and even retrieved the bucket to set on my nightstand. I'd watched him the entire time, wondering what his ulterior motives were. If he had any.

I couldn't help it; I'd never had a man dote on me without expecting something in return. But he'd never hinted at anything or acted put out even though he had to have missed work today. If fact, he'd almost seemed to grow irritated each time he caught my wide-eyed stare, as if my disbelief irked him.

I sat all the way up, leaning against my pillows and looking across the room only to jolt back when I noticed the hunched figure sitting at the end of my bed. I pressed a hand to my heart, hoping to keep it where it belonged.

"God, you scared me."

His shoulders tightened at the sound of my voice, but he

didn't raise his head. He was sitting at the edge with his hands dangling between his knees, his neck lowered and eyes closed.

"Garrett? What's wrong?"

He laughed then, or what might be called a laugh. It was more like an angry huff. He rolled his neck, cracking it, and I realized he held something in his hands. I couldn't see much past his legs, but it looked like a stack of papers.

"Layla swung by to check on you. She was heading to pick up Jamie and take him to grab some dinner. How are you feeling?" He still hadn't looked at me.

I'd slept all day? No wonder I felt rested. "I feel better. Pretty sure my fever broke."

Why wasn't he looking at me? Hell, who was I kidding, he'd missed an entire day of work because he was afraid to leave me alone. Of course, he was irritated.

"I'm sorry you had to see all that and be here."

The pages in his hand crinkled, accompanying a heavy exhale. "You know, I thought about going home earlier, but I was afraid you'd get sick again. So, I left you to rest, and I watched a movie in the living room. I found your phone sitting on the floor next to the couch. I'm guessing you dropped it when I showed up."

He crunched the papers farther. "I brought it in here so you'd have it when you woke up, but I couldn't find your charger."

I stared at his lap, brow creased, trying to figure out what he was holding and why he was upset. "I keep it in my nightstand when I'm not using it because I have to use the same outlet for my laptop."

"I know," he snapped, "I found it."

Why was he so angry…oh. *Oh.* I looked at the pages in his hands again, at the stack containing the screenshots and messages, photos and medical visits.

The blood drained from my body as ice filled my veins instead. "Garrett—"

"What the fuck are these, Madison?"

Oh God. I was going to hyperventilate. He should never have seen those. God, why did I even still have them? I should have thrown them away the day I'd realized I no longer needed them.

"They're records."

He heaved a breath as if he was in physical pain. "Madison *Walsh*," he spit, and I flinched like he'd struck me. "That's the bastard's name. Aaron Walsh." The words were laced with so much hatred, I was sure if words could kill, Aaron would be bleeding out somewhere.

"Yes."

"Explain to me why some of these are from the time you were together, and some are only a few fucking years old. Because I'm really struggling to wrap my fucking brain around it."

I crossed my legs, tucking the comforter around me as a makeshift shield. Not from Garrett, but from the topic. I knew Garrett's anger was directed at my history and not myself, but uncovering my past was agonizing.

"Aaron asked to meet up when the divorce was finalized

under the guise of giving me some of the things I'd left. They were sentimental items I couldn't replace like Jamie's baby photos, so I agreed. But he showed up wasted. I should've known better."

I looked down at my lap. It wasn't the first time Aaron had convinced me to do something I knew better than to do, but it had certainly been the last.

"That's why Jamie's so fucking defensive of you, why he shoved me away that day. He saw this shit, didn't he?"

Goosebumps covered my entire body at the pure venom staring back at me from his eyes. I couldn't get my mouth to form words, so I nodded.

He cursed, ducking his head down and clasping a hand over the back of his neck. "I'm gonna fucking kill him."

I lurched forward, stretching a hand out and placing it on the bed. "Aaron may have been the one to hurt me, Garrett, but I was the one who invited him to an apartment my child was at, knowing what he was like. I'm not saying what happened was my fault. It's taken me a long time to accept it, but it wasn't. But that doesn't make me completely innocent either."

"That piece of shit knows where you live."

I pulled my hand back, snapping, "I'm well aware."

He held the bent papers out. "Why are these printed out, sitting in your damn nightstand like bedtime reading material?"

I squeezed my eyes shut, fighting against the tears his question brought to the surface. He could've had me butt ass naked, and I wouldn't have felt as stripped bare as I did in that moment.

"I started logging incidences and printing things while we were together. I couldn't seem to find the courage to leave, so I tried to force courage by manipulating my fear instead." My voice shook, and I took a deep breath, wiping away a tear that slipped free.

"Every time I second-guessed myself, I'd pull them out and remind myself why I needed to leave. Because it was hard, Garrett. Leaving him was one of the hardest, most terrifying things I've ever done."

He didn't reply, but his face had lost its hardness. He almost looked lost as he stared at me, and I wondered if he was thinking about his mother. I pushed through, determined to explain an unexplainable situation.

"When things were bad, they were really bad. But when they were good, they were amazing. Over time, I'd gotten so used to the bad times, that the good ones seemed almost euphoric." I stared off into space, contemplating my next words.

"Being with a manipulative partner is like an addiction. But instead of a drug, you're addicted to *them*, to making them happy because it's the only time *you* can be happy. You acclimate to their behavior a little at a time, until you grow numb to it. Until it's no longer the worst day you've ever had, it's just Monday.

"Then one day they stop giving you your fix. They leave you writhing on the floor, screaming out into the void, all the while knowing, even through the pain, you're going to wake up and do it all over again. Forever chasing the high of making them happy."

Tears were now streaming down my face. The reins I'd had

on my emotions completely gone. I was too emotionally exhausted and physically drained from the morning I'd had to hide how much the admission broke me.

Garrett walked around to the opposite side of the bed and sat, leaning back until we were shoulder to shoulder. He set the papers between us, his fingers twitching toward me as if he'd almost reached for my hand.

I stared at the pages that documented my history. My pain. My humiliation. "I know it may not make any sense. It's not something you can understand unless you've lived it. Men like Aaron manipulate and gaslight and wear you down so slowly you don't see it. You don't even realize your bar has lowered until it's fucking non-existent."

"Why do you still have them?"

I sighed, brushing my fingertips up and down the corner of the papers.

"Because there were days, usually when a roach crawled across our apartment or when somebody degraded me at the store for using EBT, that I'd get so depressed I considered going back to him. Back to a beautiful home in a clean neighborhood."

"And now?"

I leaned my head on his shoulder, needing to soak up my friend's comfort and warmth. "There is no now. They were sitting in my drawer because I pulled them out the day he showed up, but I didn't look at them. I realized I didn't need to."

Garrett rested his head on top of mine, finally reaching over to cage my hand in his. "You are the strongest woman I've ever met, Maddie."

I huffed a breath through my nose, but he just tipped his face down and kissed my forehead.

"You are. There's no one in the world quite like you."

Chapter 18

I WOKE UP to something poking me.

I grumbled, slapping at the irritation. It came again, more insistent, stabbing into the flesh of my shoulder. Throwing myself onto my other side, I tried to ignore it, but it came again, this time on my back.

"Mom!"

My eyes snapped open, and I shot up, turning to look at the child who stood at the head of my bed like a scene directly out of my nightmares. "Of all that is holy, bud." I rubbed at my eyes, looking at the clock and trying to remember what year it was. "Why are you awake? What's wrong?"

"Somebody's at our front door."

I blinked, trying to focus more on what he was saying. "What?"

"Somebody's banging on our door. It woke me up."

I moved my legs around the useless dog sleeping near my ankles and dropped my feet to the floor. It couldn't be Layla. She took Sadie and went to Rick's tonight, and even if she hadn't, she obviously had a key. Maybe someone had the wrong house?

Then I heard it. Jamie was right, it wasn't knocking. Someone was banging on our door, incessantly. That wasn't the knock of someone who was accidentally at the wrong house.

It was no surprise it hadn't set off Rugpants, the sound was so hard, it sounded more like road construction than someone at the door. Whoever was there was determined to wake the dead from the graveyard down the road.

"All right, I'll go check it out. Go back to your room."

I grabbed a sweater from my dirty clothes basket, tossing it over my sleep tank and heading down the hall. The banging started again, almost in sync with my footfalls.

"Maybe you should call Garrett?"

I stopped near the couch, twisting to look at Jamie, who had absolutely not gone to his room.

"I am not waking Garrett. It's not his house or his problem, bud." I hadn't seen him much this last week, but there was still a chance it could be him. He'd never sounded like he was trying to tear my door down before, but he certainly wasn't a quiet knocker either.

Maybe something had happened to Sarah, and he'd had a drink and couldn't drive, or maybe his house was on fire, or maybe he cut his finger off chopping carrots at midnight. Suddenly, I was walking faster. I didn't even bother glancing out the window before yanking the door open in my haste to make sure he was okay.

He wasn't.

And he wasn't Garrett.

Aaron stood before me, propped against the door frame. Wasted. His shirt was soaking wet down the center and a chaotic halo of auburn hair surrounded his head. He blinked at me in surprise, his eyes looking more like glass marbles.

"There you are. You've been making me wait out here a long time." The sour tang of his breath crashed into my senses, blanketing me in a bile-like aroma.

I gripped the door, flinging it shut as hard as I could, but he threw himself forward, slamming his shoulder into the wood and sending it back toward me. The *crack* of it hitting my face vibrated down my body and back up, leaving a ringing in my ears.

My head jerked back, and I tried to retreat but only succeeded in tripping over my feet in my urgency. A firm, clammy grip wrapped around my arm, halting my flailing and keeping me upright.

"Now, see, look what you did. You hurt yourself, honey. That's what you get for being rude."

His speech was slurred, and he tried to pull me closer, but his drunken spatial awareness was garbage. All it took was a frantic yank on my end, and I pulled away, knocking him off center.

"That was a bitchy thing to do."

Ignoring the throbbing of my head, I crossed my arms to hide their shaking. "You need to leave. You have no right to come inside my home." My words came out strong, but I was a quaking mess inside.

He rubbed a hand over his lips, looking me up and down with watery, bloodshot eyes. "This game of pretend is growing…obnoxious. This little playhouse is not your home."

He looked at me hungrily, like he had every intention of stealing me away and locking me back up in his house. He hadn't even glanced at Jamie, and if that wasn't a clear indication of the kind of man he was, I didn't know what was.

I slid a hand down the pocket of my sweats, discreetly searching for a phone that wasn't there. Oh God, why had I not grabbed it on my way out? How many times did I have to make stupid decisions in my life before I learned my lesson? I'd admittedly made a lot, but answering the door at midnight without a phone on hand was pretty high on the stupidity ranking.

I stepped back, twisting so my back faced the kitchen barstools. I wanted to simultaneously keep my eye on Aaron to my left and Jamie on my right.

Jamie hadn't moved from his spot between the couch and the hallway, and I knew if I looked at him, my heart would be ripped from my chest and thrown into a nest of vipers. I kept my eyes on Aaron, knowing even inebriated as he was, he was stronger than me by a lot.

"Jamie, why don't you go to my room and sit with Rugpants, okay?" She'd been barking like crazy from the second Aaron's voice broke through the air, and it was only increasing my level of anxiety.

"No."

I dared to take my eyes off my ex just long enough to pin my son with the firmest gaze I'd ever given him. "Get in my room and shut the door. I am not asking."

I immediately looked back to the threat now leaning against the far side of the bar, and a small amount of tension released from my soul when I heard the sound of Jamie's retreating steps. I stood a small chance if I didn't also have to protect him. I could do it.

I could fight back this time.

"I'll forgive you, Madison. I promise. I'll forgive all of the last few years. Just come home."

"I'm not playing a game. I want you to leave."

His brows lowered. "No. I want to fucking talk to you. Why are you always trying to start a fight?"

Breathe in. Breathe out. "I'm not. I'm asking you to leave."

He stumbled closer, and, on instinct, I took a step back. I'd taken a self-defense class as soon as I'd healed from the last time I'd disappointed him, but I didn't actually know much more than the basic stuff I'd done to Garrett. One class wasn't going to get me out of this unscathed.

I was scared. So scared, I couldn't even sense the safe place in my mind, but I still had claws. I wouldn't make it easy for him.

I will fight back.

He continued to approach, cursing when he staggered into a barstool. I glanced back at the hall, considering making a run for my phone, but the thought of him cornering me in a room with Jamie and only one exit had me nearly gasping for air like a fish out of water.

"Please, Aaron, it's late. I promise we can talk tomorrow."

"You're lying." He was only a foot away now, pinning me

between two of the stools while he continued mumbling incoherent words under his breath.

"I'm not." I was. "Whatever it is you want to talk about, I promise we can talk tomorrow when you're—when we're both feeling better."

"Liar," he drew the word out, shaking a finger back and forth. "You think I'm drunk. You just want to kick me out like the bitch you are."

He lunged, wrapping his fingers around my neck, and pushed against my windpipe until my back bowed over the bar. He squeezed just enough for pressure to build, and I did the first thing I could think of. I spit in his face.

He yelled, recoiling, and I took my chance. Flinging my hands up, I aimed for his eyes, but before I could make contact, he dropped forward, smashing his body into mine. One of the barstools crashed to the floor, and my back screamed as the edge of the bar etched itself into my spine. I tried, but I couldn't hold back the cry that slipped free.

Using his free hand to steady himself with a barstool, Aaron leaned down, his hot, acidic breath landing on my cheek and stirring up memories best left untouched. Panic clawed its way up my throat when the hand gripping me migrated to clamp around my jaw.

"You little cu—"

My front door shot open, the hinges creaking in protest, and a freezing gust of air filled the room, introducing the six feet of male standing at the threshold. He was practically naked, sporting only a pair of checkered boxers, and his broad chest heaved in and out like he'd sprinted straight from his bed. His eyes zeroed in on me—or more specifically, the hand still clutching me—and his features turned feral.

Aaron immediately went off, cursing Garrett and calling me a whore in every drunken, uncreative way possible. He was like a defective bomb trying to detonate but failing to take anyone out. His words bounced off Garrett's statue form, tumbling to the ground.

The second Aaron released his hold on my jaw and turned toward him, Garrett moved. There was no stopping, no pausing, no taking a moment to blink. One second, he was at the door, and the next he was punching my ex straight in the face.

Aaron's head snapped back with such force, I was surprised he didn't break his neck. He collapsed to the floor in a heap at my feet, groaning and smearing the back of his hand through the blood pouring from his nostrils.

Stooping down, Garrett grabbed him by his collar, hauling him up only to smash his fist into his face a second time. I cried out, banging into the single-standing stool next to me in my effort to move.

"Garrett, stop!"

Even in the fog of his anger, he froze at the sound of my voice, locking eyes with me while Aaron dangled like a rag doll from his outstretched arm. His eyes were swirling storms of fury, agony, and despair. They flicked away from me, wincing as they looked at something over my shoulder.

My heart fell when I followed his gaze to see Jamie standing in the hall, wide-eyed. His back was plastered to the wall, both hands gripping my phone to his chest.

Garrett let the unconscious body in his grip drop to the

floor, and when he spoke, the words were hoarse. "You all right, J-man?"

Jamie's head bobbed up and down, but he didn't attempt to move from his spot.

"I'm proud of you."

The way my child's face lit up at Garrett's words of praise was all at once amazing and devastating at the same time.

I expected Garrett to look at me next and ask if I was all right or what happened, but he didn't. He didn't even look at me. He curled his arms underneath Aaron's shoulders and began dragging his body out like a corpse.

I jolted forward, my eyes darting from the morbid-looking scene before me back to Jamie. "What are you doing? Garrett!"

He continued ignoring me, retreating through the open front door and down my porch, Aaron's body thumping after him. Indignation flared inside of me, and I chased him down, closing the door behind me so Jamie wouldn't follow.

It was pitch black and freezing out, and I bounced from one foot to the other, pulling my sweater tighter around me.

"What are you—oh my God, *what are you doing?!*" I called out as he threw Aaron into the backseat of his Nova like a sack of rotten garbage and slammed the door.

"Garrett, talk to me."

He slapped both palms on his car, leaning forward to rest his head between them. Positioned the way he was, with every naked muscle in his back and legs on display, he looked like a fallen angel who'd lost his wings. It tore at me. "I'm sorry you had to—"

Flat hands turned to fists, and his shoulders tensed and

shifted. "Don't stand there and fucking compare me to him, Maddie. I am not him."

I threw my arms out. "What are you talking about, I'm not!"

"When your gut reaction is to apologize every time I help you, you're comparing me to him. When you second-guess how I'll respond and feel the need to grovel to maintain my approval, you're comparing. Stop fucking apologizing."

I pulled my lips into my mouth, pressing down until it felt like my teeth would slice through. He hadn't looked up from his car, but he might as well have laid me out. His words lashed out at me like a whip, digging into everything I was, and showing all the cracks.

I didn't know how to stop over-thinking and second-guessing. I didn't know how to be different.

"This is a little more than fixing my dishwasher or cleaning my fence, Garrett. You have a body in the back of your car, and you're obviously upset with me. You won't even look at me."

He shoved off, twisting to me with a speed that didn't seem possible. In only a few strides, he was flush against me, the skin of his stomach pressing against my sweater. His fingers dove into my hair, tangling in my curls as he gripped the back of my head and tilted it back.

"You want to know why I can't fucking look at you? Because looking at you reminds me of what you told me last week. It makes me want to rip that motherfucker out of my car and finish what I started.

"I can't look at your face without seeing the ghost of his fingerprints and remembering what they looked like on you, without remembering how you look when your eyes fog over in fear. It'll be seared into my mind until the day I die."

I subconsciously reached up, placing my hands on his chest. His grip tightened, pulling at the hairs along my nape, but I barely noticed. Hell, I was barely breathing.

"As long as that piece of shit is within arm's reach of me, I can't keep fucking looking at you, or tonight's story is going to have a completely different fucking ending."

My heart stuttered and stopped as he pulled away from me, dropping my hands to hang uselessly at my sides. "What are you going to do to him?"

"He's not your concern." He turned, running toward his house and disappearing. I didn't move until he returned. Keys in hand, he'd only thrown on a pair of jeans and untied boots and climbed into his car.

"Go back inside and hug your son, Maddie. He needs to know you're okay." And with that, he shut his door and reversed out of the drive.

I should've checked his trunk for a shovel while he'd been inside.

When I stepped into my house, my senses were assaulted by the smell of pure bliss. I walked to the couch, grabbing a blanket thrown over it, and wrapped myself in the soft fleece before venturing into the kitchen. Jamie was standing before two mugs of freshly stirred hot chocolate.

"I haven't put ice cubes in them yet so don't drink it."

I gave a tentative grin, deciding not to point out the massive billows of steam that had already hinted to that fact. Instead, I opened the freezer, twisting the tray and carefully dropping a few cubes into each.

"This was a great idea, thank you. You want to come watch something with me?"

He nodded, grabbing both mugs and carrying them carefully toward the coffee table. He disappeared into his room long enough to grab an extra blanket, and then plopped down next to me.

He needed to talk. What kid wouldn't? I was still deciding whether I should say something or let him open up to me in time when he handed me my phone.

"Are you mad I called Garrett?"

"No, of course not."

He played with the fringe of his blanket. "I know I should've called 911, but Garrett was the first person I thought of. I promise I would've called 911 next if he didn't answer."

I placed my hand over his own, stilling his movements. "I'm not upset. You did what made you comfortable, and I'm proud of you. I should never have put you in a position where you needed to make that choice. I knew better than to answer the door without checking to see who it was. That wasn't safe."

"Yeah, it was pretty stupid."

I sent a mock glare his way. "How'd you even know which number was Garrett's?" I'd never bothered changing his contact name from Sugar Daddy.

"You and Layla talk a lot. I pay attention."

I laughed, basking in the relief I felt at the hint of a smile on his face. He was handling it better than I feared, for now at least.

He picked up his mug, curling his legs underneath him and blowing the steam. "I think Garrett loves you."

I choked, Garrett's words from earlier still playing on repeat in my head. "Why on earth would you think that, you weirdo?"

He shrugged, sipping delicately at the still too-hot chocolate before grimacing and setting it back down. "He came and saved you. He didn't even put clothes on first, Mom."

"And my eyeballs appreciated it," I said, wiggling my eyebrows. He dove forward over his lap, pretending to gag, and it brought another laugh to my lips that felt pretty dang good.

"He's just a really good friend, no hearts and flowers involved." But even as I said it, the words tasted a little like ash.

Jamie considered me for a moment but seemed to accept my answer. We picked out a random movie and curled up with our drinks and blankets. An hour later, he was slumped over, mouth hanging open.

Slipping off the couch, I grabbed my phone and dialed Garrett. I walked to the small window next to the door and peeked out as it rang and rang in my ear.

"You've reached Garrett..."

"Goddammit," I muttered, listening to the rest of his answering message. I had no idea what he was doing, and I was fifty percent terrified and fifty percent undecided.

"Hey, Garrett, it's me. I'm still awake." I slid a hand down my face, cringing. Of course, I was awake, I was calling him. "Jamie's asleep now so I'm going to do some reading or something. I can't sleep. Anyway, I just wanted to make sure you were all right."

I ended the call without even saying bye, mentally hitting my head against the wall. How was it, I could make business calls every day of the week, but leaving a voicemail had me stuttering my way through a simple sentence?

Tucking the device into my pocket, I stared at the front door. Unlocking it would be monumentally stupid, and I wouldn't risk it with Jamie crashed out here, but I also didn't want Garrett knocking and scaring the pee out of him.

But that was assuming Garrett even stopped by or came back at all. I chewed on the inside of my cheek, again worrying about what the hell he was doing.

The sensation of my phone vibrating against my thigh had me jumping out of my skin. I fought with the material of my pants, trying to dig my phone out of my pocket.

"Hello?"

"It's me. Open the door."

My head whipped back to the door as if I'd be able to see him through it. Turning the lock as quietly as I could, I pulled it open, pressing a finger to my lips. Rugsy was bound to go off if he spoke, and the last thing I wanted was to wake Jamie again.

He nodded in understanding and stepped inside. He'd made the time to go home and change into his hoodie and sweats before coming over, and my imagination went wild with all the reasons he might have had to change clothes.

Knowing he'd follow, I made for my room. I crawled across my bed, slipping my arms under the comforter to uncover my lazy guard dog, petting her head as I let her see Garrett so she wouldn't bark.

He reached an arm back, pulling his hoodie over his head and revealing a plain white shirt underneath. He tossed it over the bottom of the bed before coming to sit next to me, graciously giving Rug some scratches.

"You two okay?"

I gave him a side-eye look. "That depends on what you're about to tell me." His expression flattened, and I sighed, flopping back on a pillow. "We're fine."

He rubbed his jaw, looking back at my prostrate form. "I'm glad. I've been worried about him."

I rolled to my side. "My instinct is to apologize for worrying you, but I won't." He shook his head and opted not to answer. "He told me you were the first person he thought of to call."

He cleared his throat, staring at the wall. "I'm glad he trusted me enough to call but fuck if it didn't destroy me. For the rest of my life, I will never forget the way that boy's voice shook as he begged me to save you."

Jesus. I patted the spot next to me, scooting over so he had room to lie down. Our knees brushed as he got settled and faced me, curling an arm under his head.

"I was so goddamn scared of how I was going to find you, Maddie."

"Can I apologize now?" I asked, snuggling deeper into my pillow. When I peeked up, he was glaring at me.

"Then will you tell me where you went?"

"I told you he's not your concern, Madison."

Oh, we were back to Madison, were we? Someone *really* didn't want me bringing it up. "Will you at least tell me if I need to provide you with an alibi? I'm not the best liar under pressure. I'll need to practice my statement."

He flicked me in the nose. "And what will you tell them we were busy doing at midnight?"

My pulse quickened, and I darted my tongue out to lick my

lips, suddenly feeling parched. His eyes lowered, and his stare went straight to my core, turning the switch to ON.

God, it'd been way too long since I'd had a release. I needed him to quit looking at me that way or this was going to get really awkward really fast.

"Playing bingo."

"My favorite nighttime activity."

I chuckled, turning to roll on my back and stare up at the ceiling. I couldn't keep looking at him lying there next to me. It was making my heart do stupid things. Like telling me it wanted to see him there every day, smirking at me even when I had bad breath and a frizzy morning mane.

I dove my feet under the covers to get more comfortable and enjoy the few hours I still had before work. Yawning through the words, I closed my eyes and asked, "So, *do* you need an alibi?"

He grunted. "Ask me in the morning."

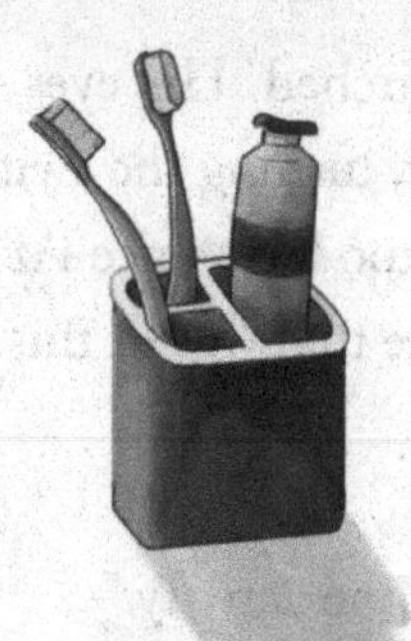

Chapter 19

I WOKE UP to something poking me. Again. I groaned, cracking an eye open before quickly shutting it again. It was still dark, so my alarm shouldn't be close to going off yet.

I sighed, determined to enjoy the last few moments of sleep, but that same sensation prodded me again.

Something was digging into my back. Rugsy often laid against me, but she typically aimed for my legs, and this didn't feel like her. I slowly reached my arm back, wondering if maybe I'd fallen asleep with my laptop still on the bed again.

My hand hit something warm and hard. And slightly rounded? What in the world? I twisted, sliding my hand up in an attempt figure out what it was I'd almost fallen asleep on.

"Something in particular you're searching for?" A rough, raspy voice asked, thick with sleep.

I dug my nails into the *limb* I was gripping, my eyes shooting open. A leg. I was touching a leg. A knee, to be exact, and it did not belong to me.

Inhaling sharply, the previous hours came flying back to me in excruciatingly vivid colors. Aaron coming over, Garrett disposing of him or who even knew what, and lying in bed together.

Ask me in the morning.

Holy hell, he'd stayed the night. Knowingly and purposefully stayed. Well, more like just a couple hours, but still, he'd come in with the intention of falling asleep.

Oh Lord, I needed to slow my roll. He was just being a friend. A friend who sacrificed his entire night to help me and be with me, but still. Just a friend.

I eased onto my opposing shoulder, painfully aware of every morning I'd ever woken up and how much of a zombie I always looked. He was sure to be tucking tail and ditching soon. Then again, he'd already seen me slick faced and puking, so who knew.

The first thing I saw as I finished my snail-like turn was an arm resting on top of the comforter an inch away from my own. My eyes traveled up its length, noticing with a mixture of both disappointment and relief that he was still wearing his shirt.

I continued my perusal, stopping at the scruffy jaw and lazy grin that greeted me. The dimples peeking out to say hello sent my heart aflutter, but it was the intense gaze, tracing every line of my face, that was going to be the death of me.

"Good morning."

"Good morning," I whispered. "What time is it?"

"About five."

Good, I still had an hour before I needed to get ready for work. Thank God I was used to running on little sleep. Before thinking better of it, I heaved a sigh, puffing my cheeks out.

The moment the air left my mouth, I froze in horror, yanking the comforter up to cover my face. Morning breath was no one's friend on a good day, but I'd fallen asleep without even brushing my teeth.

Oh, hell no.

I lunged up, knocking into his bent knees and practically climbing over him to reach the edge and jump off. Dashing into the bathroom with nothing but a quick, "I'll be right back," thrown his way, I shut the door on his responding chuckle.

Feeling minimally better after I'd brushed my teeth, I gathered my hair in a messy bun. Garrett was in my bed. Jamie could see him and would know he'd stayed over. I covered my face with my hands, what had I gotten myself into?

I splashed water on my face, giving myself a mental pep talk. I could do this. I just needed to get rid of him before Jamie got up. I opened the door, preparing myself for the eye candy sight of Garrett lounging in my bed, but the spot he'd been in was empty.

"Feel better?"

I jumped, twisting to see him standing near the edge of the bed, holding his phone. Blushing ten shades of red, I mumbled out a yes, and made my way past him to find a clean sweater.

He grabbed my wrist as I passed, twisting me to face him. His fingers brushed along the curve of my jaw, and my eyes widened, my pulse echoing in my ears. He leaned down, placing his mouth above the shell of my ear. "Then can I kiss you now?"

Like a deer in headlights, I stared up at him, slack jawed and completely caught off guard. "You want to kiss me?"

"I wanted to kiss you the moment I opened my eyes and had to bat your wild hair out of my face to see you snoring beside me."

But why? Literally nothing he'd just said was attractive. He tilted his head to the side, his tongue pushing into the inside of his cheek, and I realized I'd voiced my question out loud.

"It baffles me how a woman as beautiful and amazing as you can see herself in such poor light."

I frowned. I liked to think of myself as a good mom, and I definitely worked hard, but beautiful and amazing were pushing it.

His gaze intensified, hardening with his determination to prove whatever he saw on my face, wrong. "Have you never woken up next to a man who couldn't wait to press his lips to yours? Where just the sight of you next to him was driving him wild?"

"No. You're the first man I've ever woken up next to besides my ex."

His tongue wet his bottom lip, and I swore his chest moved a little faster. "It's really been five years since a man has touched you? Kissed you?"

I gripped the hem of my shirt and nodded, watching his eyes darken like he wanted to consume my soul. Heat flared between my legs, and I could feel my nipples hardening against my shirt.

"All this time, you've never wanted to take someone home? Just one night to release all that stress and tension I see in your shoulders every day?"

Without meaning to, I huffed a laugh, and he quirked an eyebrow in response, waiting for my answer. "Sex…" How did I explain this? "Sex has never been much of a stress reliever for me. So no, I've never wanted to take someone home."

Although, with the way he was looking at me, I was second-guessing that thought process.

He took a step closer until his stomach brushed against my peaked tips, and my lungs started working double time. "You don't find yourself ever needing release at all? Needing someone to help you find that sweet spot and press it over and over again?"

My legs were full on shaking now, and I had to squeeze my thighs together to control the throbbing that was taking over every thought in my head. The hint of a smirk on his lips let me know he hadn't failed to notice.

It didn't matter, my voice gave me away a second later anyway. "In another world maybe, if anyone other than me could find it."

His head pulled back, an incredulous look in his eyes. "Wait, you don't mean—as in, ever?"

I looked away, knowing every visible inch of my skin was vibrant red. How the hell had we even gotten here?

"As in ever. My body doesn't work right, I guess. I enjoyed sex just fine, but I had to, you know, handle things myself later." I waved it off like it didn't bother me to have spent my entire adult life feeling like I was broken.

He heaved out a sigh, brushing the pad of his thumb across his bottom lip. "I can't decide if I want to go find that bastard all over again for ever making you think it was a *you* thing, or if I want to spread you out across that mattress and show you how goddamn wrong you are."

Could you orgasm from just verbal stimulation? Because if you couldn't, I was about to be the first. I'd break the fucking records. "You want to have sex with me?"

"I want to do a lot of things with you."

He reached out to wrap his hands around my waist, but I stepped back out of reach, watching his eyes immediately shutter.

"I don't know if I'm ready for a relationship, Garrett. I wasn't lying that day to Layla. I don't have the time a relationship deserves."

His features relaxed. "I know you're new to the idea, but you don't have to be in a relationship to enjoy the feel of someone's skin, Maddie."

Looking toward the door, I rubbed my palms down my thighs. When had I started sweating? "So, you mean friends with benefits. No feelings."

His eyes flared as he approached me again, brushing his lips across my cheek. "I promise not to catch feelings if you don't."

I shuddered, goosebumps covering my neck and arms. My body had never reacted like this to someone before, and the thought of this man touching me had me wanting to climb to the rooftop and agree at the top of my lungs.

I cleared my throat, then swallowed. I opened my mouth to

say something I'd probably regret, only for a light, rhythmic tapping on my bedroom door to pull me back to the present.

Jamie. My kid was here. This is why dating was off limits for me. I couldn't be thinking about Garrett's chest, and thighs, and the hardness I'd felt, and fuck. I was in so much trouble. I put a large amount of space between our bodies, turning toward the sound.

"You need something, bud?"

"I woke up on the couch and you were gone."

I shrank in on myself. And the most self-centered parenting award goes to? "I'm sorry if I worried you, I was going to let you sleep while I took a shower." Which was kind of true, at least.

"Okay."

It was silent for a moment, and then I heard the sound of his door. I sighed, pinching the bridge of my nose. When I looked up, Garrett was smiling down at me, his dimples on full display, like he knew exactly what I'd been about to say before the interruption.

"All right, you go jump in the shower and get ready. I'll make coffee and find some breakfast for J-man."

A large finger pressed on my lips, stopping the reply from exiting my mouth. Taking his time pulling it back, he pointed to the bathroom. "Shower. I'll whip something up for you too."

Satisfied with my silence, he ripped back the covers and wrapped those bulky arms around my miniature dachshund, cuddling her to his chest, and left.

I watched him amble out and pressed a hand to my chest, wondering how much this dream would hurt when it crumbled all around me.

Chapter 20

IT WAS SATURDAY. Another game day. Jamie jogged out of his room in his uniform, cleats hanging from his hands. I looked over his thin, short-sleeve top and blew out my cheeks.

"Dude, you can't go in that, you'll freeze. Go get the long-sleeve undershirt I bought you."

He groaned, throwing his head back and wiggling his body around like an inflatable tube man. But he listened, dropping his cleats to the floor, and trudging off.

I shook my head, turning to the two people standing by the door. Jamie had asked both Garrett and Layla to go today, so we were all piling in and heading there together.

I'd legitimately feared for Aaron's life when I'd told Layla what had happened that night. She'd nearly clawed my arm off in her haste to snatch my phone and call him. I'd had to tackle her and threaten to give her a wet willy before she conceded defeat. The woman was crazy, but I loved her for it.

She was now leaned over, talking nonsense and rubbing Sadie's back. My lips tipped up at the sight but faltered when I glanced at Garrett to find him looking at me. It'd been a few days since I'd woken up next to him, and in that time, he'd had dinner with us twice.

One night I'd cooked, and the next time he'd brought over Chinese. His proposal hovered over us like an elephant in the room—an overly large elephant wearing stilettos. Every time he said my name or brushed a little too close to me, the urge to say yes would whisper in my ear.

He didn't bring it up again and neither did I, but every time he looked at me, I felt like he was undressing me. My body would tighten, my heart pounding in its cage while the air around us thickened to an unbearable degree. It was exactly what was happening now, and it was maddening.

"Ya'll are making me wish I was headed to Rick's rather than a soccer game." Layla had straightened up, and she was fanning herself, looking back and forth between us. "Holy secret tension."

"Oh, it's not a secret. She knows."

If I could have been a turtle, I'd have popped my head right into my shell. They were both looking at me, Garrett with self-satisfied humor, and Layla in wicked delight.

"I'm going to warm up the Jeep," I muttered, slipping past. I could barely handle Garrett's persuasion, but if Layla jumped on the bus—which she would—I wouldn't stand a chance.

About five minutes later, the remainder of the group climbed in with me, Garrett up front and the other two in back.

From the sounds of it, Layla was mid-way through an aggressive pep talk.

I rolled my eyes, backing out of the drive once everyone was buckled. The woman was incredibly competitive. Jamie would be lucky if she didn't end up shooting to her feet, yelling, throughout the game.

Hearing Layla finally wrap up her speech, I glanced in my rearview mirror. "You get all that, bud?"

"I guess."

I held a thumbs up behind my head. "Cool. Now chuck it all out the window and pretend you didn't hear it because if you take any of her advice, you're bound to get kicked out."

Next to me, Garrett chuckled. "Maybe take a little bit."

I stuck my tongue out at him, and he winked. Of course, he'd agree with her. Glancing back again, I saw Jamie eyeing all of us like we were a band of unruly marsupials.

"Can I just have fun?"

I rubbed my hands together, trying to keep warm. In the last week the temperature had taken a turn, but I swore it'd dropped even further in the last hour. I needed to remember to bring a blanket to the next game, or at least follow-through with purchasing a new coat. A large Thermos of coffee wouldn't hurt either.

Bringing my hands to my face, I cupped them and blew hot air between them. This game was taking forever, caffeine actually sounded like a great idea.

"Hey, I'm going to go grab some coffee, would either of you like some?"

"Is that a rhetorical question?" Layla didn't even bother looking over at me, eyes riveted to the game, her thighs in a permanent state of half squat over the bench.

I stood, looking down at Garrett and pointing at him, but he shook his head. "I'm fine. Do you want me to walk over there with you?"

"No, it's okay. Enjoy the game, I'll be quick."

I shuffled down the bleachers, thankful the audience was fairly sparse today, and I didn't have to squeeze by anyone. The concessions were on the far side of the field, but it'd be nice to move my limbs and get the blood pumping.

When I approached, a line had already formed of other parents with the same idea, but at least I could still see the field. I took my place, turning to watch as I bounced from side to side.

"Today turned out to be a cold one, didn't it?"

I nodded to myself, still watching the game, agreeing with whoever was talking.

"The boys sitting on the bench must be freezing."

I absently nodded again. I'd already thought the same thing. Most of the boys were wearing layers under their uniforms, but I was cold under a long sleeve and a sweater, so I'm sure their thin undershirts weren't helping much.

"You're Jamie's mom, right?"

Startled, I darted my eyes over to find a man standing behind me, looking at me. "God, sorry, I thought you were talking to someone else. Yes, he's mine."

"Oh good, glad I didn't make a fool of myself then." He

laughed, and his smile showed off a line of perfectly straight, white teeth. "I saw your group walk over before the game started, and it was hard to tell which of you were his parents."

I waved a hand back and forth. "Yeah, we get that a lot. The other woman is his aunt of sorts, a close family friend."

He bobbed his head, glancing at the line and moving up with me. I'd never seen him before, but he was an attractive man. He wasn't quite as tall as Garrett, but he stood a few inches above me and was sporting perfectly styled, blond hair. Relaxed brows sat over a pair of strikingly blue eyes, and a trimmed beard covered his jaw.

"I'm Michael." He held out his hand, and I hesitantly took it, unsure why he was being friendly with me. No one at school events was ever friendly to me.

"Madison."

He held onto my hand a second longer and smiled again, crinkling his eyes. "Nice to meet you, Madison. My son has nothing but good things to say about Jamie. He seems like a great kid."

That had me thawing, and I couldn't help but return his smile. "I'm glad to hear that. He's definitely a good kid, although I might be biased." I glanced to the side, noticing the line had moved up, and shuffled forward.

"We're fairly new to the area and new to the school. My son, Ian, is incredibly shy and doesn't make friends easily, but he came home talking about Jamie on day one. Jamie kind of took him under his wing, I guess."

My heart warmed. "We've moved around a bit, so he knows what it's like to be new. I'm glad to hear they're hitting it off."

"Maybe we can get the boys together sometime so they can hang out outside of class."

I certainly wasn't against the idea of Jamie having a friend outside of school. I opened my mouth to agree when something was yanked over my face. I jolted, whipping back and bumping into something firm.

Hands brushed along my arms, pulling the item farther down until it encased me. I was two seconds from shooting out an elbow when I smelled it. That familiar, musky smell I'd know anywhere.

For the second time in my life, my head was forcibly shoved through the neck hole of a man's hoodie, and I could see again. Michael was still there and was looking at me with an amused grin.

I turned to look over my shoulder and sucked in a breath. Garrett stood directly behind me, his eyes hard and heated as they locked with my own.

"Hi," I whispered.

His lips twitched. I could feel how tense he was as he looked up at Michael, but he nodded at him in greeting.

"Michael, this is my neighbor, Garrett. Garrett, this is Michael. His son goes to school with Jamie."

Garrett's eyes snapped to mine, and the look he sent me before he extended his hand to Michael had me rolling in my lips like a child caught in a lie.

Pulling the proffered limb back, he wrapped both hands around my arms and turned me, moving me forward. I'd been next and hadn't noticed, and the woman working the stand stared at me, waiting.

"She'd like a coffee with one sugar and three creams."

I looked up at him in surprise, but his hands on my arms kept me from turning around. "Make that two, please."

He nodded, handing the woman cash and taking the cups from her outstretched hand.

He transferred one to me, and I wrapped both hands around it, stepping out of the way. I looked over my shoulder to bid Michael goodbye, but firm pressure on my back had me throwing out a quick wave and walking toward the bleachers instead.

I narrowed my eyes at the man beside me, the feel of his hand hot against my lower back. "We could have invited him where we're at, I don't think he knows anyone here."

"He'll live." With the lack of concern in his tone, we might as well have been discussing the weather or the branches of government.

I grumbled. I knew Garrett naturally wasn't talkative, especially to strangers, but being new sucked. It wouldn't have killed him to be friendlier.

Garrett sighed, and I swore his fingers glided an inch up my back. "I'm sorry, I'll look for him next time."

I let him guide me back up to our seats, pointedly rolling my eyes when Layla wiggled her brows at me, accepting the second coffee from Garrett. I'm sure watching Garrett potato sack me with a hoodie was the highlight of her day.

I settled next to her, holding my cup near my face, and basking in the steam. Garrett dropped down next to me, and if I didn't know better, I'd say he was sitting a little closer than he had been before.

***

The boys lost the game. I wanted to be able to pat Jamie on the back and say something like, "It was so close!" But it wasn't. They got creamed. He was eight, so I couldn't care less who won. I just didn't want to see him upset.

Layla, on the other hand, hadn't shut up about it. Garrett and I were currently suffering through the tail-end of her rant as we stood to the side of the field and waited for the boys to be dismissed.

"I mean, honestly, if they would've just—" She stopped, nudging my arm. "Never mind. Incoming."

I glanced over, expecting to see Jamie, but what I saw was the mutts of my own personal hell descending on us. Otherwise known as Tristan and her gang.

Her face was pinched like she'd eaten something sour, and Carolyn and Lara—I still wasn't sure if those were their names—both looked uncomfortable. Tristan was looking directly at me until Garrett's body shifted a half-step closer. Her eyes darted to him, and she swallowed, turning and transforming her features into a mega-watt smile.

"Hello, Madison. How are you?"

I fought the urge to frown and give her the finger. What did this woman want? "Fine. You?"

"Cold as an ice cube and sad the boys lost their game, but I'm peachy keen." She continued smiling at me like we were fast friends, and I looked around wondering if I'd somehow dropped into another dimension.

"I wanted to let you know early, since you're always...so busy, we'll be having a party in a couple weeks for the team. I'll send little invites at the next game, but I hope to see you there!"

I gaped, only succeeding in nodding my head. She seemed satisfied with the response and flipped her hand in a wave before she and her group moseyed off to go wait for their boys.

I slowly faced my companions. "That was weird, right? Did anyone else find that super weird?"

Layla looked about as confused as I felt, but Garrett looked like a cat that'd finally caught the annoying ass canary. He was watching the women walk away, an immensely pleased expression on his face.

I glanced back and forth between Tristan's group and him. "Garrett Rowe."

"Hm?"

"Is there something you'd like to share with the class?"

He dragged his face down to mine but only tapped a finger under my chin and winked. Then he stepped past me, striding off to meet Jamie who'd finally been released from the field.

I watched him lean down to fist bump him before saying something that lit up my kid's face with a laugh loud enough for me to hear from where I still stood.

They both had mischievous looks on their faces, and Layla burst into cackles behind me. "Girl, you're in so much trouble."

I was. I really was. Because I was pretty sure I might be in love with that man.

Chapter 21

THE ROOM SPUN, circling around me like a kaleidoscope of images. I couldn't help but wonder if this was what it felt like when people said their lives passed before their eyes.

Did it spin around them in quick bursts, or did time slow down in those moments and allow you to enjoy it?

I closed my eyes, shoving off again. I could do without seeing my life flash before my eyes. Besides Jamie, there wasn't a single thing I'd want to re-experience before death. I'd die depressed and stressed out.

Sighing, I gave myself one more round before putting my foot out and stopping the chair's movement.

I stared at the time on my desktop, wanting nothing more than to grumble and crawl under the desk. You know it's going to be a long night when you're daydreaming at work about life and death. I was so over this work schedule. When I was thirty-five and successful, I sure as hell better look back and be proud of this shit.

I finished filling out my timesheet and put the monitor to sleep. "I'm about to clock out for the day, Evaline. You need anything before I go?"

"No, honey, you enjoy your weekend."

I scrunched my nose, that was highly unlikely given my schedule, Jamie's game, and midterms to study for, but it was a sweet sentiment, nonetheless. I pushed back my chair and grabbed my purse and change of clothes, making my way through the office.

I saw a few people as I passed, but most only offered a quick smile or a half-wave. Things had become different after the fiasco with Rob. He hadn't been well-liked, so no one seemed to hate me over him being fired, but they also didn't strike up conversations with me anymore. No one was necessarily rude; they just didn't know how to act around me.

It was as if the sexual harassment I'd experienced had affected *them*. Seeing me only reminded them of something they'd prefer to forget. I was no longer just a person. I was *that* person, and they didn't know what to say to me.

I stepped into the bathroom, efficiently switching out of my office clothes for my waitressing uniform before slipping back out and making my way through the lobby and to my vehicle.

I'd only recently started changing clothes here so I could drop Jamie at home without going inside. I'd felt weird about it at first, but it saved me time so I'd gotten over it pretty quick.

The restaurant had no problem with me clocking in a few minutes early, and with the holidays coming up, I needed every extra tip I could get.

Honestly, I was tempted to take a few extra guard shifts as well. Jim had already asked me if I'd be available and willing to cover more Saturdays as the holidays approached so some of the other guards could have full weekends off with their families.

The irony wasn't lost on me, and I'd kind of just stared at him before making some off-hand comment saying I'd think about it. I still hadn't decided.

The restaurant was quiet when I walked in, only a few straggling customers spread around. I waved to one of the new girls who was lazing about the host stand and made my way to the back to clock-in and store my things.

The quiet didn't last long. By five o'clock we had a full house. It wasn't Super Bowl slammed, but it kept me busy enough that the time whirred by. Five quickly turned to six and six to seven. These were my favorite kind of shifts, the fast-moving ones.

I smiled at a toddler strapped into a highchair at one of my tables, playing a game of peekaboo with my order pad while waiting for her father to dig through his wallet for his credit card.

She squealed, clapping her hands and showing me two rows of tiny teeth. Her chubby cheeks were covered in ketchup, but it was nothing compared to the globs of it I could see on her lap. I chuckled, grabbing an extra stack of napkins from the neighboring table and handing it to her mother, who gave me an appreciative smile.

All my other tables had received their meals and would be set for a few minutes before I'd need to check on them, so once I finished cashing out the small family, I headed into the back to get a head start on my side duties.

Tonight, I was in charge of re-filling ranch bottles, and I hated it. The sad truth about restaurants—this one included—was they never replaced condiment containers unless they broke. They just had us top off the bottles using bulk containers night after night. No rinsing, no washing, no emptying out the old stuff first. Just refilled and reused over and over again.

Cringe.

I was on my fifth one when Nate popped his head through the swinging door. "Hey, Curly, you got a two top at seventeen."

I tipped my head, indicating I'd heard.

"I went ahead and took their drink orders since they wanted beer, so swing by and grab 'em on your way."

"All right, thanks, Nate."

"And maybe clean up your face a little as well."

I looked up sharply, spilling ranch down my fingers. "Why? What's on my face?" I asked, wiping the back of my wrist across my forehead.

"Nothing, you spaz. I just meant one of them is sizzling hot. Like, the kind of hot I'd happily spread my cheeks for while screaming thank you."

"Jesus, stop. I'll never be able to wash that image out. Clench your butt and go make my drinks," I said, waving him off with my non-ranch-covered hand. He winked at me but did as I bid.

Typically, I enjoyed when I had an attractive, single man as a customer. I was only human and enjoyed casual flirting as much as the next lonely person, but I found myself not even remotely interested tonight. In fact, I was kind of dreading walking out there.

If I wanted a decent tip, I'd give him a couple extra smiles and stop by to chat a few times, but the idea tasted bitter in my mouth. There was certainly a hot single man I'd like to do that with, but he wasn't a random stranger.

Grabbing a paper towel, I wiped my hand free of ranch and pepped myself up before marching back onto the floor with a smile on my face.

A smile that froze almost instantly.

Oh.

Well, Nate hadn't been wrong, the man was absolutely cheek-spreading worthy. Before the table noticed me, I retreated through the swinging door, circling around the back to the other side of the restaurant, and dashed straight into the bathroom.

After cleaning up my messy bun—the bad messy, not the cute kind—and smacking my cheeks a few times, I took a deep, steadying breath. I could do this.

"Hi, guys, I'm Madison, and I'll be your server this evening." I set the two beers I was holding on the table and then placed both hands on my hips.

"Your name tag says Curly."

I pursed my lips. "They like nicknames here. You can call me either. Are you ready to order or do you need a few more minutes?"

"I don't know about him, but I'm just here to enjoy some drinks and the impeccable view." He lifted the bottle to his mouth, his tongue darting out slightly before his lips made contact, and he took a swig, eyes pinned on me.

"Oh, um. Perfect. Okay. How about you?"

The older gentleman across from him sat there trying to hide his shit-eating grin behind a menu, and for some reason it made me laugh. I had a feeling these two were going to be a handful tonight.

"Nah, but I'm sure I'll crave some fries or something later," he finally got out.

"You got it." I turned to leave but paused when fingers brushed my wrist. I looked over my shoulder, holding a knife to my heart and threatening it to calm the fuck down.

"I'll admit, Curly's cute, but I think I like Maddie better."

Licking my lips, I swallowed, meeting his gaze. "You know, you're the only one who calls me that."

Garrett's eyes flared, and his knuckles whitened as he gripped the bottle in his hand. "Then I definitely like it better."

My mouth opened, but realizing I had nothing to say that wouldn't give away the butterflies taking flight inside of me, I snapped it shut, nodding to Harry and high-tailing it out of there.

I checked on the rest of my tables and then promptly staked out a hiding spot on the far side of the bar.

Nate whistled. "That man was looking at you like you were a snack he wants to partake in three times a day. I could feel the angst from here."

I groaned, lowering my head to my arms. Of course, Garrett would not only show up when I wasn't prepared, but also turn up the heat less than a full week after my self-revelation about being in love with him.

Tipping my head to the side and gazing up at my friend, I asked, "You really don't recognize him?"

He raised his brows, grabbing a frosted mug and filling it with the perfect amount of beer to foam ratio. "No, why? Who is he?"

I groaned again, cursing Nate and his playboy habit of never remembering a single face or name. "Do you remember that night when I downed a guy's beer over his lap?"

"No. Shut up. That's the same guy?"

I nodded pathetically, knowing I needed to pick my head up and go check on my customers, but not having the courage to do it yet.

"And you *still* haven't put him out of his misery? Curly, that man wants you."

"I know," I said, flicking pretzel crumbs off the bar that'd probably fallen from someone's mouth. "He's already asked me to play the benefit game."

"*And you haven't*—okay, you're officially, certifiably insane, but we'll circle back to that. I meant that man wants you, as in, wants you forever and ever."

I shoved off the bar, steadying myself from the sudden change in equilibrium. "No, he doesn't, Nate. He already told me to my face it would be a 'no feelings' deal."

Nate flipped a few shakers, making some random

concoction that was sure to be delicious. "Even better then. You always whine about not having the time to date anyway. So, what's holding you back?"

The fact I was in love with him, and touching him would kill what was left of my beaten-down heart? Was that a good reason?

He popped the caps off two more bottles and slid them over to me. "Do something crazy, Curly. You're a mom, and a great one, but don't forget you're also a woman. You have needs, and that matters too."

I plucked them up. "Since when did you get all philosophical and shit?"

He paused mid-shake, sucking on his teeth and clicking his tongue. "Curly, I got all kinds of different sides to me. How else do you think I get all my dates?"

I rolled my eyes. Do something crazy, huh? I didn't judge anyone who enjoyed one-night stands. Nate made it his second profession, and I loved his face. But could I move Garrett's and my friendship in that direction and not want more? That's what I wasn't sure about.

But as I approached his table, and his eyes flicked up my body, I almost yelled, "Goddammit, yes!" and dragged him by his collar to the bathroom. Somehow, I don't think getting fired was the level of crazy Nate had in mind.

Garrett watched every step I took like it was foreplay for him, and I suddenly forgot how to speak. Setting the new bottles on the table, I reached to grab his empty one, but he whipped his hand out at the same time, curling his fingers around my own. He yanked the bottle toward him, and it lurched me forward until I almost fell into his lap.

I placed a hand against his shoulder, propping up my weight, and stared down at him, wide-eyed. The position felt oddly similar to the last time I'd held a beer bottle over his lap, and the look he gave me said he was thinking the same thing.

I flushed crimson, scrambling back and wiping my palms on my sides. Turning my body away from the fucking sun, I asked Harry, "You still good?"

Harry was leaned forward, his chin resting in his bear-sized hand, a suspiciously blank expression on his face. "Yeah, I'm good."

I cleared my throat, refusing to look to the man on my left who was staring a hole into me. "All right then, just flag me down when you're ready for more."

"I thought I'd already made it clear I was, but I can tell you as many times as you need to hear it, Maddie."

My ears were so red, they burned, and I'd never moved from a table faster in my life. The sounds of the brothers' laughter echoing out behind me.

The remainder of the night went on fairly well, all things considered. It didn't take long for me to have a full section, including a large party, so I was too busy to over-think Garrett's presence or his teasing comments.

He seemed to understand that, too, because the minute he saw me hustling from table to table, he toned down his gravitational pull and relaxed into his booth, chatting with his brother.

I was assisting another waitress, and had my arms covered in dishes from my elbows down, when they finally pushed out of their booth.

Garrett met my eyes across the room as he tossed cash and something else onto the table. Then he quietly followed Harry out.

I don't want to say I sprinted over the minute my arms were free, but it was possible. Tucked under a wad of cash that was way too much for their total, was a folded, wrinkled-looking paper. I snatched it up like a crack addict, reading it, then re-reading it.

I'll see you after work.

How those five words could be both thrilling and nerve wracking was as confusing as it got. I feel like he was both threatening and teasing me at the same time, and it made me feel like a fire was burning in my belly while ants crawled all over my skin. It was heady.

I stashed the note in my pocket, glancing at the window and half-expecting him to be standing there smirking at me, but he wasn't.

The fact that I was mildly disappointed should have worried me. The fact that it would have turned me on, should have worried me more.

"You going to change it up tonight, Curly? Or just take your usual?"

I stuck out the tip of my tongue in thought, Garrett's note burning a hole in my back pocket. Was he really going to wait for me to get home?

"Change it up, but nothing crazy that will hinder me from driving."

"You got it."

I left Nate at the bar and stored the broom I'd been using, switching it out for the mop. We'd closed right on time, and this was the last chore on my list.

My manager had long since stopped checking on my closing duties, trusting that I actually did them, so when I was done, I shouted a goodbye toward his office and met Nate on the patio.

"Your poison, my lady."

I took it, dropping my tired butt into the chair next to him and propping my feet on the bars between the legs of the table. "Oh my God, what is this?"

"Just a lemon drop."

"Jesus, that's good." I took a few more sips, leaning back and closing my eyes, enjoying the sweet and sour flavors mixing with the silence of the night. Sometimes you don't realize just how loud your surroundings are until the moment you finally have silence.

"Uh-oh."

Eyes still closed, I mumbled out a lazy, "What?"

"Would you say your boy toy is the murdering type?"

I cracked an eye open, wondering where his line of questioning was going, but the sight of his pale face had me shooting up and whipping my head around to see where his gaze was focused.

Garrett stood on the other side of the patio fence, his face partially obscured by the night, and his fists clenched at his sides.

What in the world was he still doing here? I set my drink down, turning my body to face him. "Garrett?"

He blinked, telling me he heard me, but he didn't tear his eyes from Nate. On the outside, he looked cool and detached, but I knew better.

"She's not interested."

Nate's eyebrows shot right up his forehead. "Yeah, I'm pretty sure even fucking Pluto knows that."

"Good."

I put a shaky hand out to stop Nate's continued rambling and tried not to panic. Why did I feel like I'd just been caught cheating? "What are you doing here?"

The skin around his eyes twitched as he looked at me, and something flashed across his face. It was there and gone in a blink, but I'd seen it. Hurt. "I told you I'd be here."

Oh god. I'd thought he meant he'd see me back at the duplex, not that he'd literally wait for me to get off work. He'd been sitting around waiting, only to find me meeting up with a different guy as if I'd just disregarded his message. Fuck. My next words tumbled out of me like word vomit.

"Nate's a friend from work."

"Good to know. Let's go."

I chewed my lip. "My Jeep is here," I said lamely.

"You've been drinking, you're not driving."

"I haven't even finished one drink. And you drank tonight too."

"Hours ago. You're not driving. Harry and I will come pick it up later." He cocked a thumb over his shoulder. "Get in the car, Madison."

Realizing I didn't have much of a choice unless I wanted to be thrown over his shoulder, I stood stiffly, scooting past Nate's chair with a muttered goodbye.

"You good to go with him, Curly?" he asked quietly.

"Yeah, I'll be okay. Thanks, Nate."

He shot a sympathetic look my way, but he didn't say anything else to either of us.

Garrett walked one step behind, reaching past my body to open the door to his Nova for me. I slipped in, eyeing the plastic bag of items sitting at my feet. The man had been working on the baby blanket for me while he waited for me to get off work. God, I was such an asshole.

He climbed behind the wheel, not speaking or looking my way as he buckled in and pulled out of the lot. The silence between us was deafening.

I didn't know what to say or do. I wanted to apologize for hurting him, but he hated my apologies. The act alone would only succeed in making him angry.

I unbuckled my seatbelt the second we pulled into the driveway, determined to at least be outside when he yelled at me, but the low tenor of his voice stopped me.

"Don't run off."

"I'm not running, I'm just getting out. We're here."

"You're unhappy."

Wait, he was worried that *I* was unhappy? He was the one in the middle of a glaring contest with his windshield. "I'm not unhappy."

"Don't lie to me. You're panicking because you think I'm mad at you. I can tell by your face."

"Maybe you don't know my face as well as you think you do because I'm fine." Great, another person who could see through me, just what I needed.

He squeezed his hands over the wheel, knocking his head back. "Jesus fucking Christ, why are you so difficult?"

"Look, don't yell at me, but I'm sorry for making you angry. I wasn't ditching you for another guy or whatever it looked like. I thought your note meant you'd see me when I got home. Nate works the bar and makes me drinks sometimes to wind down, but that's it."

My words rushed out like lifesavers being thrown at a drowning man, sounding exactly as panicked as he'd accused me of being. But I couldn't help it, I was desperate for him to understand that it wasn't what it looked like. I wasn't like that.

But they seemed to have the opposite effect. His features twisted, and he took a deep breath, holding it for several seconds before releasing it heavily. "You know, I keep waiting to have you all to myself, but every time I turn around, he's always here with us."

I looked around the car like an idiot. "Who's always here?"

"Your ex."

I flinched. "What about him?"

"I'm trying to figure out how I got rid of that son-of-a bitch, literally dunked his whiny ass in a random fucking porta-john, and yet he's somehow still here, hanging over your shoulder."

"Wait, you did what?"

"Why is he here?"

"What? You just said—"

"Why is he still in your head, Maddie?"

I pressed my back against the door, grasping at it like it could stabilize my heart. The heart he was currently exposing to the air. "What the hell are you talking about?"

"I'm talking about that fucking look on your face. Like you think it's only a matter of time before I hurt you. Like you really thought I'd scream at you for tonight just because I was hurt." He sighed. "Every time I think I'm getting you out of your shell, you let him put you right back."

"I don't know what you mean." I slapped my hand around behind me, searching for the door handle and yanking when I found it. I needed out of this enclosed space.

It'd only opened an inch before he lunged toward me, pulling the door shut and leaning down over my face.

"When I can't be upset without you wondering what I'll do, you're inviting him in here," he jabbed his finger toward my forehead.

"When we can't sit here and talk like a normal couple without you worrying I'm going to scream at you, you're letting that motherfucker pull up a chair and stay. You're seeing my actions and comparing them to *his*."

I smacked his hand away. "Stop saying that. I know you're

not like him."

"Then kick him out."

"I have."

"No, you haven't. Kick. Him. Out."

"What do you think I've been doing for the last five years?" I snapped.

"Stop making excuses and kick him out, Madison. Stop thinking about him, stop comparing people to him, stop giving the bastard the privilege of your time."

"Goddammit, I'm trying!"

His face hovered only an inch above mine, both of us staring at the other, chests heaving. My eyes stung, and I sucked in a shaky breath.

"I told you I had baggage. It wasn't some random metaphor. I like you, Garrett, more than I should, but—"

The arm across my body pulled away from the handle to grip the back of my neck, tipping my head up and allowing his eyes to rove over my face. He closed them for a split second before snapping them open. "Fuck it."

Then he slammed his lips to mine.

There was no soft peck, no hesitation, just two forces colliding. It was as if he couldn't take another second of not knowing how it felt to have his lips on me. As if his life depended on it.

I was frozen in shock, my hands glued to the door behind me until I felt the graze of his teeth surround my bottom lip, sucking it into his mouth. And I melted, molding to him like candle wax.

I wrapped my arms around his neck, pulling him even closer until the entire top half of his body covered my own. I slanted my mouth, opening for his tongue to dive in. I was a flame, pure star fire straight from space, ready to explode and take the earth with me. I dug my nails into the muscles of his shoulders, drowning in the feel of his tongue and full lips.

He pulled away, just far enough to drag his mouth down my jaw, leaving hot, searing kisses in his path before dropping to my neck. He nipped and sucked along one side and then the other until I was a panting, heaving mess. Then he was back at my mouth, opening me up and stealing every last piece of my soul.

It wasn't enough. I wanted his skin painted against my own, I wanted to hear him groan in my ear and feel his breath ghost across my skin. And I didn't just want it now. I wanted it every damn day.

It was that thought that had me coming to my senses, dowsing me in cold water. I tried to pull away, but the hand on my neck tightened, keeping me in place.

I sighed against his mouth, "Garrett."

His lips pressed to mine again, then again, growing softer each time. Once. Twice. Four times. Finally, he retracted his hand from my neck, resting his forehead on mine and brushing his hands over the curve of my shoulders.

"I knew tasting your lips would be amazing, but if I'd have known it'd be fucking life altering, I'd have kissed you a long time ago."

I dropped my hands to rest on his chest. "This doesn't change anything, Garrett. It doesn't change my past or my head or mean I'm suddenly fixed."

His eyes zeroed in on me. "You don't need to be *fixed.* I'm not expecting you to throw out your past like it never happened. I just don't want it to be forefront in your mind when we're together. I want you to feel safe to fight with me."

He shook his head, breaking eye contact and staring at my hands. "You're a fucking treasure, Maddie. A goddamn crown jewel, and everyone who meets you sees it, including your bar friend. I saw you sitting out there tonight with him, and my jealousy got the best of me. I can't stand the thought of another man claiming you before I'm able to make you mine."

Could your heart grow too large for your chest? I raised a hand and let my fingers rest against his cheek, already wanting to bring his lips back to me.

"There's no other man, Garrett. Not yesterday, not today, and not tomorrow. I just need time."

He closed his eyes and sighed, kissing my palm. "I can't promise I'll survive it, but I'll back off until you're ready. Just tell me when, baby, I'll be here."

Chapter 22

SHE GAPED AT me. "I'm sorry, he did what?"

I didn't repeat the story, instead knocking my head back to down my wine. Snagging the bottle next to her, I poured another ungodly full glass, emptying the bottle and licking the dribble from the neck.

Yep, I'd splurged and purchased an actual bottle the following morning. What could I say, I was having a crisis.

"Then what happened?"

"We both went home. Our own homes. Alone."

Layla stared at me with wide, unblinking eyes. It was rare to see her speechless. "He said all that to you, and you just went home?"

It was one of my more cowardly moments, for sure. I balanced my glass between two of my fingers, twirling it back and forth, wondering if I should actually eat lunch. "Yep."

"What in the hell is wrong with you? He's a catch. A good one, Mads. And Jamie loves him. He's always talking about him and asking if he's coming over."

I set my glass down and pushed it away from me. I needed to get my shit together and be an adult. My shift tonight wasn't going to disappear just because I'd kissed the man I was in love with and chose to have wine for a meal.

"I know he is, but it's not fair to him or Jamie for me to jump in before knowing it'll work out."

"No one goes into a relationship already knowing it'll work out. That's literally the point of dating."

I grumbled, passing by her position at the bar and throwing myself face-first onto the couch. "I don't know if I'll ever be dating material, Layla. I'm a mess."

She followed, plopping down on top of my ass. Both dogs jumped up from their positions on the floor, excited for a cuddle party, but luckily for my face, she waved them down. I couldn't help but chuckle at the way they both seemed to huff in disappointment.

She smacked my thigh. "Yeah, you are a mess. A hot fucking mess, to be exact. But that doesn't mean you're not worth it, nor does it mean you shouldn't try. You've been single for years, Mads. It's time to take a chance."

"I don't just have me to think about. You said it yourself, Jamie loves him. I can't do that to him. I can't tease him with the idea of finally having two parental figures in his life only to rip it away if things don't work out."

"Just test the waters then."

I sent a glare her way even though she couldn't see my face from her perch on top of me. "I can't sleep with him. We're neighbors. If we ended up having no chemistry, and he decided he wanted to hit-it-and-quit-it, he wouldn't be able to. He'd be stuck seeing my face all the time. Hitting-it without the quitting-it part."

"So, you're saying there was no chemistry when he kissed you?"

Even smooshed to the couch, a full-grown woman using me as a cushion, I flushed to my toes, replaying Garrett's kiss for the one millionth time that morning. There'd been more than chemistry, a lot more. I just hadn't decided what to do about it yet.

Garrett wanted me right now, but would the excitement of being with me fade after he finally fucked me? He claimed to be willing to wait until I was emotionally ready, but how long would he actually be willing to wait before losing interest? Chemistry didn't automatically equal long-term feelings.

Not to mention, had he really thought through the fact that being with me meant also being with my kid? That was a huge ass commitment for anyone.

I thought about my sweet, protective, sassy, oddball child, who was currently at a movie with his grandpa. I couldn't imagine a single person who wouldn't enjoy having him around, but I was a tad biased.

Did I want to see Garrett every day? Yes. I wanted to watch him and Jamie argue over video games and wrestle on the floor while Rugsy yapped at them. I wanted him to walk up behind me and kiss me sweetly while I cooked dinner or folded his clothes. I wanted to dote on him and be doted on.

Did I also want to strip his clothes off and see if he could back up his claim to have me seeing stars for the first time? Ab-so-fucking-lutely. Pun intended.

But as I'd learned long ago, life didn't often work out as smoothly as envisioned. In fact, the train usually went off the rails a few times in the process.

Deciding it was in my best interest to change the subject, I rolled to the side until Layla was propped on my hip rather than my rear.

"He said he left Aaron in a porta-potty."

She shifted forward toward my head, causing me to grunt and squish deeper into the couch. "As in, sat him on top of it or..."

"Or."

"Oh my fucking God, that's it. He's husband material. I'm serious, I'll take him if you won't."

I shoved her off me, laughing and throwing a pillow down on top of her. "Hearing that would break Rick's heart."

"Ugh," she groaned, sliding onto the floor like a slug. Taking that as their official cue, the dogs leapt up, stepping all over her for snuggles and scratches.

Layla had been trying to gently break things off with Rick for a few days now, but the poor guy wasn't getting the hint. She cared about him and enjoyed playing music both in and out of the sheets, but he just wasn't passing the soulmate vibe check.

Rick had professed his love the last time she'd hinted at just being friends, and she was desperately trying to avoid breaking the claws out and scarring his lovesick heart for life.

I chuckled, not feeling the least bit sorry for her. She'd done it to herself, and it was only more proof that I shouldn't jump into dating Garrett. Because if he broke things off, I already knew I wouldn't recover.

The truth was, I'd rather feel a tinge of sadness every time I looked at him and couldn't have him, rather than walk through life with a shattered heart.

It'd been an entire week since Garrett had kissed me, and we still hadn't talked about it. In fact, we hadn't really talked at all. He'd waved and asked me about my day the few times we'd bumped into each other outside, but that was it.

On Thursday, he'd even helped Jamie practice some goals out in the yard, but had turned him down when he invited him over for dinner.

I felt like in trying to save our friendship, I'd already ruined it. He'd said he'd back off, but I guess I hadn't realized he'd also meant as friends as well.

I shifted on the bleacher, rubbing subconsciously at my chest, trying to soothe the ache that had settled in and wouldn't leave. It was late morning, and Jamie's game would be starting any minute. It was the first one I'd had to attend alone, and I was feeling a little sorry for myself.

Layla had taken a gig to play music at a farmer's market in a neighboring town this weekend, and my parents were at some kind of fundraiser for my dad's work. I was whinier about it than Jamie was.

We'd all made plans to have a late lunch together later so he could tell them how it went. He'd asked me twice already if I knew whether Garrett was coming. I hadn't been able to give him an answer.

I rubbed harder, wishing I lived in one of those fantasy worlds where people could turn their emotions off. When compared to powers like flying, super strength, or speed, I'd take emotional control every time.

Huddling deeper into the blanket I'd finally remembered to bring; I propped my feet on the bleacher in front of me and rested my head on my knees. I closed my eyes and crossed my arms over my face, separating myself from the world.

To anyone looking at me, I probably resembled a woolly cocoon. Too bad I'd be the same exhausted woman when I emerged.

Laughter sounded to my left, followed by the vibrations of someone walking across the bleacher I was sitting on. "Is that you under there, Madison?"

I shot up, nearly tipping backward into the foot space behind me. My blanket puddled around my waist, and I looked up to see Michael smiling down at me.

"Oh. Good morning, Michael."

"Cold?" He stepped closer, lowering to sit next to me. I grabbed the edges of the blanket, shuffling to the side even though he already had more than enough room to sit.

I huffed a laugh I dearly hoped didn't sound as fake as it felt. The idea of small talk was already pulling on the last strings of my energy, and we'd only started.

"A little. Just waiting for the game to start."

He pointed toward the boys huddled up on the field. "Looks like they're getting ready to run out there now."

I made do with nodding.

"Do you mind if I sit here, or are you waiting for someone?"

I bit the inside of my cheek at his obvious fishing. He might as well have waved a rod and worm around, but I couldn't blame him. The last time we'd spoken, Garrett had swept in like a tidal wave, whisking me away.

"It's just me today." I turned my attention to the field. I still couldn't claim to be a fan of sports, but there was something about watching kids run aimlessly around a field for an hour or two that was almost calming. Like watching a fish tank or an ant farm.

In my peripheral, I could see Michael glance my way several times. He clearly wanted to say or ask something, but he hadn't worked up the nerve. Part of me hoped he never did, as shitty as the thought was. Anytime someone gave me a look like that, they were usually about to ask me something personal.

"Can I ask you something?"

Damn.

I dragged my eyes to him, but he was looking down at his watch, fiddling with the dials, so I looked back at the field. "Sure."

"Are you free next weekend? It's Ian's birthday, and he's wanting to invite Jamie over for some pizza and cake. I thought…maybe we could…"

His stuttering trailed off, and I frowned, twisting toward him. He was asking about a kid birthday, not dinner and a movie, so why did he sound so damn nervous? I opened my mouth to ask when, only for another voice to beat me to it.

"What day?"

Warmth engulfed my shoulder a second later as a large hand curled around it, tucking me against the jean-covered leg standing behind me. How his lumberjack of a body made it across these rickety benches without me noticing was a feat in itself. The man was stealthy as hell.

Michael looked like he'd swallowed something bitter as he replied, "Saturday afternoon."

Garrett's hands lifted just enough to grip the edge of my blanket and pull it higher over my shoulders before dropping to my biceps and rubbing his fingers up and down in a soothing manner.

"We can check our schedules. Maddie works Saturday evenings, but if you're okay with it, I have no problem bringing Jamie," he said, directing the last part at me.

Michael glanced over, but I struggled to focus on him when I could still feel Garrett's words wrapping around me. We. He said *we* would check, like we were a team, a unit, a family in the making.

There was a funny feeling in my middle that was either my heart pulling a Grinch number and growing, or there was a chance I was about to vomit.

"Yeah, I'm sure we can make it work."

Michael appeared less than happy about the entire ordeal. "Good. That's good." He stood abruptly, muttering something about needing to use the restroom. I watched him leave, wondering if he knew he'd walked in the opposite direction of them.

I pivoted my body, coming face to face with Garrett's thick thigh. I slid my eyes up his frame, raising an eyebrow in silent question.

His eyes moved over every inch of my face like we'd gone months being apart. The hand on my arm moved to my cheek, cupping it for a fleeting moment before he pulled back and tucked his hands into his hoodie. "Hey."

I couldn't hide the smile the single word brought to my face. "I didn't think you were coming."

He stepped over the bleacher, settling down next to me. "Is it all right that I'm here?"

Before thinking better about it, I placed my hand on his leg. "Of course, it is. Jamie kept asking me if you were coming. He's going to be so happy."

His eyes latched onto my hand before slowly making their way up. "And you?"

"I'm happy you're here too." I laughed awkwardly. "I thought you'd finally come to your senses and were avoiding me."

His brow furrowed. "I was trying to give you space."

I squeezed his leg once before forcing the mind-of-its-own

limb back to my lap. "I needed space from your sex eyes, Garrett, not from *you*."

Laughter tore out of him like he wasn't prepared for it, and a small glowing ember perked up inside of me. It was one of the most beautiful sounds I'd ever heard.

I stared at my child, a knife gripped in my hand, hovering over a half-sliced tomato. "I'm sorry, you did what?"

"I invited him over for lunch."

Carefully setting the knife down, I wiped my hands on a towel, turning to face the living room and my parents, who were currently chatting on the couch about something they'd read in the news.

"Here," I confirmed, pointing to the floor.

Jamie opened his mouth, but just then a knock sounded against the door, startling my parents and setting Rugsy off.

I dropped my head into my hands, allowing myself to freak out for a split second before I found my female balls and marched over. Garrett was here. To have lunch with my parents. Dear Lord, they were going to interrogate the hell out of me later.

Opening the door, I stepped back enough for his large frame to squeeze past. He looked like he was about to treat me to a sexy smirk when his eyes darted over my shoulder and noticed the other occupants in the room.

"Hey, Garrett," Jamie said, popping up next to me jack-in-the-box style.

"Hey, J-man, long time no see."

Jamie chuckled, looking at me with the orneriest face on the planet, silently saying, *See? It's fine.*

I sighed, putting my hand to Garrett's elbow and steering him farther into the house. "Mom, Dad, you remember my neighbor, Garrett."

His jaw tensed, a muscle popping, but he quickly plastered a smile to his face and stepped forward to offer his hand. "It's nice to see you again. Your grandson talks about you often."

That's all it took for my mother to melt. "Really? That makes me so happy."

My father took his proffered hand, giving it a solid shake before lowering himself back to the couch. "So, Garrett, you're in this same duplex, correct?"

"Yes, sir. In Madison terminology, we're wall neighbors."

My father chuckled. "Madison terminology. I like that."

Garrett turned away so only I could see his face and winked at me before striding off. I was still staring after him, blinking like an idiot, when my mother stepped next to me.

Together, we watched Jamie skip over to the kitchen to talk Garrett's head off while he started grabbing dishes from the cabinets to set the table.

"Wow."

"Yep," I agreed.

"You know, one might think he's been over for dinner a few times with how well he knows his way around your kitchen."

I flushed crimson. "The duplex is symmetrical. His kitchen is exactly the same, Mom."

"You know that from experience, do you?"

I twisted around, my mouth dropping open, but she'd already sauntered off, dragging my dad off the couch to head to the kitchen and help.

Lunch wasn't anything fancy, just simple sliders with salad, but as long as Garrett didn't go all caveman on it, there'd be plenty. I was a chair short, so Jamie and I shared one, each balancing on an edge as our elbows sparred for space.

"I talked to Brenden this morning. He called while we were at the fundraiser."

"Oh?" I asked, talking around a mouthful of lettuce. My brother wasn't a fan of talking on the phone, so I knew my mother had a point she was working up to.

She took another bite of her slider before she answered, putting her fingers to her mouth and giving me the universal sign for chef's kiss.

"He's going to visit for Christmas."

My fork froze halfway to my mouth. "Really? How'd you convince him to do that?" My brother didn't avoid us or anything, but his schedule was fluid and usually increased around the holidays, so he rarely made it.

She waved her hand. "He had some project get canceled so he decided it was a sign for him to finally make a trip out here."

I turned to Garrett, who was shoveling food in his mouth, listening intently. "Brenden is my older brother. He works in the film industry, so his schedule changes month to month. Makes it hard to plan trips."

My mother cringed. "Speaking of schedule changes, honey,

do you think Layla could hang out with Jamie tomorrow? We'll still have him over tonight, of course, but we got asked at the fundraiser to attend another event tomorrow, and it'd be hard to take him with us."

My stomach dropped. "She can't, she's performing at the farmer's market again." Shit. I couldn't take the day off, there was literally no one to cover for me for that shift, and it was payroll. It couldn't *not* be done.

"I'm sorry," she said at whatever expression was on my face before looking over to my dad, "Maybe we can—"

"I got him."

I turned to the man beside me, my mouth parted. "What?" I asked, even though he'd spoken clearly, and I'd felt every letter of the sentence echo inside my ribcage.

"I got him."

I shook my head, resting a hand on the muscles of his bicep and feeling the way they tensed underneath my fingers. "No, it's okay. I'll figure it out."

"I'm sure you could, just like you always do, but I want to. He and I can chill and battle it out on some games until Layla gets home."

"Oh my gosh, can I, Mom? Please?" Jamie begged, hopping up and down in his seat.

"You don't need to do that, Garrett," I said, unsure how to process his open willingness to help. He didn't even care that my parents were here and listening with rapt attention and bated breath to see if I'd relent.

"I want to, Maddie. Jamie's the coolest person I know, we'll have a great time."

I looked from his calm face to Jamie's puppy dog eyes and broke. Rubbing a hand down my face, I muttered, "I'm sure I'll regret this."

Garrett leaned over, patting me on the knee. "Only in the best way."

"All right, bud, you heard Grandma, take a quick shower and pack a bag. I'll drop you off on my way to work."

He groaned, falling backward onto the couch. "I don't get why I couldn't just leave with them now."

"Two reasons. One, because you need to shower your soccer filth off, and two, so you could hang out with me longer. It used to be you wanted to hang out with me."

He scrunched his nose like he found the idea utterly repulsive. "I think I'd rather take the shower."

I threw a pillow at his face, causing him to giggle and leap up, running for the bathroom.

"I'll get you back later, you little twerp."

Turning, my eyes met Garrett's. He was leaning against the bar, watching me with a loaded look on his face. I wasn't a hundred percent sure what it meant, but something about it had me swallowing, an equal mix of nerves and warmth building in my chest.

We stood there, staring at each other from across the room, the silence broken only by the sound of the shower clicking on and Rugsy re-adjusting the blanket she was curled under.

We hadn't been alone since the night we'd kissed, and if the look on his face was any indicator, he was thinking about it too.

I exhaled sharply, biting the inside of my cheek and pivoting away from him toward the living room. It wasn't messy since we'd stayed at the table the entire time, but I still walked around, fluffing pillows and organizing the shoes by the door. I didn't know what to say or how to feel about the tension in the air, the innate urge to grab him by his ears and eat his face.

Noticing I hadn't locked the door after my parents left, I walked over and twisted the deadbolt, telling myself to say something—anything—to break the heavy silence.

Feeling pressure on my neck, I whipped around, barely suppressing a curse. Garrett stood less than a foot away, looking down at me with that same heated gaze. Any words I might have said got stuck in my throat when he rested his hands against the door on either side of my head.

"I feel like we need to clear up a few things so we're on the same page."

I was effectively caged in on all sides, the chill of the door clashing with the warmth of his body. I struggled to find oxygen, convinced it'd all left the room. Dropping his head near the crook of my neck, he blew air along my skin, leaving a trail of goosebumps in his wake.

"So, I'm not supposed to fuck you with my eyes."

I shook my head, my cheek bumping into the side of his, while certain neglected parts of my body sparked to life with flying banners and fucking blow horns. With him this close to me, his scent filling my nose, I couldn't remember why I'd ever said that. He could eye-fuck me until I was a mess on the floor for all I cared.

"But you want me around?"

My head bobbed in answer. I wanted him around every damn day.

"Use your words, Maddie."

"Yes," I croaked, "I want you around."

"Why?"

"You're my friend."

"Friends." He hummed low in his throat. "And as friends, am I allowed to touch you?" His arms slid down the door, inching closer and closer to my body. I nodded again, my eyelids fluttering closed.

"How about kiss you?" All it would take was the slightest movement and our lips would touch. I could feel his breath mixing with my own, and it was intoxicating.

I pulled my lip into my mouth, biting down. There was a reason for no kissing, no touching. But fuck me, I couldn't remember what it was.

"Words, Maddie."

I could hear the smile in his voice, and like a dam, I broke. I lurched forward, slamming my body into his, and running my fingers through his hair. Gripping two fistfuls, I yanked his mouth to mine in a vicious kiss.

The second our lips touched, his hands were already clutching at my hips like they'd been on high alert, just waiting for the green light.

He gripped me tight, as if worried I'd disappear, but there was no need. I wasn't going anywhere. Refusing to breathe would be easier than denying this man. His body called to every part of my own in a natural, primal way, and I couldn't fight it.

I ran the tip of my tongue across his lips, and he opened for me, swirling and caressing in equal measures. It wasn't enough. My body was screaming and my mind silent for the first time in my memory. I pressed harder, imprinting him into my soul, and sucked his bottom lip into my mouth.

He groaned, lifting my leg and wrapping it around his waist as he shoved me back against the door and ground into me. Noises I didn't even know I could make were slipping out in breathy sighs across his mouth.

I released his hair and moved my hands down his body, allowing myself to feel every single muscle while he continued to rub against my center.

Giving my mouth one final sweep of his tongue, he pulled away, dragging his teeth across my jaw and down the column of my neck, sucking and licking as he went.

For the first time in my life, I sensed I could reach the brink, sensed I could shatter into a million pieces from a touch that wasn't my own. And the truth was he was barely even touching me, yet I could feel myself tightening, coiling up like a spring.

He was dry humping me in the middle of my living room with the lights on, against a cold door, and I could still imagine myself screaming out his name.

I gripped his shoulders, fully intending on hiking up my other leg so I could straddle him koala-style. I needed him to take me to my room, and I needed it now. Consequences be damned. But the second my fingers curled around his sexy ass trapezius muscles, the door to the bathroom opened.

Instead of staying where I was or shoving Garrett back, or doing literally anything else, my brain chose option Z.

Squeaking like a mouse in a trap, I dropped straight to Garrett's feet right as Jamie stepped out into the hall. My ass hit the ground, the impact reverberating through my tail bone all the way up my spine. I winced, raising my head only to get an eyeful of Garrett's thighs and the enormous bulge straining there.

"Mom? What are you doing?"

"*Jesus.*"

"You're doing Jesus?"

Garrett's deep, hearty laughter hit my ears, and I tipped my head back to see him clamping a hand over his mouth, trying and failing to hold it in. The sight hit me straight in the gut, and I joined him, laughing my ass off, sprawled at his feet.

"I don't get it."

I rubbed my eyes with the pads of my thumb and pointer before looking toward my narrow-eyed child. "Nothing, bud."

He raised a brow, shaking his wet head and walking toward us. "Then why are you on the floor?"

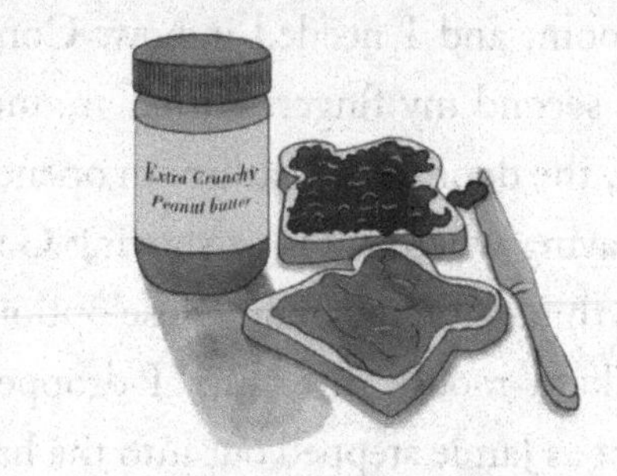

Chapter 23

WALKING OUT THE front door that morning was one of the hardest things I'd done in a while. Not because I didn't trust Garrett with Jamie. I did. Probably more than I should, given I'd only known him for a few months.

What was hard was admitting I needed help from someone I didn't consider family and actually *accepting* said help. Layla was the only one I'd ever allowed past my barriers in that way, but I'd known her my entire life.

Accepting help from someone, especially a man who clearly had interest in getting into my pants, was fucking hard. I obviously considered him more than just a friend, and I knew intrinsically, since I'd not only entertained the idea of him having Jamie, but allowed it, I trusted him more than my mind wanted to let on.

But no matter how hard I tried, how hard he worked to

prove his motivations were good, I struggled not to question them. Did he truly want to help and enjoy Jamie's company, or was he trying to butter me up so he could get in my pants, shatter my heart, and never speak to me again?

Okay, that was dramatic, but still. I clenched my hands around my steering wheel, banging my head against it a few times to loosen some brain cells from wherever they were hiding. I needed to get a grip.

I'd tried texting Garrett a few times during my shift to check on them, but after the first two times, he'd effectively told me to fuck off.

Me: How is everything??
Sugar Daddy: Same as the last 2 times you asked.
Me: What are you guys up to?
Sugar Daddy: Shouldn't you be working?
Me: I am.
Sugar Daddy: Then focus on your job and let me focus on mine.
Sugar Daddy: If Jamie beats me again because I'm distracted checking my phone, I'll spank the shit outta you.

I might have hyperventilated at that point. In fact, I was sure of it. That was the only explanation for why my next reply only further encouraged his line of conversation rather than ending it.

Me: …
Me: I'll run.

Sugar Daddy: Go ahead, baby, I'll enjoy the view.
Sugar Daddy: And then I'll spank you twice.

I was lucky I didn't crack my screen when I dropped my phone.

Hours later, I still didn't think my heart was pumping properly. I'd pulled open our thread when I'd clocked out of work to let him know I was on the way in case Layla still hadn't arrived, but I'd seen that text again and instantly closed out. Nope. I'd officially put away my Bad Bitch pants and replaced them with my Cowardly ones.

So now, here I was, parked in the driveway, beating my head on a steering wheel instead of walking into my house. Layla was home, her Miata parked right on the street in plain sight, but I had no idea if Garrett had left yet.

I thought about texting Layla and asking, but she was a conniving wench, and if he was there, she would one-hundred percent tell him I was outside hiding.

I glanced at the clock. I didn't have long before I'd have to head back out for my night shift. I needed to go inside and spend a few minutes with Jamie before I had to change and leave again.

I may or may not have opened the door slower than the drip of molasses. By the time I'd actually stepped through, Layla, Jamie, and both dogs were all staring at me from their curled-up positions on the couch. But no tall caveman in sight, thank God.

I dropped my purse to the ground, kicking off my heels and dragging my butt toward them, only to collapse on the floor. How was it my evening was only starting, and I was already emotionally and mentally done? It was nights like this that I was thankful I didn't have to try to focus on any schoolwork.

"Did you have fun today, bud?" From my position on the floor, the coffee table obscured my view of him, so I just posed my question in his general direction.

"It was awesome, he's got so many cool games, Mom. If we ever win the lottery, I want a PlayStation. Oh, and he made me a peanut butter and jelly sandwich for lunch with *crunchy* peanut butter! And he taught me how to change the air filter for the house because he said our landlord is an individual unworthy of the oxygen occupying his lungs."

I blinked, rolling my head back to look at the ceiling and laughed. "Of course, he did."

The man shared a love of crunchy peanut butter, one of the few things Jamie liked that I refused to buy. It was game over. I stood no chance against the power of crunchy peanut butter fans.

Layla leaned her weight on the coffee table, hovering her head over me. Her hair cascaded down and tickled my face as she spoke. "Do I even want to know what's got you all giggly down there?"

I groaned, kneading my fingers into my temples. Between Garrett and Jamie, I was pretty sure men were going to be the death of my sanity.

"You really don't."

Jamie's voiced popped up behind her, "I bet it's because I was talking about Garrett."

"Ooo," she sang, lifting an eyebrow at me. "Is that so?"

"Yep," he said. "I'm pretty sure I caught them kissing the other day."

I shot up into a sitting position, narrowing my eyes at the

little devil who was conveniently hiding behind Sadie.

Layla's expression was so giddy, all she needed was a bag of popcorn to complete the package. "Kissing in plain sight, Mads? Tsk-tsk."

Jamie pretended to gag, holding a finger to his open mouth. "It was gross. He kissed her so much, she fell to the ground."

The gleam in Layla's eyes had me up off the ground and booking it to my room.

Someone was watching me. I could feel it. I'd always been able to, like a sixth sense guarding my back. The hair on my neck would raise, and a cold sweat would slither down my spine, conflicting with the sweat accumulating along my hairline. It'd always been my warning that Aaron had followed me somewhere and there was hell to pay.

I twisted around for what felt like the tenth time in an hour, eyes darting to every corner of the restaurant trying to find the source of the feeling. I wouldn't put it past Aaron to have watched my house and followed me to discover where I worked. It's how he operated. For him, lines were meant to be crossed, rules broken.

But as much as I trusted that sixth sense, the one that'd never been wrong, my gut said it wasn't him. Aaron never hid. He'd always *wanted* me to know he was there, wanted me to know he was angry so I could stew in the knowledge I'd disappointed him again.

So, I brushed the feeling away, rubbing my hands up and

down my arms and heading toward the bar to get a new round of margaritas for a Girls' Night group at one of my tables. They were loud as hell and there was a good chance they'd be too tipsy to tip well, but they were having the time of their lives.

"Hey, Nate, think you can throw together a good nonalcoholic drink for me to go with those?"

"What on God's poor, polluted earth for?"

"The designated driver for my table of women looks like she's contemplating lying in traffic. That level of friendship deserves a reward."

He laughed, turning to grab some pineapple juice and grenadine. "You got it, Curly."

The five dollars the drink cost me had been worth it, not just for the grateful smile it'd put on the poor woman's face, but also by the gracious tip she'd made sure to leave on the table. Sometimes it literally paid to be kind.

I finished clearing off their table when I felt it again. I whipped around, causing the customers next to me to glance my way, but again I saw nothing. I rubbed at the side of my face, feeling like I was losing my mind.

I snagged a coworker's arm as she walked past. "Hey, I only have two tables right now and they're both set for a while, so I'm going to step out real quick. Will you come find me if I get seated?"

"Sure."

Thanking her, I crossed the restaurant toward the bathroom, deciding to pee and splash some water on my face first.

I'd just wrested a paper towel from the finicky dispenser

when the bathroom door creaked open behind me. I stepped to the side to free up the sink and turned, my eyes landing on the male body standing right inside the doorway. I jerked back, whacking my shoulder against the dispenser.

My heartbeat picked up until I was sure it was visible, and my breathing became unsteady. I knew someone had been watching me. Where in the hell had he been this entire time? His tall ass, Henley-wearing hunk of a body wasn't exactly easy to hide.

Squeezing the paper towel like a stress ball, I tried to clear the lump in my throat. "Jesus, what is up with you and scaring the shit out of me? A man your size has no right to move as silently as you do."

Garrett tilted his head, slowly taking me in.

I swallowed. "You're giving me sex eyes again."

He smirked, removing his hands from his pockets and rubbing one against the shadow covering his jawline. "On a scale of one to ten, how creepy would it sound if I told you I came to watch you work?"

"A solid ten."

He took a step forward. "What if I said I came to watch you work because I couldn't stand the thought of going an entire day and night without seeing you?"

Oh God. Oh God, oh God. "That'd drop it to a six or seven, maybe," I said, mentally raising my arms and yelling hallelujah when the words came out steady.

Another step. "What if I told you the thought of waiting all night to taste you again was too much for me? That I was going out of my mind remembering what it was like to sink my teeth into that perfect lip of yours while I pulled it into my mouth."

I inhaled, but it was shaky and did nothing to settle the tingles that had erupted, centering in a very specific spot. "Three."

He was directly in front of me now, and I was very aware that at any point someone could walk in and see him practically pinning me to the wall. Instead of causing me to panic as it should have, the knowledge only seemed to spur on my arousal, allowing it to practically take over.

"And if I told you I'm half-tempted to sit you on that counter, cover your mouth, and prove to you you're meant to be mine, one thrust at a time?"

"I'd probably be fired."

He dipped a single finger into the collar of my shirt and pulled, and like a marionette, I moved with it. "Give me a number, Maddie."

A number? I couldn't breathe, let alone math.

His hand rose, curling around the side of my throat. Not squeezing, just resting while his thumb gently pressed on the underside of my chin. "You can pretend all you want, baby, but I know you feel this too."

He ran his thumb up my chin and glided it over my bottom lip, popping it out from the cage of my teeth. "Your body gives you away, and I can't resist it."

He closed the small distance between us, placing a soft kiss to the corner of my mouth, then the other. His teeth gently gripped my lip, and the moan I released was long and husky.

His reaction was instant. He swallowed the sound, one hand cupping the back of my head while the other snaked around to grip my ass.

He kissed me roughly, passionately, stealing my breath while gifting me his own. I never wanted it to stop, wanted to live in the moment forever, but just as quickly as he'd began, he pulled back. His eyes were hooded, and his chest rose and fell rapidly against me.

He didn't say a word as he leaned forward one last time and brushed a featherlight kiss to my forehead. And then, just like that, he was gone.

I watched him go, incapable of moving for several minutes, drowning in the feral lust still clawing at my core. I couldn't believe I'd allowed that to happen, but at the same time, my eyes were begging the door to open. For him to come back.

By the time I left the bathroom, I'd been seated. Twice. The waitress I'd asked to find me had checked for me in the back, but apparently that's as far as her detective skills had gone. Which was probably a good thing considering what she might've seen if she'd found me.

I walked the entire restaurant in between orders, looking for my neighbor turned stealthy stalker, but he was nowhere in sight. If it weren't for my raging woman boner, I'd have thought I'd imagined him.

Watching a new group scoot into one of my booths, I tipped my head back and sighed, ignoring Nate chuckling behind me. I was so ready for this night to be over. I reached into the right pocket of my apron, searching for a pen since my last table stole my other, when a wad of something at the bottom touched my fingers.

Weird. I kept my cash and notepad in the left pocket, and

only my pens on the right. I frowned, pulling it out. It was a roughly folded piece of paper. I had no idea what it might contain, but only one person had been close enough to me to put it there.

There were only four words, written in a familiar, scratchy handwriting.

Stay with me tonight.

My second nemesis of the night stood before me, firm and unyielding, deliberately blocking my path and laughing at me. I glared at it, grinding my teeth. I'd kick it if I didn't think I'd shatter my kneecap. Motherfucker.

My first nemesis had been easier to conquer. I'd gone home immediately after work, skipping my usual drink with Nate, never more thankful that both Layla and Jamie were already in bed.

I'd tip-toed through the house, conscious of the still-sleeping mutt curled up in my bed. I'd immediately started a slew of soft words when I'd entered my room so she'd know it was me, and that's when nemesis number one made its appearance.

My clothes.

What was I supposed to wear? Was I supposed to dress sexy because we both knew what would happen if I showed up? Or was that too obvious? Was I supposed to wear what he always saw me in, sweatpants and fuzzy socks? Or was I supposed to show up in my work clothes?

I glanced down, lifting my shirt and giving it a whiff. Yeah, no, that wasn't happening. I smelled like a basket of buffalo fries dipped in ranch. Delicious? Absolutely. But not the kind of delicious I was going for.

When a man went down on you and peeled your clothes off, you wanted him to say you smelled like flowers, not fucking spicy garlic.

In the end I opted for a quick shower without washing my hair, and my normal sleep clothes—minus the fuzzy socks. Those weren't sexy no matter how you wore them.

And now here I was, standing on Garrett's porch, freezing my ass off in a thin top and pajama bottoms, staring at his door. I couldn't open it or even knock. I'd tried. I had ants crawling all over my nervous system, and my limbs were apparently made of pure lead.

In essence, I was nervous as hell. So, since it refused to open sesame, I was stuck glaring twin holes in it, cursing it like the little bitch it was.

It was the vibration of my phone that finally had me dragging my eyes away from my opponent.

Sugar Daddy: Why are you glaring at my front door?
Me: It's mocking me. Why are you spying on me through it?

The offending door was pulled open, and the way my mouth instantly dried had me silently apologizing to it, begging it to shut again. Standing right on the other side, giving me the strongest fuck-me gaze I'd ever been on the receiving end of, was Garrett. Sweatpants hanging off his hips, bare feet on the floor, white t-shirt wearing, messy-haired Garrett.

I never stood a chance. I shivered, toying with the hem of my top. "I came."

Hazel eyes flashed, and his smirk grew, but he said nothing as he stepped to the side and ushered me in. I paused right inside the entry, crossing my arms over my chest and looking around while he latched the door behind me.

"It's a little trippy to see my house, but backwards." It was almost an exact mirror of my side, but more bachelor-y. No kid blankets or dog beds, no frames on the walls or stacks of used coffee mugs. It was depressingly empty of life, and I suddenly understood why he'd once said my side felt homey to him.

"What do you use the other two rooms for?"

He circled around toward the bar. "One is a guest room, and the other has my gym equipment."

Ah. That made sense given the muscles I'd previously felt up. "I don't think I ever asked, but what made you decide to rent a duplex instead of purchasing your own place?"

"I'd always lived on the Marine base in the past. I've never purchased a home before. Doing so felt too permanent, and I wasn't sure I wanted to stay."

I nodded, passing his couch and running my hand along the top. Fear of permanent decisions was something I could empathize with.

"Will you stay?" he asked.

Twisting to look at him, I frowned. "Like tonight or in this state in general?"

Another smirk. "The latter feels a little heavy, so let's go with the first."

I decided to grow a pair and ask him straight up. "Look, Garret, are you sure you want this? To cross this line? Like, I'll understand—"

"Baby, I've wanted you from the second you straddled my lap and swallowed half my beer in one go. Just the image of your lips wrapped around that bottle has got me off on numerous occasions."

I huffed a quiet laugh. "You didn't even like me then."

"My body knew what my head hadn't realized yet."

I stalled again, clasping my hands in front of me. "What if it ruins our friendship? You'll be stuck seeing me all the time."

"Maddie?"

I looked up hesitantly. Regardless of my rambling fears, I didn't know what I'd do if he agreed. I wanted him. I wanted his body, his mind, his heart, all of it. I wanted him so badly I thought I'd explode without him.

"Unless you'd prefer the floor over my bed, I suggest you get your ass in my room."

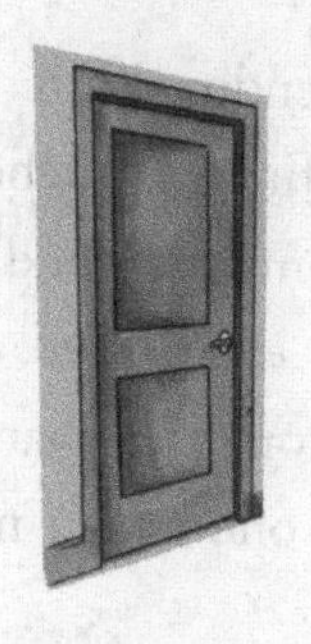

Chapter 24

THE CLICK OF the door echoed out into the silent room, reverberating through my body. I could feel each pump of my heart as it raged against its cage.

I couldn't yet bring myself to raise my head, nervous of what I'd see in his face and how it'd compare to the way he might look at me after. Instead, I watched his bare feet slowly eat up the space between us.

"Eyes on me."

My head snapped up, eyes locking on his with that single demand. When his voice lowered to that deep, gravelly tenor, I wasn't sure there was a thing I could deny him. And by the smirk curling at the corner of his lips, I was fairly certain he knew it.

"There you are."

He grazed his hand across the side of my jaw, the feel of his calluses against my skin sending butterflies loose in my stomach. He continued until his fingers reached the back of my head, tangling into the curls at my nape and gently pulling.

My head tipped up even more, throat bared to him, my mouth forced to part from the sharp angle. His other hand gripped my hip, and in one rough movement, he yanked me flush against him.

"Caveman much?" I tried to joke, resting my hands on his chest, but I could feel his hardness against my stomach, and my voice betrayed me, coming out airy and quiet.

"You'd be surprised how primal my thoughts are when it comes to you." He lowered his head enough to brush his lips across my forehead, down my nose, pausing over my mouth.

I licked my lips, wanting to close the distance, but unable to move my head. "That sounds a little dominant."

He still didn't kiss me, and I swore I could feel my sanity fissuring. But then the hand on my hip relaxed its vicious grip and traveled down the curve of my ass. Slowly. Like he was memorizing the shape. "You'd like it that way, wouldn't you?"

I couldn't immediately form an answer, my mind zeroing in on the hand that was now tracing small circles over the fabric covering my upper thigh. "What way?"

"Rough."

I nearly combusted. Straining my neck, I again tried to move my head forward, but he held firm, his smile growing sinful. His fingers danced back and forth across my leg, teasing me but never venturing farther up. I rotated my hips, grinding against him, seeking any form of pressure.

He *tsk*ed me, lightly pinching the inside of my thigh. "Use your words."

I glared up, curling my fingers and digging my nails into his chest. "Yes, I'd like it rough."

"Yeah?"

He lifted that teasing hand, slipping it past the waistband of my pants and gliding down my center with the firm pressure I needed.

"I believe it, because something tells me an independent woman like you wouldn't appreciate being treated as though you were breakable."

He said the words right as his fingers slid just low enough to discover the obvious arousal saturating the fabric of my panties.

A guttural groan escaped his lips a split second before they smashed against my own. It wasn't a gentle kiss or even a heated one. He devoured me, simultaneously plunging his hand past that final barrier to press his fingers to my clit.

I bucked, my mouth parting on a moan, and he didn't waste a second to thrust his tongue in. Using the grip on my hair, he tilted my head, placing me exactly where he wanted while lowering his fingers to slide through me.

He murmured filthy words against my lips, and I felt them everywhere, setting me even more on fire. I ground harder against him. I'd never been this close to an orgasm with someone other than myself before, and I craved the experience. I *needed* it, more than I needed air.

He paused, his fingers resting against my entrance and his

lips hovering over my own, sharing breath. His eyes searched mine, and for a moment I thought he was going to pull away from me.

My forehead creased, confusion warring inside me, wondering what I did wrong. But then he barked out a sharp, "Fuck," and plunged a thick finger inside me.

I cried out as he rocked his hips into me, slowly easing in a second finger until both were buried to the knuckles. "You're so tight, Maddie."

The sensation burned, but only for a moment before it was shadowed by the rapidly rising pleasure he was coaxing out of me. I didn't know it could be like this with another person. My body felt like it might burst if I didn't have more of him.

The man still had control of my head, so I reached up, grasping his face with both hands and yanking him to my mouth, practically attacking him in my impatience. He responded enthusiastically, his tongue dancing in my mouth in time with his fingers as he stroked them in and out of me.

We stood there for what could've been minutes, hours, days, eating at each other's mouths as he finger-fucked me. Both of us pressed forward like we wanted to climb into the other's skin, and even then, we'd still never be close enough.

"You need to get control of yourself, baby," he said when he finally pulled back. His eyes roved over my face, taking in every minute detail while he continued his relentless torture, leisurely working his fingers all the way out and circling my clit before sinking back in.

I moaned, eyes still closed, clawing at his chest. "Why?"

He tightened his grip on my hair until I opened my eyes and met his hungry gaze. Swiping hard up my center, he jerked his hand out of my pants and placed both fingers in his mouth, sucking them clean.

"Because I'm not down there yet, and you're wasting it all."

"Oh God."

Releasing my hair, he moved to wrap his fingers around my jaw and leaned down to whisper in my ear.

"That's your one freebie. Once I have you naked, the only name I want to hear you call out is mine. You need to send up a prayer when I make you scream? I want it to be to me."

He slammed his lips onto mine in another scorching kiss, both of his hands skimming down my sides to grip my waistband. I whined when he took his mouth away, but the sound turned into a gasp when he dropped to his knees, taking my bottoms and panties to the ground in one fluid motion.

I was completely bare from the waist down, and he wasn't just seeing me naked, his face was literally inches away from said nakedness. I tensed, squeezing my thighs together to hide, but that only earned me a stinging slap to my ass cheek.

"Ow!"

He curled his hand behind my left knee, lifting my foot out of my rumpled clothes and resting my leg over his shoulder. Leaning his head back, he unabashedly took me in, his eyes darker than I'd ever seen them before. He seemed to be trying to implant the image of me in his mind, and I'd never felt more exposed—or more turned on in my life.

He circled my clit with his thumb, watching the movement

with the same intensity he did everything. "This is mine."

Circling one final time, he slid his thumb down through me until it met up with my ass, spreading my wetness around the rim before retreating back up. I might have been vividly hallucinating at that point.

"The next time you get wet over me, you better sit on my fucking face until I feel my soul leave my body and tap out." Then he was on me.

The first touch of his tongue had my spine arching, and when he swirled the tip around my clit, my head fell back as I panted. By the third thrust of it inside me, I wasn't just seeing stars, I was mapping out entire fucking constellations.

Balancing on only one leg, I sank my fingers into his dark hair, fisting it at the roots to steady myself. He didn't seem to mind the pain. If anything, he sped up.

He plunged two fingers back inside me as he focused in on my clit, licking and sucking at it until my senses mixed and I was hearing smells and seeing tastes. "Oh fuck, I'm going to—"

"Do it." His words vibrated against my core, and then he sucked *hard*.

I broke, clenching around him and yelling out his name among a multitude of incoherent sounds. He never stopped his ministrations, letting me ride his face like an animal as I fell apart.

"Holy shit."

"Baby, that wasn't even the half of it." He gave me one final lick, all the way up with the flat of his tongue, before standing and cradling my head.

I looked into his eyes, and the desire and affection looking back at me made me feel powerful. I reached up and encircled my hands around the wrists framing my face. "Then give me the rest."

His nostrils flared, and he brushed a soft kiss to the corner of my lips. "I want to. I want you so badly I could saw through these goddamn pants, but I need to make sure you understand something first."

"Okay."

"In here, I will take control because you and I both know you need it that way in order to turn your mind off. I will learn your body better than my own and have you writhing and begging me for more."

He caressed his thumbs across my cheeks and down the line of my jaw to press on my chin, forcing my lips apart. "But outside this room, Maddie, you fucking own me. I will worship the very ground you walk on if you'll only let me."

Closing the distance, he kissed me, and it was gentle and thorough. He molded himself to me until I could taste, not just myself on his tongue, but his soul.

He only removed his mouth long enough to drag my top up over my head, then he was back on me. His hands were moving up and down my back, pulling me in and pressing my stomach against the hard bulge fighting against his sweats.

Diving under his shirt, I ran my fingers up his torso, feeling every ripple of muscle as I made my way up to his chest. I raised his shirt high enough to catch a glimpse of his nipples, waiting for him to lift his arms and allow me to remove it all the way.

But he didn't budge, the control freak apparently taking his claim seriously.

I pouted. "I want to feel you."

When he still didn't move, I pressed an open kiss to the divot between his pecs, darting my tongue out to taste his skin. He shuddered, his hands lowering to my bare ass.

I refused to be the only one naked. Continuing to kiss his skin, I worked my way across the muscle until I reached my goal. Digging my nails into his sides, I twirled my tongue around his nipple before pulling it sharply into my mouth.

He lost it. Reaching an arm back, he yanked his shirt over his head, tossing it to the ground. I raked my greedy eyes over his skin, trying and failing, to fight back my smile.

"Keep giving me that shit-eating grin, and you'll be eating something else in a minute."

My core turned molten, wetness pooling between my thighs, begging for what he could give me. I pressed them together, not to hide this time, but to provide me with any form of friction.

"Promise?"

His hands came around to squeeze my ass, and he lifted me, wrapping my legs around his waist and kissing me fiercely as he carried me to the bed. I thought he'd lay me down and crawl over me, but he didn't. Instead, he tossed me on the mattress like a bag of flour, and a startled laugh burst out of me.

His smirk disappeared, and he stared down like he'd just seen a glimpse of heaven. "That fucking sound."

His fingers moved to his waistband, and I watched hungrily

as he shoved both his sweats and boxers down his legs.

My eyes were riveted to his hard length, watching it rise to attention as his clothing dropped to the floor. He was huge. Granted, I didn't have a whole lot of experience to compare him to, but even I knew he was a fucking magnificent specimen.

A bead of liquid appeared at his tip, and I instinctively licked my lips, wondering if this was how he'd always make me feel. Because seeing him stand there at the foot of his bed, gloriously naked, I couldn't imagine a day when I wouldn't want him.

I moved up onto my knees, crawling toward him until I was an inch away. I sat back on my heels, staring up at him under hooded eyes and wrapped my hand around his base.

His eyes fluttered closed, and he groaned deep in his chest, rocking his hips and slowly fucking my fist. "Tighten your—yeah, just like that, baby, damn that feels good."

"I promise my mouth will feel even better," I said, swallowing back my nerves. I'd never been one to talk dirty in the bedroom, and I'd definitely never *wanted* to give a blowjob before. But the way Garrett touched me and looked at me made me feel sexy and alive.

I wanted this man in my mouth, wanted to make him see golden gates and hear trumpets. Honestly, he could thrust deep enough to gag me, and I'm pretty sure I'd thank him.

His eyes snapped open, and his mouth parted. I shifted back, bending my head down, but he stopped me with a firm hold on my jaw.

"I told you, you're not in charge in this room, Maddie. You

want my cock buried in your throat, you're going to do it my way."

I sucked on my teeth, narrowing my eyes at him and squeezing his shaft. With all the mock sweetness I could muster, I purred, "Yes, sir."

One second, I was kneeling on the bed, hand wrapped around him, and the next I was on my back. Gripping my legs with both hands, he spun me until my feet were in the center of the bed and my neck rested over the edge, my head tipped upside down.

Positioned as I was, his heavy length hovered right above my nose, and I found myself second-guessing my brazen behavior. I didn't have a sensitive gag reflex, but I'd also never tried to take on Garrett Rowe's monster dick before.

"If you keep looking at me like that, I'll cum all over your face before I've even passed your lips."

"Now wouldn't that be a shame." I grinned up at him, or at least I tried to. I couldn't see anything else with his cock in my face.

"Open your mouth."

I thought about demanding he say 'please', but I wanted it just as badly as he did. I opened wide, wrapping my arms around him and gifting myself with two handfuls of his rounded ass.

He pushed into my mouth, inch by glorious inch. Sealing my lips around him, I teased him with the tip of my tongue as he slowly eased in and out. His groans mixed with his salty, musky taste like a damn aphrodisiac.

"Good girl, fuck, that's it."

By the tremor in his legs, I could tell he was struggling to hold himself back, but he maintained his steady movements, and that just wouldn't do. I swirled my tongue around his tip, sucking hard, and he jutted forward, picking up speed.

Lying with my head resting on the edge of the bed, I was completely at his disposal as he fucked my mouth in earnest. I couldn't pull back or control the speed, I could only open my throat and enjoy the ride.

He leaned over me, continuing his erratic thrusts, and reached out to roll one of my nipples between two fingers, pulling ever so slightly. My nipples had always been incredibly sensitive, and I moaned around his shaft.

He moved to my other nipple, and I was a writhing mess. I'd have been begging him to fuck me if I didn't have a mouthful. Wanting to set him on fire the same way he was doing to me, I reached up, cupping his balls and giving them a light squeeze.

He bucked, ramming sharply down my throat and making me gag. "*Fuck.*"

He pulled out, my lips making a popping sound at the sudden break of suction. He moved so fast, my mouth was still agape when he cradled one large hand behind my neck and the other under my ass and launched me to the center of the bed.

He hovered the bulk of his body over me and stole my lips in a possessive claim. He plundered my mouth, sucking and sweeping like he'd lost all control. He maneuvered himself until he prodded at my entrance, and only then did he pull back to look down at me.

"Tell me you want this."

"I want this."

"Tell me you want me."

I hesitated momentarily, scared to admit it out loud. But in this case—in a purely physical sense—I felt safe admitting at least that truth. "I want you."

He pushed in an inch, teasing. I wiggled, lifting my hips, desperate for him to fill me.

"Tell me you're mine."

I smacked at his chest. "Just fuck me already."

"No."

"Garrett, *please*."

He reached up, pinching my nipple and making my back arch, seeking the stimulation. "Tell me you're mine, Madison."

"Goddammit, I'm yours, I'm fucking yours!"

In one forceful thrust of his hips, he impaled me. I cried out, unprepared for the sudden stretch of my inner walls.

He let out a long, drawn-out groan, leaning his forehead on mine. "You feel so damn good, baby, you fit me like a glove."

I heaved in breaths, tensing up from the unfamiliar pressure. It wasn't anything more than a mild discomfort, and he stayed still, letting my body acclimate. "You could have done that a little less caveman-like."

"I told you, you're not breakable." He pinned me under his gaze. "You want to know why no other man could ever get you off? Because you've never been theirs. You've only ever been mine. Your pussy was fucking made to take me." He flexed his hips, driving his point home.

"And I'm going to spend the whole night proving it to you.

Tell me you're ready."

I nodded, probably looking like a bobble-head with my eagerness. "Yeah, I'm ready."

"Thank fuck." He pulled out slowly, watching my face for any sign of pain, and when I didn't give any, he drove deep, all the way to the hilt.

Some people had sex. Some made love. But Garrett? He fucked, and he fucked hard. His grip on my hips was bruising, and he slammed into me again and again in a punishing rhythm, obliterating the friendship zone into nothing but dust.

I writhed under him, apologizing for wrongs I'd done, promising anything under the sun, and begging him to please not stop, don't ever stop. He wrapped my legs more firmly around his waist and leaned forward to kiss what little brains I still had, out of my head.

He built that tingling up again, one grind, one thrust, one circle of his hips at a time. The pressure was almost too much to handle, and I wondered how I ever could have enjoyed sex before him. He played my body like an instrument, watching my face and adjusting his motions.

And just when I thought I couldn't take any more, his fingers found their home on my clit, circling with quick, firm pressure until I hit oblivion, clawing at his back and biting his shoulder to smother my scream.

Before the sensation had fully disappeared, he was flipping me onto my stomach and raising my hips until I was face down and ass up for him. With two hands gripping me, he leaned forward and swiped his tongue through my entrance before rising and slamming back into me.

"Bite down on the comforter."

He didn't have to tell me twice. I'd barely buried my face into the bed when he moved, rutting behind me like a man unhinged. I curled my fingers into the blanket, holding on for dear life as he destroyed me in the best way possible. I'd begun to fear my body might actually give out when he suddenly pulled out and hot spurts landed across my lower back.

He'd pulled out.

Oh God, I hadn't even thought about that. Me. *Me*. It hadn't even crossed my mind to ask him about protection or—

A hand slid up my spine, brushing the now-frizzed curls off my neck. "I can feel you freaking out from up here, baby. I know we got a little carried away, but I swear to you, I'm clean."

I exhaled jaggedly, what in the hell had I been thinking?

He lowered my hips to the bed and pressed a quick kiss to the center of my back before disappearing into his bathroom. He returned a minute later with a damp cloth and gently cleaned me up before pulling me into his arms.

Neither of us said a word. I could tell he wanted to, but he must have known I was at my mental limit for the moment because he just tucked us in and curled his naked body around my own. Holding me close.

I was panicking, yes, but not over what he thought. Having unprotected sex without an adult conversation about it first was irresponsible and stupid, but I was on birth control, and he'd pulled out. I also trusted Garrett. I trusted that he never would have touched me if there was even a chance he was unclean.

No, I was panicking because of the level of love I felt for this man. I wanted to give him my heart, bruised and battered as it was, and the thought of giving the last remaining piece away without the guarantee it would be safe was terrifying.

I wasn't sure if I was brave enough to risk it. So, I burrowed closer to him, desperate to enjoy the last dregs of euphoria, basking in the feel of his hands running up and down my skin.

In case it was the only time it happened.

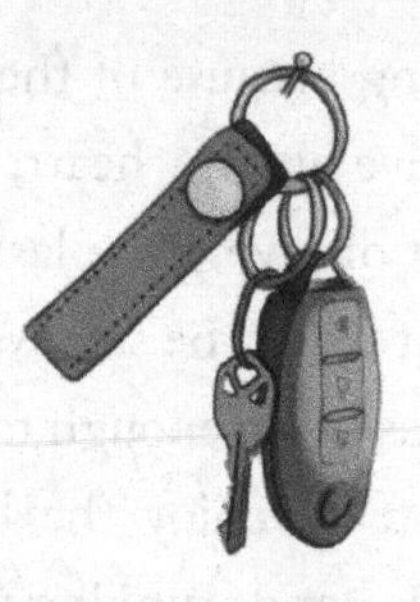

Chapter 25

WHOEVER FIRST DECIDED alarm clocks needed to be decked out with mini foghorns was the devil. The sound was sharp and loud in my ear. I stirred, grumbling and squeezing my eyes shut.

Wait.

My alarm was set to the radio, not ear-splitting beeps. I shot up, eyes punching open to dart about a room that wasn't mine. I was at Garrett's. I'd fallen asleep at Garrett's. Oh fuck. Oh fuck, oh fuck, oh fuck.

Fingers brushed down the length of my spine. "Calm down, baby, it's fine. I set the alarm for five, you're not late."

Getting to work on time was vitally important, but not at all what was on my mind. I needed to get home before Jamie woke up and noticed I was gone. I needed to shower, and chug an entire pot of coffee, and get my shit together, and *oh my fucking God.*

The groan I emitted was loud and positively indecent. Garrett's hands had come to rest on my shoulders, and he was kneading them in a way that might have been more pleasurable than his touches from the night before. Okay, that wasn't true, but holy magic fingers.

"You're so tense, Maddie. It'll be all right, it's not like you live far. We can go over there as soon as you're ready."

He was right, I knew he was right, but the thought of Jamie finding out I'd stayed here prevented me from relaxing. Garrett's thumbs slid down to massage my lower back, and that had me straightening to a rod. I was naked. I was butt ass naked.

Un-pretzel-ing myself from him, I leapt off the bed, crossing my arms over my chest as my head whipped left to right, searching for my clothes.

"Maddie."

I ignored him. Ignored his cute nickname and sexy morning hair. If I looked at him, I'd melt like I always did, and I'd never get out the door. In the span of one night, I'd had unprotected sex and slept at a man's house—regardless of how close it was—and didn't think twice about setting an alarm, myself. Not only could I have been late to work, but I would've left Layla to handle getting Jamie to school.

Finding my shirt, I snatched it up, roughly shoving my head through. This was why I didn't date. I needed structure, I needed boundaries and rules. I wasn't sixteen anymore, I couldn't be this irresponsible.

"Maddie, look at me."

"I can't, I need to go. I need to shower and get ready and get Jamie to school."

"I'll help you, just slow down."

He lowered his long legs to the floor, and I twisted farther away, refusing to allow myself to indulge in his deliciously naked form. "I don't need help; I just need to find my damn pants."

A heavy sigh sounded behind me. "Maybe I'm wrong, but that sounds like you could use a little help then."

"No, I don't," I snapped. I cringed, hating myself for taking out my anxiety on him. It wasn't his fault I was here. I'd walked over on two very willing legs. But I had a tendency to get angry as a defense mechanism when I was emotional.

"You're overreacting a little bit, don't you think?"

I didn't reply, finally spotting my underwear and pants near the door and charging for them. How did I explain that this scenario was exactly what I'd feared? That this was one of the reasons I'd tried to hold him at a distance?

I'd spent my entire life giving up things for other people, and the thought of depending on someone, of falling in so deep that I forgot about my responsibilities, scared me.

I yanked my pants up, already aiming for the door when a hand wrapped around my bicep.

"Goddammit, Maddie, wait a minute. Let me get dressed, and I'll help you."

I turned to him, blinking back my shame and the burning in my eyes. "I don't need your help; I just need to go home."

He'd only had a chance to slip on boxers, and he was standing there staring at me with a look of determination. But underneath, I sensed a sliver of disappointment, and my heart twisted.

"I know you don't. You could take over the world without a

lick of help, and I'd watch from the sidelines, rooting you on, but that doesn't mean you don't deserve it. You're making excuses so you can tuck yourself back into your shell. Don't do that, don't act like last night didn't happen."

A tear slipped free, and I dashed it away angrily. I hated that I cried when I was overwhelmed. "Last night did happen, and it was amazing, Garrett. But I can't be the type of person to have an unplanned sleepover without even thinking about the child I have to get to school in the morning."

I swiped another tear away as they fell faster, forcing myself to maintain eye contact even though it was killing me. "I can't do this; I can't be the person who puts a man and a relationship before myself or my kid again. Especially when you have so many reasons to walk away."

He pulled on my arm, drawing me in closer, and placed his hands on my cheeks. "I'm not going anywhere, Maddie. I want you; I want everything about you, the good parts, the bad parts, and the annoying as fuck parts, I want it all."

I shook my head, disbelieving. "What if the bad parts outshadow the good ones?"

"I'll still want you."

"You say that, but you're not thinking it through. My shit isn't going to disappear the moment we're official. What if Aaron comes around again? That's drama you don't need in your life."

He snorted. "Trust me, he won't. But I'd still want you."

For my own best interest, I decided to file that foreboding comment away to question later. "And then there's Jamie's sperm donor. Eventually I'll have to go to court and try to terminate his rights again, and that's even more drama, and money, and time, and—"

"I'll hold your hand every step of the way and still want you."

I sputtered; the man couldn't be serious. Even *I* didn't want to date someone like me. I pushed harder, determined to prove I was right.

"I can't do sporadic sleepovers with you because I have schoolwork, I can't go out to dinner on the weekends because I work, I can't go on trips because I have a kid to take care of. Hell, we haven't even been on a real date. I'm not girlfriend material, Garrett. I'm a walking disaster."

He chuckled, his eyes drifting to watch his thumb wipe a stray tear from my cheek. "Yeah, you are."

I hiccupped. "Then why are you pushing this? Why do you want it? Have you met you? You could have literally anyone."

His eyes clashed back with mine, heat and intensity staring into me. "Because I love you."

I reared back, my wide eyes blinking up at him like he'd told me the sky was made of cheese. "What do you mean?"

"I mean, I'm in love with you, and I'm done pretending I'm not."

"But you said you wouldn't catch feelings."

"I lied." He shrugged like we were talking about the weather, like he hadn't just decimated my world and every fabricated truth I'd been clinging to.

"And I know you feel it, too, even if you're not ready to voice it out loud yet. I know you love me, and I'm not going anywhere."

I squeezed my eyes shut, scoffing. Of course, I wasn't ready.

I hadn't even been able to voice it out loud in the privacy of my bedroom yet.

"So, what? You'll just wait for me to be ready? To get my shit and my life together? No matter how long it may take?"

"No, baby, I won't wait for you."

Even though it's exactly what I'd expected, what I'd pushed for, my heart still faltered, and my lungs seized up as I tried to step away.

He gripped me harder, digging his fingers into the side of my neck. "Waiting indicates I'd willingly watch you walk away with the blind hope you'd come back. I won't do that."

He tilted my head back, forcing me to stand flush against him. "But I will follow you anywhere, baby. I'll run a never-ending race for you. Name the distance. I'll go at whatever speed you let me. I'll sprint, walk, or crawl to get to you. I will *never* give you up."

My heart was gone, my ribcage empty. I wasn't sure if it was currently a melted puddle at my feet or if it was now in Garrett Rowe's chest. All I knew was it was no longer mine. I placed my hands over his, holding them to my face. "You're insane."

"Probably."

I laughed, the sound broken and wet. Leaning forward with our hands still cradling my face, I rested my head on his chest. I soaked up the feel of his skin, and the way his body seemed to both tense and relax under my touch.

"Baby, I'm not asking you to forget your responsibilities or put me first. I wouldn't let you even if you tried. Which is why as soon as you get your head out of your ass, I'm going to go over with you and help."

I shuddered, breathing in his smell and analyzing my mental wall, or in his words, my shell. "Tell me again that you want this, Garrett."

"I want this."

I smiled against him, tearing that barrier down piece by piece with both hands. "Tell me you want me."

He leaned my head back so I was looking at him, and he smirked, fire licking around his irises. "I want you. I'll tell you every fucking day if you want."

Rising up onto my toes, I brushed a featherlight kiss to his lips. "Tell me you're mine."

"I'm yours."

His voice was low and thick, and it vibrated across my lips in a way I never wanted to forget. I wasn't ready to say those three words back yet, that final piece of wall loosened but still in place. But I wanted to work toward it. Together.

"I don't want you to run a never-ending race for me. I don't want to be the kind of woman who expects that. I refuse to do that to you."

His breath hitched, his hands clutching at me like after everything he'd just laid at my feet, he still worried I'd walk away from him. "What are you thinking then?"

"That maybe we can meet halfway."

Chapter 26

My FATHER THREW the ham at me.

Not on purpose of course, but intention didn't matter much when I was staring down at the splatter of carcass fluids on my breasts, dress, and feet.

One second he was raising it from the counter, and the next he was tripping and launching it at me. It'd barely touched the ground before he was kneeling, grabbing the greasy—probably still delicious—bundle, and turning it like it needed to be checked for injuries.

I hadn't moved a muscle, my arms still splayed out on either side of me. I was trying to decide if I should be offended by the outrageous cackling and snorts coming from my audience or laugh along with them.

My dad glanced from me to the ham, back to me. "Ten-second rule, right?"

Someone choked, and I looked over to see Layla fanning her face, wine dripping from her nose as my mother lurched across the table for a napkin.

Behind them, through the opening between my parents' kitchen and the living room, I could make out my brother and Jamie hunched over controllers, arguing over a game and completely unaware of what was happening.

Dropping my arms, I exhaled, blowing out my cheeks. I side-stepped over the sticky mess left on the floor and headed to the roll of paper towels on the counter.

"Don't worry, everyone, I'm fine. My boobs are still intact, and my dress is only semi-ruined, but I appreciate all the concern."

I yanked a few sheets loose, patting them over my chest, trying to do what I could with what I had. I couldn't be too mad about it; I would've laughed too. However, this dress really was one of my favorites, so I hoped it'd at least wash out.

"You know, if you wanted meat thrown at your breasts, you could have asked." The words were whispered over my shoulder from lips hovering a hair's breadth above my ear. It sent a shudder through me, and I couldn't help but arch my neck slightly even as I laughed.

"For shame, Garrett Rowe, we're at a holiday dinner."

"We could always leave, and I'd give you a different dinner." His hand slid between us, and I barely held in my yelp when he pinched my ass.

I reached back, whacking him on the thigh. "If you can't behave, I'll send you home without any dinner at all."

"As long as I get dessert when you get there." He leaned

down, stealing my laughter with a searing kiss before sauntering off to help my dad do who knows what with the rogue ham.

I cleared my throat, smoothing down the skirt of my dress and twisting around. Both Layla and my mother were watching me, amused smiles on their faces, and I was an instant tomato.

Ignoring them, I busied myself with finishing the last of the prep work to set the table, desperately hoping Garrett kept all his dirty jokes to himself during dinner.

Garrett and I had been seeing each other for a month now, but we'd agreed not to be anything official. We just saw each other almost every day, and on days I worked too much, he'd hang out with Jamie instead.

The longest we'd spent apart was the week he flew to California with Sarah and Harry to spend Thanksgiving with his mother. He'd invited Jamie and me to join, but I'd already promised Jim I'd work the holiday guard shift and had to decline. I regretted it every day he was gone.

But still, we'd agreed to no label, no serious commitment. Sure, he'd stared down Michael when the poor man had tried to catch me alone to talk. And sure, I was pretty positive I'd cut the tongue out of any woman who tried to hit on him, but regardless. We definitely weren't official.

I hadn't told him I loved him yet, even though the words hovered over my mouth every time I looked at him, and he hadn't repeated the sentiment to me since the first time. Even so, I doted on him every chance I got, and he fucked me like no one's business behind closed doors.

Not official…at all.

Garrett was careful what he said and did around Jamie, but

he considered me fair game in front of anyone else. It was after he'd set me on his lap and curled his body around me to block the wind during Jamie's last game that my parents had invited him to spend the holiday with us this year.

Fine…we might have been a tiny bit official.

Dinner had gone much better than the prep had. No one threw anything, nor did Garrett make any more comments for my mother and Layla to swoon over.

Luckily for me, they hadn't been able to see the hand he'd kept on my thigh almost the entire meal.

My brother and Garrett had hit it off quickly. The three-and-a-half men spent a good portion of the evening talking video games and new releases while us ladies indulged in a healthy amount of wine. It'd been one of the best evenings I'd ever had, ham stain and all.

We'd just finished cleaning up and dishing leftovers in to-go containers for everyone when I slipped away to the bathroom. I hadn't looked in a mirror since I left my house, and I had a feeling, between the wine and how often Garrett played with my curls, I probably looked a mess.

I stepped in, but barely finished turning the knob when the door swung back open, nearly taking me with it. I darted back, making room for the bulk slipping through.

He leaned against the door, shutting it behind him, and smirking at me all the while. "Hey."

"Hey."

"Fancy meeting you here."

"You almost hit me in the face."

He dragged me forward against his body, his hands sliding down my ass as his eyes sparked with a mischievous glint.

"On a scale from one to ten, how romantic would it be if I told you I wanted to whisk you away for the night?"

I cocked my head to the side, scrunching my face. "A four, given we can't do that, so you'd only be teasing me."

"What if I told you your parents asked me if they could have Jamie tonight to watch some Christmas movie that's on TV?"

My heart picked up, my pulse thrumming beneath my skin. They'd asked him instead of me for permission, as if they saw us as equal partners. As if they knew I trusted him to answer on my behalf.

"What if I want to watch the movie too?"

"We can do whatever you want, baby. But I was thinking we could swing by a coffee stand for hot chocolate and then drive through the ritzy neighborhoods to look at Christmas lights."

There was a kaleidoscope of butterflies inside of me. I might have floated to the ceiling if he hadn't had such a firm hold on my rear. "And after that?"

"I'll take you back to my side and make love to you as many times as needed to have you drenched and blissfully sated." His hands tightened, and then he was lifting me and setting me on the counter, my legs instinctively wrapping around him.

He stood pressed against my center, his large hands resting on my thighs. "Then after all of that, I'll revert to my stalker-like tendencies and watch you sleep while you're curled into me emitting those sweet, happy sighs I love."

My hand drifted between us, and I rubbed the heel of my palm along the erect length straining against his jeans. "What if I need something a little rougher to feel blissfully sated?"

"Then I'll shove your panties in your mouth to keep you from waking Layla next door and fuck you into oblivion anywhere and everywhere you want."

I might as well have been the sixth Great Lake with how my body reacted. His words brought back a slew of images that were best not remembered at a family gathering, but my mind latched onto them with filthy glee anyway.

Turned out, Garrett had a thing for sinking his fingers into me elsewhere while he fucked me from behind. The act would send him into a desperate frenzy, and he'd pound into me so violently I was pretty sure I'd learned a new language. By the devilish gleam in his eyes, I had a feeling it might be more than his fingers fucking me there tonight.

I squeezed my thighs around his waist, wishing we were already home. Snaking my fingers around his head, I brought his face down to me and demanded his lips. He readily obliged.

When we finally broke apart, it was only far enough for me to utter, "Nine," against his mouth.

He chuckled, letting his hands wander up my sides. "Damn, still only a nine? What would make it a ten?"

"Tell me you love me again."

His hands continued sliding over my ribs, and he smiled against me. "That's easy then. I love you, fuzzy socks and all."

My reply poured straight from my chest, no nerves, no second-guessing, no over-thinking. No wall. He was mine. And I'd only ever be his. "I love you, too."

His head reared back, and his hands shot up to grip my face and tip it. His chest rose and fell heavily against me, and his eyes were two glittering hazel pools.

"Say it again."

"I love you, Garrett Rowe."

He crashed his mouth to mine, sealing my words between us like he needed to taste them on his tongue. He spoke in between kisses, "Home first, then Christmas lights."

I giggled, pushing him back. "We both know we'll never get back out to view lights if we go home first."

Home. Because that's what it was, *our home*. Our belongings might have been separated by a wall, but it was only a wall. We'd yet to let those stand in the way.

"Fucking hell," he groaned, helping me off the counter and readjusting himself. He looked mildly in pain as he set his hand on the doorknob. "Meet me at my car in five minutes, or I'm coming to find you."

"Promise?"

He smirked. "Countdown's already started, little mama. I suggest you run."

I've never moved faster.

Epilogue

HEAVING FORWARD, I curled my spine, trying in vain to roll into a sitting position. I failed, flopping back onto the mattress when the round weight on my stomach was too much. I tried again, grumbling out a curse.

"Seriously, Garrett, I have to pee so bad, move!"

He laughed, a dimple peeking out at me from where his head laid on my torso. He wrapped his arms tighter around me and turned, snuggling his face down toward my lap.

"If I wet this bed because you won't get off me, I'm going to rub your nose in it like a dog."

He playfully bit my thigh and chuckled harder when I swatted him. "Learn to curb your wine intake when we have get-togethers, and you won't spend half the night emptying your bladder."

I shoved his head this time, kicking and thrashing my legs, wiggling them out from under his weight. I made it as far as a foot before his arms grew vice-like and he rolled, taking me with him. Stopping in the center of our bed, he pinned me beneath him, letting me feel a hint of his weight but holding the bulk of it off me.

A hand slid down my side, curling around one of my legs and wrapping it around his waist. "You know, a full bladder can heighten pleasure."

I scrunched my nose, pressing my palms against his chest. "Is that actually true?"

"I feel like we're in a prime position to find out." He rolled his hips, eliciting a groan from me.

"Garrett."

"Maddie." I could hear the smile in his voice.

The man had been mine for over a year now, and I couldn't get over how lucky I felt every day we'd been together. He still technically lived next door to us, but you wouldn't know it since he slept in my bed every night. I didn't mind it. I'd never get enough of him.

I was just as head over heels in love with him as I had been all those months ago. He treated me like a queen during the day and his own personal whore at night, and I'd never been so fucking happy in my life.

But I'd also stab him in the damn foot if he didn't get off me soon.

"You won't remember what pleasure is, if you don't extricate yourself from on top of me."

Another roll of his hips, firmer this time. "Baby, I'd love to see—"

Three quick raps hit my bedroom door. "Mom, Layla's home. She's waiting outside and said to hurry up if we want a ride."

"We're coming, bud!" I pinched the underside of Garrett's arm. "We're going to miss our flight, you giant ass caveman."

"There'll be another one if we do. My family can wait." He raised his arm, cupping the side of my face, and running a thumb along my cheekbone. Pressing his lips to mine, he whispered onto them, "Are you nervous?"

"About peeing all over myself? Yes."

He tugged on my earlobe. "About meeting my mother tonight."

I tilted my head, letting my eyes roam over his face, from the harsh cut of his shadowed jaw to the dark mess of his hair. "Not really. I made *you* like me. How much harder could it be?"

He smiled, finally shoving off me and helping me up. "She's going to love you. Now go pee before you make us late," he said, smacking me on the ass.

I was still glaring when I made my way into the bathroom. The man drove me crazy, absolutely batshit crazy. But I loved every moment of it because, crazy or not, he was everything Jamie and I needed.

Life before Garrett hadn't been perfect, but I'd come to accept it, and with his help, I'd finally stopped letting my past affect how I saw myself and my future. Life wasn't meant to be perfect. A candle couldn't change its shape without first burning.

I wouldn't have what I have, be the person I am, without my past.

I'd been a mother for almost ten years, and yes, eight of those years were really fucking hard, but what were eight years in the grand scheme of things? I'd take twenty hard years if it meant I got sixty good ones with Garrett after.

I washed my hands, thinking back to that Christmas I risked giving my heart to him. So much had happened since then. I'd graduated *summa cum laude*, gotten hired at a youth correctional facility as an intake coordinator, and quit every other job. I still had the dream of helping teenage mothers, but I was taking life one step at a time.

I no longer froze when my phone went off, worried who might be calling. I didn't check around corners wondering if someone like Rob might catch me unawares. I didn't work seven days a week, didn't stay up half the night studying, didn't miss out on Jamie's events, and didn't shy away from opening my soul to my boyfriend.

I still had people judge me for my history, especially with Jamie catching up to me in height, and the moms at school would never like me no matter how much Garrett threatened them, but I was doing better at not giving a shit. My little family was happy and that was all that mattered.

Happily ever after didn't always mean pregnancy and a diamond ring. Sometimes it also meant only working forty hours a week and discovering who I was as an adult and as a woman. Who I was as *Madison*, outside of who I was as a mother and a friend.

And I was okay with that. More than okay.

Even if the tungsten wedding band hidden in my suitcase said differently.

Walking out into my living room, I paused at the mouth of the hallway, watching my boys drag the suitcases to the door. Jamie's face was lit up while chest-deep laughter bubbled out of him at something Garrett had said. The love of my life reached over and ruffled Jamie's hair before glancing up and winking at me.

I might not need a ring for my happily ever after, but I did need Garrett Rowe, and tonight I was going to make sure he knew it.

Chapter 18½

Garrett

MADISON'S LUSH, PINK lips wrapped around the neck of my bottle, and she threw her head back, letting the liquid pour down her throat like a fucking siren sent to lure me straight to hell. I took in those lips, perfectly sealed around the bottle's mouth, took in the way her fingers held the base in a firm grip, and shuddered. She'd look fucking glorious swallowing my cock.

Her legs hovered over me, an inch or less from touching mine. The urge to grip her thighs and slam her ass down on my lap so she could feel exactly what she was doing to me was too much for me to bear. I lifted my hands, more blood rushing south at the thought of—

Riiing. Riiing. Riiing.

I groaned, lifting my head off the pillow and squinting my eyes at the small device that dared to pull me from sleep. I glanced at the clock next to it and cursed, rolling over. Whoever was calling at this hour could fucking wait.

What—or more accurately who—was waiting for me just on the other side of my consciousness was far too tempting to risk waking up any further than I already had. When the incessant ringing ended, I readjusted myself and sighed only for it to immediately start back up.

I flopped onto my back, patting my hand across the side table for my phone. I yanked on it, letting the charging cable fall to the floor with a dull *thunk*. If this was a drunk dial from Sarah, I'd put a damn snake in her car.

Caller ID: *Maddie*

I launched into a sitting position, my pulse already picking up even before I hit the answer button. It wasn't uncommon for Maddie to be up late studying, but she'd never called me before. That fact alone had me halfway to panicking by the time I raised the phone to my ear.

"Maddie?"

"Garrett!" The voice broke, hitting a higher pitch at the end of my name.

"Jamie? Is that you?"

"Garrett, he's here! He's here and he's angry and I'm scared."

I threw the comforter off my lap, twisting to lower my feet to the floor to stand. "Jamie, calm down. Who's there? Where's your mom?"

"*He has her!* Please, Garrett, he'll hurt her, don't let him hurt her. No, no, no, he's yelling now. *Please, Garrett!*"

The world stopped. Every feeling, every sensation, every thought I'd ever had frozen in time as I moved. I didn't feel my shoulder slam into the wall as I hurled myself out of my room. Didn't feel the bite of the air against my naked skin when I leapt from the porch, nor the loose gravel digging into the pads of my feet as I ran.

Nothing mattered but her. Getting to her and making sure she was okay. I'd barely made it up her steps when something crashed, and my heart left my chest. It shot straight through my throat, splattering across the door between us like blood on a blank canvas.

My fist wrapped around the knob just as I slammed my foot into the wood and kicked it open with every bit of desperation coursing through my soul.

Movement to my right caught my attention, and my veins turned to ice when my eyes latched onto the scene before me. The red-haired, stick of a man I'd met once before stood in their home. The same man who'd gotten in my face and sneered as he told me Maddie was his wife. The same man who'd been the cause of every record of pain in her drawer.

Aaron motherfucking Walsh, and he currently had his hand around Maddie's jaw.

My Maddie.

She was dressed in her pajamas, a sweater hanging loosely over her shoulders. Her thick curls were wild and untamed, framing her face and accentuating her wide brown eyes.

I was going to kill him.

The piece of shit went off, but I didn't take in a word. All I saw, all I heard, was motherfucking red. Like a bull after a flag, I was on him. The feel of his nose crunching under my fist was one of the most satisfying moments of my life, a fucking high I wanted to keep chasing. I wanted to do to him every single thing I knew he'd done to her. I wanted to make him beg.

I snatched him up from the ground, smashing my fist into his face a second time, but a voice behind me speared through my narrow-eyed vision. A voice that would reach me from the bowels of hell itself. I whipped my head to look at her, spotting Jamie standing in the hall, and immediately dropped the unconscious man.

"You all right, J-man?"

He nodded but didn't move.

"I'm proud of you." And I was. It took a lot of guts for him to call me, and I knew how hard it had to have been for him to not be able to help his mom. The kid was going to be one hell of a man one day.

His face relaxed at my words, and it was all I needed. Curling my arms under the man's shoulders, I dragged Aaron Walsh toward the door.

"What are you doing? Garrett!"

It took every ounce of determination in me, but I ignored her voice, continuing out and down her porch. I couldn't see her right now, not with this fucker's body between us.

She followed me, continuing to call out as I shoved his body in my backseat. I couldn't take it, couldn't take the goddamn despair in her voice. I knew, before she even uttered her next words, I knew she was about to apologize, and it tore me apart.

I leaned my head on my Nova, breathing in deeply. "Don't stand there and fucking compare me to him, Maddie. I am not him."

"What are you talking about, I'm not!"

The worst part was she truly didn't see it. She couldn't see the broken lens with which she viewed men. She was so used to the scratches and cracks; she couldn't remember what it was like to have clear vision.

The thought only made me angrier, and I lashed out, spearing her with verbal arrows because I wanted to fix it. Not fix *her* but fix everything that had ever been done to her, and I couldn't.

"This is a little more than fixing my dishwasher or cleaning my fence, Garrett. You have a body in the back of your car, and you're obviously upset with me. You won't even look at me."

Jesus, I was going to throttle this woman. I shoved off my vehicle and moved to her, pressing my body firmly against hers. I tangled my fingers into her hair, forcing her head back and ignoring how the act called to my baser instincts. How it made me want to pummel the waste of a man in my car, and then take Maddie home and fuck her until she forgot he ever existed.

I ripped more of my heart out for her, telling her exactly where I stood and what would happen if I looked at her a moment longer. I nearly convulsed when she responded by placing her hands on my chest, but I didn't give in.

"As long as that piece of shit is within arm's reach of me, I can't keep fucking looking at you, or tonight's story is going to have a completely different fucking ending."

I pulled away, swallowing a growl when her first words after that were to ask about her ex.

"He's not your concern," I snapped. And with that, I walked away, leaving her standing in the driveway. I knew exactly what I was going to do, and I sure as hell wasn't going to do it naked.

It was almost pitch black out, the surplus of trees around the park keeping most of the natural moonlight from seeping through. I parked as close to my goal as possible, the dirt path illuminated by a single, dull light pole.

Grabbing a half-empty water bottle from my cup holder, I stepped out, tucking it into my back pocket and pushing my seat forward. I stared down at the prone form sprawled across my backseat, thankful he at least hadn't vomited during the drive.

Just the sight of him had me raging again, and I wished I had a fucking cigarette. I'd quit smoking when I realized Jamie lived next door, and I didn't regret the choice, but moments like this sure as hell made quitting harder.

I leaned down, digging through his pockets until I found his phone and pocketed that as well. Then I yanked him out, not at all gently.

He grunted when his body dropped to the asphalt but didn't start to wake until I'd already hauled him several feet over onto the path.

"You know," I said, speaking calmly as I stopped next to the structure and stripped him of his pants. "I didn't get it. When

Maddie told me about the shit you put her through. I didn't understand how any man could enjoy humiliating and hurting someone."

I gripped the hem of his shirt, ripping it up and over his head. His arms twisted violently, and one of his shoulders popped from the sudden movement. He cursed, his words slurred as he kicked out and nailed me in the shin, but I didn't care.

I welcomed the pain, welcomed even the smallest bite of agony from this piece of shit because Maddie had taken worse. Survived worse. Grown from worse.

I clutched a fistful of his thick hair, yanking him up to my level and staring at him through empty eyes. "I didn't understand it then, but I get it now," I said before whacking the side of his head against the dirt-spattered blue wall next to us.

He cried out, dropping to the ground and vomiting liquid bile all over his naked legs and hands. I stepped away, flinging open the door and propping it with a stone. Then I snatched his ankles, avoiding the spots where puke-drenched leg hair stuck to his skin.

At this point, he was barely conscious again. I heaved and maneuvered his limp body inside the porta-john, smacking my elbows against the plastic walls and biting back my urge to gag when something squelched as I dropped the douchebag's feet into the hole. I leaned the upper section of his body to the side, his head lolling against the back wall.

I removed the water bottle from my pocket, throwing the lid on his lap and pouring the frigid liquid on his face. He heaved in a breath, spurting, and whacking his cheek against the wall.

Letting the empty bottle fall, I removed both our phones from my other pocket. I swiped on the camera on each and started duplicate videos of his face as I leaned down. I waited to make sure he was at least halfway focused on me before I spoke.

"Aaron Walsh, this is your only warning. I have documentation, both written and photographed, of your physical and emotional abuse of your ex-wife, Madison. It is thorough and graphic."

I ground my molars together, fighting the desire to punch him in the face again as those pages flipped through my memory on repeat. The bruises, the threats, the fear. Fuck, if it didn't kill me every time I thought about it.

"If you so much as think of her again, tonight will seem like a frat-house prank compared to what I will do. If you return to her home, you will have thicker medical records than she does. And if you *ever* lay a finger on her again, you won't even make it to the hospital."

I clicked the videos off, tucking my phone back in my pocket and throwing his next to him, the echo of it against the plastic loud in the enclosed space. "Do you understand me?"

"I hear…I hear you, man." His words mumbled out through his swollen lips, and part of me reveled in it. The part of me that had come alive the second I'd seen his motherfucking hand gripping Maddie's face.

"That's not what I asked," I said, grabbing and twisting his arm. "I said, do you understand me?"

"Jesus fu—*fuck!* I understand."

I released him, brushing the smear of blood across my knuckles on my jeans, ready to ditch this piece of shit. I wanted to go home and check on the little family that was intent on stealing my goddamn heart.

"Madison Hartland does not exist for you. She never has and never will. She was never fucking yours."

And then my fist met his face again.

Next in the Meet Me Halfway Series

Interconnected Standalone #2

Between moving across the country to help her best friend and building her music career from scratch, Layla is pretty dang proud of what she's accomplished.

She's booked every weekend, and her name is quickly becoming well known in the area.

So it comes as a shock when her booking agent slowly stops calling her. That is, until she runs into the musician who's been stealing her gigs.

She can't deny he has a voice to die for and the body of a god, but neither helps the fact that his personality is pure poison.

Their exchanges never fail to boil her blood, but it's a game she starts to look forward to, and she's determined not to back down first.

She always thought she wanted the sweet love she sings about. But with every quick-tongued remark and heated glance, she realizes sweet might not burn the way she needs.

And what better way to stoke a fire than with a little bit of hate.

About the Author

Lilian T. James was born and raised in a small town of Kansas until she finished high school. Enrolling at a University on the east coast, she moved there with her son and obtained degrees in Criminal Justice, Social Work, Psychology, and Sociology. After graduating, she met her husband and moved to the west coast for a few years before settling back in Kansas in 2022. She has three kids, one miniature dachshund, and has been an avid fantasy and romance reader her entire life. Lilian was finally able to publish her first novel, Untainted, at thirty-years-old and has no plans of stopping.